An Unusual Courtship

The Brazen Burrells, Book 2

By
Lynne Connolly

Dragonblade Publishing, Inc. is an imprint of Kathryn Le Veque Novels, Inc.
P.O. Box 23
Moreno Valley, CA 92556
ceo@dragonbladepublishing.com

Produced in the United States of America

First Edition January 2023
Trade Paperback Edition

ARE YOU SIGNED UP FOR DRAGONBLADE'S BLOG?

You'll get the latest news and information on exclusive giveaways, exclusive excerpts, coming releases, sales, free books, cover reveals and more.

Check out our complete list of authors, too!

No spam, no junk. That's a promise!

Sign Up Here

www.dragonbladepublishing.com

Dearest Reader;

Thank you for your support of a small press. At Dragonblade Publishing, we strive to bring you the highest quality Historical Romance from some of the best authors in the business. Without your support, there is no 'us', so we sincerely hope you adore these stories and find some new favorite authors along the way.

Happy Reading!

CEO, Dragonblade Publishing

Additional Dragonblade books by Author Lynne Connolly

The Lyon's Den Series
Lyon Eyes

The Brazen Burrells Series
The Only Honest Man in London (Book 1)
An Unusual Courtship (Book 2)
On Christmas Day in the Morning (Novella)
The Lair of the Burrells (Novella)

The Daring Dersinghams Series
A Touch of Silver
A Hint of Starlight
A Trace of Roses
A Bunch of Mistletoe
A Whisper of Treason
Past, Present, Future (Novella)

Chapter One

EVEN THOUGH SHE lived in luxury these days, Juliet Burrell often sighed in relief when she left Whiston House. Sometimes she yearned for the simpler life her family had led before their wildly successful Season last year.

One of her sisters had become the Duchess of Whiston, and the other the Countess of Knowsley. As for her, she was still Miss Juliet Burrell—and glad to be so, she told herself several times a day. Especially when Bianca and her Duke were having one of their noisy arguments.

She hurried down the gleaming white marble steps and headed for the corner of the square, where cabs often lingered in search of a fare. Her footman McCarrick strode effortlessly behind her. Sometimes Juliet yearned to be tall, like her sisters, but then, she wouldn't be able to walk through a crowd unnoticed. People queued up to see Bianca and Viola when they appeared. Juliet was accepted as part of the trio, the Three Graces, as some wag had called them, but Juliet knew she was not as startlingly lovely as her sisters. Not that she minded—much.

People jostled her, but she was used to that now. She pulled her crimson pelisse closer around her, an instinctive gesture against the press of humanity and the slightly chilly weather.

Better than last year, when the sun rarely showed its face. But not much.

Reaching the corner, she glanced around. Sure enough, a cab stood by the side of the road. The brown horse looked exhausted, poor thing, its head drooping and its shaggy mane too long for comfort. Its owner sat hunched over on the high bench, holding his whip upright like a ship's mast. He'd pulled a battered beaver hat around his ears.

He'd do. As she approached the cab, McCarrick overtook her and opened the door, his gnarled face grimly displaying disapproval as his mistress climbed into the vehicle. McCarrick had come down with them from Edinburgh, but he'd been with them longer than that. Ever since their Dublin days, when they'd been adventurers, living on their wits and little else.

"Ludgate Hill," she told her footman. "I want to go to Bloomberg's bookshop." Where she'd meet her friend Maria Richards—Lady Maria Richards—and they'd have a blessed hour together browsing in the stacks.

She settled back against the lumpy, worn leather squabs, prepared to amuse herself with the city. The journey could take quite a bit of time, being three or four miles from her current residence in Mayfair.

The carriage lurched as McCarrick jumped up behind. Her footman refused to travel with her. "Bain't right, miss," he said when she'd asked him. "We'll be there soon enough."

So she had the cab to herself, in all its leather-cracked, fish-stinking glory. She'd known worse. Watching London pass by the window gave her time to think and observe, two of her favorite activities. London always held something to fascinate the onlooker, and Juliet had always been an observer rather than a participant. She'd enjoyed going along with the plans her mother made for them, even contributed herself, but she had to admit a quieter life suited her better. At least, she thought it did.

The carriage set off with a jolt. They went up Davies Street, crossing Brook Street on its way to Oxford Street. A glance at one house there took her back to last year in an instant. The Burrells had lived there when they'd first arrived in London and had found it half-empty as the previous tenants had helped themselves to the furnishings. The landlord delegated an agent to see the damage, but their butler had sent him on his way.

Then the landlord himself arrived. He was so tall he put a crick in her neck when she looked up. Lord Langston had left London last year. She hadn't seen him since. Considering they had not met above half a dozen times, she never understood why she'd missed him. Perhaps because he had seen through her façade to the woman beneath. She had few friends like that, and most of them still lived in Edinburgh.

"Men don't like women cleverer than they are," her mother had warned her. "Now you're looking for a husband, you could bear that in mind." So she'd closed her copy of Paine's *Rights of Man*, and opened *Glenarvon* instead. Written by Lady Caroline Lamb, it depicted all the scandals and secrets of London society, so thinly disguised she needn't have bothered giving them new names. The repercussions were still reverberating through society. Her husband had taken her away, and nobody spoke of her any longer, except in hushed tones behind the shelter of a fan.

McCarrick insisted on handing Juliet down from the vehicle at St. Paul's.

"At least it didn't rain." She glanced up at the leaden sky. People had labeled 1816 "the year without a summer," and they'd been right. So far, this year promised to follow in character.

"Aye, ma'am, at least there's that."

She used to try to provoke McCarrick into a response, laughing, reciting moving poetry, or simply running off so he had to chase her, but little made him break into more than a half-smile. The soft hint of Ireland sometimes tinged his voice, but she had no idea where he'd come from any more than when she'd first met him.

On impulse she asked, "Where were you born, McCarrick?"

"Cork," he said, and that was another mystery solved. She'd

only had to ask.

Smiling, she turned away and smiled even broader when she saw the wooden sign over the shop door. "Bloomberg." That was all it needed to say. Although modest in size, it was still larger than many others that crowded the area. Some ramshackle stalls even sought the support of the Cathedral, saucily claiming a part of the walls for themselves. Bloomberg had a proper establishment, on the site of the stall where his father had set up shop half a century ago.

Even the ding of the bell warmed her heart. She nodded to the proprietor, who doffed his hat to her before heading for the area at the back of the shop with the political and philosophical treatises. Bloomberg did not care what she bought, only that she bought something, and she never left his shop empty-handed. That made her one of his favorite customers, or so he'd told her.

Maria hadn't arrived yet, even though she'd told Juliet she'd be there early. Ah well, she would arrive soon. Maria's mother, Lady Rotherham, encouraged Juliet to read with her, as she said Juliet would help to broaden her daughter's mind. So Juliet decided to browse a little more, pick a few books for later reading, and see if Maria turned up.

By the time Juliet had stacked three books on the counter, Maria was very late. Juliet didn't give up, however, not until the clock had chimed the half hour. Evidently, Maria was not coming.

They took turns choosing books to read, and this time it was Juliet's turn. Maria invariably chose a novel. When Juliet once chose a political treatise for their mutual read, Maria gave up halfway through. This time Juliet settled on an account of a soldier's adventures, which she'd seen on her last visit to the bookshop and thought might capture Maria's interest. She had arranged to meet Maria here today so they could make their purchases together, but she didn't mind making the selection alone.

Because the book was slim, she couldn't find it at first. Eventually she located it on a shelf of books crammed closely together.

She breathed a sigh of relief. But as she reached for the book, so did somebody else. A larger, warmer hand covered hers.

She knew that hand. It belonged to somebody she had danced with last year, someone who'd smiled on her and *seen* her. For those twenty minutes she had not been a scandalous Burrell sister, or the lesser of the Three Graces. She'd been Juliet. She treasured the memory.

How she knew his touch she couldn't begin to say, but she did. She recognized it immediately.

She turned around.

Lord Valerian, Earl of Langston, stood so close that his warm, masculine scent filled her senses as soon as she turned to face him. She flattened herself against the bookcase, but it didn't help. Words left her. She could only stare up into his dark gray eyes. She closed her mouth.

Lord Langston wasn't what society would consider handsome, not with his lean face and sharp nose, but every inch of him was male. She felt it, sensed it, and responded as she most certainly shouldn't have. Her body warmed, and heat spread from her decently covered bosom to her face.

He stepped to one side. "Miss Burrell!" He bowed, as much as he could in this narrow space.

She bowed her head in return since a curtsy was impossible. "Lord Langston."

His pause made her look up, in the process nearly hitting his chin with the brim of her bonnet. "I beg your pardon," he said. "I was wondering if you needed that book?"

She glanced down at her hand, and the slim volume in it. "Yes, I'm afraid I came here to buy it."

When she looked back up, he was smiling. "No matter. I can find it somewhere else, or perhaps they have another one." He showed no sign of withdrawing or even taking another step back, and he was still smiling. "It's been a while since I saw you last, Miss Burrell. Have you been keeping well?"

She longed to ask where he'd been, but she dared not. He

might rebuff her. He was a diplomat, moving between important cities in Europe, carrying secrets, perhaps. He might not be able to tell her where he'd been. Nominally, Europe was at peace after the depredations of Napoleon, but it was far from tranquil. So she merely said, "I am well, thank you. Evidently you know my sister Viola is married." Or he would not have called her Miss Burrell, but Miss Juliet.

"Yes, that happened before I went away. And your other sister, the younger one, is a duchess now."

Of course he would know. "Yes, she is. My mother and I live with her."

"That was my other question, because you did not hire my house in Brook Street this Season," his smile turned wry, "and its beautiful contents."

The replacements for the stolen furniture had been top quality but hideous, especially the drawing room suite. "Indeed. that furniture was most distinctive. No thief would dare to steal it, for it would scream its identity to anyone they tried to sell it to."

She made an effort not to smile, but he must have seen something, because he laughed softly. "Ah, Miss Burrell, I've missed your conversation. Yes, I agree, the furniture was dreadful. Despite its quality, the fashion for Egyptian-style objects has passed. At least, one must hope so."

Had he really missed her conversation? Perhaps he'd said it because she made him laugh. Although she tried very hard, Juliet seemed cursed to say the wrong thing at the wrong time. Her comment about the furniture had obviously conveyed her true thoughts. She was glad he hadn't been offended.

He stepped back and indicated the passage out of the bookshelves, allowing her to go first.

They went to the counter together. Mr. Bloomberg pushed his spectacles up his nose and put his newspaper down. "Ah, good morning, my lord. Welcome back. We have not seen you for some time."

"I've been away. Unfortunately I was too late to obtain this book. Do you have another copy?"

He glanced at the slim volume in her hand. "Naturally, my lord. *The Trials of a Common Soldier* has become quite popular recently." He narrowed his eyes. "I have no idea why, but perhaps you can tell me after you've read it."

Lord Langston pursed his lips. "Perhaps," was all he said.

Mr. Bloomberg quickly produced another copy of the book. Then he wrapped Juliet's purchases in brown paper, and tied string about it, ending in a loop so she could hook it over her wrist if she wished. "There you are, miss," he said. He didn't know her name and she had never introduced herself. There was no need. Juliet was rather pleased there was no "beautiful Miss Burrell" nonsense here.

Lord Langston took both parcels and opened the door for her, watching her walk through before following. It closed with a thump behind them as McCarrick appeared. The shop was too small to hold attendants, and Mr. Bloomberg did not allow anyone who had no intention of buying inside his establishment.

As Langston paused to put on his gloves, McCarrick silently took her parcel from his lordship and stepped back, with the clear intention of not letting her out of his sight. Despite the presence of the great cathedral, Ludgate Hill was not the most agreeable of places. The road was wide and the pavement narrow, to allow the passage of the incessant traffic. Mostly public coaches drove through here, the large ones that traveled all over the country and the smaller cabs. Horses and carts as well as single horses and riders added to the confusion. Still, somehow, they usually managed to avoid an impossible tangle.

"Shall we walk for a while?" his lordship said without giving McCarrick another glance. "I should like to renew our acquaintance."

He'd disappeared almost overnight, without a word to her or anyone else she knew. Certainly Viola's husband, who was quite friendly with him, had remained tight-lipped about Langston's whereabouts. If Whiston did know, he wasn't telling anyone.

Juliet decided to be blunt. After all, she had nothing to lose. He obviously hadn't thought enough of her to let her know where he'd been. "You left so suddenly. I had no idea you'd gone until your butler told me."

He stopped, stared at her. "You called at my house?" he asked, his voice raised over the sounds of traffic.

"I—yes, I did." She hadn't wanted to let him know his abrupt disappearance had alarmed her, but she'd blurted it out before she had time to think. "I knew I shouldn't, but . . ." She subsided into embarrassed silence.

His harsh features relaxed into a smile again.

Through the chaos they walked, McCarrick trailing behind them, until Langston swung around a corner and Juliet found herself in a narrow street running at right angles to the main thoroughfare. An inn stood to their right, and a brick wall to their left. It was much quieter here, and he slowed their walk to a stroll. The street was too narrow to allow the larger vehicles to pass, which was a relief. There was no pavement here, but a series of posts separating the pedestrian from the carriages and horses, giving barely enough space for them to walk abreast as they left the noise of wheels on cobbles behind them. "Now we can talk without shouting. You said you called at my house?"

"Yes." She looked away, but there was nothing to look at except a blank wall, so she stared ahead. "I was worried."

"About me?" he sounded astonished.

"Indeed, why should I not be?" she asked indignantly. "I did not know where you were. I'm sorry if I overstepped the mark by going to your house, but I had no intention of going inside. All your butler would say was you'd been called away from home."

"I see." He sounded amused. His response did not help her mood. "Well, I admit I did think of contacting you, but as you so eloquently inferred, my departure was sudden—an emergency. Then it went on far longer than I'd originally foreseen." He paused, and they strolled for a few yards without speaking. She let him collect his thoughts. "There is no harm in my telling you now. I was called upon to go to Paris immediately to cover a crisis."

"There was a crisis?" That did not sound good, considering recent events on the Continent.

"Indeed there was, or the potential of one. The new King of France is unpopular in certain quarters. The Ultras are gaining in strength."

"The people who want to restore an absolute monarchy?"

He glanced at her. "Precisely. And his brother is gaining in confidence."

"The Duc d'Orléans?" She'd read something recently. "You mean his attempt to increase his followers and make demands?" There had been disturbances in the streets of Paris.

"Just so. I was called in to help reconcile the brothers. Take the situation off the boil, so to speak." He paused while they negotiated a dip in the road where the cobbles were missing. "You are remarkably well informed, Miss Burrell."

She shrugged as they resumed their walk. "I read the papers." Politics interested her. Keeping people safe and happy interested her.

"Indeed, ma'am, you do. I had thought—" Whatever he had thought, he thought the better of speaking of it and waved it away with a gesture of his free hand. A cab rumbled past, the driver glancing around at them when Lord Langston gestured, but he did not slow down. "No matter. Yes, you are correct"

"And you were the one called upon to help?" she prompted, fascinated with his involvement in the business.

"Yes. Years ago, when the king was in exile in this country, I was assigned to him as a messenger boy. He insisted on someone of high rank. For some reason he took a fancy to me and sent me on many errands. You know his physical condition?"

"So large he can barely walk. Yes," she said bluntly.

"It doesn't seem to bother him, and indeed, why should it, when he has servants to carry him? And viscounts to run errands for him," he added with a smile.

"So because he knows you, they wanted you to deal with the situation?"

He nodded. "Especially since I'm in the diplomatic service. We needed skilled negotiation to reconcile the brothers."

After the recent conflicts on the Continent, nobody wanted to see a return of war. Juliet appreciated Lord Langston's humanity.

"How can they throw the peace away when they've only just achieved it?" she demanded. "All that death, all those places destroyed, all for one man's ambition, and they want to return to chaos?"

He smiled. "I don't believe it will come to that. You follow current affairs regularly?"

All the reminders her mother had given her had come to naught. Heat rushed to her face as she realized she'd said too much, but she attempted to minimize the damage. "Not as much as you, sir, I'm sure."

"No, don't spoil it." He touched her hand where it lay on his arm. "I've enjoyed talking with you. I had not thought you took an interest in those matters—politics and such. You showed no inclination before."

Ah. Yes, he would think so. "Mama suggested that a gentleman would not appreciate the notion that his wife might be more—informed—than he was."

Another silence before he said, "And you three sisters were desperate to find husbands, were you not?"

"Desperate?" She tried to pull her hand away, but he held it firmly.

"You misunderstand me," he said. "I do not mean to insult you, merely to understand your situation. You had very little when you first arrived and made no secret of it. If anything, that was to your credit in my view, because you appeared as what you were—and are. Your beauty was legendary. It still is."

She would not deny his assessment of her family. Indeed, how could she, since it was the truth? "We did not think it fair to try to fool potential husbands that we had money or position."

"But you considered it fair to hide your intelligence?"

"I merely chose not to disabuse people. Indeed, it would have been hard for me to do so without being rude, since they were so determined to believe we were empty-headed."

His shout of laughter echoed off the brick walls. They had passed the inn and were walking past a line of small, soot-blackened, terraced houses. "You're a budding diplomat, my dear Miss Burrell!"

He guided her around, and they strolled back. "I'm waiting for a new assignment," he told her, "so I will be in London longer this time." He paused, and stared at her, his eyes narrowed. "Ah. May I?" Reaching into his pocket, he came out with a clean linen handkerchief. He wrapped the cloth around his forefinger and touched her jaw.

"What are you doing?"

"Cleaning a bit of smut," he said absently, dabbing the spot. His touch felt like fire on her skin, even through two layers of fabric. Three really, because his gloves would be lined. But through all of it she felt him, as if he was touching her skin to skin.

He glanced up from his self-assigned task into her eyes, smiling. "All done," he said. When he unwrapped the handkerchief, he nearly dropped it, but she caught it deftly and stared at it. "I appreciate the assistance, my lord. I'll have the linen laundered and returned to you." She slipped it into her pocket. London's chimneys constantly wept the black, greasy smuts that were the result of the coal fires. The handkerchief certainly bore the evidence of one.

She might also sleep with it under her pillow tonight, but that was her business and nobody else's. They resumed walking, her hand resting on his arm. "How is your lady mother?" she asked.

"Ah." He paused. "She is back in London. She said she has done so as a favor to me, returning from her new home in Brighton. I suspect she'll lease that one, since her reason for being there has gone."

"I thought she had decided to retire from London," she said. If Lady Langston had not been very well-connected, and wealthy in her own right, society would have turned its back on her years ago. Juliet had never met her, but her reputation went before her. Her discreetly scandalous affaires had not affected her son's career. Probably because she was linked in one way or another to half the royal families of Europe—the ones the Bonapartes had left alone, that was.

"She did, but that ended, and she discovered Brighton was a terribly vulgar place." He smiled indulgently, and his face transformed from harshness to a strange beauty, his mobile mouth softening and his eyes gaining a sparkle she hadn't been aware of before.

"Don't you mind your mother having affairs?" she asked before she could control her unruly tongue.

"Not at all," he replied as if she had not been unconscionably rude. "They keep her happy and less likely to spend time redecorating, which stops me tearing out my hair when she buys hideous Egyptian furniture."

She had to admit he had very glossy, thick hair, currently swept back into a neat style she could not identify. Although undoubtedly dressed well in a dark gray coat, darker waistcoat, and pantaloons—just the thing for town wear—nothing made him stand out. A single fob on his watch chain, polished Hessian boots without gold tassels, and a gleaming beaver hat completed his outfit.

"I'm sorry," she muttered. "I shouldn't have asked such a personal question about your mother."

"No matter," he said softly. "I would much rather have at least one friend who speaks their mind and tells the truth. My world is so full of half-truths and dissimulation, I find a straightforward conversation refreshing."

They had reached the end of the alley, arriving back where they started.

She held out her hand for him to shake. "Thank you, sir. I

enjoyed talking with you again."

At her nod, McCarrick stepped to the edge of the pavement and held out his hand to hail a cab. He was about to put his fingers to his mouth to whistle one up, when Lord Langston held up a hand. "Wait. You are surely not planning to travel in a public vehicle?"

Facing him, she raised a brow. "Why not? I dislike sedan chairs, and so it is either a cab or walking."

"Is there not a family carriage you can use?"

They came from such different worlds. Indeed, Juliet thought nothing of hiring a public vehicle, but she answered him politely enough. "I'm used to it, and it's something I can do without fuss. Every vehicle in Whiston's stable bears his crest, so I can't travel without being noticed if I take one. Bianca took the best carriage this morning to go shopping in Bond Street, but I had no mind to go with her."

The other brow went up, arched and fine, winged like—well, like Lucifer. "You turned down shopping in Bond Street for a visit to a bookshop?"

"Of course."

"I see. I would be honored to take you home. Fortunately I'm in the phaeton today, so you need not worry about propriety."

"Since it's a vehicle open to the weather?" She glanced up. "I do see the sun is about to make an appearance. A bashful one, it is true, but it is lurking with intent behind that cloud." Her comment gave her time to think. Yes, she could go with him. It would be better than a cab stinking of fish or worse, and she would spend more time with him. "Very well, sir. Thank you."

"I told my groom to bring the carriage here at two," he said. He pulled his watch out of its pocket. Gold, she noted, but plain and without enamel or jewels—a watch made for use. He flipped the cover open. "He should be here any minute."

As he spoke, the Cathedral made its presence known. The creaking, clicking sound which presaged the announcing of the hour, followed by the initial *bing-bong, bing-bong* of the bells made

Juliet grit her teeth and clench her fists. "At least it's only—" she managed before the second peal started. The four quarters duly chimed, the great bell sounded its first *boom!* "Two o'clock," she managed to get out before the second one.

His lordship smiled through the ordeal, not even trying to speak. He looked over her head as the brief silence was replaced by the usual chatter, shouts, and grinding roll of carriage wheels. "Here it is."

Indeed, there it was. The carriage looked as if it would fall apart at the first breath of wind, but of course it would not. A miracle of the carriage-maker's art, drawn by two high-stepping, glossy chestnut horses, she could only admire the equipage. "My sister Viola would love this. She enjoys driving."

"What about you?" he said, as the groom pulled up before them with only the slightest touch on the reins. "Do you enjoy driving?"

"Sometimes. I prefer riding." Unlike Juliet, Viola was a veritable magician with the reins but disliked riding as she had a small deformity that made riding difficult. Her husband was giving her lessons, she said, but Juliet got the sense that more than riding horses was involved in those lessons.

"Allow me to help you up," he said, moving closer. "The footrest is a little slippery. I would hate for you to fall."

He came closer, in the shadow of the carriage, and she only had the warning of a twinkle in his eye and a wicked grin before he bent and kissed her.

It was nothing but a brush of the lips, could easily have happened accidentally. It had not. Her lips tingled, and she closed her eyes briefly as he bent and cupped his hands to act as a step up to the high seat.

It was a kiss—she could not be more certain. His groom stepped down and handed his master the reins as Langston rounded the carriage and leaped nimbly into the driver's place. "Consider it your fare," he murmured, as he clicked his tongue and set the horses into motion. She sat there, staring ahead of her.

He'd kissed her. The tingles spread from her lips through her whole body, bringing her alive. She was not even aware if McCarrick had jumped up behind with the liveried groom. She was so confused.

She needed to recover herself. Quickly. "My footman will not suit your carriage," she said. "He is not wearing livery today."

"I'm sure both he and I will survive the indignity."

That made her smile.

"At least this isn't a high perch phaeton," she said. "My sister drives one of those. Her husband bought it as a wedding present for her. It terrifies me."

He nodded. "The cobbled streets in the City are quite a challenge for a vehicle as delicately balanced as that one." He paused as he deftly took a corner, not too close, not too wide. "And they are spectacular. People stop to watch them pass. That's not my style."

"I noticed," she said dryly.

Glancing at her, he grinned. "Perceptive woman! I prefer not to stand out too much."

She stifled her giggle and after another glance, he raised a brow. "Yes, I know. I'm a few inches over six feet. But I cannot help that, and I can't spend my life sitting down."

Mortified, she said, "I did not mean to comment."

"I daresay I'm sensitive to it, being so much taller than other people. It's a damned inconvenience." He shook his head slightly. "Now it's my turn to beg your pardon."

"And mine to tell you I do not mind in the least. I have a brother in the military. He is careful around us, but I've heard some curses that are not only strong, but also inventive. And sometimes in French."

"Ah yes. French, the universal language."

Which it was, even though France's star was currently dimmed. "My French is quite good, considering I've never been there."

He switched effortlessly to French, but she had no problem

understanding him. He only asked if she planned to stay in London long, and she answered in the same language. *"Oui, tant que ma sœur veut rester en ville."*

He turned back to English. "Excellent, but your accent is execrable."

"I have never had the practice I need to perfect it. My brother speaks it well, but he is often away."

"Where is he now, if it is not a state secret?"

"America."

He nodded. "The United States, one presumes, rather than Canada."

"Yes." She smiled when she recalled her brother's response to his posting. "He had wanted a theater of war. More opportunities, more action, he said. More booty. However, now he and his wife are there, he enjoys it, or so he said in his latest letter. He is on a diplomatic mission, he says, but I've no idea what that means."

"It could mean anything." He slowed the carriage when the road narrowed. "Diplomacy covers a multitude of sins."

His answer fascinated her. What could those sins be?

"However, we are currently negotiating a new treaty with the United States. It is slow work, and I heard the envoy, Sir Charles Bagot, is not liked by all."

"But he is a highly competent and experienced man," she said. "I read the accounts of his achievements in the papers."

"Indeed," he said. "I try to follow in his footsteps."

He swung around the corner, and there they were. "You said you were staying at Whiston House?"

"Yes, with my sister and her husband."

He drew up outside the house smoothly. She was almost sorry to be home. "Thank you so much for the ride, sir."

He got down to help her to alight. No kiss this time. Grosvenor Square was busy, but not frantically so, and people would have noticed.

Pity.

Chapter Two

ALL THE WAY to Berkeley Square Val felt her presence. That kiss . . . he should not have done it, but with her lips so close and her heavenly scent reminding him so much of their acquaintance the year before, he couldn't help himself. Before his hasty trip to the Continent, he'd thought himself close to a courtship, but matters turned out differently. Now he was back, and here she was, more attractive than ever.

Which was most unfortunate, since he was on his way to propose to another lady.

When the Foreign Secretary, Lord Castlereagh, had asked him last year if he had considered taking a wife, Val took it as a signal. His service in France had been well received, and he was ready to move on with his chosen career. Ambassadors and Envoys generally had wives. Besides, when he'd returned, he'd been so tired that he would have agreed to anything. Which is probably how Maria's mother had persuaded him into the match. Now he was expected to call and make his proposal formal.

But what he'd just learned numbed Val. He'd chosen Lady Maria for a variety of reasons. She was well connected, a sweet girl, and he'd thought her well versed in current affairs. When Lady Rotherham had asked him to collect *The Trials of a Common Soldier* on his way to visiting her daughter, he'd taken it as a sign that she was a good choice. The book was well thought of, and it indicated she had wider interests than novels and shopping, which would be an asset in a diplomat's wife.

However, after the encounter at the bookshop and subsequent conversation, he suspected that Lady Maria had learned much of her discourse from Juliet Burrell. The comments she'd made as they'd walked sounded like some he'd heard from Lady Maria.

But he couldn't change his mind. He was too busy, too involved in public affairs to concern himself much with private ones. And the combined efforts of Lady Rotherham and her daughter had brought him to the brink. He'd spoken to Lord Rotherham. The marriage contract was all but signed.

He gave Miss Burrell another regretful thought. She was remarkably lovely and, it seemed, intelligent. She understood that he couldn't speak about much of his work. Not many people did—men or women—which often left him alone and isolated.

He waited until she had gone into the mansion on Grosvenor Square, the butler bowing her in. As her footman followed her in with her parcels, the man glanced up, and although he did not meet Val's gaze directly, his shrug told Val a great deal about what lay inside. Rumors abounded about the Duke and his wife, their rackety ways, their shocking extravagances. Some stories were stronger than rumors. Val assumed they were too wild for him, and had not sought them out, nor the Duchess's unmarried sister. Now he regretted that.

Sighing, he took the reins and set off for the house of his prospective bride. He drove past the line of white-stuccoed houses, turned the corner, and drove past another line of them. Fine, spacious establishments, suitable for the highest in society to spend a few months every year, and very different to each other inside, but outside, they were all the same, right down to the shiny black front doors and the brass knockers.

He climbed down outside the Rotherham house, tossed the reins to his groom in exchange for the small package containing the book, and ran up the stairs to the front door, which was opened before he reached it. They'd been expecting him.

"Good afternoon, my lord," the stately butler intoned, as he personally took charge of Val's hat and gloves, "Lady Rotherham is expecting you. You will find his lordship and her ladyship in the large saloon. I will summon a footman to take you upstairs."

Since the houses had a very similar layout, Val hardly needed anyone to show him the way, but he went along with the custom. Manners and customs must be observed, especially below stairs. So he followed the liveried footman upstairs, past portraits of previous earls and countesses, all glaring unsmilingly at him, and to the drawing room.

The house was decorated in tasteful pastels, ivory, and creams for the most part, with a few marbled accents and gilded trim. Very fine gilded trim, so nobody could accuse the family of being vulgar. Labeling a person vulgar was worse than being called scandalous or shocking, or even poverty-stricken. Vulgarity was akin to calling someone common. Something to make a person shudder, Val thought with a wry smile, not shuddering at all. In his experience, vulgar, common people could often have more integrity than the ones who considered themselves superior.

The footman flung open the door with a flourish, bowing as Val walked through. His lordship rose, and came toward him, hand outstretched in welcome. Her ladyship remained seated, her daughter by her side. Was he expected to propose to the poor girl with her parents present? It was not unknown, but not something Val looked forward to, or was prepared to tolerate. He wanted a private interview with her.

Maria was a pretty girl, with quiet but dignified address. But quiet and dignified should not have been enough. He wanted a partner, someone to share his interests and become the perfect ambassador's wife, if such a creature existed. He had made a mistake here, and he was about to pay for it.

"Lord Rotherham, it is good to see you again."

"I am happy to see you looking so well," his lordship returned. He was a man of considerable weight, both in his person and his dignity. As far as Val could learn, his wife was the real power in the household, and she made decisions her spouse would go along with, as long as he was not troubled too much. Considering Lady Rotherham had married off four daughters already, every one a good match, he could only admire her efficiency and skill at finding husbands for her brood. She had one more out this Season and another, her last, to bring out next Season.

She graciously held her hand for him to kiss. "Ah, welcome, Lord Langston. I trust your usual robust health is intact?"

As expected, he bent over her hand, but did not touch his lips to her skin. Only the gesture remained, not the act. "Very much so, my lady. And I do not need to ask to see the same."

Lady Rotherham nodded, the lace on her cap fluttering.

After he exchanged bows with his lordship, finally he turned to Lady Maria. His heart sank. Only today, when he'd met Juliet Burrell again, had he begun to doubt his choice, but the moment for indecision had passed. Perhaps she had hidden depths.

They conversed on the weather, on the Regent, and appearances at court. "Not as spectacular as last year, of course," her ladyship said, "when the three Burrell girls made their debut. It would take something remarkable to best that." She smiled at her daughter. "But they turned out well enough. We had thought they might be impostors or charlatans, but although they are still making scandals—at least one of them is—they are acceptable."

To a lady as dignified as Lady Rotherham, "acceptable" was a high compliment.

"I brought a book for Lady Maria," he said, watching his potential bride flush prettily. Lady Rotherham held out her hand. He put the parcel in it. She laid it in her lap and held out her hand again. Her daughter handed her a letter-opener that had lain conveniently on a side table next to her. Almost like a play.

Her ladyship slit the string and unwrapped the parcel, revealing the slim volume. "*Trials of A Common Soldier*? I trust it is perfectly respectable? Common soldiers are not known for their propriety."

"Quite acceptable, my lady, I assure you," he said. "Nothing of a shocking nature."

She sniffed. "I am delighted to hear it." She flicked through the book, reading a few words here and there. They waited in silence. Lord Rotherham drank his tea and put the cup back in the saucer.

The click seemed to bring her ladyship down to earth. She closed the book, handed it to her daughter, and got to her feet. At last. Her husband followed, and Val rose. "We will leave you for ten minutes," she announced, and glided out of the room, followed by her husband. Val watched them go.

Would Maria turn out like her mother? God, he hoped not. Maria's older sisters were pleasant enough, so perhaps it wasn't set in stone. He could take comfort from that thought.

Ten minutes didn't leave him much time. He'd hoped for longer, so he could coax her into a little more conversation, or a few chaste caresses. He wanted to know what she was like when her mother wasn't present. More than ever, he felt pushed into this.

He stayed on his feet and held out his hand to her, inviting her to join him. Maria put the small book aside and stood. "Thank you for the book," she said, her voice barely above a whisper. "My friend Juliet Burrell and I read together. She is educating me, although she does not see it that way." Her blush increased, her cheeks reddening. Had she ever been alone with a man she was not related to before? She stood a foot away from him, not taking his hand. This was going to be more difficult than he'd thought.

And of course Juliet Burrell had to enter the conversation. Of course she did.

"How does she see it?"

"We take turns choosing books. I confess, the last book she chose defeated me, although I did not tell her so."

"What was it called?"

"It was Thomas Paine's *Rights of Man*," she said. "I found it rather dry."

"I know it." He'd read it a number of times. It had a direct connection to his chosen profession. No matter—enough of Paine. Time to pay the piper. "You know why your parents left us alone, do you not?"

"Yes." She met his gaze briefly, then looked away. "Mama says you are going to offer for me." Evidently the prospect did not fill her with joy any more than it did him.

"Indeed. Will you let me ask?" Before she could answer, he went on, grasping at the last straw he had. "If you feel I will not make you happy, then I will not ask. If there is someone else you would rather have, or if you do not find yourself interested in me, then I beg you, tell me not to pose the question." He paused, but she remained silent. "I leave the decision up to you. We do not have to decide it today, if you would rather not."

"What would you tell my mother?"

"That we need a little time to become better acquainted." Thus condemning himself to endless tea-drinking sessions and poetry salons—perhaps not those—and balls, and oh, God, Almack's. Maria did not appear at all ready to make a decision as momentous as this. Perhaps upon reflection she would decide she did not wish to marry him.

A vision of Juliet Burrell floated through his head, and he could not entirely rid himself of it. However much he reminded himself of the Burrell sisters' scandalous behavior and their lack of connections, Juliet firmly remained there. But he could not involve himself in those scandals at this stage in his career. One false step was all it would take.

Maria was frowning, looking like a confused rabbit, sweet and vulnerable. He did not savor the idea of himself as the predatory wolf, but that was how she made him feel.

"I—that is . . ." She lifted her head, gazed at him, and drew a deep breath that stirred the pin-tucks on her chemisette, but stirred nothing in him. "Mama said—I mean, I would like you to ask, Lord Langston."

So here they were. He liked her, but he had not thought her bashful. When he'd met her in public, she'd behaved in a perfectly composed way. Was something else wrong?

Having begun, he could not withdraw. "Then, Lady Maria, I have the utmost honor to ask you if you would consent to become my wife." He went to her and took her hand. It was cold.

She gazed up into his eyes for the first time. Determination filled the light blue. "If you please, sir, then yes."

Her answer fell like a hammer on his skull. but he liked her, he reminded himself. They would learn to deal together well enough, he was sure. He lifted her hand to his lips, and at that moment, as if they had heard her response, the door opened to admit her parents.

His fate was set.

Chapter Three

A KISS, ESPECIALLY one so brief as could be considered accidental, should not mean so much, but Juliet treasured the moment when Langston claimed his kiss. Surely he could not be indifferent to her?

While her maid helped her put on the pretty muslin afternoon gown, Juliet let herself dream. They conversed so easily, as if they understood one another implicitly. Juliet tried to come down from her perch in the clouds, not to put too much on the meeting. She was not of a romantic turn of mind, she told herself, but it did no good. Apparently, where the Earl of Langston was concerned, she was.

She sat at the dressing table to allow her maid to put up her hair. A year ago, she'd have been scrambling with her sisters, sharing one maid, and attending to each other. Now, in this lovely bedroom decorated in the shades of mid-blue that suited her so well, she had a maid of her own, space to stretch out, and a bed to herself. Despite all that, she missed those days, though she suspected it was only in retrospect. Would she go back if she could?

Probably not. Her eldest sister, Viola, was blissfully happy with her handsome husband. Her younger sister Bianca was still working on it. Juliet had received flattering attention from a number of gentlemen last year. This year, she could choose a husband, or wait until next Season, because she had that luxury now.

Her maid finished twisting the last curl into shape and stepped back. "Thank you, Banks," she said as she rose, and smiled. Banks knew her job, although Juliet knew she would not hold on to her if she did not acquire a husband of good rank. Maids drew their status below stairs from the rank of their employers and if Juliet did not marry well, Banks would be off to another employer at the end of the Season. A titled one.

Outside her room, she nearly collided with her mother. Mrs. Burrell had lost her harassed, tense look and blossomed in the last year into the mature beauty she should always have been. Even though her family was not clear of scandal, they were no longer on the edge, no longer threatened with dire poverty. Her son was married to a duke's sister and rapidly rising through the ranks of a prestigious army regiment, and two of her daughters had married peers of the realm.

"You're looking pretty today, dear," she said. "That shade of green suits you, and Banks was a real find. She knows exactly how to dress you."

They walked toward the stairs together, passing glass cabinets filled with costly porcelain, soft silk carpet under their feet. "You mean I don't?"

"I mean, my dear, that you never cared. You could present yourself if the occasion demanded, but normally you'd be as likely to cover a silk gown with an old shawl that clashed horribly as you would be to appear in something better."

She pouted. "I liked that shawl. Now I can't find it anywhere."

"There's probably a beggar down at the docks grateful for the warmth," Mrs. Burrell said with a smile.

"You did it!" Juliet stopped long enough to turn to face her mother and poked a finger into her chest. "You got rid of that shawl! I knitted it myself!"

"I know, and you were forever sewing up the holes. It was a

disgrace." Her mother was unrepentant, clearly, but Juliet felt the loss. She'd held on to the ragged shawl from their sojourn in Ireland, then Scotland and London. It was a tangible reminder with the past, and now it had gone. But she couldn't explain it to her mother, because Mrs. Burrell didn't think that way. She didn't have a sentimental bone in her body.

"Oh," her mother said, stopping her. "I heard from Viola today. After the Season, we will go to her house in the country for a while. Does that suit you?"

To see her sister in marital bliss with her beloved husband while she became a fifth wheel in another household? "Of course, Mama."

Suppressing her sigh, Juliet moved on, and went into the breakfast room. Otherwise the informal dining room, it was an attractive room overlooking the garden on the ground floor and held a large round table and a long sideboard, on which currently reposed a selection of dishes. Footmen moved from sideboard to table as they sat.

The fine linen tablecloth was already stained with tea and coffee and scattered with crumbs. Their host and hostess were up early, for a change, which meant before noon. Bianca looked up from her place next to her husband, her eyes bright. Suspiciously so. Had they had another argument? Juliet and her mother exchanged a glance.

Letters, mostly bills from the look of them, were scattered around the table and floor, as if someone had disturbed the stack. The Duke of Whiston looked up with a smile. "Good morning, ladies." He indicated the spare seats, and Juliet and her mother moved to join them. The Duke's dazzling good looks were only surpassed by his wife's. They'd helped him get out of a lot of trouble in the past, but every day his creditors moved closer, and his allies moved further away.

A footman pulled one out for Juliet then returned to the sideboard to get her food.

"You're looking pretty today," her sister Bianca said. She was wearing her wrapper, a frothy concoction of lavender and lace, the shades suiting her fair beauty. Her hair gleamed in the rare sunlight streaming through the window behind her.

"Thank you. You always look pretty," Juliet said.

"She does, doesn't she?" Whiston grabbed his wife's hand and brought it to his lips. She smiled softly, and it had to be said, a trifle wearily. "But then, my wife always looks pretty."

True enough. Bianca was spectacularly beautiful, to be precise. Younger than Juliet, though not by much, she had eloped with Whiston the year before and now they lived in bliss and debt. But, as Bianca had airily told her, "Dukes can do that."

Many of the bills scattered around were duns, overdue payments that would most likely never get paid. Mrs. Burrell kicked one aside with her foot. Whiston glanced down. "I should get a secretary, I suppose. The last one left," he announced. That explained the mess. The secretary would have gathered them up and put them on His Grace's desk. If he could find room for them. Whiston had already filled the drawers. "I should have a bonfire," he added. "Many of those bills are out of date. I generally pay them when I can." His fellow peers first, the traders who made his clothes, his carriages, and his shoes last.

The doorbell clanged. A few moments later, a servant came in, but he was pushed aside by their visitor. "Good morning, Arthur," said Whiston, as if he couldn't see their guest was in a state of high dudgeon. "Do sit down, dear boy. Have some breakfast."

Bianca lifted the teapot. "Is tea good for you, or would you prefer coffee? Beer?" she added when the man did not reply. "Ah well." She smiled and waited, the perfect hostess.

Arthur Carrington was Whiston's heir, at least until Bianca produced one. He was ostentatiously dressed even in this land of frills and furbelows, and his full mouth was pursed into a moue of disapproval. As usual. He strode to where Whiston lounged next to his wife and threw a paper down in front of him, narrowly missing Whiston's plate of scrambled eggs and grilled kidneys.

Whiston heaved a ponderous sigh. "What is it now?" He did not touch the paper but looked at his cousin. "I do wish you'd tell Bianca if you want tea. Her hand will drop off at the wrist if you make her brandish that teapot much longer."

Arthur glanced at Bianca and nodded. "No sugar," he said. "Thank you," he added as an afterthought.

Bianca poured a cup for him and pushed it over without another word. She turned, half-showing him her back. "You're going out today?" she asked Juliet.

"Here! Look at it!" Arthur said to Whiston.

"Just to see Maria," Juliet answered absently. "We have a new book to read."

Arthur went into his tirade. It was like a storm breaking, a relief and an annoyance. "How can you spend so much in such a short time? Why on earth do you need another clock when your house is crammed full of them? The estate cannot bear such extravagance!"

Whiston made him wait. He ate a mouthful of what must have been cold eggs and signaled the footman to remove his plate. "What I spend and what I do not are not your business." He had suddenly turned into the Duke, his golden beauty cold and distant. He could pull on that part of him at will, like a coat covering his usual affable self. Profligate though he was, Whiston never lost sight of his position and the dignity due him. He never allowed others to forget it, either.

"Arthur, you are no longer my trustee," he continued, forestalling another tirade. "You ceased to have any jurisdiction over me ten years ago, when I came of age. I fail to understand why you continue to pester me. You have your own life at the Foreign Office. I suggest you concentrate on that."

Carrington straightened his back, as if he'd shoved a rod down the back of his coat. "As your heir, I still have an interest in the estate."

"Not until after I am gone," Whiston had lost all sign of amusement or affability. Nothing remained but the blond god who adorned the space at the top of the stairs—the portrait taken when he attained his majority. "Even then, it is doubtful you will inherit." His glance at Bianca needed no words, nor any comment about filling his nursery. As far as Juliet knew, Bianca had not fallen pregnant, but eventually she would.

With a gesture worthy of a prince, he indicated the untidy table. "You may stay to breakfast, if you will, but only if you keep your opinions on topics that are none of your business to yourself."

Carrington made a sound like "humph," and gave his neck-cloth a tweak. "My appetite has entirely gone. I will bid you and your rag-tag band good day."

Before Whiston could answer, he'd gone.

The front door slammed as Whiston resumed his seat. "Good riddance," he murmured as he picked up his knife and fork. "The man forgets himself." He shrugged. "Well, we can forget him now."

However unpleasant the visit, Carrington had a point. The bills were getting out of hand, and nobody seemed concerned about it. But having just witnessed the Duke's response to his cousin, Juliet did not care to add anything. Being referred to as "rag-tag" went without a comment.

Juliet excused herself as quickly as she could and went upstairs to find her pelisse. When she came back downstairs, she found her mother in the hall, already wearing her outer clothing. "Were you planning to walk to Maria's?" she asked.

"I thought I might. It's not raining, and I could do with the fresh air."

"I'll come with you. I thought I might persuade Lady Rotherham to take a walk in the park. McCarrick and Walsh are waiting outside."

"You should have said you wanted a walk, Mama. I'd have gone with you instead."

Her mother laid a hand on her arm. "No need. I know how much you enjoy your visits to Lady Maria."

After a hiatus last year when Viola had snatched Lord Knowsley from under her nose, Lady Rotherham had continued her friendship with Mrs. Burrell. In Lady Rotherham, Juliet's mother—who had a positive genius for unearthing the freshest of gossip—had another valuable source for her passion. Once their existence had depended on their mother's ability to unearth morsels of gossip, but now Mrs. Burrell pursued the activity because she enjoyed it. Not that she would ever admit it.

They didn't speak again until they were out of the house and in the square. Mrs. Burrell heaved a sigh. "That's better."

"What is?"

"Getting out of that house. I fear Bianca is suffering. She was wearing face paint at breakfast again."

"She's very clever at applying it. And she enjoys it." Juliet had not taken to face paint, except for a little rice powder occasionally. Bianca had never used it before, but she'd taken to it now. Juliet suspected she knew what her mother was about to say.

"It is more than vanity, and you know it. He's distressing her and making her cry. I believe he is straying from her bed." The words came as both a shock and a release. At least Juliet wasn't the only person thinking that.

Juliet felt a burden taken off her shoulders when her vague suspicions were finally articulated. "By the noise coming from their bedroom, I think she knows and is not happy about it."

Her mother pursed her mouth. "There is no excuse for his behavior. Bianca is the sweetest girl alive. I hope she is defending herself, which I would approve of." She linked her arm with Juliet's. Hers was shaking. "I have more than once been tempted to interrupt them and take her part, but I cannot. They are married, and Bianca must fight her own battles." She glanced back at the house as they walked away, quickening her pace.

"I don't know if it's something he does on a regular basis." Her mother fixed her society smile in place and nodded in response to the Marquess of Huntington, who lifted his hat to the two ladies. Juliet was not aware she had also been smiling until he passed and they could talk again. She lost the smile.

"Women are expected to accept such behavior," her mother continued, "but this was a love match, and trumpeted abroad as being so. Bianca is still remembered as the poor girl on the edge of society. She can expect humiliation and more if it becomes known."

"What can we do? How can we stand by and let this happen?"

Her mother shook her head. "We must support her and provide what she needs when she asks for it. It is all we can do." They walked to the corner in grim silence. "Nobody is allowed to come between husband and wife. Whiston could order us out of the house, and then everything could get worse, with us out of the way."

With her suspicions confirmed, Juliet badly wanted to do something. Anything. This was her sister, not some poor woman she'd read about in the paper. "He resents her," she said. "When he ran away with Bianca, he had no intention of marrying her. He had that young heiress primed and ready. Bianca was merely a distraction."

"Until Gerald stepped in."

Bianca was paying for her thoughtless decision now, but Juliet would not abandon her. "We will have to devise a scheme to help her. I cannot see her suffer like this. She adores him. How can we see her so unhappy?"

"I will talk to her about the situation," her mother promised.

They arrived at the Rotherham house, set in prestigious Berkeley Square. Mrs. Burrell stopped outside the house and took both her daughter's hands, pressing them warmly. "And you. I wanted to talk about you. You know Lord Langston is back?"

Looking into her mother's eyes like this, Juliet could hide nothing. "Yes, I know. I met him yesterday at the bookshop. He brought me home in his phaeton."

"You like him, do you not?"

"Yes, Mama. And he was—friendly yesterday."

"Was he now? Well, we will see what comes out of it, but do

not be too rash. I like him, though. I think he would do very well for you."

They went up to the front door and plied the knocker.

A FEW MINUTES later Juliet was with her friend, and her mother had borne Lady Rotherham off to take the air. The ladies had barely passed in the hall, but Juliet detected triumph in her ladyship that put her senses on alert. Something had happened to elevate her mood. She gave Juliet a beaming smile, but Mrs. Burrell hurried her off, so she did not stop to talk.

Juliet went upstairs with the maid, who promised to bring tea. In the pleasant small parlor that overlooked the garden, she found Maria staring out at the buds and new leaves of spring. A pretty woman, who would always look younger than her age, she had filmy fair hair and pale blue-gray eyes. She had the kind of beauty that was often overlooked, and her meticulous good manners did not help her to leave a mark. Juliet thought she had found a true friend in Maria. Her good sense overlaid Juliet's intelligence, and stopped Juliet complicating every matter to extremes, something she was wont to do.

She went to Maria's side, putting her book on the table in front of the window. Maria seemed enthralled by the actions of a bird outside, a small brown sparrow who hopped from branch to branch of the ash tree at the bottom of the garden. "I think she's building a nest," Juliet murmured.

"Who? Oh, yes." Maria turned to her and forced a smile, one that looked grotesque with her reddened and glistening eyes.

"Maria! What is wrong, my dear?" Juliet would have embraced her, but Maria shook her head and held her off.

"It is my own fault," she said. "All my fault. I had not realized . . . too taken up with my own emotions . . ." She shook her head.

"Tell me," Juliet insisted, deeply concerned. "Start at the beginning."

"I should be the happiest of women, as the saying is, and in different circumstances I suppose I would be. I will do my best, but I was expecting something entirely different."

Juliet frowned. "Maria, you're not making sense. What do you mean?"

Maria's lip trembled as she said, "You may wish me happy, Juliet."

"Oh!" That at least made sense. Lady Rotherham had introduced Juliet to society last Season. The Burrells had dominated events then, and several young ladies went unmarried, overlooked in favor of the sensational Burrells. This Season Maria had been receiving the attention she deserved from several young men anxious to make her acquaintance. Had she selected one of those, or had her parents chosen for her?

"Mama said he was the best suitor out of all of them, and they were convinced he would treat me well. But how can I marry him when the man I truly love is in his employ? How can I see my dearest Walter every day and not think of what could have been, had I not been so foolish! For when she told me, I thought his lordship was speaking for Walter, not for himself. Walter had said, you see, that he would talk to his lordship, and ask for his help."

"Walter?"

"Walter Norris. He is of good family, his father is Sir Henry Norris, who lives in Hampshire. He is a magistrate, but unfortunately takes no interest in politics and does not hold a seat in Parliament. It is Walter's dearest wish to become a member of Parliament, or some other political post, so with his father's reluctant permission he came to London to serve as a secretary to a man of affairs. He found an excellent post, and he has been prospering. I met him in the Park—he kindly picked up my glove when I dropped it, quite by accident, and not at all purposefully as I have seen other ladies do. He walked with me for a while, and

Mama said he was an interesting young man but far below my touch. She believes he would not be able to make me happy. But oh, Juliet, he would, he would!" She was babbling now.

Juliet took her friend's elbow and guided her to the sofa, where she sat her down and took a seat by her side. "Slowly now, Maria. You have fallen in love with a young man called Walter Norris, who is a promising person in politics. Is that right?"

Maria nodded vigorously. "But he has no fortune to speak of. He is not the eldest son, so he can expect very little when his father dies. And he has no inclination for county matters. He would rather till the fields than manage them, he says." This time her smile was soft and did more to convince Juliet of her feelings for this man than anything else. But she was wary. While not the greatest heiress, on her marriage Maria would bring a generous settlement to whoever married her. This Walter might be looking for money and blinding her with protestations of love, as Whiston had to Bianca. He'd promised her the moon, and brought her debts, infidelity and an empty title.

"So he is not wealthy," Juliet said, carefully choosing her words in case she made Maria cry. "And he wants to marry you? Are you sure, Maria, perfectly sure that he doesn't want what else you can bring to the marriage?"

Outside, the birds were putting on a special concert, but Maria seemed oblivious of them now. She frowned. "I'm sure. Walter wants to wait. He says he cannot afford to support a wife until he can find a parliamentary seat, but he fears that might not be for a few years yet. He must prove himself, he says." She clutched Juliet's hands again, holding them tightly. "I am willing to wait, but when his employer asked to see me, I thought he had found a way. Mama told me that his lordship would propose, and I must accept him. But I thought his lordship wanted to ensure my feelings for Walter are sincere. They are, dear Juliet, every bit!" Tears fell now. Maria let them fall. One after the other, they tracked down her face.

Juliet could not bear it. Producing her own handkerchief, she dabbed at the tears on her friend's cheeks. "Don't cry, dear. I am sure something can be done." Only, she realized too late, it was not her handkerchief. It was the one Langston had given her. She would have to launder it again now before returning it.

"I want Walter now!" Maria declared. "I don't want to wait for years. Mama is at me all the time to find a husband, and she said she was talking to a gentleman she thought would suit me very well. But you know, Juliet, I would far rather be happy with Walter in a hovel than in a palace with another man, seeing Walter every day and being unable to even touch him!"

Juliet suspected Maria had saved up her tears for this visit, freely as they flowed. So the lord who had employed her beloved Walter had come to pay his own suit?

"And you accepted Lord . . . Lord . . ."

"Langston," Maria helpfully supplied. "He asked me if I wanted to marry him, if I wanted him to ask me to marry him. Before he came Mama impressed on me that I must behave myself and find a match this Season, because she still has Lucy to provide for next Season, and I will be twenty next year and entirely on the shelf!" She shuddered.

Juliet sat still and numb. There couldn't be two Lord Langstons, so she had to conclude this was her Lord Langston, the man who had stolen a kiss yesterday and raised her hopes again. And all the time he'd been coming here to propose to Maria. He must have been on his way here even then. How could he do such a thing?

A great shiver went through her.

"What is it?" Maria asked.

"Nothing. Someone walked over my grave," she said, using the old saying to find her voice again. "So Walter Norris is employed by Lord Langston?" Who had shattered the lives of two women, not just one. Yesterday Juliet had begun to hope again. Now all that left her. Hope slammed the door and refused to return.

"He is Lord Langston's parliamentary secretary. He has other secretaries, of course, because he is a diplomat and he needs to know about the countries he works in, as well as knowing what is being discussed in the House. And he is so often somewhere else and cannot attend Parliamentary sessions. That's another thing, Juliet. If I marry Langston, I will not be in England much. He will take me with him when he goes to outlandish places. He says his next assignment is likely to be Russia, and how am I going to bear being apart from Walter for all that time? For he must stay here, you understand, to send his lordship regular reports on the doings at Westminster."

Now she had started to talk, apparently she was finding it hard to stop. Like a bolting horse, Maria let her words gallop all over the place. "I will see Walter soon. We meet in the park, and Mama seemed happy for us to walk and talk. But perhaps she thought he was acting as a go-between for his employer!"

She took the handkerchief from Juliet and dried her tears herself. "I would go today, but you were coming, and I was most anxious to see you. I don't know what to do, Juliet! I accepted him before I knew what I was saying, I was so shocked, and then Mama and Papa came in and they were so happy, and Mama started talking about bride-clothes, and I didn't know how to tell them I did not mean it at all."

"You accepted Langston without even telling him about your Walter? Why did you do that?"

"Mama would not let me marry Walter, I knew it, so I thought if I accepted his lordship, I could keep them all waiting until Walter was ready. But Mana immediately started to make plans for a speedy marriage."

"Is there nothing you like about Lord Langston?"

"He's kind, and very polite, but the wife of a diplomatic man must be so well informed. I daresay my head would explode. I do not travel well at all, you know, and I would be traveling all the time."

"Wouldn't you be required to do those things as the wife of a politician?"

Maria shook her head. "Walter says he would not expect me to hold political salons or anything like that, just to host dinners and such. I can do that standing on my head, you know, for Mama has taught me forever."

Juliet could believe that. While her friend babbled on, she sat, watching, thinking, her mind far away.

The news had numbed her to the point of insensibility. She had fallen asleep dreaming of Langston last night, and that brush of his lips against hers. He had now gone beyond her touch.

And she was angry, the kind of anger that simmered inside on a slow burn, only to emerge at the worst possible moment. Yesterday he must have gone from the bookshop straight to Maria. The book he'd bought was resting next to hers on the side table. So when he kissed her, when he walked with her, he was planning to come here. He had not even bothered to tell her, either. Surely he should have done that, at least? He knew who was to receive the book, so why trifle with her?

Last year, before Bianca had run off with Whiston, Langston had shown an interest in Juliet. He'd waltzed with her, walked with her. When he'd disappeared, she'd been unhappy, but he'd told her yesterday why he'd gone, what he'd been doing. Was he even telling the truth there or was it just one more subterfuge? She didn't know what to believe.

Maria had at least stopped crying. She'd crumpled the hand-kerchief in her hand, sodden with her tears. A flare of anger shot through Juliet. Let Maria keep the damned handkerchief. She had no use for it now.

Maria sniffed, then blew her nose in a most unladylike fash-ion, but she certainly needed it. "What can I do?"

Time to give her honest opinion. "You have committed your-self now, Maria. Unless—did he force you?"

She shook her head. "He asked me if I wanted him to pro-pose. I did not know what to think. My mother was in alt when he called, and she must have known, because he would have spoken to my father first. I could have persuaded her to accept

Walter in time, especially if I finished the Season without a special suitor, but Lord Langston caught me by surprise, and instead of saying no, I said yes." She stared down at her lap.

"Well, you have said yes, and so be it," Juliet said.

She would not repine. He didn't deserve it, for one thing, leading her on, deceiving her in effect, by not telling her where his expectations lay. At least he had not made her a dishonorable proposal. Both her sisters had received them from the men they'd married, with very different results. Juliet had not.

And she would not be marrying Lord Langston.

Chapter Four

"YOU ARE VERY quiet this morning," Mrs. Burrell remarked, reaching for the coffee-pot. "Are you well, my dear?"

"Perfectly," Juliet answered tightly. She refused to tell her mother she'd cried herself to sleep last night. That part of her life was gone. If she had to meet Lord Langston and Maria together, she would. She'd even wish them well, however much it hurt her. Nobody would see her pain.

"You haven't forgotten we're holding a dinner tonight?" Bianca asked. She looked paler than ever this morning, but at least she was not wearing as much paint as yesterday. She sounded more herself, also.

"We'll be there," her mother said.

Her son-in-law rattled his newspaper but added nothing to the conversation.

"The Regent said he might drop by," Bianca said. She buttered her toast and attacked her plate of food with vigor.

The Regent for dinner? Well, it wouldn't be the first time. The fact that nobody commented on it revealed that. Juliet did not like the Regent, but she kept that opinion to herself. He leered at her and assumed he was the best ruler the country had ever had. The way he claimed credit for other people's deeds irked her. Not that she would ever say it aloud, even when only family were present. Perhaps he wouldn't come. He rarely did.

"I asked Langston to come," Whiston said, from behind his paper, "but he told me he would be having dinner with his future parents-in-law. Did you know he was getting married?"

"Lady Rotherham told me yesterday," Mrs. Burrell said, "but I was not sure if the matter was public or not." She glanced at her daughter.

Aware she was being watched, Juliet ate her breakfast steadily.

"I assumed Lady Maria told you," her mother added to Juliet.

"Yes, she did." Juliet put her knife and fork down as steadily as she could manage. "But she was not entirely sure about her decision. However, she has said yes, so she must go ahead with the marriage."

That made Whiston lower his paper and Bianca stop eating. He fixed his attention on her, his mouth quirked up in that attractive way that made women stare. "A bit stodgy, Langston, but a sound man with a very pretty fortune. Lady Maria is fortunate in her choice."

"I think he overwhelms her a little." Even now, Juliet did not want to betray her friend's secret. At first she had wondered if she should, or even could, do anything about it. In the small hours of the morning, however, she decided she would let matters take their course. After all, Langston would treat Maria gently. She would come to appreciate his worth in time.

A sense of doom hung over her however, and she could not shake it. Her own profound disappointment sank in deep and threatened to overwhelm her.

"I thought he was sweet on you last year," Bianca said, "but then he disappeared without a word, and we moved on." She shot her husband a coy glance. "Did we not?"

"We did indeed." Putting his paper down, he took her hand, gazed into her eyes, and pulled her over for a kiss.

Juliet looked down. Their displays of affection often embarrassed and annoyed her, but they did not worry her as their fallings-out did. On the whole, it was better this way.

Her mother cleared her throat and got to her feet. "I think I've had enough breakfast. Juliet?"

As she rose, Bianca said, "Oh, that hat you bought the other day? I said I would make you a gift of it, so could you let George have the bill? He can put it with mine. After all, I bought two hats!" She giggled, and Whiston, who still had her hand, brought it to his lips.

They left the room and Mrs. Burrell led Juliet upstairs and to her chamber. She wasted no time after she closed the door.

"Now," she said. "What happened with Lord Langston? Do not presume to fob me off with excuses. Tell me."

Juliet had prepared herself for this interview but even so the name hit her hard. She fought to retain her calm demeanor while she searched for the right words. "I saw him on Monday when I was buying the book Maria and I had decided to read together."

"And he told you then?"

"No. He could hardly tell me before he'd asked her, could he?" She turned away on the pretext of examining herself in her mother's dressing-table mirror. "Ambassadors need well-connected wives with no scandal attached to their name."

"I see." Her mother's hard tone told Juliet that she understood the implications. "Not one who lives with a scandal-ridden sister and her husband, connected with the Regent's set. Or one who arrived last year without knowing anyone in society, with a small dowry and no relations of note. That won't be what the Foreign Office wants."

Juliet turned around. For her pride's sake, she still tried to hide her pain. "Maria will be perfect in that regard. She knows everyone, is related to half of them, and is sweet and obliging." Her mother folded her arms, her silk gown rustling. "And yet she will sink into the background. If Langston had wanted a brilliant career, you would have suited the role much better. Not that he knows it. You hide your light under a bushel, Juliet. You always have."

"You told me to," she reminded her.

"I did not!"

"You certainly did! You told me that a man would not want a wife cleverer than he was, advised me to be circumspect. No bluestockings, you said."

Juliet distinctly remembered her mother's warning. The thought riled her. "It was not my fault, Mama."

"No indeed! Apparently he has chosen duty rather than personal inclination. He is a fool. You would have made the better bride. Admit it, you were already halfway in love with him."

Juliet swallowed. More than half, if truth be told. But her mother spoke the words she had been thinking. He'd chosen his bride for his career, not for himself.

Her mother went to the window and lost herself in thought. Her room overlooked the street, but she said she liked it that way. And it was true that she loved being a part of life and watching it around her, rather than seeking out the peace of the garden side. Not that anything in this house was very peaceful. "I see Lady Greene is wearing her appalling puce shawl again. It makes her look bilious. She is such a pleasant woman, but I do not know her well enough to give her the hint."

She let the curtain drop and turned back to Juliet. "You, on the other hand, never need a hint. You present yourself perfectly. And since Langston is out of the running, we must look about this year. Even without your sisters you are attracting a court of men." She picked up one of her gossip-sheets. She had a library of them, all neatly arranged in leather folders in her powder-room, ready for her to consult when needed. Now she knew personally the people she had read about for so long.

"I will make a list."

Inwardly Juliet groaned. Her mother's lists were notorious amongst her children. True, they had kept the family going in hard times. It had been a perpetual challenge living from hand to mouth in rented lodgings, since their grandfather the viscount refused to have anything to do with them and their brother was in the army. Those years had been difficult but exciting when they'd had to live on their wits.

But those times had finally gone. Juliet could even consider living life on her own. Thanks to her brother's rapid promotion and the booty awarded him from Waterloo, she had saved enough of her own to buy a small house, perhaps share it with her mother. For the first part of her life she'd wanted that above all things, but now her ambitions were grander. She recognized the part of her she had suppressed for so long: she wanted a husband, but she also wanted to be useful. She didn't want to be a wife who stayed at home stitching exquisite embroidery, but someone who made a difference in her world and had a partner who would encourage her. She'd thought Langston could be that man, but clearly she had been severely mistaken.

Now, with respectability, came the prospect of waiting. Last year she'd dared to think that would come to an end, but perhaps this year instead. Perhaps she'd meet someone she liked as much as Lord Langston. Perhaps.

"You can do much better than Langston," her mother said, coming over to press a kiss on her cheek. "We will make sure of it."

⤜⟫⟫⟫⟪⟪⟪⤛

WHEN JULIET WENT downstairs to take the bill to Whiston, she found him in his study—not a typical place for him to be—and he had a list which he was frowning over.

"Ah, Juliet, do come in." He tossed the list on the desk, which was covered with mounds and stacks of papers. "I'm sure my cousin is wrong about what I owe." He grinned and waved to a seat. "I daresay he has not taken my debts of honor into consideration. In any case, I had a particularly good evening at the tables, and I'm settling a few of these." He waved his hand over one of the piles of paper, dislodging them. "I must find myself a new secretary. Will you sit?"

Juliet had no choice but to take a seat. She held out the bill. "I only came to bring you this."

He took it and grimaced. "Why do bonnets and hats cost so much? No, don't reply. My mother spent a fortune on them, and now Bianca is following in her footsteps." He dropped the bill on top of the collapsed pile. Were they all bills? "You are happy here?"

Juliet looked around at the beautiful mahogany furnishings, the Boulle desk, shining brass carefully inlaid into the wood, the clock with its gleaming gilded figurines. Like all the other furnishings, gold and gilding predominated. Expensive and tasteful, but to Juliet's eyes, too much of it. She lied through her teeth. "Of course. We are living in luxury now. My mother and I are very grateful to you."

"Hmm." He arched his elegantly manicured fingers, tapping the nails of his forefingers together, a man in thought.

Whiston was almost as dazzlingly handsome as his wife was beautiful, and his charm had helped him throughout his life. Being a duke did not hurt either. And yet, under all that glossy veneer lay a man who seemed to resent the world for some reason Juliet was unable to explain. He'd been born into a world of privilege that he did not even understand and couldn't appreciate—he'd never known anything else. But two generations of debt, both his and his father's, had brought the dukedom to the brink of disaster. Perhaps living on that brink excited him in a way that other things didn't.

"We must look about this Season and find you a husband," he said.

What was the obsession with marrying her off? Juliet had no intention of rushing into marriage now she didn't have to. Why should she? "I'm sure one will turn up."

Whiston nodded. "We could look outside London. I have an acquaintance, someone my father went into business with." He shuffled through the papers, dislodging more of them. "Here it is. He wrote to me, offering a pretty sum to buy me out of the business. I shall, of course, accept his offer. I have no idea why my father considered it proper for a duke to take a venture in the north—we have no property there. But if he has this kind of wealth, he could be a prospect."

He picked up a sheet with an air of triumph, and a few more dropped to the floor. "Fraser, that's his name. One of the Yorkshire Frasers, which I presume is why my sainted father chose to invest in whatever it was. Relative of the Marquess of Stonyhurst. A rum character, the Marquess, but rolling in gold. This Fraser, they call him the Midas of the North, so he's rich, too." He glanced at the paper. "Whatever the business is, I have no interest in it, but he is of good family. I shall write to him, accepting his offer, and invite him to London to settle the matter with my solicitor. You could meet him." He flashed her a bright smile. "It might come to something, it might not."

Juliet did not like the idea of being foisted off onto an unknown northerner, as if she were nothing but part of the bargain. She wanted to marry someone she at least knew. Knowing how changeable Whiston's mood could be, she said nothing, but bent to pick up some of the papers.

One was in French. "You have property in France?" she said, handing it to him.

"Is that what it says?"

"Yes." He gave it back to her, and she read it more closely. "This is the deed to a small villa, close to the coast in Calais." She returned the document to him again.

"Ah!" His face cleared. "I won it last week at the card table." He put it aside. "That's an asset I can sell."

She gave the rest of the small stack of papers to him without a word. He muttered his thanks as he glanced at the top one and shuffled them all into a leather folder. "Blasted French," he murmured. Again, he gave her that beautiful smile. "I never truly attended to my lessons, you know. What point was there learning French when we were at war with the devils? Why shouldn't they learn English if they want to talk to us?"

A generation ago every nobleman learned French as a matter of course, but then, they could travel there and experience the place. However, the world had suffered a profound change since then.

He opened a drawer of his desk and crammed the papers into it until no more would fit, then he found another and proceeded to stuff it full. Only a few papers now remained, including the one from Fraser and the dressmaker's bills Juliet had just added to. She wished she had not. She would not give him any more but would take care of them herself. She did not wish to add to her sister's worries. Today they were all sweetness and light, probably because of the good night on the tables and the offer from the unknown Fraser. Tomorrow it could be thunderstorms, and Bianca might need to resort to the face paint at breakfast again.

Chapter Five

V AL DID NOT go into the Foreign Office on Whitehall every
day. He didn't need to, since he was one of the gentlemen
who worked there. Besides, he had other duties. Having spent
most of the last year abroad, he had a lot of estate business to
catch up on. Today, however, after finishing with his personal
affairs and delegating tasks to the relevant members of his staff,
he set out to see what was happening at the Foreign Office.
Besides, the day was a fine one, if cold for May, and he needed the
exercise a brisk walk would give him. By the time he arrived, the
fine day had turned murky again and rain threatened.

Val passed through the main gates into the forecourt and
glanced at the windows ranging around it. Recently he'd
wondered if he should draw back and attend to his own affairs,
but he could not bring himself to do so. He loved the work and
knew that once he began reading about events in the papers he
could not be a part of, he'd regret his decision. So far, he'd
received significant assignments, but they were well within his
capacity and did not lead to anything else. But greatness lay on
the horizon, he was sure of it.

And here he didn't have to explain himself, because the people around him already knew what he was talking about. He
didn't have to watch their eyes glaze over as he explained
something that should be blindingly obvious, and he didn't have

to answer repetitive, stupid questions and be utterly polite while doing it. He belonged here, as he did not anywhere else.

His new wife would find difficulty settling into this world. Why the devil had he gone ahead with the proposal, especially after discovering whose opinions she relied on? No answer to that, especially after that kiss, or rather, those two kisses. But he had, and that was that. No point repining over it.

Climbing the stairs to his office, he passed the likenesses of several ambassadors, current and past, who had made a difference to the world. Titles and honors were subservient to their abilities here. He liked that.

He found his Parliamentary secretary waiting for him in his office.

"Ah, Norris," he said. "Do take a seat. Was there anything in the session today to concern us?"

Walter Norris was frowning. "Only that push to continue to suspend the Habeas Corpus Act to better control the riots."

"I can't agree with a move like that. The rioters would be better controlled by giving them food and decent working conditions," Val commented. He practiced his opinions and had seen better than average production on his estates as a result, but not everybody agreed with his methods. Arguing the point would win him very little, since it was not covered by his current brief.

"Indeed, sir. I would urge you to attend the sessions."

"I believe the situation has been decided already," Val said, sitting behind his big desk. "There is little I can do to change it. They would regard me standing up in Parliament to discuss that topic like a donkey on its hind legs, I fear."

Norris smiled but placed the single sheet on which he had summarized yesterday's proceedings on the tooled leather top of the desk. "There was little else of note."

"Thank you. Did you hear anything about affairs abroad?"

"Not today, sir." Naturally Norris knew of Val's desire for the Russian post, but matters had gone quiet in that quarter, which probably meant the people who would make the decision were sitting in small rooms together making the shortlist of candidates.

"Then I won't keep you." As Norris got to his feet, Val added, "Would you consider coming with me, if I get a posting abroad?"

Norris's shocked face told him what he wanted to know. He didn't need the words, but he listened to them anyway. "Sir, you know my interests are here at home. I would vastly prefer to retain my concentration on domestic affairs, but if you feel that you need me, then indeed I'm flattered, and I would give it profound consideration."

In other words, he didn't want to go, but he would, because a man had to earn a living, and Norris depended on his salary. If he did obtain the position, Val would let him go if he could find a suitable place that would use his talents. Or—the thought occurred to him, not for the first time—he had a Parliamentary seat in his control that he could make available. The current incumbent had privately told Val he wanted to retire. Norris would make an excellent MP, and God knew Parliament needed more of those.

He leaned back, staring at nothing after Norris bowed and withdrew.

Losing the man would be a blow, but he could persuade Norris to continue his superb summaries of the day's events. Or he might find someone else before he let his man go, so Norris could train him. Parliamentary secretary to an earl was a plum job. Too many applicants used it to further their own careers and feather their nests. Norris was not one of those.

Val glanced at his desk. He had a folder to go through, mostly about Russia. He wanted to be abreast of affairs there when the call came. If it came.

After a tap on his door, Castlereagh entered. He rarely waited for a response for his knock. In any case, his lordship, as Foreign Secretary, could go wherever he pleased in this building. Castlereagh had made a lot of enemies, but even they could not ignore his brilliance. The tall, slender figure with its shock of gray hair was not easily overlooked, but he rarely noticed when people stared after him. Val had seen him work as the main negotiator at the Treaty of Vienna and, despite the man's lack of oratorical skills, admired his achievements there.

He got to his feet and bowed. "Ah, yes, Langston. I was passing, so I thought I'd drop in."

"May I do anything for you, my lord?" Val did his best to quell his rising excitement.

"Humph. Yes, well." He fumbled in his pocket and came out with a piece of pasteboard. "The Regent is holding a reception at Carlton House. Several dignitaries will attend—I'll send you the details. I would greatly appreciate your opinion on them. Here's your invitation."

He had to mean the state dinner for the Polish delegates currently visiting Britain. Val's heart rose. "I will of course be delighted to attend."

Castlereagh gave a distracted nod. "And I heard you were recently betrothed. Bring her too, will you? The Regent will expect it. We'll all be pleased to meet her."

Val bent his head over the pasteboard invitation that Castlereagh handed him in order to hide his excitement. "Thank you, my lord. Of course we will be there."

"Hmm, yes, thank you. If you need any more information, do let me know."

It seemed having a betrothed wife brought immediate results. At least as far as his career was concerned, his decision was a success. This would be an interview, a chance for Castlereagh to look him and his betrothed over, to see if they could hold the position planned for them.

As the door closed behind the Foreign Secretary, Val punched the air and let out a silent whoop. He would forget his personal concerns. At least one part of his life was going right.

IF VAL HAD thought he could avoid a confrontation with his mother by keeping the house busy and full of guests, he should have thought again. As he was getting ready for one of his mother's convivial and large dinners, the lady in question walked into his bedroom without knocking or sending a request to see him. As usual.

"Mother, I could have been stark naked," he said in mild reproof.

She shrugged. "I've seen you naked before. I don't think the sight of you now would give me an apoplexy." She glanced at his valet. "Good evening, Compson."

Compson bowed. "Good evening, my lady."

"So you're getting married," she said to Val, after nodding to Compson. "It might have been more respectful of you to tell me, since you'll no doubt want me to move out of the Hall and retire to the dower house." She folded her arms.

Val took his time. He was sitting at his dressing table, having his hair brushed by his valet. For the last ten minutes he'd been staring at his own reflection without seeing it, trying to plan his future.

"You look, Mama. Do you have a new friend, or is this for me?"

Lady Langston had a succession of lovers, the latest one Val knew about having resided in Brighton. "Foolish boy! Nobody since James. I adored him, you know, but apparently he did not reciprocate. I will not waste my time on a man who doesn't appreciate quality when he sees it."

So James had taken other lovers. His mother was monogamous, and she expected the same from the men she spent time with. One at a time was her style, unlike others of their mutual acquaintance. Tonight, in ruffled peach silk and gauze, she looked half her age. Well, perhaps ten years younger than the fifty she admitted to. Her riches had brought many suitors to her door, but she had never remarried, nor expressed any desire to do so. "I tried that," she'd told him once, "and it did not suit me."

Val agreed with her. His father had not made his mother's life easy. Nor his own, for that matter. "I thought it was time I married, Mama," he said, coming back to the idea of his own nuptials. He nodded to Compston to dismiss him. The man stuck his nose in the air and muttered something about gold studs for his cuffs as he went in the direction of the dressing room.

"She is coming to dinner tonight," he said mildly. "And her parents, too—Lord and Lady Rotherham."

Lady Langston closed her eyes and groaned. "In this way you ruin my convivial dinner. She will disapprove of every dish served and every guest sitting down to it."

Val picked up the nail buffer, more for something to do than any need for it. "I look forward to the clash of philosophies."

His mother snorted. "I'm not discussing Socrates tonight," she said, "though Plato would be more appropriate. I doubt Lady Rotherham has heard of either."

"Neither had you until you fell in love with a philosopher," he answered. Her erstwhile lover had published several small monographs on the subject of Platonic philosophy. Val thought them tedious and obvious. Wisely, he'd kept quiet on the subject.

"You love this girl?" his mother said, in a softer tone than before. "Did you propose to her impulsively?"

He spared Lady Maria a brief thought. "No," he confessed, because his mother would see through any subterfuge. He could persuade politicians and world leaders to do what they did not want to do, but he'd never been able to fool his mother. "However, she is appropriate. The family has useful connections. She's pretty, a biddable girl, and appears to know enough about politics and international affairs." Though not as much as he'd thought. "I imagine she will learn the duties of a diplomat's wife without too much trouble. I want someone ready to step into the work."

She sighed and turned away. "I'm disappointed in you, my son. You know what agony is caused by a poor match. You are doing neither her nor yourself justice. I want better for you. Lady

Maria is a sweet girl, rarely puts a foot wrong. If you had fallen in love with her, I could understand. But why rush into something when your heart is not involved?"

He had done his best to rationalize his choice of Lady Maria. It was true that her mother's scheme to trick him into thinking Maria was more knowledgeable than was the real case irked him, but she was still a good candidate for a diplomat's wife.

"Mama, there is only what is possible." He pushed the image of Juliet Burrell out of his mind and closed the door on it. That prospect was gone. "Marriage is a partnership and need not be a love affair."

"Yes." She clasped her hands together and Val knew she was thinking of his father. She had loved him. He had not loved her. In Val's observation, love matches led to great unhappiness.

Even so, he was attracted to Juliet Burrell. Too much, if truth be told. She was not well-connected and had nothing but beauty and a modest dowry to bring to a marriage. And her bright mind, he amended. She was not to be thought of, he told himself, even as he thought of her more.

He recognized—and lamented—his mistake now in thinking Maria the clever one, although he would not admit it to anyone, least of all his mother. He didn't trust her not to meddle. Although her marriage to his father had failed, his mother remained hopeful of finding the one true love of her life—who probably didn't exist—and he knew she wanted that for her son, as well.

He stood and faced her, his expression impassive. "Shall we go down to greet our guests, Mama?"

AFTER RECEIVING A frantic note from Maria, Juliet hurried to the Rotherham house. The butler greeted her warmly as he let her in, but she didn't linger, only rid herself of her pelisse, hat, and gloves as quickly as she could. Hurrying upstairs, she found Maria in the small parlor, and again, Maria was weeping, a handkerchief screwed up in her hand.

"Oh, Maria, please don't cry! What did you mean in your note, 'I can't carry on any longer'?" She'd feared the worst.

"Juliet, I just can't marry him!"

Again? "But you did promise him."

"I know," she said miserably. "And I've tried to accept it, truly I have, but it's no use."

"Then cry off."

"Mama will find somebody else so fast. And I will never see Walter again, and I'll never find a man to love!"

Juliet took her by the elbow. "Come and sit down. Tell me all about it, and we'll see what we can do."

As she allowed Juliet to lead her to the sofa, Maria muttered, "Nobody can help me now."

It seemed a bit dramatic, but Juliet didn't know exactly what Maria had been through. Had her parents beaten her, or bullied her? Was she run ragged from sleepless nights? She was young and sheltered. Although only a few years older, Juliet had been through much more. Her adventurous life had hardened her, made her more able to bear hardship and setbacks. Why, she had not wept at all last night.

She moved aside the sad piece of overworked knitting that lay on the sofa and sat, taking Maria's trembling, damp hands. "Now, what has happened?"

Maria swallowed. "Last night we attended a dinner held by Lady Langston—my betrothed's mother."

"Yes."

"It was awful!" Tears began to flow again. "Oh, I cannot! They talked about foreign countries, spoke in French and Spanish and even German! They all knew so much, I was completely at sea, and I fear I showed it, too. I can't stand it!"

If they deliberately talked over her head, Juliet did not think much of that behavior. "What about Walter? If you marry him, you'll be expected to learn."

"Yes, but he is at the beginning of his career. We will learn together. I want him so much I am close to eloping."

"Has he suggested it?" That alarmed Juliet—fortune hunters typically suggested elopement.

"No!" she wailed. "He will not do it. He says it would be a betrayal. But what of the betrayal of our happiness?"

To Juliet, that sounded promising. This Walter could have had what he wanted, but he had rejected the idea. That spoke well of his character.

Juliet was Maria's only close friend, the one person who listened to her, so she had to be careful what she said now. And she could not admit her preference for Lord Langston to Maria, or her friend might suspect her of ulterior motives and send her away, never trusting her again.

And she would hardly be able to blame Maria if she did. Juliet barely trusted herself. "You must speak to him—Langston, I mean. Explain yourself, tell him you've reconsidered." Honesty would be the best way to approach him.

Maria sprang up from the sofa, and strode around the room, wringing her hands, the image of a tragic Shakespearian heroine. "I can't! I don't know where to start, and I don't think he would listen to me."

"He is a gentleman. He won't cry off. You must do that if it is to be done." An ugly thought struck her. "Has he kissed you? More?" Had he come from kissing her to kissing Maria, perhaps even making love to her?

Maria shook her head. "Not really. Only on the cheek, as friends do, and once on the lips to seal our agreement. That was how he put it. He doesn't have a romantic bone in his body. How can I marry a man so cold and unfeeling?"

Juliet kept her thoughts to herself. She had never thought of Lord Langston that way, although she'd heard him described in those terms by others.

Maria clasped her hands and faced Juliet as if a supplicant in prayer. "Please, Juliet will you talk to him?"

"Walter?"

She shook her head, curls bouncing. "No, of course not! Lord Langston!"

"No, Maria, I will not. You know I cannot." How could Maria expect her to do such a thing as to go to Lord Langston and beg him to release Maria from their engagement? Lady Rotherham would hate her, and with good reason.

"Langston is to go to a state dinner next week, and he expects me to go with him. Oh, I cannot, truly!"

"If you will not break it off, then you must go," Juliet said firmly. How could Maria even think of treating Langston this way? "You will learn." Both his way of life and how to love him. "Speak to your Walter. You see him in the park, you said. Then go tomorrow and walk with him. Perhaps he has some sway with his employer and can advise you. Otherwise, you must say goodbye to Walter Norris."

All it needed was for Langston to become aware of how Maria felt about him. He wouldn't force her, Juliet was sure of that. But Juliet could not be the one to tell him. Maria must do that for herself.

"Yes, I will talk to Walter, try to persuade him to change his mind and elope. Surely if we run off together, nobody can do anything about it."

Maria turned away and plied her handkerchief. When she turned back, her face and eyes were dry again and her face was more composed, though her eyes were red-rimmed and swollen. Cold compresses would take care of that. Juliet had been in that place before. Maria would live through it, just as she had. Indeed, she would have to live through it again.

"You cannot do that, Maria," Juliet said firmly. "Eloping leads to regret. It would ruin your Walter's career, destroy the work he has done, and wreck your own reputation."

"Oh, but I cannot think of anything else! I had no idea my mother would want the marriage so soon and prevent us the chance to prove Walter's worth!"

"Be true to yourself," Juliet told her, ignoring the foolishness of Maria's plan to use her betrothal time to prepare the way for another suitor. "That's all you have to do. Be strong, stand tall, and remember who you are and what you want. Either accept the marriage with Langston or reject it to his face."

That was all she could say, all the advice she had to give. When she was sure Maria had recovered from her upset, she left, her friend's words ringing in her ears: "Yes, I promise. I will take your advice, be strong, and be myself. Thank you, Juliet."

Then, perhaps, everybody could move on.

At least Maria seemed to have remembered her status. If she appeared at the dinner next week with eyes as red as the gown at the bottom of her clothespress, people would think she was being forced into the wedding. All she had to do was say no, and then her torture would be over. True, she might face a difficult time, but all that could be coped with.

Juliet had enjoyed Maria's innocence and her lack of pretension for one so high born, but perhaps she'd mistaken the softness and sweetness. Perhaps it was weakness after all.

Chapter Six

FOR THE NEXT few days Juliet went about her life, shopping with her sister, listening to her arguments with her husband and then the embarrassing making-up, and accompanying her mother on her relentless rounds of salons, balls, and garden parties. The latter were the worst, because although this spring was marginally warmer than the one the year before, the fine fabrics and slim silhouette demanded by fashion gave her permanent goose bumps.

On the Monday after her last talk with Maria, she received a wrinkled, tear-stained note that had been delivered in the night. She had to read twice before she could take it in. She was sitting in her bedroom, and her maid was arranging her hair for the day. If she'd been given it at the breakfast table she'd have betrayed herself to her mother and sister.

As it was, she leaped to her feet, and ran to the bed where her maid had laid out her gown for the day. Or part of it. "This won't do. Get me something plainer and sturdier. I need to—" she waved her arms in frustration. She couldn't say what she needed to do, or the word would be around Mayfair as fast as her maid could run to the next house.

Banks hurried to her side, spitting hairpins onto her palm "Madam, we need to finish your hair first."

With a "Tcha!" of exasperation, Juliet returned to the dressing table. "Hurry, then. Just pin it up. I'll be wearing a hat." She was supposed to be walking in the park with her mother, but that would have to wait.

Knowing her job, Banks did as she was bid, and went to the bed. "I can add a spencer to this, ma'am. Would that suit?"

Since she might have to wait for something else to be pressed and prepared, Juliet agreed to the pale green sprigged muslin. It wasn't too distinctive.

Maria's letter had been brief.

Juliet,

You inspired me. Knowing what your sister and mother did, I decided to take my fate into my own hands. You will not see me for some time. My dearest Walter and I are fleeing to the border. We should be well on our way by the time you receive this note.

All my love, your friend Maria

Friend? Not after this escapade. Good Lord! What on earth had entered her head now? Was it entirely filled with feathers? And, oh no—Lord Langston would be humiliated, especially at his state dinner. His wife-to-be eloped rather than marry him. She had to get to the Rotherham house and then to Langston's. Someone had to stop them.

The spencer Banks produced was warm enough, a good cloth lined in silk. It would have to do. But instead of pretty jean half boots, she settled for leather, ignoring Banks' complaint that they didn't match. "We had the other boots dyed to suit this gown," she protested.

Juliet ignored her. "Tell my mother, if you please, that I've been called away on an errand. I will be back shortly." At least she hoped she would.

With the stoic McCarrick trailing behind her, Juliet left the house on foot, hurrying to the Rotherham mansion. She remembered to smile and nod at people who greeted her, but she stopped for nobody.

When Bianca had eloped with Whiston, they had given out that her sisters were ill, and could not be disturbed. That story had held—barely—until Bianca returned to London in triumph, her husband by her side. It could have ended so differently, but they'd all done their best to make the story into a fairytale rather than admitting the reality, which was more sordid and more dangerous. So Maria would not have known the truth of it, and it was too late to tell her now.

She ran up to the front door and plied the knocker with vigor.

The stately butler opened it himself. "Lady Rotherham is not at home," he said, and would have slammed it shut had Juliet not had the foresight to shove her foot in the gap.

"She will be at home to me," Juliet said.

From inside came a strident voice. "Let her in. I'll speak to her."

Reluctantly the butler allowed Juliet and her footman inside, barely opening the door before he closed it firmly behind them.

"In here," Lady Rotherham snapped, and Juliet followed her voice into a small room that was all business. A large desk dominated the space, a small and neat pile of papers waiting for the attention of his lordship, who was not present. Juliet wondered where he was.

"I got this," she said, thrusting the note at Lady Rotherham.

The lady, dressed as carelessly as Juliet, as if she'd closed her eyes and grabbed the first thing she could find, made a sound of disgust, but she took the note and read it. "My daughter will return unmarried. My husband has gone after them."

"When did you know?"

Her ladyship did not reply. Instead, she pulled a scrap of cloth from the pocket of her sadly creased mustard-yellow gown and thrust it at Juliet. "I have been meaning to talk to you about this. You gave it to my daughter."

Juliet unfolded the cloth. A linen handkerchief, rather large for a woman. With misgiving, she touched the white monogram embroidered on one corner, more a laundry identifier than a mark of distinction. but it still had the initials VL. Entwined in fancy script, but still most definitely there.

She swallowed. "I came by it by accident," she said. "I got something in my eye, and his lordship removed it for me. I promised to have it laundered and returned to him."

Her ladyship snorted. "A likely story!" She spun around and stood by the door. "I always knew I should have gone with my instincts and cut you and your family when you Burrells first appeared in London! Your sister might be of high rank now, but she's the most scandal-ridden duchess who ever existed."

Recalling the many mistresses of Charles II who wrangled titles out of him, Juliet doubted it, but she was too wise to say anything. Though not wise enough to retrieve that handkerchief, apparently. She had been so angry when she'd heard Maria's news, that she hadn't wanted to touch it again.

Since her ladyship was blocking her exit, she had to listen.

"You will be received nowhere by the time I have done with you. Your advice no doubt encouraged my daughter to take this disastrous course. I will not receive you in this house again, nor will my friends receive you in theirs."

Since her "friends" included most of London's elite, that would be the end of Juliet's career in the ton. Strangely, now the penny had finally dropped, Juliet felt nothing.

Lady Rotherham wrenched open the door as if it owed her money and stood by it.

Juliet stalked out. What was the point of trying to explain? Lady Rotherham wouldn't believe anything she said anyway. She was looking for somebody to blame. And to come to the conclusion she had with no more proof than a handkerchief, she must be desperate indeed for a scapegoat.

Juliet hadn't even taken off her hat and gloves.

For the second time, the butler opened the door. Just as Lord Langston, hand raised as if to knock, walked in.

Followed by a young man holding the arm of Lady Maria Richards.

Chapter Seven

LANGSTON MET JULIET'S eyes and nodded, as if they shared a secret. That was completely ridiculous, Juliet knew. She realized she was numb with shock and wanted nothing more than to go away and cry somewhere, just let out her feelings before putting on her brave face again.

Apparently she had no time for that.

Without a word, Lady Rotherham stepped aside, so her unexpected guests could crowd into the small office. She would have stepped across Juliet's path, preventing her going in, but Langston forestalled her. "I'm glad to see you, Miss Burrell. I believe you have some part in this business."

Did he think she was responsible, too? Juliet shrugged to herself and went in, trying to ignore her ladyship's triumphant stare.

Lady Rotherham was smiling now. "My lord," she said, acknowledging him first.

He ignored her but addressed Juliet. "Miss Richards says she sent you a note."

"She did, but it is now in Lady Rotherham's possession."

He turned his attention to Lady Rotherham, who gave him the paper. She shot a glare at Juliet. "This person has been poisoning my daughter's mind with talk of elopement and foolish dreams. She is dangerous, and I advise we have nothing more to do with her."

"On the contrary," Langston said smoothly. "I believe she tried to dissuade Lady Maria from her plan. At least, that is what Lady Maria herself told me. She said when Miss Burrell refused to help her, she decided to take matters into her own hands."

He was as cool as everyone else was agitated. The young man standing with Maria's arm through his—presumably Walter Norris—put his hand over Maria's in a soothing gesture.

Langston continued. He held the room. Juliet had never seen Lady Rotherham so overwhelmed, so—speechless. "Lady Maria went to my secretary's lodgings. He has rooms close to the Houses of Parliament, as well as a place in my household. There she declared she would kill herself rather than go back home."

Juliet winced. She couldn't help it. So dramatic and unnecessary!

Lady Rotherham addressed Juliet directly. "You knew?"

"She asked my advice. I told her any such course would be unwise. I never dreamed she would—"

Lady Rotherham cut Juliet off. "Maria! Explain!"

Her daughter, traces of tears inevitably on her cheeks, quavered as she spoke. "I'm sorry Mama, but I cannot marry Lord Langston. Not while I love Walter so terribly much."

"Nonsense, child! Mere nerves, that is all!" Her ladyship's voice was back to its usual slightly louder than needful timbre. Smoothly, seemingly in charge of herself once more, she said, "She will recover, my lord. I have to thank you for your swift and discreet behavior in this matter. My poor girl is overcome by the honor you do her, and I can promise she will not do anything of that nature again. When you are wed, you may instruct her on proper behavior."

Langston's raised eyebrow stopped her. "I fear marriage between us will not be possible, ma'am."

The chilly tones created a pocket of silence enveloping them. The only sound was Maria's sniff, until Lady Rotherham found her voice. "I'm sorry, my lord? Is it not even more urgent to celebrate your union?"

He lifted his chin, and since he was a tall man, he could stare down his nose to great effect. He could probably intimidate a room full of dignitaries with that stare. "I beg your pardon?"

Lady Rotherham was made of stern stuff. "You gave your word."

"Under certain circumstances."

"Are you reneging on that promise?"

Fascinated, Juliet watched the duel.

"We made no formal promises. No ceremony, no contract signed."

"It is ready for your signature, with exactly the terms we discussed." Lady Rotherham folded her hands and stared at him through half-closed eyes, haughtiness in every inch of her compact body. "Honor demands that you sign." Turning her head slowly, she met Juliet's gaze. "I believe we can dispense with your presence, Miss Burrell. This is a family affair."

"No, Mama!" Maria cried. Nobody took any notice.

"Would you escort Miss Burrell home, Mr.—Mr. . . ." she spread her hands helplessly.

"Norris," the secretary supplied helpfully.

Langston glanced at his employee and shook his head. "Norris is not finished here."

Her ladyship bridled. "Has he not done enough? While I appreciate his perspicacity in bringing my daughter to you, I would rather we discussed the rest of this delicate matter behind closed doors."

Langston turned his attention to the entrance. "It looks closed to me. And the interested parties are here. Lady Rotherham, I cannot marry your daughter. I cannot marry anyone with such a dislike of me. Also, with regret, I must tell you circumstances have changed."

The short hush was filled with Lady Rotherham's wordless fury. Her voice, when she did speak, was dangerous. "In what way, my lord?"

"Oh, Mama!" Big-eyed, Maria's gaze went from Norris to Langston and back. "I fear I transgressed."

Now Juliet knew what a frozen silence sounded like. Somehow it was worse than a normal silence and held both ice and fire. She shivered and clenched her fists to stop it. Something awful was happening here and she was in the middle of it somehow. "I told Maria not to do anything rash," she said.

"She did, truly she did! But I could not think of another way!" Maria was so young, not just in years but in heart. Sometimes Juliet wished she was like that, but with the life she'd had, she would not have lasted long. As before, once Maria had started talking, she pushed on. "My lord, I didn't mean to insult you or to hurt you, but I could not tell you what was in my heart. I went to dear Walter to seek his advice."

"And he took you to his lordship," Lady Rotherham said firmly, "whose mother kindly invited you to stay, did she not?" Whether it was true or not, that was what Lady Rotherham wanted to hear. Maria had been away for a night that had to be accounted for.

The subsequent pause lengthened uncomfortably. Langston was standing by one of the office's two chairs—both unoccupied for all the turmoil in the room—but he moved to stand closer to Juliet, where she stood alone, facing Lady Rotherham. "He brought Lady Maria to me this morning. Not last night."

Lady Rotherham closed her eyes briefly. "I am sure you are mistaken, my lord."

"No, he is not." Maria's quiet voice confirmed. She lifted her hand and dropped it again. She was visibly shaking.

At last Maria had found some courage. All her life Maria had been controlled and instructed by her mama. Juliet did not underestimate the bravery Maria showed at that moment.

Norris broke in, moving a little closer to Maria, as if to protect her from her mother's wrath. "I could not persuade her to go."

"Oh, don't spoil it, Norris," his lordship drawled. "You behaved like the perfect knight errant, except for a few hours." He smiled at her ladyship but there was no humor in it. "So you see, ma'am, I cannot marry your daughter."

Lady Rotherham glared at Maria and swept around restlessly—no mean feat in this crowded room. "We can still go ahead with our plans," she said. "We may wait to see if there are any—results."

Juliet didn't miss Langston's warning glance to Norris, though she wasn't sure anyone else caught it. His secretary closed his mouth. "I will not take another man's leavings," he said. "I hate to be quite so direct, especially since my profession is not known for it, but that is the bare truth, I regret to say, ma'am." Before her ladyship could interrupt, he went on smoothly. "However, I had intended to provide Norris with a Parliamentary seat I have in my gift. He is a talented politician with a great future before him. I am naturally unhappy to lose him as my secretary, but needs must. I am sure you will come to be proud of him."

Lady Rotherham turned back around with a swish of her silk skirts. "There is such a thing as breach of promise." Her face was stony, set rigid.

"So there is," Langston said. "And you are welcome to drag your daughter's good name through the courts. I would not advise it, however." He held out his hand, and without overthinking, Juliet took it. "I will leave you to discuss the details," he said.

Somehow he'd managed to maneuver them both closer to the door, though Juliet had no idea how he'd done it. He opened the door and ushered her through it, one hand at the small of her back. He turned and bowed. "I wish you both well," he said to Maria and Walter Norris who stood together like a shield. "Please contact me later, when you've settled matters here."

JULIET DIDN'T COME to herself until she was in the passenger seat of Langston's curricle and they were bowling away from the Rotherham house. "Lady Rotherham will never speak to us again," she said, still stunned by what had just happened.

"We can only hope and pray," he replied calmly.

"How can you appear so unaffected?"

He turned his head and smiled at her. "We'll discuss it in a little while. But at the moment all I feel is relief." He turned his attention back to the road. "My mother will corroborate what I told her ladyship. We did not see Lady Maria until this morning. I'll take you to visit my mother. She has a great desire to meet you."

"I have met her," Juliet replied, struggling to keep up with the abrupt change of subject.

"Not properly."

Clearly he was in no mood to be gainsaid, so she sat upright and stared ahead. "I have something I need to discuss with you."

"Yes, we have a lot to talk about, do we not?" he said affably.

Neither of them opted to have their discussion in public. Instead, as they drove past the lines of white stucco-fronted houses with shiny black doors, they nodded to acquaintances, smiled, and discussed the weather. Nobody gave them more than a second glance.

They arrived at his white house with the black door. Juliet had plenty of time to examine it while he brought the horses to a stop, climbed down allowing his groom to take his place, and walked around the back of the carriage to help her down. But instead of giving her his hand, he reached up, caught her around the waist and lifted her down.

Juliet could not suppress her gasp. Half shocked, half pleased, she looked up at his face. He was smiling. She liked his smile, the broad, genuine grin that transformed his features from stern to merry.

"Yes," he said, as if acknowledging her frisson of arousal. Was he feeling it too?

He said nothing more but stepped back and led the way into the house. The door was already open—his butler would have seen him coming. As they climbed the stairs, wide enough for them to walk abreast, Juliet tried to come to terms with what had happened and what would happen next. If the Burrells were shunned by Lady Rotherham, even cut, they would need the support of Lady Langston, someone she did not know well, to cope with it. She couldn't rely on her sisters' help. Viola was in the country, not planning to come up for the Season, and Bianca was close to being refused admission to any number of houses.

He led her into a spacious, white-painted entrance hall. The usual portraits adorned the walls, with a large one at the half-landing, where the stairs turned to go up. The staircase rose either side of the hall, creating a grand entrance. She swallowed.

"Tea, please, Fotherington," he said to the butler as Juliet handed her bonnet, gloves and pelisse to the footman dressed in the Langston livery of slate blue and silver.

"Your lady mother already ordered a fresh pot," Fotherington replied. His bald head, only relieved by a fringe of close-cropped gray hair, shone in the light cast by the skylight above them.

"Very well. I'll take Miss Burrell up to see her." He turned to her, his smile not so broad as before, more formal.

She touched the soft, matte fabric of his dark blue coat as she took his arm and tried not to reveal her nervousness, keeping her expression schooled and her breathing regular. She felt like a princess for the short journey up the stairs. Calm came back to her with every step.

The doors to the main drawing room directly in front of them were flung open by the footman on duty. Langston grinned. "Thank you, Taylor." So he knew the names of his servants. Many did not concern themselves with such details, especially London servants who might change from one Season to the next. His casual use of the name pleased her.

The drawing room was mainly ivory, with discreet touches of gold. The room looked out over the square, the trees and greenery providing a pleasant backdrop, the rails in front reminding visitors where they were: in a graciously appointed house in a privileged part of the greatest city in the world.

By the fire, two sofas were set opposite each other, and on the thick rug between them a low table was covered in a veritable feast. Tea was the least of it. Her ladyship, a willowy woman with fair good looks that belied her age, stood in a single, gracious movement and held out both her hands in a welcoming gesture. "My dears, do come and make yourselves comfortable. We're *en famille* today, no irritating visitors to repeat gossip we've heard twice already!" She continued to talk in a soothing flow until they had taken their places before the fire. She glanced at the burning coal. "I know, a fire in May! But at least the weather isn't as bad as last year. Perhaps we will even get a summer, imagine that!"

After serving the tea herself and offering scones and slices of cake which both Juliet and Langston refused, her ladyship resumed her seat. "Now, before you say anything pleasant or proper, do tell all. Are you persona non grata with the pompous Lady Rotherham? If it were not for my own standing in society she'd delight in cutting me."

She made the whole situation sound like a lark rather than a matter that would define peoples' lives. Somehow that approach made Juliet feel better. Like her own mother, Lady Langston had a robust, practical approach.

"She accepted our explanation," his lordship told his mother. "She believes her daughter and poor Norris spent the night together unsupervised."

Her ladyship sighed. "Good. That makes matters so much easier."

Juliet gaped "You mean she didn't?"

Smiling, Lady Langston shook her head. "Norris brought her here. Just after one o'clock in the morning, so strictly speaking we didn't see her until this morning. She spent what was left of the night under this roof, and just in case there was any rumor of impropriety with Valerian, my poor son spent the night elsewhere."

Langston covered his eyes with one hand. "In Brook Street. That pink room, oh my eyesight will never be the same again!"

His mother laughed. "I rather liked the furnishings when I had them, but I do admit the novelty wore off quite quickly. Anyway, it serves you right for being so blind regarding Norris and Lady Maria. A man like you couldn't see what was under your nose?"

He shook his head. "I suspected nothing until last night. I did suspect her emotions might be engaged elsewhere, but not there. And Norris, blast him, never let on either."

"But you told Lady Rotherham they had compromised each other," Juliet said.

"Part of a diplomat's skill is to tell lies," Lady Langston pointed out.

"And to avoid them whenever possible," her son added. "Lies are difficult to support. I did not actually tell her, I let her draw the conclusion."

Juliet could not help but admire what they'd done. Of course Langston could not marry Maria if there was any chance of Maria bearing Norris's child.

"Besides," Langston added smoothly, "they spent at least an hour together before he could get her out of his lodgings. It would be ungentlemanly of me to suggest they did anything other than talk, however. And untruthful, too. That girl can cry."

"She can," Juliet said fervently.

"The poor creature should never have been put in that situation," Lady Langston said.

Her son shook his head. "I asked her if she wanted me to propose before I did it. She said yes."

His mother shot him a piercing stare. "I still want to know why you asked her." She shrugged. "But I will not ask again. It is over now, and we have to deal with the aftermath." Without warning, she turned her attention to Juliet. "What do you think? Why would my son the diplomat ask for the hand of a young girl obviously unsuited to the life?"

Juliet was not used to such plain speaking outside her immediate family circle. And not even much of that recently. But someone had asked for her opinion honestly, so she'd give it. "She most likely gave the impression of being better read than is in fact the case. With the encouragement of her mother, I've been reading books with Maria. Our habit was that for every book of philosophy, philosophical thought, or history that I chose for us, we would also read a novel or a book of poetry. I'm afraid she did not finish most of my choices, not even some of the poetry, but she devoured the novels. Lady Rotherham said I was bringing a touch of culture to Maria."

"Bringing her daughter up to scratch." Lady Langston paused to help herself to a scone and lavish it with jam and cream. No thin slices of bread and butter for this family at teatime. Despite the tension tightening her stomach, Juliet could have managed one of those scones. Her ladyship must have seen something of her thoughts on her face and nodded to her. "Don't stand on ceremony. It's hours until dinner time."

This time Juliet did as she suggested and plied her dessert fork with good effect. The food soothed her. That scone was baked particularly well, soft and crumbly.

His lordship did not partake but watched the women and sipped his tea. "Lady Rotherham had her eye on me from the beginning of last Season."

"Before then," her ladyship said, "but you left for Paris. When you returned, she took her chance. Evidently, she had Miss Burrell here instruct Maria but without telling her why." She tutted, the sound emphasized when she put her dessert fork on to her empty plate. "She would have made you both unhappy. That poor girl needs someone entirely different. You expect the people around you to hold their own," she told her son. He grunted but did not deny it.

"I only knew I'd made a mistake recently," he admitted. "Or rather, realized it."

Juliet was remembering that walk by the bookshop. He'd encouraged her to talk, and she had.

"But Lady Maria is in love with a politician," Juliet pointed out. She had finished too, and she felt much better with something in her stomach. Breakfast was a distant memory. "She will have to cope with the political world if she marries him."

"*When* she marries him," Lady Langston corrected her.

"He is a gentle man and kind," Langston said. "Also astute. He won't expect more of her than she can give. He will be a credit to everyone, I predict. I'll give him the seat I have when it becomes vacant later this year."

"Has Horrocks decided to resign?"

"Yes," he told his mother. "He says he's too old to care anymore. I planned to persuade him to stay another year, because I wanted to give Norris more experience, but he will need that seat now he's to become a married man." He lifted one shoulder in a half-shrug, reminding Juliet how powerful those shoulders were. His clothes, although understated, must be beautifully tailored. They followed the contours of his body but magically gave the impression of someone slender, willowy even. Which, as she had reason to know, given how easily he had lifted her down from the carriage, he was not. "We have merely helped him with his ambitions. I daresay the Rotherhams will help him, too."

"At any rate, your unfortunate misalliance has come to an end."

With a move so graceful it made Juliet suppress a gasp of admiration, Lady Langston rose from her sofa. "I saw how much you enjoyed that scone. Allow me to ask my cook to write the recipe down for you. Perhaps the Whiston cook can do something with it."

Her son rose to open the door for her. What would happen now?

She found out when he closed the door, which he rightly should not have done, because it left her alone with him.

"Now," he said, advancing on her. "We have something to

discuss."

"Oh!" What on earth did he mean? She was still reeling after the evidence of contrivance worthy of her mother. "I thought that was the end of it. Unless you want Maria after all."

"Would I have gone to such lengths if I did?" He resumed his seat, far too close to her. The hairs on her forearms rose. "I blame myself. I should never have proposed to her. The union would have made both of us unhappy. But I had no idea that she had been stuffed with knowledge rather as a tutor crams a pupil facing a stiff exam." He grimaced.

"I'm sorry," she mumbled.

"Not your fault," he said. "You had no idea what they were doing. I exonerate you completely."

She shook her head. "I should have guessed something." She could see now that she'd been so eager to have a friend, someone outside her beloved family, that she'd chosen to believe only the best of everyone's intentions. Before London, the Burrells had been on their own, and while they loved each other, their acquaintances had been just that. With her sisters settled, Juliet had felt alone, solitary. She'd welcomed Maria's friendship, too eagerly as it turned out. Despite his words, she still felt guilty.

He took a breath. "I have a problem of my own to solve."

"Oh? P-perhaps I can help." She couldn't move any further away; she already had her back against the arm of the sofa. And she did want to make amends. Although she understood she'd been fooled by Lady Rotherham, she still felt partly to blame for this mess.

"Perhaps you can." His smile came, the soft, warm one. "In two days' time, I have a very important dinner at Carlton House. Not to put too fine a point on it, but this is an interview for the post of Ambassador to Russia."

Ah. She had forgotten about Maria's dreaded state dinner. "I am sure you'll do very well." Carlton House, the Prince of Wales's residence could be a daunting prospect even for him, apparently.

"They expect me to attend with an affianced wife," he continued.

"Can your mother not substitute for Maria?" She was doing her best not to imagine herself in the role. He probably meant to ask her if she knew someone who might suit. Juliet did have a good acquaintance with most of the young ladies husband-hunting this Season. "Or did you want me to suggest someone?"

"No need," he said. "I want you."

Chapter Eight

HE REALLY MEANT that, God help him. In every sense. His erection was straining against his pantaloons, so much he had to keep his legs crossed, ankle over knee, to conceal it. An embarrassing response, but one he did not seem to have any control over. He wanted her quite desperately.

He must concentrate on persuading her if that expression of incredulity on her face was real.

"Me? What can I do?"

Her voice rose in pitch, but he pretended not to notice and tried a new tack. "Did you suggest that she run off with Norris, as Lady Rotherham seems to believe?"

"No!" She glared at him, color tingeing those divine cheekbones. Without her sisters present, Juliet would always be the loveliest woman in any room she entered. With them, she was one of the three loveliest, but he had never responded to them as he did to her. "She told me of her plan, but I said that was foolish in the extreme."

"So you knew about Norris?"

"Yes." She bit her lower lip, worried the plump flesh with her teeth. "But Maria swore me to secrecy. I was the only person she trusted. How could I abandon her? Maria is the sweetest-natured girl in the world, far too biddable for her own good."

"But not as bright as her mother wanted me to believe."

"No, she is not. I did not know what Lady Rotherham planned. I only thought she wanted me to help Maria develop her mind a little, that's all. People do that," she added helpfully.

She was still clutching her dessert plate, her fingers white at the tips. Gently, he tugged it from her grip, but she resisted, held it tighter, until she realized what she was doing. She released the china with a muttered apology. He suppressed his laugh.

"No matter." He put the plate on the table to join the other remnants of his mother's mid-afternoon feast.

He was annoyed that he'd allowed a woman like Lady Rotherham to deceive him. Had he wanted to be fooled? Juliet was right. Maria was so sweet-natured she would probably have run herself into exhaustion trying to please him and become the perfect ambassador's wife. And she would still have failed. As the wife of a young, promising politician, moreover one that she loved, she would have a much better chance of reaching her potential and being happy.

"I've not seen them together before," she mused aloud "but he seemed very protective of her, which is what she needs."

"If she becomes more like her mother, she may not need that forever." He watched her, drinking her in. "We shall see. Fortunately, not with me. I won't pretend with you, Juliet. I will not insult you so."

He had never used her first name before, and he saw the impact. Her glorious blue eyes opened wide, and her lips parted, but she said nothing, only snapped her mouth shut.

He longed to touch her, to feel her body under his palms. Her attention went from his face to his hands and back again, as if she could read his thoughts.

"I have a dilemma. I am to attend a state dinner. I'm sure Maria told you of that, perhaps expressed her apprehension. I think the prospect of it might have been what pushed her to drastic action."

She met his gaze. "Yes, she did. Did you encourage that fear?"

"Maybe a little. Only to show her I would expect such events to occur frequently if she married me." He was not ashamed of that. Maria had needed to know.

"It was not well done of you, my lord," she said with deliberate formality.

"It was necessary."

"For what?" The spark of anger on her friend's behalf emboldened her. "To scare her half to death?"

His lips tightened. "To make her future role clear."

"And done in that highly formal way you use so well!"

That made him laugh. "Ah yes! Formality is part of my everyday life. Does it bother you?"

"Not in the least." The corner of her mouth twitched, as if she would smile. "Would you have gone forward with the marriage?"

He nodded. He'd have had no choice. "I chose to propose to her, so I would have borne the consequences. I'd have done my best to make her comfortable in the role of wife to a diplomat, but I don't think she would ever have settled to it."

"If she marries Walter Norris, will she not face the same thing?"

He shook his head. "Unlikely. Domestic affairs are also changing, but here she will be on familiar ground, with her family around her. Norris is at the start of his career, and his wife will not be under the kind of scrutiny afforded the wife of an ambassador. Or even in my current position."

"And what is your current position?"

She needed to know, but he was so unused to sharing that part of his life that he hesitated. He arched a brow but answered her. "Consul, envoy, sometimes nothing at all." He lifted one shoulder in an elegant shrug. "My role is the same."

"Which is?"

"To manage the covert activities of the consulate or embassy." He stopped, evidently waiting for her response.

"Spies?" She didn't know whether to be appalled or thrilled. "Are you a spy?"

He laughed again. "I'd make a terrible spy. Besides, gentlemen don't spy. They just supervise the ones who do."

"Lying for their country?"

"Exactly." He wasn't laughing now. "And dying for her, too. They usually lay in unmarked graves in foreign countries. Most are attached to the army but a very few, the select ones, you might say, work on their own. Most route through the consulate or embassy. We have the communication channels they need."

"What if a gentleman discovers something he should not know? By accident, perhaps?" she asked, curious.

"If he has any sense, he comes to us. They usually do. And he tells us what he knows, then goes about his business and pretends he had nothing to do with the matter." He shrugged. "We do a great deal of work with codes, too." He hated that part of his work, the subterfuge and the lies. It was a strong factor in his deciding to leave it behind for the Ambassadorship.

"Oh! I used to enjoy word puzzles. I have not done any for a while, but I found them fascinating. Not that I could do anything as complex as a code."

"Don't be too sure. You are an intelligent woman." He leaned forward, and touched her hand, testing the waters. Their conversation had done nothing to dampen his desire. He still wanted her badly. At least he would try to claim a kiss.

She tried to snatch her hand back, but he closed his larger one over it. If she truly wanted him to let go, he would. "Don't," he repeated. "Simply be yourself, don't try to be anyone else. I shall send you a letter in code, and we will see how you do. Would you like that?"

"Yes," she said and then bit her lip. "I should not have said that."

"Why not?"

"Because—because . . ." She tailed off.

Because she'd been told that clever women didn't catch husbands. Because she was ashamed of her own intelligence. Anger stirred when he thought how she'd tried to suppress what she was, what she enjoyed. He would see to that.

"Did you really have no idea that Maria was being compelled to accept your proposal?" she asked.

"Not really," he said. "Suspected maybe. But suspicion isn't evidence. That was why I asked her if she wanted me to propose. But must we continue talking about her? I thought we had moved on."

She made to rise. "I should be going."

He stood with her and towered above her, at least a head taller than she was. He still held her hand, and he used that to tug her closer. "You could come with me on Thursday. In fact, I expect you to."

"Expect?" She glared up at him. "Expect, sir?"

He smiled, softening his demand. He did not want her angry with him. "Indeed I do. As matters lie, Maria has left me in a dilemma."

"Why?"

"I need a wife. Or rather, a betrothed wife. I am expected to arrive at the dinner with one, and this promises to be important for me."

Juliet caught her breath. Did he really mean to marry her? Or no, perhaps he only intended to use her while he needed a partner. Either way, she could not take Maria's place. Could she? "Why do you need it?" she asked him. "Ambassadors don't need to have wives."

"This one does," he said firmly. "Lords Liverpool and Castlereagh strongly prefer it. And the Tsar has expressed his preference for dealing with married men. I am not the only candidate for the position of Ambassador to Russia, and the others under consideration are married. If I arrive at that dinner without a betrothed in tow, I will not be considered for the post."

"And you want it."

"I do," he confirmed. "But that's not the only thing I want." Bending his head, he tightened his arm around her waist and brought her hard against his chest. When her mouth dropped open in shock, he took advantage of it, and kissed her.

Cupping his cheek seemed natural, at least that was where her hand went, as if it knew what she wanted. And she responded, oh how she responded to his kiss. He gave no quarter, and she loved it, reveled in his passion. He touched her lips with his tongue, caressed the soft flesh and pushed inside.

Valerian kissed like an angel, or a devil—she didn't know which, and at the moment she didn't care. She slid her other hand around his waist, more to hold on and stop herself falling to the floor. That brought his lower body closer to her and his hard rod pressing against her stomach like a hot brand, one that marked, but caused no pain, only desire and passion.

He touched her tongue with the tip of his, teased it, played with her until she reacted, shyly at first, then with more confidence, especially when he gave a low groan. The sound vibrated deep within her, right through her and she shivered.

Immediately he finished the kiss and loosened his hold on her. When she did not move away, but instead moved closer, he slid his arm around her again, and pressed a kiss to her forehead. They stood together, the only sound in the room the quiet tick of the clock and their breathing. Carriages rolled past outside, and the sound of distant voices reached her ears, such a commonplace thing she seldom noticed it.

His shoulder was right there, so she rested her head on it.

"So is that a yes?" he asked.

"When you put it like that, I can hardly say no."

He kissed her again.

Chapter Nine

"**S**UCH A CATCH," Juliet's mother crowed. "You're to be a countess!" Juliet sat with her mother and sister in the small parlor, having a cozy afternoon together which was all too rare these days.

Bianca looked up from her embroidery. She was smiling. "Yes indeed. In some ways Juliet is the most fortunate of all of us because she will see the world. Or parts of it."

"I didn't know you wanted to travel," Juliet said.

Bianca tucked her needle into her work and gave her sister her full attention. "I did not know. When we were younger, we certainly traveled, but it was uncomfortable and on occasion frightening, even though Mama persuaded us to see it as an adventure. Now, with the consequence I can demand, and servants to attend to my every need, I see a great deal to commend it. I would like to go to Paris. I'm told it's a marvel, even though some of it is still under construction. "Where did you say your husband to be is to be sent?"

"Russia, he thinks," Juliet said, "but I don't think I will be his wife by then."

"And why not?" her mother demanded.

"Because I was a material part of Maria crying off. I agreed to attend the state dinner as his betrothed, because he is expected to bring one. He needs a wife, he says. He *says*," she repeated, because she was not at all sure he was not bamming her. She didn't know him well enough to know what he really meant to do. That ambiguity made her nervous.

"He will not cry off," Mrs. Burrell said. "Gentlemen don't do that. So it is your choice. Do you want him?" their mother asked.

Juliet was firm. "I won't entrap him into something *he* does not want." God forbid she did that.

"So you *do* want him!" Bianca shifted to look at Juliet, and the movement dislodged her shawl from her shoulder. It slipped down her bare arm and she bent to retrieve it. With her face turned away, she said quietly, "People say I entrapped George."

"You didn't," Juliet said instantly. "He entrapped you."

Finally, Bianca straightened, her shawl in her hands. "He says I did."

"He's wrong," Mrs. Burrell said, her voice hard. "He took you away. Whatever else we might have been, we were always respectable. He had no right to do that."

"No." Bianca stared down at her hands. "His main concern now is the lack of an heir."

"Ah."

"He says it must be my fault, because before we married he had a mistress, and she had his child." She said it quickly, as if she wanted to get it over with, keeping her head down as she spoke.

"How dare he!" their mother said. "How dare he say such a thing! You have barely been married a year, and he says that?"

Bianca swallowed. "But it's true. One of the reasons George was eager to be married in the first place was to cut out his cousin Arthur."

"I thought it was the debts," Juliet put in.

"Well those, too, of course. And the woman he'd planned to marry brought a fortune with her. If I can't even give him an heir, what use am I?"

What had happened to her sister, the joyous Bianca who had never encountered a problem in which she could not see the happy side? This dispirited, downtrodden woman was the very opposite. Juliet had never seen her sister so dejected, so beaten. She wanted to cry, but what good would that do?

Their mother laid a hand over that of her youngest daughter. Her voice gentled. "Bianca, do not let him blame you for this. Or for anything else, come to that. Keep fighting, keep asserting yourself. I know it's hard, but don't let him lay you low like this."

"I do try." A tear fell on the back of their mother's hand. "But he's right about the baby. And I want a child so much, too."

"It might yet happen, my love. Some people have to wait for a while. Your brother did not make his presence known until your father and I were a year married."

Bianca lifted her head and stared into her mother's eyes, her own wide with shock. "I didn't know that! May I tell George?"

"If you feel you must."

Juliet didn't like this. Her sister should not have to excuse herself, to accept blame for something that might not be her fault. Why should she do it?

At least now she understood the arguments and disagreements, and she was proud of her sister for fighting back. But how long could she continue to do so? How long before she was beaten down and made to accept the blame for other things she was not responsible for?

"With an heir, Arthur and his mother at least would stop worrying him. You know they have threatened dreadful things, like accusing him of madness. If they have the ear of the committees involved, they could have him committed. He is not mad, truly he is not! And now he says it was my fault he did not marry the heiress he needed. The estate has great, gaping holes of debt, but he had to marry me."

"It was his choice to run off with you. Therefore it was his choice to marry you," Mrs. Burrell pointed out.

Whiston had eloped with Bianca with no intention of marrying her. Powerful friends intervened, one in particular, and left him with no choice. If not for those friends, he would have abandoned Bianca and gone for his heiress, a sweet girl who had yet to make her debut in society at the time. The affable, high-living duke had a dark side that marriage had not relieved him of.

"I think he is a weak man," Juliet said, voicing the thought that had haunted her since they'd come to live here. They had spent the winter in Whiston's huge country seat, so they had been effectively separated, on the other side of the house form the newlyweds, but even then Juliet had noticed the poor maintenance of the place, as if appearances were everything and a sound structure meant very little. Water had come through the roof in the winter storms, and nobody had discussed repairing it.

Like the rest of Whiston's property, the house in London, while lavishly appointed, had weak spots, places where the stairs were not entirely safe on the upper levels, faded paintwork and fabrics, nothing cared for properly after it was bought and put in place.

And now these accusations and arguments. Since silence had fallen, she continued with her thought. "He does not face problems—he runs away from them. The foolish pranks, the rash escapades, all excuses for not thinking. It's as if he's constantly running from all of his responsibilities."

Her mother shot her a warning glance, but she could not prevent Bianca's outburst. "He is not weak! Only sometimes his problems overwhelm him. And we are part of those, you know. He cares for you both," Bianca continued. "He truly does. He considers you part of the family." She grimaced. "Which reminds me, Arthur and his wife and mother are coming to our dinner tonight. I'm sorry."

Bianca paused and looked at her sister, sudden worry creasing her brow. "Don't tell him I told you about his troubles or the other child. He would throw you out of the house."

"And then you would have no friends here," Juliet said. She and her mother could easily find somewhere else to live—they were not the poverty-stricken adventurers of the year before—but then her sister would be alone. How could they leave Bianca with no support, nobody to bolster her spirits and take her side?

After a few minutes more of conversation about dinner and the guest list, it became clear that Bianca had closed up again and would not share any more of her worries. She refused to answer further questions, and soon it was time to go upstairs and dress for the evening.

Juliet longed to have someone she could talk to about all this.

JULIET TOOK MORE care than usual over her appearance for that night. She even surprised Banks by saying, "No, not that one. Is the pomona green ready?"

Banks lifted the pink silk Juliet had just rejected carefully from the bed. "Yes indeed, ma'am. I shall fetch it directly." She sounded pleased.

The pink looked too young to Juliet. She wanted to give a more mature appearance. After dinner, all the guests were to attend Lord Rotherham's birthday ball and it would be her first one as Langston's betrothed. Perhaps her last, she reminded herself, if he only wanted her for the dinner she owed him. She would make it count.

In all honor she would have to cry off, but it would not be easy. He trusted her to do that, which was flattering, but it left the burden on her shoulders. With the example of her sister strongly in the forefront of her mind, she determined that she would not force him to do anything. Condemning herself to a husband who would resent her, and use that initial resentment to push her further down into her personal pit of despond? No, thank you.

She just had to keep her head and try to forget how immensely attractive she found him. Remember, he went from kissing her directly to Maria.

"WILL YOU HOLD her to the engagement?" Lady Langston asked her son as he helped her down from the town carriage outside the Whiston residence.

His head shot up and he met her gaze before he realized she had said it to gauge his reaction. The sudden, unexpected question that came out of nowhere. She'd taught him the trick many years ago, and he used it to great effect in his work, but she'd caught him out now. She must have seen the blaze he was too slow to damp down.

"Ah," she continued when he did not answer. She slipped her hand through the crook of his arm as they walked up the broad marble stairs. "So you do want her."

"My feelings towards her are immaterial, Mama. If she wishes to cry off, then she must." He would not tell anyone how he felt about Juliet, not even his mother. He didn't trust it himself. They had no more privacy as the front door was already open and they were walking through it, so he was spared from having to say any more.

On the surface, the Whiston mansion was a grand example of a London residence. The hall was spacious, and marble staircases rose on either side of the area to the cross-landing above. but the paintwork was thin in places, showing a shadowy suggestion of the plaster beneath. Above, the plasterwork was yellowed with age. The red carpet on the staircases was thinning in the middle, the area of most use. But the candles in the huge chandelier above their heads were all lit, and there was no paucity of servants to attend to their needs.

"Bad management," her ladyship mouthed to Val as she removed her hat and handed it to a maid. He tended to agree. Last week he would have considered the state of the Whiston house none of his business. Now, he needed to take an interest as one of the inmates here had become quite important to him.

They chose the left-hand staircase and went up, guided by a liveried footman. His uniform was too large for him and had not been altered to fit better. A new servant, a sign of an exodus of domestic staff? Perhaps that was stretching speculation too far.

The family and other guests awaited them in the drawing room. Langston nodded to a few he knew. There were twenty guests in all, and their hosts and houseguests made it an even two dozen.

Val would have gone straight to Juliet, but the Duke forestalled him. "Have you met Mr. Carrington, my heir?"

"Yes, I have. At the Foreign Office," Val said, and forced a smile. He preferred to avoid Carrington. As usual, he was dressed ostentatiously, in a blue superfine coat and heavily embroidered satin waistcoat. What hair he had left was puffed and teased so much it resembled spun sugar more than real hair. That was not, however, why Val disliked him. Carrington was puffed full of his own self-importance. His pomposity, self-righteousness, and his talent for getting nothing done while appearing to be busy irritated Val beyond measure. However, since Carrington's work included being a liaison between various offices, Val met him far more than he would like.

Nobody would know from his pleasant smile and bow. "Delightful to see you twice in one day, Carrington."

"Mutual, I'm sure," Carrington replied. He held a quizzing glass, though he did not level it at Val. "Have you met my wife?"

"I believe so, my lord," Mrs. Carrington said before Val could answer. "At the Devonshire dinner."

Since the Devonshire dinner had catered for sixty guests, Val did not remember. He would not have been seated close to them, but he smiled and said, "Of course," and bowed again to the thin woman dressed in layers of silk and lace.

"And my mother, Anna Carrington." Carrington indicated the woman standing on his other side, whose size, height and girth, seemed to make up for Mrs. Carrington's bird-like qualities. Not that he would have commented on that feature, but if the caricaturists ever had cause to depict them, they would fall on the contrast with rapacious avidity.

Val bowed over the lady's hand.

"Pleased I'm sure, sir," she said.

Interesting she did not consider it necessary to use his title before moving to the less formal "sir." Generally, Val didn't care what people called him, but the assumption stroked him the wrong way. Perhaps because he did not like Carrington, he was prepared to dislike his wife and mother. Something he should guard against. Unthinking biases did not work well with diplomacy.

After the introductions he was free to greet his betrothed. He loved the shy flicker of her eyelids and the warm smile. He kissed her hand, making sure his lips made contact with her skin, and felt her light shiver. "Good evening, my lord," she said.

"Good evening, Miss Burrell." He did not move away but drew her hand through the crook of his arm. Short of kissing her full on the mouth, he could not have made his partiality more obvious. Perhaps he could steal a kiss later. He'd thoroughly enjoyed the two they had already shared—yes, he was counting them—and he wanted more.

They went through to the dining room. Here, the lavish furnishings were balanced by the grubby paintings and the light film of dust on the chandeliers. Val, used to attending to detail, marked it but made no sign that he had.

By some miracle, or clever management by Mrs. Burrell, Val found himself sitting next to Juliet, with Mrs. Carrington on his other side. Sublime to . . . well, he must not allow his prejudices to show. He would practice his diplomacy. After all, he'd sat through worse dinners than this, though the food served varied from uneven to excellent. Whiston stood to carve the beef, making a show of swiping knife against fork, laughing with his wife. "My skill at carving is only surpassed by my painting."

"I didn't know you were a painter," some wag spoke up.

"I'm not," Whiston replied to laughter. Val laughed along with the others and noted that Whiston was lying about the carving. He did it well and neatly. He took a serving and found buttered carrots and a fricassee nearby to supplement his meal.

He helped the ladies on either side of him to food, and leaned back to observe, his usual habit.

"You are to be congratulated, Langston," Lady Westbrook said, from across the table. Trust her to know. If Lady Westbrook did not know something, the wags said, it was not worth knowing.

"Thank you. I'm a fortunate man."

Lady Westbrook glanced down the table to where the Duchess was holding court, sparkling, attending to the people at her end of the table in equal measure. More skillful than Val would have given her credit for. Possibly a little too sparkling, however he saw no sign of intoxication by alcohol, laudanum, or even laughing gas, the latest society craze. Her eyes were clear, and her hands steady. Perhaps it was just the excitement of the occasion.

Next to him, Mrs. Carrington went still, and stopped the methodical application of food to mouth, her concentration for the last ten minutes. "I heard you had proposed to Lady Rotherham's daughter. You know, the older one who is out, not the one who is about to come out."

Val picked up his wine and took a sip before replying. "I wonder who told you that? Whoever did, they were mistaken. I admire Lady Maria, but as a friend, not a future spouse." He sensed that Mrs. Carrington was fishing. She had heard something, and she wanted confirmation.

"Really?" Lady Westbrook, not to be outdone, raised a quizzing glass, and then dropped it back in her lap. "I gave the tales no credence, but it is always good to hear a true confirmation or denial."

"That depends upon which you prefer," Val said.

Laughter rippled around the table, but Val did not join in. Disconcertingly, her ladyship turned to Juliet. "Miss Burrell, how do you feel about the current state of affairs?"

"In what way?" she asked sweetly.

"The turmoil in Europe—the state of France, for instance."

A difficult subject. King Louis XVIII's subjects were not impressed in the country he claimed he was born to rule, but he was a British ally. "I think everyone is exhausted. Even now, with Waterloo behind us and the great Treaty signed, there are matters to resolve."

He liked that answer. Very diplomatic.

"So you read more than the gossip sheets," Lady Westbrook said. Next to Val, Mrs. Carrington gave a derisive snort loud enough for the people around her to hear.

"I always have," Juliet said, as if she had not heard Mrs. Carrington.

Val felt Juliet's tension as if it were his own but let her have the lead.

"I believe your daughter also takes an interest in current affairs," Juliet said.

Her ladyship shot her a sharp look. "Indeed she does. I discourage gossip."

"Oh, but it's such fun!" Mrs. Burrell, sitting next to Lord Westbrook, protested. "The danger is in believing everything you read. As long as a person bears that in mind, and treats it as an amusement, there is little harm. People are always going to gossip and speculate, so an outlet is useful sometimes. And those poor people employed to write it must make a living, I suppose."

"At our expense," Lord Westbrook said. "It is an imposition I do my best to depress. We allow no gossip sheets in my house." From the knowing look his wife gave him, along with her sweet smile, he did not know the half of what went on in his house.

Val took a moment to appreciate the Duchess's clever arrangement of guests. Since he was bringing his mother, he presumed they agreed to invite a few older guests. The Carringtons could not be left out, obviously, but there were also Lord and Lady Westbrook. She was a great arbiter of society knowledge, and sometimes its wilder gossip. He was generally quieter than the others, but when he spoke, everyone listened.

By keeping the seating informal, the Duchess had been able to keep the older contingent in the middle and put the younger set on either side. Very clever. Perhaps Juliet had similar skills. Poor Maria would have had no idea how to seat guests with this kind of subtlety.

After dinner, the men did not linger over their brandy and port. As was his wont when in the society of people he did not count as intimates, Val watched and learned. Tonight he learned little, except that he disliked the Carringtons even more than he had before. Carrington's pomposity was only surpassed by his toad-eating ways. Val detested both traits.

When they went through to the drawing room, the ladies were evidently waiting, because as soon as they appeared, the Duchess hurried over to organize the exodus to the Rotherham ball. Held ostensibly to celebrate Lord Rotherham's birthday, but in reality it was meant to mark the betrothal that would now never happen. But they could not put off the event. Invitations had gone out—far too many to stop cancelation. And if Val and Juliet did not attend, rumors would abound.

Val had brought his own carriage, which he shared with his mother and his betrothed. As they climbed into the carriage, they heard a sharp snap.

"Oh botheration!" her ladyship said when they had settled. "I've broken my fan. Would you mind awfully if we stop at the house so I can collect a new one?"

They murmured compliance, and after Val delivered the new instructions to the coachman, they set off, the ladies sitting together facing the horses, Val opposite them. Since they headed in the opposite direction to the other guests, their progress was quicker. At the house, her ladyship only waited for the steps to be let down before hurrying indoors.

Val gave Juliet a wry grin. "Apologies for the delay." He picked up the discarded fan which his mother had abandoned on the seat. It drooped, a lopsided, expensive trinket ruined in an instant by his mother's quick thinking. It wouldn't take much pressure to break those ribs. Dropping it, he looked up at Juliet and reached for her hand. She let him take it and showed him a polite, society smile.

"We don't have to go," he said softly. "I have a box booked for the Season at the theatre. We could make an appearance there and keep people at a distance."

"No indeed!" she retorted. "We must go."

"It is likely we'll receive a hostile reception," he warned her. "I would not wish to see you distressed or as tense as you appear now. I promise that my mother will have no objection if we decide to go elsewhere. Let the gossip die down, and give society a chance to accept us as a couple."

"A pretend couple," she said, her smile wavering.

Was that it? He didn't think so. But both he and his mother had noticed the way Juliet's jaw tightened, her manner more stiff and formal as he handed her into the carriage and she sat bolt upright. The glance he'd exchanged with his mother was all that was needed, and the fan became a victim.

"Let's put that aside for now," he suggested. He didn't have time to discuss his shockingly passionate response to her presence, or what that might lead to. "Tonight we aim to become an established betrothed couple in society. Agreed?"

She nodded.

"We don't have to go to the heart of the matter to establish that. Being seen in public will be enough to fill the print shops and gossip sheets. Let them talk at the ball. My absence will explain what they need to know."

She swallowed and stared at her hands before raising her gaze to his face. "I think we should go. The ball is to celebrate her father's birthday, after all, not only Maria's betrothal." She met his concerned gaze steadily.

Pride welled within him that she was prepared to go through with this, despite the tension she was clearly feeling. "If you're sure?"

She nodded. He gripped her hands more firmly and had almost forgotten himself so completely as to draw her closer for a kiss, but at that moment the door opened, and the footman let down the steps for his mother to alight.

She glanced at them. "No, don't bother to hand me up. Higgins can do that."

And they were on their way again.

"One must assume her ladyship has the good sense to announce her daughter's betrothal to the excellent Mr. Norris, a talented young politician everyone should watch," Lady Langston remarked as she settled her skirts.

"Yes," Langston said. "I fear she may not have your good sense, though, Mama."

"The Duchess is charming. I enjoyed her company and her conversation," his mother went on, "but is she always so animated?"

"Not always, but her marriage has thrust her into a new milieu. She has had to adapt quickly," Juliet said.

Val would have called the Duchess's mood febrile rather than animated. Perhaps the Duchess was merely nervous. If so, he would be happy to reassure her that she had done very well by mixing the generations and managing any possible conflicts. But she was not first in his mind at the moment.

As the carriage neared the Rotherham house, Val's thoughts turned to the challenge ahead. "If Lady Rotherham has any sense, she will acknowledge us, and behave as if she knew about our betrothal all along. A misunderstanding merely."

"She might not," Juliet said. Her fingers shook as she folded them in her lap.

A pang of guilt struck him. "I can still escort you back to Whiston House if you wish."

Her answer came without pause. "Maria is my friend, and she needs my support. I want to see her happy."

"Don't you care how you will be painted?"

Juliet's laugh startled him. "No. We Burrells are used to being misinterpreted." She closed her mouth firmly as if stopping herself from adding anything else.

As new entrants to society, as parvenus, they would have

faced a number of uncomfortable situations. He could understand that—like when he'd entered a conference chamber when the outcome was not certain. And she was to face yet another one now. He was glad he'd given her the choice, and proud that she took the most effective—and most difficult—course.

"We started the hare running by appearing together and attending a dinner at the Whiston house for the first time," he said. "Now for the main event. After that, we should be able to go forward. We must wish Maria and her betrothed well, be seen together in public congratulating them."

"Yes. But what if they refuse us entry?"

The suggestion rocked Val, and from his mother's echoed, "Refuse us entry?" he knew she felt the same way.

"They will not," he said firmly. "I do not think we have ever been refused admission to an event, have we, Mama?"

His mother laughed. "Speaking for myself, I do not go where I am not likely to be welcomed." She flicked her new fan open and addressed Juliet directly. "My son has no conception of what being shunned and cut means. You must know I conduct my life as I wish and have done so since my son achieved his majority. I have had reason to avoid people, but on the whole the people I avoid are not those I wish to associate with anyway."

She spared Val a glance. "However, my son is the soul of propriety and has lived all his life in the bosom of the great and good. He might be refused admission to Almack's for wearing pantaloons instead of breeches, but he has good company. Wellington himself was turned away once for exactly the same reason. I tired of perfect propriety some time ago."

She was referring to her affairs. He should talk to Juliet about that. The idea made him uncomfortable—not the affairs but trying to explain the complex relationship he had with his mother to someone else.

His mother closed her fan with a snap. "We have arrived, so we shall see."

Chapter Ten

T HE ROTHERHAM HOUSE was fully decorated for this ball.
Torches flared outside the house, and straw laid on the
street helped to muffle the sound of rumbling carriage wheels as
the many guests arrived. The door lay wide open, revealing the
glow of many candles. They were among the early arrivals, but
even so the house was busy. So different to when Juliet had
tripped up the stairs every Wednesday to visit her friend Maria
and read yet another book with her.

Those days had gone. Whatever the outcome of the current
situation, Maria would not require her services any longer. For as
far as Lady Rotherham was concerned, that was what she'd been
doing: tutoring Maria to become a suitable wife for Langston, to
spend her life making intelligent conversation with the great and
good.

The way she'd been taken-in angered Juliet. She'd thought
Maria sweet and guileless, but she'd been wrong. Surely Maria
must have known about her mother's scheme to use Juliet to
make her more attractive to suitors. If she'd been told, Juliet
might even have gone along with the plan for her friend's sake,
but not the deception.

She would take part in this charade tonight, and then assess
her situation. Once Lord Langston had secured his position, they
might be able to quietly allow their betrothal to lapse and fade

away in the English summer. He needed a well-connected wife experienced in society matters and the world of the diplomat. Juliet fitted none of these criteria, and they both knew it.

They got out of the carriage, Lord Langston personally handing down his mother and Juliet, then they went into the house. Far from being turned away, the butler even bowed to Langston, though he and his footmen were still busy helping guests out of their outerwear and carrying it away.

Juliet savored the sight of the paintings and the tiled floor, reminders of happier times spent here when she was still under the illusion that Maria wanted her as a friend. Whatever happened tonight, it was unlikely to be pleasant. Happy memories notwithstanding, she rather wished she could leave.

Langston escorted his mother up the stairs, as was proper, and Juliet followed after. This early in the evening they might expect a receiving line, but private balls did not always have them, and Lady Rotherham preferred mingling with her guests. People glanced at the trio, but nobody addressed them directly, other than to acknowledge their presence with a nod or a small bow. There was no room here to properly bow and curtsey in any case. Maids stood at the top of the stairs and more footmen guided the guests to the drawing room, which would become the ballroom for tonight's event.

Everywhere Juliet looked, candles gleamed and crystal chandeliers glittered. Everything was beautifully maintained and in its rightful place. It was quite unlike Whiston House, where a few discolored patches showed where paintings had been sold and inferior ones put in their place, or where the servants had not bothered to clean the cornices properly.

Had her mother arrived yet? Yes, she caught a glimpse of her mother's emerald green satin when she glanced behind her to the hall below with Bianca and Whiston. She always felt safer when her family was around.

The odious Carringtons followed Whiston, but one couldn't have everything. They had perfected the art of criticizing without saying a word. Quite a feat, but not one she would want to emulate. Langston paused to speak to someone, allowing the others to catch up. Bianca leaned over to murmur one word in Juliet's ear. "Together again."

Juliet's heart warmed. Indeed they were.

"We'll tour the room," Bianca said. "Spread the news and gauge reactions."

A good plan.

A quartet played country airs in one corner. The room was already comfortably full. People dressed in bright silks, satins, and lace, jewels glittered under the light of a hundred candles, ancestors watched them from the walls. All was as it should be. At the far side of the room, Lord and Lady Rotherham were holding court. Maria stood by her mother's sofa, her head lowered, her hands clasped tightly over her fan. She'd break it if she wasn't careful.

Mrs. Burrell nodded to Lady Rotherham before the press of people obscured their vision. Juliet would have started across the room, but her mother put one hand on her arm. "No," she said. "Don't."

His mother turned to Langston. "You go."

His gray gaze roved over Juliet's face then passed to her mother. "You will look after her," he said, and walked away.

Alarmed, Juliet said, "What's wrong?"

"She didn't nod back," Mrs. Burrell said. "And young Norris is not with them." She and Lady Langston took Juliet to a group of people who acknowledged their presence and began a conversation, one she barely attended to, while Bianca and Whiston continued their circuit around the room. Danger sparkled along with the king's ransom in diamonds strung around prosperous necks. Juliet's modest string of pearls adorned hers, as they usually did.

Her mother steered Juliet toward another group. From the other side of the room Bianca laughed, that unmistakable trill she used to such good effect, but tonight laced with prickly edges.

The same prickles danced over Juliet's spine, a sense of uneasiness, an awareness cultivated in the ballrooms of Dublin, Edinburgh, and now London, with a few places in between to add a touch of spice.

Juliet and her mother strolled slowly up one side of the room, stopping to talk to people, and then through the door at the end to the next room, smaller but still elegant. On the other side, Lady Langston mirrored their actions. "In the old days," her mother said, "Your status depended on how far you could get in the enfilade of rooms. Until you reached the state bedroom, and that was the holy of holies."

Juliet had heard this before, but she smiled, as if her mother had said something clever. "These days nobody sleeps in the state bedroom."

"I daresay they prefer something a little more comfortable. Ah, Lady Graveney!"

They exchanged more meaningless conversation, the how-are-you-is-the-weather-not-appalling words that had ceased to mean anything half a room ago. Juliet waited for the summons, the footman politely asking them to leave, the chill as they followed him to the door. Juliet knew how that felt all too well. Her sister was a duchess, and even a rackety duchess occupied a level that gave her some protection. But she was still Miss Burrell. She was nobody.

They continued around the room, pausing to admire the flowers lavishly laid out, draped, and put into vases on delicate stands. They paused several times to converse, even though a few people skirted them. As they approached the Rotherhams this time, there was a definite drop in the volume of nearby conversation.

"Should we leave?" Juliet murmured. Langston had not come back. He'd been gone at least half an hour, and he wasn't with the Rotherhams. She couldn't see him anywhere. Her throat tightened even as she smiled.

The quartet struck up for the first waltz. People moved to the sides of the room, and a few swept onto the floor. The waltz, elegant, danced only with one partner, demonstrated affection, or was supposed to. Was Juliet about to see Langston escorting Maria onto the floor? *Where was Walter Norris?*

Juliet did not need to look around now to know who touched her elbow. She released the breath she was holding. "Our dance, I believe," Langston said, guiding her on to the floor.

Relief flooded her. He'd come back to her.

He danced well, but so did she. They did not have to mind their steps. He gazed down at her, smiling. "Her ladyship kept me by her for a while, explaining to her son why Paris was still unsafe for visitors. I could not oblige her by agreeing, but I can see why she wants to keep him by her."

She didn't care about Lord Greenfield. She had no interest in the pompous idiot whatsoever. "I thought you'd gone."

"Gone where?"

She tried to shrug, remembered she was dancing, and took the turn he led her into. "Do you always think the worst of a situation?" he asked, eyes gleaming.

"The worst?"

"Did you believe I would return to Lady Maria after the pains I took to get rid of her?" His lip twitched. Annoyance. "I don't scruple to tell you that Lady Rotherham is a fool. She had the perfect opportunity to put it about that her daughter jilted me because she preferred my secretary. That information would not have reflected well on me, or on you, I might add. Instead, Lady Rotherham has not even invited Norris!"

The news shocked her. "Why would she not do that?" To Juliet that was the height of absurdity. "After what Maria told her?"

"Either Maria has let slip where she really spent the night, or Lady Rotherham has decided to wait upon events. Or she doesn't believe her daughter." He smiled in greeting to a couple as they danced past. Juliet tried to follow his example, but she feared it was more of a grimace. However, his presence steadied her. Her feeling of despair, the dread of yet another night of snubs slid away, returning to the darker recesses of her mind.

"That gives us a position of strength," he added in a conversational tone as he performed a perfect turn. "We know the truth. Both the complete truth, and the one we provided her mother. If we allow that partial truth to become known, no man will come near Maria for the rest of the Season, for fear he would be harboring a cuckoo in his nest. If Lady Rotherham chooses to spread spiteful gossip, we have the power to retaliate."

If anyone underestimated this man, they would do so at their peril. She felt sorry for anyone who chose to oppose him.

"Poor Maria!" she said.

"Indeed, poor Maria. Her mother is destroying every prospect she might have. And now we're seen waltzing together and will be sharing another dance later . . ." He watched her reaction closely.

"You want two dances?"

"Two waltzes, or a waltz and a quadrille. I won't settle for anything less. Three dances, even. You are a delightful dancer, and I would seek you out for pleasure alone. Lady Rotherham may be determined to prevent our two friends from coming together, but she has no control over me. Although she did try." He glanced over her head to the corner her ladyship occupied. "Maria is still standing there. I saw her ladyship signal to the musicians to play the waltz as I was standing close to Maria. I came to you instead."

"I didn't see you," she said in a small voice.

"I saw you." His smile made the room an intimate one. "If Maria's mama destroys all chances for her, she may relent by the end of the Season and let her marry Norris. Or we could contrive to throw them together. Let them compromise one another in reality this time."

"My lord!"

"What?" He looked down into her eyes. "And don't you think it's time you called me Val? I do not want to stand on ceremony with my wife!"

She kept her expression steady, but it was an effort. "I'm only your affianced wife for tomorrow night. And maybe a little time after."

"Keep telling yourself that. I'm applying for a common license tomorrow."

A common license dispensed with the banns and shortened the waiting time before a marriage. Shocked to the core, Juliet stumbled. He supported her and led her back into the dance. "But this is a temporary arrangement, my lord—Val!"

"Is it?" He danced a few steps in silence. "Well, you may think so, and if you cry off I cannot stop you, but I'm still getting that license."

His smile would be the death of her. As it was, she had to work hard to retain her sangfroid. Her tension when he'd left her and not immediately returned was ridiculous, as was her delight when he came back to her side.

Yet a doubt had entered her mind. Could he mean it? "You cannot want me for a wife after rejecting one of the best-connected ladies in society. You need a wife who knows people."

His fingers grazed the bare skin below her short, puffed sleeves. Juliet had to repress a shiver of pleasure. He could play her like a violin, if only he knew it. "Allow me to know what I need. Good connections are always useful, but I have plenty of my own, you know."

"I will be your betrothed until tomorrow night," she reminded him, as well as herself. "I do feel I owe you that. And I will do my best to help you. But once you have your appointment, you will need someone who can offer you more. I am not insensible of the good it will do me, either, being seen in those exalted circles." She was trying hard to be sensible, she really was, but it was difficult when he was looking at her like that, when he was holding her so close.

She had not even noticed the interested gazes following them around the room until the music stopped and she found herself being openly observed. Curiosity and speculation filled the eyes of the people watching them. Before they left the floor, he murmured to her, "We will behave with perfect propriety."

His comment made her laugh—he must know how agitated she was.

He took her back to her mother, who was conversing with the younger Lady Jersey, one of the Lady Patronesses of Almack's. "Truly?" Mrs. Burrell trilled a laugh. "They thought Lord Langston was interested in Lady Maria? Well, Lady Maria is a dear friend of my daughter, so naturally he would find himself in her company, though I cannot understand how society could have supposed anything else. Do you not see how devoted his lordship and my daughter are to each other?"

She turned, as if unaware of their presence, but of course she'd known all along. "Ah, here they are. You see?" she said to her ladyship, one of the greatest gossips in all society. She could be relied on to spread the news. And her mother's account was clever, because it was simple. Arranged marriages were all well and good, but not when neither party was interested in the union once they'd become better acquainted. Juliet had thought of using such a disaffection as an explanation, but her mother had come up with something better.

Lady Jersey perused the pair standing before her. "Indeed. You make a pretty couple, I have to say. Better than . . . but never mind that! Langston, I must pay a visit to your mother, now she has returned to London. She always has the best gossip, and I have no idea what your chef does to make cucumber sandwiches so delicious, but she does. In fact, I have just come from her. She's in the card room, trouncing Lord Leverson at picquet."

"My mother enjoys a hand of picquet," Val said. "I'm afraid I only play moderately. My interests lie in other areas."

"Indeed they do," Lady Jersey said. "My word, this Season is turning out to be even more interesting than last. All this and a royal child to come later in the year! Do excuse me, I'm sure I see my husband beckoning." They watched her pass through the crowd, a smile here, a nod and a few words there, but her progress was steady. "Very skillful," Mrs. Burrell remarked. "Well, I think that is enough. We can retire now."

"I had hoped to speak to Maria," Juliet said.

Two pairs of eyes fixed her in their astonished gazes. "You must not," her mother said. "Don't even try. Not while her mother is here. I tried to approach Maria earlier while you danced. Her mother turned her away from me."

"She is being forced—" Juliet protested. She flicked her fan open and spoke behind it, so people could not read her words. "Manipulated. What kind of friend am I, that I cannot offer my sympathy and aid?"

Mrs. Burrell turned in a swish of silk and headed for the door. Val and Juliet followed her. "Not here, not now," Mrs. Burrell said. "Give them a few days. Her ladyship might yet come around."

They found Lady Langston in the card room, still holding her own. "I shall stay, if you don't object," she said after Langston told her they were readying to leave. "Lord Dupont is here, and I have not seen him for this age!"

Satisfied she'd be happy remaining where she was, the others escaped from the house faster than they'd entered it. By some miracle Val's carriage was already waiting outside, and they gave a mutual sigh of relief once they were moving.

"That was difficult," Mrs. Burrell said, leaning back against the squabs. "Bianca and George did not even stay for the dancing—I saw them make their escape early. I thought it best to stay longer to help get the right explanations moving, but I don't think we could have done any more tonight. Poor Maria!"

Poor Maria indeed.

Chapter Eleven

WAS IT POSSIBLE to be more nervous than this? Juliet's hand shook as she lifted the hare's foot and applied a light dusting of powder to her face. Of all the situations she'd faced in her life, she couldn't remember being so nervous before any of them. Not sneaking out of their lodgings in Dublin when they couldn't pay the rent, not walking out into high society in homemade gowns and cheap jewelry, not even her presentation at court last year. Because every time she'd been with her sisters and her mother. Their solid unit had always ensured they had someone to talk to, someone to be with. Tonight, she was on her own.

Juliet put the hare's foot down and studied her appearance. Her maid had dressed her dark hair in the latest style, an elaborate confection of glossy curls, gathered up as if done carelessly, but nothing was out of place, and every pose she took displayed a different aspect. Her gown was blue to match her eyes, overlaid with delicate Indian muslin which had been embroidered with tiny flowers by an expert, something they couldn't have afforded last year.

While Banks fixed a pretty spangled pin to her hair, Juliet mentally went over the political points she'd memorized. She could hold her own in most conversations, or at least add a point or two to show she was not entirely ignorant. She had found out as much as she could about Russia, but the British newspapers did not seem to take much interest in Russia now the war was over.

When she went downstairs, he was waiting for her. She had not heard the doorbell, and even in a house this large, she'd have heard it. No doubt the butler had kept a watch. Val had probably not rung the bell at all.

The sight of him, dressed immaculately in dark blue superfine and buff evening breeches, sent a jolt through her. But then, he did that whatever he was wearing. He smiled up at her, watching as she came down the stairs. Her mother and sister were there, too. They had eaten earlier than usual, and without guests, which was easier because the Duke was away for a few days, visiting a friend. The house felt much lighter without him. Now they were dressed for the theater, and after they would go to a ball at Lady Durham's. They had made sure Juliet knew their plan in case she should want to join them later. Juliet doubted she would go anywhere else after tonight's event, however.

"Charming," her mother murmured.

"Beautiful," Val said.

"I was trying for elegant and discreet," she said.

"You are elegant, discreet, and beautiful," he answered. "No, I take back discreet. Your beauty is far too spectacular for discretion."

The Burrell sisters had been labeled "beautiful" last year, and Juliet had grown used to hearing it, but to have it spoken now by someone she respected, and with *such* a gleam in his eyes, meant much more to her.

Val dipped a hand into his pocket and drew out a slim case. "I thought you might like to wear these."

That case could only hold jewelry. When he opened it, she caught her breath at the glitter of diamonds. But not the large, flashy type. This was an exquisitely delicate necklace, with matching earrings twinkling on either side. The filigree work was interspersed with fine, clear diamonds, so delicate she dared not touch it before he twirled her so he could remove her pearls and fasten the necklace in its place. She unhooked her simple earrings so her mother could put the new ones in for her.

"So clever," Mrs. Burrell murmured. "Beautifully made."

Juliet stood before the mirror in the hall and admired the way the stones caught the light, as if she were wearing stars around her neck. She finally dared to touch it. "It's lovely."

"I'm glad you like it."

She turned back to him. "I'll take great care of it."

"I know you will."

They were lovely pieces, and she would greatly enjoy wearing them until it was time to return them.

He led her outside to his carriage, and they climbed aboard. "Should we not have a chaperone?" She had expected someone to be waiting in the carriage, especially as he'd told her mother there was no need for her to change her plans.

"We are betrothed," he said firmly. "A little license is allowed."

Even though the carriage windows were not covered and they did not touch, she felt vulnerable and excited. And not all of it was because of the upcoming dinner.

The journey to Carlton House was so short it was hardly worth taking, but it would never do to arrive on foot, even though they had done so perfectly happily last Season. The footmen opened the door and let down the steps so Val could alight and help her. Then they had to traverse the ritual of removing hat and outer clothing, which did nothing to soothe her nervousness. Her heart was stuck in her throat. How on earth could she breathe properly, much less consume a banquet?

"Relax," he murmured in her ear when he helped her remove her cloak.

As if she could, especially with his hot breath warming the outer rim of her ear. She would try, and she was well practiced in putting on a face that revealed nothing of what was going on inside. An essential requirement of this gossip-keen society.

Compared to the crushes they usually attended, this was

almost stately, but then again, not many houses could compare with Carlton House. Ostensibly this dinner was to celebrate the announcement that the Prince Regent's daughter, Princess Charlotte, was expecting a baby in the autumn. Naturally, everyone was delighted, and the excuse did give opportunities for occasions such as this, a chance for statesmen and politicians to meet on neutral ground.

Unsurprisingly, the Princess of Wales would not attend. She'd left the Prince shortly after their nuptials, and neither was eager to resume the relationship. Princess Charlotte was not there, either. As the butler explained to her, "His Royal Highness thought it best for Her Royal Highness to rest, as she has a slight cold. She sends her apologies."

A convenient cold, no doubt. The Princess never had a taste for formality, although she bore it well enough.

And there, at the head of the huge double staircase, talking to his guests, was the Regent, his sister Princess Augusta Sophia by his side. Most people did not mention the fact that the Prince of Wales was as wide as he was tall, at least not to anyone who might repeat the words to the man himself, but there was no denying it. One might call him portly if one wanted to flatter, but the cartoonists made hay with his size, his pomposity, and his multiple affairs every day. He had recently returned to his mistress, Mrs. Fitzherbert, who naturally could not be his hostess for the formal occasions. She probably counted herself lucky.

The air was thick with heavy perfume and gossip. As they reached the Regent, he smiled, his thin mouth stretching into something that looked genuine. He wore as much face paint as Bianca had earlier tonight, though not so carefully applied. His brown wig was slightly askew, and as they approached he scratched his forehead, nudging the offending object a little more out of place.

As Juliet rose from her curtsey, Princess Augusta Sophia bestowed a smile on her. The gossip was that she had privately married Sir Brent Spencer five years ago, but if she had, it had never been announced. However, considering the way her father had clung to his five girls, refusing to allow them to marry, Juliet hoped the rumors were true, and the Princess was happy now. She certainly appeared to be. She was a well set up woman, soft brown hair cut to curl around her face, and friendly brown eyes.

"Ah, Langston, good to see you. So you're back from your travels, eh? You never seem to spend very long in any place, so I hope you can stay until the end of the dinner tonight!" the Regent joked, and the people around him dutifully laughed.

Val smiled. "All in the service of the Crown, sir. And I am delighted to do so."

The Prince lifted his quizzing glass and stared at Juliet through it. She lowered her eyes and sank into a deep curtsey. As she rose, he said, "Ah yes, you're one of the Misses Burrell, aren't you? I recall it now. Adventuresses, some called you." He nodded and lowered his glass. "Though I did not do so. And how are you this evening?"

It was barely five o'clock, but she would not comment on that. Dinner was to be at six, unconscionably early, but the Prince preferred it that way. "In good health, Your Highness." A wave of sweet violets, from the lozenges he constantly imbibed, swept over her, the undisguised sickly aroma of rotting teeth beneath that.

"Humph. Good to hear." He turned back to Val, penciled brows raised.

Val answered the unspoken question. "Miss Burrell and I have recently become betrothed, sir. The invitation was for myself and my affianced bride."

His brow cleared. "Ah, I see. Well met, ma'am." He fixed her with a stare, unapologetically studying her, his gaze lingering on her breasts and then her face. "I can't recall when I met you last, but I never forget a face as lovely as yours."

Juliet kept her eyes lowered. "Thank you, Your Highness. I am the sister of the Duchess of Whiston and the Countess of Knowsley, so perhaps we met at one of their receptions? And the

Duke has entertained you to dinner before, I believe."

"Yes, of course!" He was all smiles now. "Your sister the Duchess is a charming lady. You do not resemble each other closely. Her hair is spun gold, and yours . . ." he paused, clearly groping for words.

"Wild honey," Val suggested. "The dark kind that you can find in the woods."

"Or perhaps satinwood," the Regent said. "Yes, that is a perfect description."

Val bowed. "It is indeed, sir. Perfect."

Beaming at his well-worn metaphor, the Regent glanced around at his splendid surroundings. "I must apologize for greeting you in what amounts to a rookery. I have determined to move to Buckingham House, but the architects and workmen are kicking their heels. However, if one wants good work, sometimes one must wait on results. Art cannot be rushed." He beamed. "I have long been accustomed to doing so. I am the soul of patience."

Not from what Juliet had heard, but knowing the gossip that circulated about the Burrells, she wondered how many stories about the Prince were true. In any case, she saw no rookery. Only white and gold magnificence, more gold than white. Masterpieces hung on the walls, the marble statues sat stately on their pedestals.

They passed on as the Regent greeted someone else, a not-so-tactful hint for them to leave the presence.

She smiled up at Val. He smiled back. "You're doing well." When they were out of anyone's hearing, he added, "I still prefer the wild honey comparison."

"So do I."

They went up the grand staircase in perfect accord.

THE CRIMSON DRAWING Room lived up to its name. All the walls were covered in the same crimson satin damask and drapery which also matched the furnishings. One long wall was broken by windows, the opposite by large paintings set at intervals. Whatever else the Prince was, his taste in art was exquisite. Everything was trimmed and fringed with gold. The chairs were all occupied, but most of the company were walking around or chatting in groups. Juliet took notice of the groups—Lord Liverpool and his coterie, then Lord Castlereagh and George Canning's. "I can't see our Russian representatives, but a few from America are over there," Val said.

They were all men, mostly dressed conservatively, as was the man by her side. A few stood out. The fashion for high, stiff collars and elaborate neckcloths still prevailed, some ensuring their owners could not turn their heads. Juliet had seen this all before, but not these people. A different air hung about the great room, one of self-importance, the affairs of nations. And here she was, in the midst of them.

"I see the Duke of Wellington," she murmured. The tall, unmistakable figure stood at the other end of the room, surrounded by acolytes. His drooping lids and hooked nose could not belong to anyone else. Juliet had not yet met him, but as she moved towards the Foreign Secretary, she felt his regard.

Turning her head, she met his eyes. And understood. As if she knew him, she saw his sorrow, his triumph, and his clear sight. Nobody here could claim half his achievements. And, she saw from one fleeting glance, he knew it. He'd let her see that.

"Would you like to meet my cousin Freddie?" Val asked as he led her through the room. "He's an army man. Made Major General this year." He spoke with pride.

"Oh, yes, that would be interesting. My brother Frank is a colonel."

He walked slowly to a group by the window. Two of the men wore military dress, one in the gold and blue uniform of a hussar regiment, the other in a dragoon's uniform. After bows and curtseys had been exchanged, Juliet found herself talking of her brother Frank. "He is a colonel in the 8th Hussars," she explained.

"The 8th, eh?" the dragoon officer said. Major General Howard was as tall as his cousin Val. He sported an extremely fashionable Brutus haircut, and his magnificent uniform was brushed and polished to perfection. The gold buttons could blind a person, were they not put in the shade by the rows of gold braid. The fur-edged pelisse worn over one shoulder was equally lavishly adorned.

The man in the hussar uniform, a Lieutenant Colonel Cathcart, could have been a model for a Hyde Park soldier, the kind kept for parades and show, but Juliet knew the 8th had seen heavy action in the recent war and suspected he had too. "I'm Queen's Own, myself. Seventh," he explained, "but I daresay you'd know that. You know I met your brother when he was a mere major." He huffed a laugh. A major, especially one capable of retaining his commission after a field promotion was not to be sneered at. "Excellent soldier. He'll surpass all of us at this rate."

"It's kind of you to say so, sir. He is currently in America on a diplomatic mission." She screwed up her nose, making the Lieutenant Colonel and Major General Howard laugh.

"Ah, but diplomacy saves lives," Val said.

"So does the army."

Val arched one fine brow. "We could talk about this all day."

"And we have," his cousin said, clapping him on the back. "Clara isn't here tonight, but she sends her regards. She's near birthing our third. Good sort, Clara," he added, addressing Juliet. "You'd like her. Had our last baby nearly on the battlefield, but she popped him out and was up and about the next day, seeing to the wounded."

"Goodness!" The way he described the event made Juliet smile, but the mental visualization of it added an edge of horror.

"Freddie is my heir," Val explained, "and his burgeoning family ensures the succession."

"We don't think of them that way," the Major General said,

sending Val a darkling look. "I'd rather you made your own succession."

Val looped Juliet's arm through his. "We could be on the way to fulfilling your wish."

His words made the people in the small group pause. Juliet even heard a gasp. "Well, ain't that good news!" Major General Howard bellowed, giving Val another clap on the back.

"I think we'll move on before you turn my back black and blue." but Val grinned as he said it, every inch the proud husband-to-be.

If only it were to be so! Obviously now their connection would need to go on longer than one night, since Val was acknowledging it so freely. Perhaps she should invent a quarrel between them in due course.

As they went further up the room to where the Foreign Secretary stood, she murmured, "You should not. The news will be all around London tomorrow."

He pressed her arm closer to his side. "Good. In any case, they will gossip anyway."

She would have no more opportunity to talk to him about it here. She could only fret inwardly until they left—too many people were listening. She couldn't risk saying anything that would sound wrong, even if it was right.

Lord Castlereagh greeted her warmly. "I am delighted with Langston's choice," he said, once everyone had congratulated the happy couple. Each time they did, it shamed Juliet, both because she knew they were feigning the engagement, and because deep down she wanted it to be true. More than she was prepared to admit.

Dinner was announced—not just announced but trumpeted by two footmen proudly liveried in red and gold. Juliet nearly jumped out of her skin, giving everyone except herself a spectacle to laugh at. Castlereagh took her arm to steady her. "You didn't warn her?" he asked Val.

"I never thought to," Val said, his eyes wild with unspilled laughter.

"Sometimes he has each course announced in the same way," Lord Castlereagh told her. While the notes of the fanfare echoed, he leaned closer and murmured, "Don't let him take you to see the conservatory, ma'am."

She didn't need to be told who "he" was. While the Regent was not a randy young buck any longer—in fact the results of a life of debauchery were evident in his face and figure—he still took mistresses and entertained ladies. Perhaps if the Prince had one of his women here to keep him busy instead of his sister, Juliet would have felt less uncomfortable at this warning. She had not been insensible of his speculative gaze earlier and would have appreciated someone who could distract him.

A footman arrived to show her to the person taking her into dinner. She didn't know him, but he was an older gentleman who leered rather than smiled at her. "I had a notion I might meet one of the lovely Miss Burrells before the Season was out," he told her, taking her hand and brushing his lips against her skin.

Juliet repressed her shudder and forced a smile. "There is only one Miss Burrell now," she said.

"So I'll have to be quick." He patted her hand.

Juliet maintained her smile but with some effort. She did not recognize his name, but for all she knew this could be one of the important men deciding Val's fate. They were going into dinner by rank, not by actual importance so it was impossible to discern his role in this gathering.

The dining room in Carlton House, or to be precise, the one used for formal occasions, was part of the lavish state apartments. The magnificent room sported classical columns and red velvet draperies with a long table groaning under the weight of the silver gilt set pieces depicting fountains and gnarled tree trunks with silver grapes hung improbably from their branches. And that was not counting the place settings, glasses, finger bowls, gold-edged plates emblazoned with the royal coat of arms. Juliet silently thanked her mother, who long ago ensured all her girls would know which silverware to use, and how to eat the more difficult food offered to them.

A footman stood behind every chair. There must be fifty of them. Juliet's place was halfway down the lower part of the table. She let the footman seat her and counted the glasses. Val sat much further up. She didn't know how on earth anyone was to judge them together if they were so far apart, but it was the way of society and not unexpected.

She settled down to what turned out to be just over three hours of feasting and conversation. Instead of a quartet, an octet serenaded them during the meal. Better than the bugles. She talked about the situation in Europe, or rather, let the gentleman to her left contradict everything she said, accepting his labored explanations of current politics which she neither needed nor asked for, with every appearance of meek acceptance. She would rather have told him how wrong he was, but until the table was cleared, the tablecloths removed, and dessert served, she did not learn that he was merely a friend of a friend of Lord Castlereagh—nobody who would affect Val's fate.

The gentleman on her right, however, a younger man with far more address—and it had to be said, better table manners— proved convivial. He introduced himself as "nobody of importance," but Juliet doubted that. He was a gentleman, for all that he was in trade, but his trade could not be ignored. Providing uniforms for the army, he informed her, had made his fortune. "My brother is in the hussars," she ventured.

"Ah, we make those uniforms," he said. "All that gold bullion makes me wonder how they can wear the uniform and still fight. But they do so, and good for them."

"You did not fight in the army, sir?"

"No, but I knew plenty who did." Sadness filled his eyes, so she did not pursue that line of conversation. His expression spoke of loss.

If she wondered why a mere cloth manufacturer should have a place at the Regent's table, Val disabused her when finally—

finally!—they left the dining room and Val could join her again. The orchestra moved into the drawing room with them after dinner, and Juliet would be forced to endure another hour of conversation, but at least she could share it with Val. "Ah, Fraser," he said, shaking hands with the man. "Good to see you. I trust you protected my betrothed against the advances of Sir George?"

"I did my best," Fraser said, smiling. "But I believe Miss Burrell is perfectly capable of taking care of herself."

"You are right." Val let his gaze flick over her, but Juliet knew he was watching her closer than it appeared. "He can be a little busy. I was somewhat concerned when you were given to his care. Why were you sitting so low down the ranks, Fraser? Isn't your uncle a marquess?"

"Don't remind me," Fraser answered. "We don't make much of the connection. True, I'm his nephew, but I hardly know him. Technically I'm in line for the title, but I don't live on the expectation."

"A nephew is fairly close," Val said. "Does he not ask you to visit the estate?"

Fraser dismissed the relationship with a careless wave of his hand. "My father was merely the disgraced third brother who ran off with a woman my uncle did not approve of. My sisters and I have made a good life for ourselves. We have no interest in the title of a man who detested our father for marrying into trade."

Val raised a brow. "Rather old-fashioned of him." The two men then exchanged a few words about Fraser's manufactories and the people he employed.

"I believe they use slaves in America," someone said nearby, lifting his handkerchief to his nose. "Should you like that, Fraser?"

"Not at all," he answered promptly. "I have no personal experience of it, nor do I ever want to." His features shaded. Something was going on here, something she'd missed.

In support of her dinner companion, Juliet rushed to his defense, and to cover the awkward silence that had dropped.

"When we were disembarking at Bristol on a—visit we saw slaves being brought ashore. Some of them could hardly stand." She'd never seen people so broken. The chains that shackled their legs and linked them one with another had made her ache to step forward and loosen them. Raw patches showed how long they'd been wearing them. They drooped and carried a stench that someone had told them sneeringly was "natural," but she later learned was a result of being chained together in the hold for the long journey from their home country. "I would not wish to be responsible for putting anyone in that state," she concluded.

The small silence around them told her this was her first faux pas of the evening, only broken by Fraser's quiet, "Well said!"

A man cleared his throat. While slavery was abolished, the trade was still legal. No doubt someone engaged in it was standing nearby.

"I thought they could not be brought ashore?" another lady asked. The conversation seemed to be gathering in all those within earshot.

"I believe Bristol has special warehouses that are not officially British soil," Juliet told her. "At least their quarters on the ships get hosed down before they take the second part of their journey."

"To the Americas," Val concluded, his voice grim, his brows low over his eyes. He took her arm. "My betrothed and I are as one in this," he continued. "We do not condone the trade."

"But without it, where would the economy be?" Sir George asked.

Fraser spoke up. "Where it is now," he said. "In the ditch."

Not for everyone, though. The people in this room would not suffer from the rural depression the Corn Laws had done nothing to abate.

No doubt Juliet would be blamed for starting the conversation. "Unsavory," she heard someone mutter.

"Well," said the lady, "the abolition movement has already achieved a signal victory. Perhaps it is going too far to expect any more."

Val opened his mouth but closed it again.

Had she destroyed his chances with her thoughtless words? Castlereagh would certainly hear of their remarks. Juliet had no idea what his views on the slave trade might be, but thinking of those poor souls in Bristol, she was almost glad she'd said it.

After that, a footman whispered something in his ear, and Val made their excuses and bore her off. For a moment Juliet thought they'd been discreetly asked to leave, but no. Val took her to a group where the Regent was holding forth, with the Duke of Wellington standing to his left.

The Regent beamed when they approached. "Ah, the beauteous Miss Burrell!" he said, smiling broadly. "I trust you have had an interesting evening?"

At least here she could try to atone for her remarks in the other room. Though she would not apologize for saying them, since she meant every word, perhaps she should not have said them. Not here and not in these circumstances. She would do better now.

She curtseyed. "It has been delightful, sir, and a great honor." She'd been instructed to call him "sir" after the first "your highness."

"You and your sisters created quite the stir last year!" He sounded as if he'd thought up their scheme himself. "Most amusing. And I see my friends were not exaggerating." He paused as if he expected some praise for his observation. To her surprise, he received it. Well, he was a prince, after all, and the ruler of the country. Presumably there were always people nearby who would applaud him.

He went on while she tried not to stare at his brown wig. "I thought you might care to see some of the rarest plants in the country. I have been collecting them for some time, and my hothouses contain some wonderful specimens." This less than subtle invitation was obviously the one she'd been warned of, and his practiced tone told her he had issued it to more than one lady.

Nobody seemed surprised.

Juliet thought rapidly. "Oh, Your Highness! That is an honor I never thought to be offered." Around them, the conversation had muted. People were listening. "Why, I cannot wait." She turned to Val in an impulsive way. "My dearest, did you hear that? His Highness is too kind, offering us this treat! Should we get up a group?" She would babble.

The Regent had gone pale, at least she thought he had, because his face paint seemed to fade. "Such kindness!" She tried to simper, though that was not something she was used to. "Oh, Your Highness, do you know about all the plants? I would love to hear about them. I adore flowers, they add such distinction to a room!"

When he held up his hand, she subsided, stared at the floor and kept the stupid smile pasted to her face. "I fear the plants may not appreciate so many all at once," the Regent pronounced. "They are rare examples, and perhaps I spoke too hastily."

He looked around for agreement, which he found readily—it must be tiring to spend all day agreeing with him. She doubted he would call on her again, and Juliet tried not to sigh her relief. While this was not the first time a man had tried to entice her away from the press of the crowd, it was the first time she'd had to deter someone so exalted. "We must of course consider the plants," she said. "You are most wise, sir."

"You must study the art instead," he said. "I doubt you will find a finer collection anywhere else."

That served as a dismissal. As Val guided her away from the royal presence, someone murmured "Well done!" as she passed.

Surely not the Duke of Wellington. But since it had not been Val, and he was the only male close enough, it must have been.

Chapter Twelve

VAL LEANED BACK against the squabs and closed his eyes. Juliet was tempted to do the same. The evening had exhausted her, but she would be home soon, and in her bed. She could hardly wait. She felt a stir and she looked to see Val's arm stretched out, his hand open, palm up. It seemed perfectly natural to slip her own hand into it. Their fingers threaded together and folded over. "You did well," he said without opening his eyes.

She wanted him to achieve his heart's desire but feared she'd ruined his chances.

"Several people commented on your appearance and your conversation. All favorable." He paused. "Some in a backhanded way, it has to be said. As in, 'She's a Burrell, is she not? I thought they were beautiful dolls, but this one has something about her.' And no, I'm not going to tell you who said that."

The comment didn't surprise her since they'd presented themselves to society precisely in that way last year. They had not fully understood that many men of high rank would require more than a lovely face and good manners.

"Do you think my babbling to the Regent deterred anyone?"

"Not in the least. You escaped from that particular predicament quite neatly. He fancies himself as a ladies' man still. I would have been forced to follow you and then God knows what would have happened."

Tonight had forcibly borne in on her that this man was at the center of affairs, clandestine and otherwise. Men who featured in the newspapers every day thronged those huge rooms tonight, like drawings come to life. Yet none had taken her in obvious dislike, none had asked her to leave. The last was the one she feared the most, particularly after her bruising experience with the Rotherhams. That fear had chased her all her life. And it was not just a fear for the Burrells, but sometimes a reality.

"And the slavery issue? I should not have said what I did. I thought I'd ruined it for you. It is not a proper discussion for dinner."

"You spoke the truth. That is the main thing."

His approval meant a great deal to her. She closed her eyes too, enjoying the simple companionship. When the carriage finally stopped, she put her hand down to steady herself and noticed they were not where she expected.

"What are we doing here?" They were in Brook Street, at the house Val owned and had leased to them sight unseen. This was where everything had started for the Burrells.

He met her gaze. "I want to talk to you. Properly. Everywhere we go there is always someone else. Tonight, I don't want to be interrupted."

His words sounded ominous. She did not mistake him. He wanted to talk about their betrothal. He said he'd applied for a common license, but she still was not sure that he wanted her in that way. Marriage was an important step, and it was for life. And Val was a thoughtful man who had no doubt given a great deal of consideration to this step. Perhaps he wanted to tell her that this arrangement was temporary after all.

The thought sent her stomach plummeting, but better that than to live with false expectations. The notion did not cheer her, but she allowed him to help her out of the carriage with a steadiness she was not feeling inside. When the footman had folded the steps up and closed the door, she received another shock when it drove away.

Val wasted no time leading the way up to the front door. He produced a key and unlocked it. She had not entered this house for nearly a year, but entering it took her straight back in time. The scent had changed, though. Instead of the miasma of damp and mold permeating the whole place, she smelled lavender polish and the faint scent of oranges. They'd spent a whole morning last Season studding oranges with cloves to counteract the house's natural odor.

Nobody waited for them, and there were no lights. A tinder-box and candles in simple sticks waited on a brass-topped table set just inside the front door. He lit a couple and handed her one. "I feel like an explorer," she said.

"Perhaps we are." His deep voice echoed around the hall, empty but for a few simple pieces of furniture, as clean as they'd left it. "I ordered the place cleaned and maintained, though most of it is under holland covers."

He glanced up. The lantern hanging from the ceiling was wrapped in a cover, too. "I employ a married couple to look after the place, but I told them I might come in this evening." His gaze returned to her. "They will not disturb our talk unless we wish them to."

Talk? That was all he wanted? Was this not an elaborate way of discussing the end of their connection?

"Come." He took her to a small parlor at the back of the ground floor. This was where the sisters and their mother sat around the large table, laying out fabrics and sewing enough clothes to see them through the first month of their Season. They'd shared their dreams in this room and confided their problems.

Val went around the room lighting the candles in the wall sconces. "They opened this room for us," he said. "We may have privacy here. My mother is at home, and she would be agog if I took you there. I did not think you would wish for that." He sat his candle down and leaned against the table, putting his hands on the edge.

"You want to discuss tactics?" She rested her own candle on a small table near the door where she still stood and folded her arms.

Val must have sensed her unease. "Don't you trust me?"

"Yes, I do." Juliet trusted very few people, but he was one of them. "But I don't know why you brought me here. Or why you sent the carriage away."

He grimaced. "Because if my carriage, with all its equipages, footmen, and crests stayed outside this house for too long, people would speculate."

"What if they saw us coming in here together?"

"Then we must bear the consequences."

Easy for him to say. If she were seen here, speculation would turn to outright gossip, and she would be finished. But she trusted him, had gone where he led. "My position isn't as secure as yours. I'm a female, and I am not part of any great family." She turned away. Going home on her own did not appeal, but it was better than calling the carriage back and increasing the chances that someone would see her leave in the crested vehicle. She could probably find a cab or a chair. Or even walk.

His hands landed on her shoulders. "I have not forgotten." She sucked in a breath and stood completely still. "Turn around, Juliet."

Reluctantly, she did so. Even though he'd released her, he was closer, close enough for her to see the dark ring around the lighter gray of his pupils, a tiny scar on his jaw. He regarded her steadily. "If you wish our arrangement to come to an end, you must cry off. I shall not do so."

"Of course." She understood that. "You must tell me when—" she couldn't finish her sentence. The words were too hard to say.

"Never?" He quirked a brow.

She stared at him. "What do you mean?"

Speaking very slowly, enunciating every word carefully, he said, "I would prefer us to marry."

"Why?" The word left her lips before she properly thought about what she should say.

"Any number of reasons. Most of all, because I want you."

He could have her without making the commitment. This close to him like this, she could deny him nothing. Surrounded by his scent, his presence, his sheer masculinity, she wanted him as she had no other man. But like her sisters, she'd vowed to be no man's mistress. "Is that why you brought me here? For a little clandestine amusement?"

"Tcha!" Releasing her from his thrall, he turned and went to the window, as far away as he could get from her. "I won't insult you that way. It's more than physical. I like you, Juliet, I respect you. I can think of no other woman who has the qualities you do." He spun around, confronting her. "Do you think I say this lightly? The first time I saw you I wanted you. Remember last year when your mother insisted on seeing me after finding this house burgled?"

She nodded. He'd come to see what kind of person had hired his house. "Nobody knew us then. And for a few weeks people were not sure. I heard my mother called an abbess." The only kind of abbess in this country was the kind that ran a house of pleasure. That comment had hurt.

"I knew from the start. Quality isn't just defined by birth, and truthfully, not all the people born to the great houses have the quality you and your sisters possess."

The reality was slowly seeping in, destroying her defenses. "You mean it? All of it?"

"Yes."

She swallowed. "Do you think I'd make a good diplomat's wife?"

Crossing the room once more, he stood before her, then clasped her forearms gently. "You will make a good wife to me. That is what's important now. So what do you say?"

The last barrier fell. Juliet surrendered. "I say yes."

His lips covered hers, gently at first, then increasing in pressure. Juliet had to tilt her head back and clutch his shoulders to keep her balance. Her head spun, her senses scattered, as did her common sense. He slid his hands along her bare arms, stroking her as he might a cat, feathering over her wrists before he lifted her hands away and settled them on his waist, under his coat. Somehow her hat became dislodged and fell to the floor. And still he kissed her, as if he would never stop. Not that she wanted him to.

She opened to him, pressed her body against his and felt his heat sear through their clothes. When she ran her hands up his back she felt his responding shudder through the fabric of his shirt and waistcoat, and her gloves. "More," she mumbled, when his lips left hers to press tiny kisses on her cheek, her ear. "I want more."

Val lifted his head. "How much more?"

"All. Of. It."

He groaned. "You're sure?"

"Shut up and get on with it." She tugged at his shirt. Gentlemen's shirts were long, she knew that much from sewing them for her brother, and Val was a tall man, but she wanted—needed—to feel his bare skin under her hands. He growled low and busied himself with undoing the tiny buttons fastening her Indian gauze overgown.

"Wait." He drew back, dragged his coat and waistcoat off, tossing them to the floor. Then he pulled his neckcloth off, heedless of its careful folds, unfastened the stud at his neck and his cuffs, letting the glittering items fall before he pulled his shirt over his head.

Juliet caught her breath. He was magnificent. She might have even breathed the word aloud, she wasn't sure. His muscles positively rippled as he reached for her. Folded in his arms, she took her fill of his warm, smooth back, exploring the way he moved and reveling in the power of him.

They kissed, and this time she tasted, their tongues dancing, swirling as he made short work of the hooks at the back of her gown. When they parted, he pushed the short sleeves down her arms, letting the garment fall free. And still there were layers to struggle through. She wore light stays that he unfastened.

He drew back when he touched her breasts for the first time. Cupped one and teased the nipple with his thumb. "You are breathtakingly lovely," he said. He looked, and she drew her chemise further down, loosening the drawstring to show him more. "I'm a fortunate man."

Juliet grinned. "Yes you are."

Laughter, shaky with passion, linked them both.

"I want you so much, but I won't …"

"Won't you?" covering his hand with hers, so they both felt her heart beating, she looked him straight in the eyes. "I want you to. I want us to do this."

Val closed his eyes and moaned softly. "How can I resist you?"

"Don't even try."

A mirror hung over the mantelpiece. A sparkle caught her attention, the glitter of her new necklace in the light of the candles, dim but sure. Returning her gaze to the man in front of her, there was also light enough to see his face when she pressed against him. The relief was indescribable, the touch of yearning flesh to powerful muscled chest, the way he held her shoulders while he kissed her again and dealt deftly with her skirts. They were rolled up above her waist and he was touching her, stroking her crease, delving deeper with each caress until he reached her center, the place no man had ever seen, much less touched, before.

His lips left her, and he watched her as he fumbled with his falls, freeing himself. "Touch me," he whispered, sharp and urgent. "Please."

He sounded as desperate as she felt when she slid her hand between them, careful not to push her skirts back down, and felt the hard flesh that would make them one. Curling her fingers around him, she explored the way his skin slid, pushed down to the tight sac, explored in wonder.

"You have not done this before," he said. A statement rather than a question, but she was happy to confirm it for him.

"No, I have not."

With a slight smile curling his lips, he moved closer, put his hands around her waist and pressed her against the wall behind her. "Hold on," he murmured. "Sweet Juliet, hold tight."

His shoulders proved perfect for gripping while he brought his body to hers and began their journey. She gasped, feeling his strength as he nudged and pushed, each movement tightening the tension in her body, until as if bursting a balloon, something gave and he surged within her.

Not without pain, however. It lanced through her, burning. As the tears escaped from her eyes, he kissed them, took them for his own as he claimed her. "Oh God, we should not be doing this, but I can't resist you, can't stop. I must have you, Juliet."

"Yes." She gasped for breath, doing her best to accommodate all of him, but he kept coming, until he stopped, deep inside her.

With her pain receding, she could concentrate on what they were doing. He pushed back in and this time it barely hurt at all. The next time it did not hurt, but something else began deep inside her, matching the sensitivity outside. The sensations merged so she could not tell where that growing warmth inside her came from, precisely.

Time meant nothing anymore.

And still he thrust, withdrew, and thrust again. Nothing mattered but this, that he feed their growing passion, urging the warmth into a conflagration she could do nothing to stop. It rushed at her, engulfing her, as he slammed his mouth over hers and cried out into it, as he throbbed deep inside her.

Clinging together, they panted out their passion.

Val was still holding her as they recovered. Slowly, he came back to himself, wondering what the hell he had done and why. What he'd planned as a proposal, followed by a few kisses, had changed into something else. Once he'd touched her skin he'd become an unthinking beast, but not so much of one that he had not attended to her every move. If she'd said no at any part, he'd have stopped, however much it would have killed him.

For a man who prided himself on his civilized behavior, Val had turned into a person he hardly recognized.

Juliet was so light, so beautiful, and so damned responsive. With just enough sense to prepare her, he'd ignored his better self, pushed it aside in order to take her.

"We should have gone upstairs. I'm sorry your first time was so—uncouth."

Her soft chuckle warmed his ear. "I give you leave to be uncouth again." He felt her wince when he withdrew, "but not tonight."

"I'm sorry I caused you even an instant of discomfort. I should have taken you upstairs to bed, not rutted against the nearest wall. Truly, I am sorry."

"Don't be. It was utterly thrilling. Who cares about a stuffy bed when we can have this?"

Her hair tickled his chin. He could stay there all night but if they did that, everyone would know. "Come on, sweetheart. We have to at least try for respectability."

Slowly he lowered her and waited until she'd found her feet before he stepped back. When he grabbed his shirt, prepared to sacrifice it to clean them both, she'd done something clever with her shift, tucked it between her legs somehow. He watched, his mind still fogged by passion as she neatly retied her stays by pulling the ends and fastening them at the back. "As long as I can get my gown back on," she muttered.

Val found his handkerchief which served to clean himself. There wasn't a lot of blood. "I've never done this before."

She lifted her head, eyes wide. "What? This?"

He smiled at her shock. "I've never had a virgin before."

"Ah. Yes, I was, wasn't I?" She sounded positively smug.

Dear God, what had he turned into? He'd meant for them to have a decent conversation. Conversation? She turned him into a man he barely recognized. But tonight they had taken an irrevocable step. They could not turn back now. He'd just have to learn to control his passion for her, to steer this marriage back to the rational union he yearned for.

Passion inevitably led to destruction.

She was almost dressed, and he was still half naked. He had to hurry to catch up with her. He flung his shirt over his head and thrust his arms through the sleeves. "I'll take you home when you're ready. We'll accelerate our plans. Next Wednesday, I think. I'll go down to Doctor's Commons in the morning."

He heard her gasp. What did she expect? They had just made their wedding inevitable, and the sooner the better. He'd made his bed. He couldn't wait to lie in it.

Chapter Thirteen

HAVING CREPT INTO the house and found her mother and sister not yet back from their ball, Juliet thought she'd escaped nicely from her predicament. She'd dragged her hat down over her ears to hide the mess she'd made of her hair, wrapped her evening cloak around her disheveled clothing and managed to get to her room without people noticing. The night was a lot younger than she'd thought, which worked to her advantage, as she'd pulled out most of her hairpins and tugged off her outer clothing by the time Banks arrived with a can of hot water.

She woke up the next morning to find her mother sitting at the end of her bed.

Juliet blinked awake.

"Do you have anything to tell me?" Mrs. Burrell said, and from the stern set of her face she did not mean the dinner.

"Ah . . . um . . ." Juliet sat up and dragged her nightcap off. Her hair in its nighttime braids fell over her shoulders. She flicked them back, using the exercise as an excuse to collect her thoughts. "I did not sit with him at dinner, of course, but I met an interesting man called Fraser—"

"You and I both know I don't mean that. Is there any reason why your stays weren't tied in the usual way? Banks tells me the knot was wrong. She ties it in a different way."

Juliet groaned. That such a small thing should give her away! But she would deal with something else first. "I will be sorry to lose Banks. She was a good lady's maid. But I won't accept taletelling and gossip." She shrugged.

Her mother nodded. "I thought you'd say that. As it happens, I agree. A lady's maid should be discreet. However, since she was not, what do you expect me to do? Ignore what she told me?"

"Why did she tell you anything?" Desperately, Juliet hunted for a distraction, but found none.

"She said she was deeply disturbed and she thought it her duty to tell me. As a good Christian woman. Yes, she said that."

Juliet picked up the end of one braid and began to unravel it, avoiding looking at her mother. "A shame. I'll give her a character, but I'll say she is a good Christian woman who believes in her duty to the head of the household."

"I'm not the head of this household."

Juliet waved away the quibble and started on the other braid. Her mother had always used this as a tactic, accosting her children before they were properly awake to discover what she wanted to know. On the whole, Juliet did not mind, but this morning she'd have preferred some peace.

"Well, you do not need to worry, Mama. I'm marrying Lord Langston. He says as soon as Wednesday, which I think is foolish."

"What?" Her mother stood and strode around the room restlessly. "Wednesday? How can we arrange anything by then? The wedding can be private, but hardly so a wedding breakfast. And a ball to celebrate! What were you thinking to agree to that?"

She remained silent on that point. She was sure her mother could work it out for herself.

"Mama, if you want something to do, could you put a light to the fire?" The weather was still unseasonably chilly, although they had yet to see snow flurries this May, as they had last year.

Unlike most women of her social position, Mrs. Burrell knew how to lay and light a fire. They all did. With a grunt of acquiescence, she reached for the tinderbox on the mantelpiece. "It's too soon. People will talk."

"We'll say that he expects a new appointment shortly, and he wants to marry before he takes it up," Juliet said. They'd agreed on that excuse on the short drive home.

"Hmm. It will serve, I suppose. And the need to put Lady Maria Richards in the background, although nobody will say that outright." She stood, watching the tiny flames lick over the wood, reaching for the more substantial layer of coal. "But everybody will be thinking it. I feel sorry for Lady Maria, but not sorry enough to believe that union would have been anything but a disaster."

"Apparently the reading sessions we have been doing recently were enough to fool Langston into thinking that Maria was well-read and had an interest in politics."

"Instead, it was you putting those words into her mouth," her mother said. "I see. Well, we must do our best with what time we have. I will visit his mother this morning, and we will concoct a scheme between us." She turned. "I cannot understand why Lady Langston is never shunned. Ever. She may go anywhere and do anything. She takes lovers, travels on her own, has an utterly outrageous taste in furnishings. Why does her son not correct her? She can hardly help his precious reputation."

She'd wondered about that part herself, but she had an answer for the others. "She's from one of the greatest families in the land, and she is possessed of a fortune in her own right. Her legacies are for the most part in trust, so her son cannot touch them. Not that he wants to," she added after a reflective moment.

"Well he should. I like the woman, but it cannot be denied that she has some very odd starts. Look at that furniture in Brook Street!"

Juliet rustled the sheets, sweeping them back with a flourish to hide the results of the heat rising to her face when her mother mentioned the scene of her . . . she did not want to call it deflowerment. It meant so much more to her. She had not lain back and allowed him to do what he would. She was as much a participant as he, and secretly she was proud of it. The ritual bedding was completely destroyed now. And she was only a little sore this morning.

Her mother went to the door. "We have a lot to arrange. I'll tell your sister and her husband, and I'll start the household moving." Her mother, the ever practical, who had taken everything in her stride. This was but a small matter in her scheme of things.

"And ask the agency to send me some maids to interview," Juliet said.

JULIET'S NEXT CALL was to her brother-in-law, since her sister had not yet risen. He was sitting in his study, looking the picture of elegance, but his surroundings let him down badly. The same plethora of papers littered his desk. Perhaps he'd tried to tidy them, because some were in piles, with heavy objects set on top to hold them in place. There were still too many of them.

"I'd like my bills back, please," she said after he'd waved her to a seat. "I'll deal with them." She did not want to go into her marriage bringing debts in her wake.

"They're nothing." He glanced around and sifted through a few pieces. "I can't find a thing anymore." He tossed down the pen he was holding, splashing the nearest document with ink. He didn't seem to notice.

These days, since she'd learned of his behavior towards her sister, Juliet was more wary of the Duke. Bianca had sworn her to secrecy, so she could not speak to him the way she wanted to. For her sister's sake, not for his. "It can't be a bad thing."

He shrugged. "I had to do something after my cousin's last visit. He had the effrontery to read me a lecture, but he did actually help me do some tidying." He waved a hand over the piles of weighted papers. "At least I know which accounts are urgent now, and which can wait. I'll work through them. I had an excellent night at the tables, so I'll pay a few while I have the wherewithal." He leaned forward, his eyes sparkling. "And there's another venture. You won't have heard of it. I only arranged it yesterday."

That sounded ominous to Juliet. She pasted on an interested expression. "Do tell."

"You must swear to keep this to yourself until we have it arranged." At her nod, he continued, "a race, a steeplechase if you will. We have them all the time in the country. So why not in town?"

"Because it would disrupt the traffic?" she ventured.

"Pah, we can deal with that." He grinned, his mood buoyant. "We're doing a steeplechase. We have to do it soon before word gets around.

How could he live like this? She would never sleep if she owed so much to so many people. And he was planning a mad race? "There's money to be made in this, too," he continued. "The betting book at White's is already open, even though we've kept the details vague." He chortled. "It spread like wildfire last night."

Another start. One that sounded more dangerous than the others, but of the same kidney. She didn't want to know more, but she feared she would need to.

"When do you plan to announce it?"

"Oh, soon. Publicly, probably one or two days before, so that entrants can be established and bets made. But we won't say precisely where until the day itself." He clapped his hands, delighted by his news.

She decided to move on to her own tidings.

"I have other news for you, sir." Juliet had always remained proper in her address to Whiston. Careless though he was, Whiston still preferred it and, truth be told, so did Juliet in this case. But then, if she had ever walked into a room full of men and called his first name, George, at least half the room would turn around, so perhaps it was practical.

"Do tell," he drawled, reaching for his snuff box. God knew how much that gold, diamond encrusted, enameled trinket had cost him. He certainly did not. The price would probably cover the whole of one of those piles of bills.

"I'm getting married. Next week."

"Good God!" He clicked the box shut and tossed it to join the pen on the table. "Langston, I presume?"

"Yes." She sat primly, her hands folded in her lap, and prayed he would not want to embrace her. She didn't want him anywhere near her.

He sat up, grinning. "Congratulations, he's quite a catch. Good man, too. Why the haste?"

She had her answer ready. "Because he expects an appointment abroad shortly, and he does not want to leave without me."

Whiston nodded. He seemed to accept it. But then a sly grin curved his lips. "Are there any other reasons?"

She did not pretend to misunderstand him, but she did pretend to be offended. "Sir! Lord Langston is a gentleman!"

He raised a brow. "So am I, and look what Bianca and I did. Does my wife know?"

"I told Mama this morning, so I presume she does." Bianca would be up by now, or her mother would have barged into her room and told her anyway.

"If you need any help with the legal niceties, I stand ready. The dowry and marriage contract, for instance."

She suppressed her horrified shudder. "There is no need. I'm of age, and before he left for America, Frank left the contract ready for me to sign. But thank you for the offer," she added hastily.

"Good." He shuffled some of the loose papers and picked up a bill. "And when you see Bianca, ask her why she needs quite so much French lace, hmm?"

Thank heaven she did not have to depend on him. She had

trustees to handle the financial side, her brother's legal men, and she knew the details. Unlike other men, her brother did not consider his sisters to be as children in finance. Though she would have to mention it to Val.

When would she see him again? Tonight at the theater or before then? The fact that she had parted from him a few scarce hours ago, not even a day, meant nothing to her heart. She missed him already.

※≫≫≪≪

"Goodness, how exciting!" Bianca, still dressed in a white and frilly lace wrapper that made her look even younger than she was, came towards her with hands outstretched. "I am so happy for you! But Mama says you wish to marry next week! How on earth will you do that?"

"Quietly," Juliet said. "And yes, I'm happy too." She was, too, bubbling inside with excitement.

"Were we going shopping today? I think we should. You will need so much. Did Whiston tell you his plans? The race? Oh, I totally forgot to ask you how your dinner went. I was so excited when Mama told me your news."

She bustled to her dressing table, where her maid was busy laying out her cosmetics. All those pretty pots and cut-glass jars, adding up to something dangerous. At least today Juliet could see her sister's lovely face. No dark shadows under her eyes, just as she was before her marriage.

Bianca was almost frenetic with busyness. Perhaps just over-excitement at her sister's news. While Bianca could sail along like a stately galleon if she chose, her natural temperament was to the bubbly.

She waved at the pots and bottles. "I won't be needing those today," she said, a note of triumph entering her voice. "The pink sarsenet, please," she told her maid, who nodded and left the room. When the door had closed, Bianca faced her sister, beaming. "George apologized to me, you know," she said. "Business was upsetting him, and he was not happy. He cannot organize, poor dear, so he is looking in earnest for a secretary. Truly, he was most contrite and promised me he would not stray again. He said he was deeply ashamed. So you see, you may leave me to go to your new home in a perfectly content frame of mind."

Oh yes, of course, Juliet recalled, she would be moving. Events were catching up with her, and while the momentous events from last night dominated her thoughts, she had to bring herself to consider the practical. Not moon around thinking of what he did, and what she did . . .

There she went again. Firmly, she pulled her thoughts back to the here and now. "And the race? Can't you dissuade him? It's madness!"

"Oh, it's put George in the best of moods!" Bianca said gaily. "It's just a notion. It might never come to pass. If it does, it will be carefully arranged and regulated."

Juliet doubted that, although she was too wise to say so.

"And you, becoming Lady Langston!" Bianca whirled around, her loose robe floating around her. "Lady Rotherham will be mad as fire!" Bianca went back to the dressing table and opened her jewelry box, lifting first a string of agate beads, then a pretty coral necklace. Her better jewelry was kept in separate velvet-lined boxes. This box contained the pretty but nearly valueless trinkets they'd first owned when they came to London. Juliet owned a similar box, and like her sister, sometimes she still wore them. However, Bianca was a duchess and should perhaps wear the better jewels. Though it was true that she and her husband were not what a person thought about when they imagined a duke in all his pomp and power. Whiston could have power, if he chose to use it, but he did not. Instead, he thought up pranks and starts, a boy who had never properly grown up.

"We have so many exciting things to discuss, do we not? You

should write to Viola. She might want to come to the wedding."

Viola certainly would if she could. She was increasing, and although she planned to come to London to give birth, since that was where all the good birth attendants were, she and Knowsley had not planned on a full Season. Juliet and her mother had planned to visit them in the country in time for Viola's confinement, but that might not happen for Juliet now. She might be in Russia.

Chapter Fourteen

V AL COULD BARELY keep away. He was happy to find an excuse to call, almost merry when he called for his curricle. He hadn't seen Juliet for a day, while he'd been harassing his lawyers to prepare all the necessary documents. He'd have married her with nothing formalized, but he owed his estate and the people he employed due process. He'd have had to do it anyway if he was to take a post abroad. Fortunately, he had a group of people he could rely on to run his estate and property in his absence, so he set up the process formally. It still took too long for his liking.

Staying away from her also gave him a chance to try to put her firmly in his mind instead of his groin. It didn't entirely work. He came to the conclusion that he needed to let the lust he evidently felt for her abate, He would keep her at a distance until he could control his desire for her. That would do.

After making early calls to secure the church and ensure the legal arrangements were in place, he contacted his man of business, whose screwed-up lemon-face only made him more determined to go ahead with his plan, though he'd managed to wrangle two extra days out of Val. So Friday it would be.

His idea of a rational marriage, of finding a woman he could be friends with, had gone out the window in that fateful house in Brook Street. But his stubborn soul made him continue in his plan. Perhaps they could confine their passion to the bedroom and continue as friends outside it. For in Juliet he'd found a delightful friend, one with whom he could discuss affairs that bored everybody else. He would always treasure that.

The passion he wasn't so sure about. He didn't know how to manage that part.

After finalizing the details with his lawyer, Val went back to the house for breakfast. His mother had only just risen, as evinced by her lacy wrapper and the cap covering her curling-rags. She still looked lovely, but Val freely admitted he was biased.

His mother declared her delight and surprise at the early date. "I've never known you behave so impulsively before," she'd said, applying herself to a full plate of breakfast. People who did not know her might be surprised at the amount of food the delicate Countess could put away, but Val took it as part of the paradox of the woman who bore him.

"I'd thought Wednesday, but I've had to agree on Friday."

"A whole two days later!" she exclaimed in mock surprise.

"It's necessity," he said. "If I am offered the position in Russia, the post is immediate."

"And you don't want to leave her behind." She studied the piece of pork chop on her fork, frowning, before she popped it into her mouth and chewed.

Val took the opportunity to tuck into his own breakfast, because he knew the peace would not last for long.

"I am glad, of course," she said fifteen minutes later when she had an empty plate and a fresh cup of tea. "And relieved it was not Lady Maria. She would have driven you to despair in six months."

"Unfair, Mama!" Maria could have been molded into the wife he needed. She was highly susceptible and eager to please. But she would have been hard work.

"Not at all," his mother said tranquilly. "That girl is wily and deceitful. I know she appears to be sweet and innocent, but I have no confidence in that verdict. Her intelligence is also not of the level you require."

Considering recent events, he had no compunction in agreeing with her. The fact that he had been deceived so thoroughly still irked him, though.

His secretary would make a much better job of the molding, simply because he loved Lady Maria. He would see Norris later today, another task he had to settle. He'd already informed his man of business he would need a new Parliamentary secretary, since he had decided Norris would take the vacant seat in his gift. Finding someone so reliable and intelligent would be quite a task.

"I will do what I can to reconcile Lady Rotherham to her daughter's choice of husband," his mother said, leaning back in her chair and pushing her plate away. They usually ate breakfast without servants present when it was just the two of them. "Tricky, because although she isn't giving us the cut direct, we're not invited to her upcoming dinners and parties. However, she cannot ignore us forever. Perhaps her daughter has made inroads."

"Perhaps she has, but I doubt it." He cradled his coffee between his hands before taking a sip. "I assumed her mother would agree to an immediate wedding, not defer the date. The two are determined on each other, so it can only be a temporary separation."

His mother raised a brow. The dark wing of it, so like his own, added to her character. "Lady Rotherham will cast about her for a suitor."

"For all she knows her daughter is carrying Norris's child."

She snorted in derision, something very few people had the pleasure of witnessing. "If Maria has not given in to her and admitted the truth."

"I believe Norris will keep her on the right path. He knows how much that story means to him. If they learn the truth, the Rotherhams will have her married off to someone else in a trice. Part of it is because her ladyship did not choose Norris herself."

She frowned. "I will think about it." She put down her cup.

"I'm sure I can contrive something." She brightened. "Do you think that Maria would actually go through with a seduction, if it's with the man she loves?"

A mental picture of Juliet, loose hair curling around her shoulders, pearly skin exposed and open to him flashed into his mind. He closed his eyes, trying to dispel the highly inappropriate vision, but the part of him that remained with Juliet would not let it go. He cleared his throat. "Perhaps."

He opened his eyes to see his mother watching him shrewdly. "Either you cannot wait, or you have chosen not to wait. I cannot decide which."

"It is not a matter you should concern yourself with, Mama," he said with all the dignity he could muster, which admittedly was not much. but he was not a diplomat for nothing.

She smiled but said no more on the subject. The rest of the meal was devoted to wedding arrangements, with his mother promising to call on the Whiston household to see if she could assist in any way.

VAL MADE HIS way to the Whiston house immediately after breakfast, to try to avoid the fashionable visiting hour, when the house would no doubt be thronged with curious visitors. They needed to prepare their strategy.

He found his betrothed alone, in a small parlor which showed a few signs of neglect. A sofa and two chairs in a slightly old-fashioned style were set before the fireplace. A bureau that did not gleam with polish stood against one wall. The mirror above it was spotted, and the table in front of the window held a sewing basket and some dog-eared books.

A family room. He was touched that she would receive him here, in a room obviously not intended for show. And there she was, dressed simply in a mid-blue muslin gown and plain white linen. "You're as fresh as the morning," he said, going over to her and taking her in his arms.

"Bianca is fending off the guests," she murmured, her breath stirring against his chin. "They won't come here."

"Good."

He kissed her but took care to keep his greeting gentle and sweet, as a man should greet his betrothed wife. "I'm sorry for Brook Street," he said when their lips parted. "I'll never forgive myself for treating you so roughly."

"Why? Didn't you enjoy it?"

Her response jolted him into laughter. "Very much. but to treat you that way was beyond acceptable. You had not . . ."

She grinned. "I enjoyed it. It is by far the best way, I think. Taking me by surprise." She placed her palms on his chest. "Don't give it another thought."

"I treated you like a—"

"Well, if that's how men treat their mistresses, I can see why they would do it." She tapped her fingers against his waistcoat. "Truly, Val, you helped me surmount a fence I was not looking forward to jumping. Now it's done, and I am looking forward to the next one."

There seemed to be little else to say, so he kissed her again instead. That seemed much more to her taste, and it certainly was to his.

The second kiss lasted much longer than the first one. With every kiss, every embrace, she reacted more naturally, with more eagerness. He slid his hands over her elbows, slipping his fingers under the short sleeves of her gown, to stroke her skin and feel her warmth.

"You are so lovely," he murmured.

"I'm glad you came."

"I brought my curricle in case you should like to drive out." Easing her away, he dipped his hand in the pocket of his greatcoat and brought out a package. He'd wrapped it himself, so the brown paper was rather rumpled and the string awry. but it held together long enough for her to pull the loop away.

The fine fabric spilled into her hands.

When she unwound it, she found the gauzy overgown she'd left behind last night. Almost completely transparent. "Oh! My goodness, I had quite forgotten!"

He smiled, recalling how he'd found it. "It's somewhat crumpled but I found no damage. Remarkable, considering the rough way we treated it, and how careless we were." He'd almost ripped it off her.

She pulled the garment over her hands. There was almost no impediment to his view, although that "almost" was what fascinated him. "It's a special Indian muslin, very precious, very expensive." She lifted her gaze to his face, her blue eyes dancing with mischief. "I can't remember the proper name, but we bought a bolt of it from the captain of a ship in London docks."

A vague memory stirred. "Can you remember the name of the vessel?"

After a pause, she told him. "The Dawn Trader."

Val grinned, then laughed. He turned away, trying to control his reaction, but it was hopeless. He put his hands on his hips and let go until the tears came.

"What? What did I say?" she demanded.

He lifted his chin and sucked in deep breaths, letting the air fill his lungs, and stopped his laughter that way. He turned around, and went back to her, putting his hands on her waist as if they belonged there. "I used to own the Dawn Trader."

"Oh." She sifted the gauze in her hands. "So this really belongs to you? We bought it from the captain. He said the main cargo had been disembarked."

"It had. Spices and tea. The ship was also carrying commissions from other clients. Your fabric was part of that, but it had not been paid for. You paid for it, so it's yours." He felt nothing but pride for her resourcefulness. And something else. He could not deny that desire stirred inside him, as strong as last night but now he was prepared for it. He wanted to see her in that overgown and nothing else.

"Mama said that Cerisot the seamstress had ordered a bolt of the stuff, but it never arrived. This was most probably it." She drew in a breath that made her chemisette rise enticingly, the shadow of her flesh under it forcing him to push his desire more strongly away. "We had other fabric and trims, too. We couldn't afford to make a complete set of gowns that the three of us needed for the London Season. We'd made things before, so we set to. We had most of it done in a week." She glanced at the muslin. "We could not do detailed work, like the embroidery on this one, so we've had that done since. We decided we would make a virtue out of the plainness and call it elegance."

She put the delicate over gown aside, draping it carefully over one of the chairs. "There was so much of it. We made shifts and overgowns and still had plenty left for underwear," she said as she turned back to him.

He sucked in a breath. "Chemises? Night-rails?" he added hopefully.

"Not respectable, Mama said, but we made some anyway."

The thought of her wearing something so transparent under all her clothes pushed his body into another strong reaction. His erection rose along with his longing until he had to remind himself he was a civilized man. "Wear one on our wedding night. Please?"

She stroked the tip of one forefinger over the fine stuff, and this time he knew for sure she was doing it on purpose to tease him. She must know the effect such a vision had on him. "I could. I do have one."

He walked over to the door. "Then we have a choice. We may remain here for a scandalously long time, and we will emerge somewhat ruffled, or you may fetch your hat and gloves, and we will tool around the Park and talk about the arrangements for the wedding. You must choose because I cannot."

"Well, I do need to go to the Royal Exchange."

To his disappointment and relief, equally mixed, she decided to fetch her outdoor things and drive out with him. On the one hand, he did not want to cause any scandal, but on the other, he longed to repeat what they had done last night. Just with a little more finesse.

Once they were in the curricle and bowling through the streets in the direction of the Royal Exchange, she made a confession. "Mama knows."

"Knows what?" Although a notable whip, he almost let the reins slip when he suddenly realized what her mother knew. "How?"

She laughed. "I was so careful, but Banks spotted the knot on my stays wasn't the one she used when she helped me dress. So she told my mother."

"Hmm." A chatty maid could be a dangerous thing, especially in his line of work.

"I dismissed her. I'll give her a character, but I will not employ any servant who carries gossip and tittle-tattle, especially to my loved ones. My mother listened to Banks but agreed with me. So I am yet again without a maid." She peeped at him, but by now he had his features under control. "I will find one by Wednesday."

"Friday," he corrected her. "Unfortunate, but putting it off until then means we can have all the legal arrangements done with. My man of business nearly had a heart attack when I informed him this morning, so I allowed him another two days. Are you disappointed?"

"Do you mean it? Can we truly marry so soon?"

"I already have a common license, and I spoke with a cleric, a friend of the family, this morning. He assures me it can and will be done—in his church and at ten in the morning."

"Goodness!" She swallowed.

"Indeed. I thought I might have to purchase a special license from Doctor's Commons, but I did not wish to evoke any suspicion in the minds of our friends that we had . . ."

"Anticipated the wedding," she finished for him.

"Precisely." He took a sharp corner briskly and without turning the curricle on its wheel. "I can barely wait."

"We have the race to get through before then."

"Race?" He took another corner and slowed the horses to a walk. The narrow, crowded streets of the City were no place for a brisk trot. Even as he turned, two urchins darted across the road, ignoring the piles of horse dung that lay there, waiting for the sweepers. Horseshit pebbled the side of the curricle as he avoided them but fortunately didn't reach as high as the seats. Val ignored the effects, only releasing his breath when he saw the urchins scampering along the other side of the road, pulling faces and swearing at him.

The distraction had not deterred him. "Race?" he repeated.

Juliet pulled her attention from the urchins. "The markets race."

Foreboding crept its way up Val's spine. "I heard something in the club, but I paid little attention to it." He was too busy trying to impress the Foreign Secretary to concern himself with foolish bets, whatever they were.

"Whiston was one of the initiators. A steeplechase around the three main markets in London. They made the final arrangements in White's last night, so the news will be everywhere now. It will be tomorrow at noon. Whiston solidified the details with his co-conspirators," Juliet finished grimly.

"I'm sorry?"

"The race is to begin at Covent Garden, outside the church. As many as wish to take part must be there with their carriages and a pair of horses at noon. When the adjudicator gives the word, they must race to Billingsgate Market, where they will collect tokens. There are only six tokens so anyone who doesn't secure one must drop out. They proceed to Smithfield Market, where another adjudicator waits with three tokens. After that, the first to return to Covent Garden is the winner. Apparently, London is too sadly dull for a fellow." She closed her mouth on a snap and stared down at her hands, folded in her lap.

"What? That is pure insanity!"

"Yes." She drew in a deep breath. "As the few people initially allowed into the plan have constantly said. It was the talk of White's last night, apparently."

He rarely went to White's, not being fond of deep play and wild behavior. He'd heard a little in Watier's but he hadn't taken much notice. Certainly not enough to grasp then the sheer horror of what lay in store. His gorge rose. "They must be out of their senses. Someone will be killed. Several someones."

"They are mad," she said gloomily, "and too much so to call it off. The arrangements were initially made with the greatest secrecy, because if the magistrates get wind of it, they'll put a stop to it. Do you think we should tell the magistrates?" She raised her gaze to his face, a hopeful expression in her cool blue eyes.

"No," he said shortly. "They would probably join in the betting. And before you say it, the Runners won't care. Neither will the Watch." He drew the horses to a gentle stop outside the Exchange. "Though maybe someone will tell them anyway. Did you hear that, Frisby?"

The tiger riding up behind them answered. "Not a word, me lord. The wind was in the wrong direction, you might say."

He climbed down and tossed the reins to Frisby, who was no help at all. "I daresay you have money down on the race?"

"Aye, maybe. The grooms is all of a tizzy, what with their masters and all getting ready. If you ask me, me lord, it's the worst kept secret in London. If the magistrates don't know by now, then they're deaf, dumb and blind."

"An interesting concept. Since Justice is blind, we may assume the rest."

Bribes will have been dispensed. He went around the back of the curricle to lift his betrothed down, but she was already on the ground. "Pity. I was looking forward to that. My tiger is under the impression the magistrates probably know already. You can't deter Whiston?"

She shook her head. "He's mad for it. I've tried, Mama has

tried, but that only makes him worse."

A chilling thought struck him. "Will you or your sister be taking part?"

He was only partly relieved when he received another shake of her head. "I'm keeping Bianca company, but we will most likely watch it from a good distance."

"See that you do."

The thought that Whiston had climbed into another scandal was only made worse by imagining Juliet run down and lying bleeding by the side of the road. This race would not be a gentle trot, or even a gallop. It was much worse.

Friday was not soon enough to get her out of that house.

Chapter Fifteen

MINDING HER ASSURANCE to Val, on Monday, the day of the steeplechase, Juliet dressed in her plainest carriage dress and bonnet and joined her sister in a hack to Covent Garden. Bianca was in fine fettle, eyes sparkling, wearing her newest hat, a white straw lined with white pleated silk, with pink and white rosebuds rioting over the brim. So much for the discretion Juliet had hoped for.

Val had escorted Juliet back to the house after their shopping expedition, and delivered a blistering lecture to Whiston and Bianca, one Juliet counted herself privileged to hear. Such precise language, such icy blasts of disapproval awed her, but they had not affected Whiston one jot.

So here they were, standing by the church. Bianca had opened her parasol and planted a kiss on her husband before he laughed, patted her arm, and strode to his lightweight curricle, which had been stripped of all but the essentials for the race even though this would not be a test of speed, but of dexterity and skill. If nobody ended up dead, it would be a miracle.

Other vehicles lined up, some with the insignia of the Four Horse Club and other clubs that had sprung up in its wake. Whiston had a huge nosegay in the buttonhole of his double-breasted coat, which signified one of those clubs, but Juliet neither knew nor cared which one.

Horses champed at the bit, stamping, waiting for the command to start the race. The starter stood by the side of the road, pistol primed, and a flag in his other hand just in case nobody heard the pistol shot. There must be at least twenty entrants to this piece of foolishness.

"Ah, there you are."

She spun around. "I didn't think you planned to attend."

Val did not look happy. His eyes were cold. "I did not. But I could not leave you alone for this ordeal."

Bianca laughed at him. "This is an adventure, a lark, not an ordeal. And we are not exactly alone." She indicated to where three footmen in livery stood silently behind them.

"Alone," he repeated firmly. "Without escort. I look after what's mine."

"I'm your property now?" Juliet's lips thinned.

"Not precisely," he said distantly, "but you have given yourself to my care." He watched the carriages lining up. Everything from gigs to high perch phaetons. "What kind of idiot brings a high perch phaeton to a race?"

"Not my husband," Bianca said. "He had all the trim stripped from his curricle, the padding from the seats, everything that would slow it down." A touch of pride colored her voice. "He really wants to win this race, and that is not only for the prize money which is considerable now. The betting is sky-high." She laughed, rather high pitched, drawing her sister's attention.

She was bright-eyed, alert, everything Juliet wanted her to be. But she disliked the feverish quality to her sister's appearance. As if the fine line that usually defined Bianca had blurred.

She was frowning over the conundrum when a commotion made her turn her head to where the carriages waited. Voices were raised in furious argument, and a whip was raised, its tip curling wickedly over the heads of several carriages.

"I don't like this," Val said. "There will be some mischief if the organizers aren't careful to control it."

As he spoke, someone rushed up to the carriage and grabbed

the whip. Its owner expostulated furiously, his high collar obscuring their view so they could not identify him. "Better than a raree show," somebody behind them remarked. Juliet doubted that the owner of the usual raree show in Covent Garden would agree.

With a chorus of his fellow competitors ringing in his ears the owner of the whip was forced to withdraw. That took some time, with carriages drawn by high-spirited horses moving out of the way. "Well, there's one thing" Val commented. "You can tell who has control and who doesn't. It will make the odds easier to calculate."

He sounded so cool, while Juliet became increasingly agitated. Standing outside a coffee house, the upper window festooned with male figures draped over the sill, shouting their bets to the wandering tallymen below, the square filling with more contestants by the second, Juliet felt far from safe. She wished she had not come, although she could not leave until her sister did. She wouldn't abandon her to this mob. She wished she'd brought her white parasol, the one with the long spike at the tip.

The noise rose every second. "We should probably step back," Val murmured in her ear. "They're preparing to set off. It won't be pretty."

Bianca overheard. "I suspect many of these people are only here to watch. From what Whiston told me before he left home this morning, only thirty carriages are entered in the race."

Only thirty? Juliet did not say it aloud, but in her opinion that was about twenty too many. London roads were not built to take that kind of traffic, all going full speed and all at once. Dread entered her heart. "People will be killed," she said.

"I doubt it, though I suspect there will be a few sore heads by the end of the race," Bianca said tartly.

"Not to mention broken limbs," Val added. "Let's step back a few feet."

Covent Garden Piazza was one of the largest open spaces in London, barring the parks. Even so, today there was little room to move. By dint of backing up first, using his larger body to ease a way through, and incorporating the bulky footmen they'd brought, Val managed to draw them further back, until they were right outside the coffee house.

Juliet looked around in alarm. The press of humanity around them did not include her sister. "Where is Bianca?"

"She would not come," Val said. "I saw her shake off the footman who went to her, but he followed with her, so we must hope she is safe. She no doubt wants to wave off her husband."

"I'm sure she does."

By now Juliet understood what was happening between Bianca and Whiston. If Bianca did something of her own volition, it would invariably be wrong. If she had not gone to see him now, he would certainly have complained, probably at dinner when others could hear, perhaps framing it as a joke. His criticism of her was constant and unrelenting, even when she was doing nothing wrong, comporting herself impeccably.

It was hard to notice at first, but now she knew what to look for, Juliet could predict it. To the world, the Duke of Whiston was the wild, handsome scion of a noble family, but Juliet knew differently now. So did their sister Viola, now their mother had written to her. The kind of ill-use he was employing was not actionable in law, nor was it something many would regard. But Bianca was less self-assured now, not as confident as she had always been. Her husband's treatment of her was having an effect. Even her expostulations and the arguments were less frequent and quieter, as if she were beginning to accept his treatment of her, his assessment of who she was and should be.

Did he know he was doing it, diminishing her with every comment? Of that she was not sure. It might not be a deliberate plan of action. Perhaps it was all born of his desire for her to be perfect in his eyes.

Today, however, he was more concerned with his driving and reaching the end of the race. He even thought he'd win, despite several famous whips having accepted the challenge. The crowd stirred and murmured, the stink of humanity mingling with the powerful perfumes the wealthy used to try to drown the odors of life. A waft of delicate lavender reached her, breaking through the earthier smells for a bare instant then was gone, before she could discover who had used it.

The cacophony rose, and finally, a shot echoed around the square.

The signal to start.

A sharp *crack!* followed the explosion of the gun. Juliet jerked around, trying to go onto the tips of her toes to see over the heads of the people in front of them. Something flew into the air—a piece of wood, a large, curved piece, spinning like a missile as it headed straight for them.

The world spun as Val picked her up, and turned around, presenting his back to the flying wood, moving quickly as he barged his way through the door at the front of the coffee house and right through the spectators gathered there. Inside, he dumped her on the floor and yelled. "Close the doors!"

Something smashed outside, and people screamed.

Only then could Juliet get her bearings. The smell of stale beer, coffee, tobacco smoke, and humanity assailed her nostrils, as twenty or more pairs of eyes leveled at her. And the hush as they entered. Not one that lasted, but the unusual sight of a woman in a coffee house, followed by the smash and scream outside, shocked them into temporary silence.

Juliet brushed herself down and pulled her bonnet into place. Thus armored, she looked out of the mullioned window at the front of the house. All she could see was a press of bodies. "Bianca—where's Bianca?"

"We lost her for now," he said tersely from behind her. "We can do little to find her until this commotion has died down." He moved closer to the glass, and being closer and taller, he could see more. "The carriages that are still intact have gone. They went up King Street, at least most of them did. There are probably some knowing sorts who went the other way. I can see debris. My guess is that someone's wheel broke or one carriage collided with another."

"Aye," said someone, a man unabashedly standing on a settle, clutching the high sides for balance as he also peered through the window. "Lord Seaton and Mr. Darraway are shouting and going at each other like street fighters. Presumably it was their carriages that met." A few men groaned and tore up scraps of paper. No doubt their bets were now useless. Wisely, Juliet remained silent. In this bastion of male privilege, she was best that way. But nobody seemed too concerned at her presence. They had accustomed themselves to the shock of a female in their midst.

The man standing on the settle continued. "A few people are lying down. They must be hurt, to lie on that filth. They never clear those cabbage leaves away properly." The morning market provided most of London's fresh fruit and vegetables, and although they were gone, the stalls folded and propped against the sides of the square, they left evidence of their presence in the form of vegetation which grew slimier and more dangerous to the unwary as the day went on.

"I see Mr. Perceval over on the other side of the square. He doesn't seem hurt, and his carriage is intact. Perhaps he thought better of it."

Her heart contracted. Was Bianca hurt? Did her footman have the sense to take her out of the chaos? Through her worry for her sister, Juliet was still glad to be here with Val. His speed and swift action had startled her in the moment, but he had protected her, even while the world was erupting around them. He was standing now where he could stop her if she decided to leave to look for Bianca. Was that on purpose? She rather thought so.

All she could do was listen to the man who could see more than most. He listed names and descriptions of people who were injured or left behind. None of them sounded like her sister.

Val came back to her. "We'll look for her, I promise." He glanced at the footman who had accompanied them. He moved to the back of the shop and spoke to a waiter who, a moment later, was carrying a tray over. Val handed her one of the plain white cups. "Drink. The coffee is fine here. The milk too."

That was worth knowing. London milk was sometimes so adulterated there was no actual milk in it. She sipped, cautiously at first, but then with appreciation. She needed something, and although coffee was not ideal, it was certainly something.

The man on the settle climbed down to raucous laughter. They could see daylight between the spectators outside as the crowd began to thin, and people started to move again. "Daresay the magistrates will have something to say about that," the man said. "Did they know it was happening?"

"Probably paid off," someone else commented.

The first man glanced at Val, who did not catch his eye and did not add to the conversation. Instead, Val glanced at the footman again, who nodded and went outside. Several other people left as well. Now the coffee house was less crowded, two men could stand and allow Val and Juliet to take their seats. Juliet sipped her coffee and listened.

Their footman returned in short order. "They're in a shop two doors down," he told them. "Watson got Her Gr—your sister away safe, ma'am." He bowed. Avoiding the title made sense. It would only attract unwanted attention.

Juliet made to stand, but Val reached over and pressed her back down, his hand on her arm. "Finish your coffee. We know she's safe."

"Am I pale?"

"As my mother's face powder." When he smiled, she had no option but to smile back. Relief filled her at the news. She addressed the footman. "Did you see her husband?"

"Got away safe," the servant assured her. "In the first group to leave, or so Watson said. She was all for following him, but Watson managed to persuade her to wait." He lowered his voice. "Billingsgate next, then Smithfield. She wants to go to Smithfield to watch him."

Not wise. Juliet exchanged a glance with Val, who shook his head. "We'll see what can be done. She should go home and wait there."

When they left the coffee house, passed by the groups of gossiping people, and found Bianca, Juliet's sister absolutely refused to go home. She'd lost her hat, but the rest of her seemed intact. Her cheeks were flushed with excitement. "Go home like a good little wife?" She laughed. "I cannot think of anything more tame. Why should I let George have all the fun?"

"You call this fun?" Juliet demanded.

"Well, exciting, at any rate," her sister said, displaying her adorable pout. It was wasted on her sister, and Val didn't appear impressed. "I thought I would go to Smithfield and see him there. And he expects me here when he returns."

Not *here*, in a milliner's shop, surely. Hats on stands stood on every surface, and the owner of the establishment stood by the window, hands folded. She was beaming like a parson who'd just found a guinea in the collection plate. Which in a way, she had.

"Well!" Bianca said, smiling. "I need a new hat, so we're in exactly the right place."

"Indeed," Juliet said dubiously. Her hands went to the ribbons of her bonnet. When she removed it, an assistant stepped forward to take it. The least they could do for the woman who'd given Bianca shelter was to buy a hat or two. Then the woman could tell her other customers that they'd shopped here—far better compensation than a mere monetary consideration.

Juliet settled on a puce number that would make her mother recoil in horror. But it would not match her blue pelisse, so she could give a reasonable excuse for not instantly wearing it. She had a good mind to give it to her mother just to see her reaction.

"Whiston will be hours," Juliet reminded Bianca as they perused the bonnets on display. "You cannot wait here and impose on this lady any longer."

"There will be somewhere appropriate to wait," Bianca said airily.

"Coffee houses, whorehouses, shops," Juliet said. "You could go home and then return in an hour or so."

A riderless horse still running free thundered through the square, but nobody followed it. "This is chaos," Val added. "Let me take you both home."

Juliet could only sense disaster in this entire business. She took her time choosing the hat she had already decided on, the violently puce bonnet. She enjoyed the winces of her sister, who at least knew her dues and chose an equally hideous number, a straw decorated with the most inauthentic daisies Juliet had ever seen.

They let the proprietor box them up, using all the "your graces" in the world. They even allowed the lady to mention their presence here today. Two of the three Burrell sisters, and the other only absent because she was not in London! Goodness, how her fellow milliners would stare!

"If you wear those hats, people will certainly stare," Val said as they closed the door of the shop behind them. He set a comfortable pace to King Street, now clear of racing carriages, where he had ordered a carriage to wait. Watson waited with the elegant vehicle. Val personally helped them in. As she took his hand, Val murmured, "Not long now."

Juliet couldn't wait.

ONCE INSIDE THE carriage, Bianca had flatly refused to go home. By way of a compromise, they had undertaken a shopping expedition to the Royal Exchange so she could buy a proper replacement for the hat she had lost. That task complete, Bianca insisted they return to Covent Garden. Val had gone away on a few errands while the sisters shopped, but after two hours surely the place would be back to its normal, more rational self and would not pose further threat.

People were waiting as they arrived—not as many as before—but an air of anticipation filled the air. Shouts from King Street announced the arrival of the carriages. Bianca reached for Juliet's hand.

Then, with a sweep of wheels, two carriages—one Whiston's—swept around the corner. The crowd cried out, shouting names.

The carriages were neck-and-neck, driving around the three sides of the square to return to the fourth, the church.

Another carriage followed, but it was too far behind to catch them up in time.

Whiston was in front, then the other man, then Whiston again. Two men stood in front of the church doors. The adjudicators at the finish line.

Whiston and the other driver passed the church and finally drew their horses to a halt at the end of the square. Whiston didn't hesitate, but leaped down, tossing the reins to his groom, who, of course had been waiting there all this time. The horses were tired, their heads drooping, sweat flecking their once glossy coats, but they were alive and uninjured. And although Whiston was disheveled, he was also alive and safe, and speaking now with the adjudicators.

Bianca flew to him. He seized her in his arms and subjected her to a smacking kiss.

Juliet stood there, temporarily at a loss. Everyone seemed to have forgotten her. Men and women stood around, watching the racers in awe, as if they'd done something heroic. After a moment's hesitation, Juliet walked over to join them.

"Dished!" Whiston told them, and now his smile was wry. "The adjudicators swear Landry came first, but I'm not so sure. We rounded the piazza together, so it depends on where exactly the finish line is."

The tall Lord Landry smirked. "It is where we agreed. Come, Whiston, admit it. I beat you fair and square." He favored Bianca and Juliet with a smile of his own, knowing and superior. Juliet had the very strong urge to smack it from his face, but she was not a violent woman, or so she kept telling herself.

"Congratulations," Bianca said to his lordship, forcing her own smile. Although she stood close to her husband and they were both smiling, Juliet sensed the tension, as if a cord tying them to one another was pulled tight by an unseen hand.

"Aye, well," one of the adjudicators, Sir Henry Smythe-Fotherington said, with a smile of his own. "It was close, no denying that, but we are both agreed—Landry had it by half a head. If you would care to call on me in the morning, Lord Landry, we can settle up. There's a deal of prize money, more than we originally agreed. Your share of the bets adds to the pot. And it's no small thing, Your Grace, to come so close to beating such a notorious whip."

"We shall have to arrange a rematch," Whiston said smoothly, but beneath those fair good looks lurked a flash of anger, a spark which could easily be fanned into flame.

"Indeed, sir, but not this circuit. We have run it now. We must agree on another."

Whiston bowed. "I thought it exceedingly challenging. We lost fully half the entrants and more simply gave up. No doubt the papers will be full of the exploits tomorrow."

Sir Henry cleared his throat. "And the magistrates will be after our blood. Do not forget, gentlemen! It was an impromptu encounter, if you please!"

"Even though White's books were filled with bets yesterday?" Whiston asked silkily.

"Speculative," Sir Henry said, dismissing the comment. "Everyone knows the books are full of bets that never reach completion."

Nobody knew any such thing. If a bet was entered in those sacred books, it was brought to a conclusion, one way or another. But nobody ventured to contradict Sir Henry.

"Time to go home, darling," Whiston said to Bianca. "Unfortunately, the curricle is all but wrecked, but I've sent for the town carriage. It should be here by now."

Knowing she would not have to tolerate such behavior for long, Juliet joined Bianca in the town carriage, and they waited for her husband to conclude his business before going home to face the wrath of their mother.

⫸⫷

AND ANGRY SHE was. "You should never have gone," she berated them, after they visited her in her bedroom, where she was getting ready for dinner. "You both have more hair than wit. Do you truly wish to make your reputation worse?" she asked Bianca, then turned on Juliet. "And you, the future wife of a diplomat! They will bury you alive if you insist on participating in such idiotic scrapes! You must behave with dignity and stateliness at all times if you are to take your place in that community!"

Recalling the dinner at Carlton House, Juliet wisely said nothing. She'd have found more success in the hothouse if she'd taken up the Regent's offer. If one could call it success. But she did say, "Val came to see the start of the race and to take care of us." The information mollified her mother, but only a little. And she had not seen the hat yet.

Bianca excused herself first. "I only came to reassure you that we are both perfectly well. And capable of handling our own affairs," she added, after a significant glance at Juliet. "The race was merely an escapade. Nothing scandalous happened, except I bought you what is probably the most hideous hat in London."

"Oh no," Juliet said, finding her voice. "I must lay claim to that. I will have them brought to your room, Mama, and you must judge for yourself."

"Then why would you buy them?" Mrs. Burrell demanded.

"Because a milliner kindly gave me shelter in her shop when the crowd became a little too rowdy, and we had to thank her somehow."

"Why not just tip her?"

Juliet smiled, recollecting the fussy little woman. "I thought she deserved more. She now thinks she is a fashionable hat maker, and she will no doubt put a sign in her window."

"And you'll be associated with hideous hats," her mother said.

"Half the tradesmen in London have claimed we patronized their establishments, when we have done nothing of the kind," Juliet answered. "What's one more?"

Their mother shrugged. In her it was an elegant gesture, one she could turn into a flirtatious move. Juliet had tried to copy it many times, but never succeeded exactly. Mrs. Burrell intended it now as an indication of her lack of interest in the subject. "If anyone asks you about today's disgraceful display, you will say you disapproved of it, but you could not put a stop to it. I fail to understand why you attended in the first place. It is not at all the thing to appear in the middle of a rowdy group of men, demanding to watch a spectacle you should never be a part of."

"Lady Lytton took part," Juliet said mildly.

"Lady Lytton is not far from a man herself," her mother said tartly. "She never dresses properly, struts around London as if she has every right to frequent coffee houses and such and declares she will remain single until the end of her days. Her only virtue is her wealth. You surely cannot wish to emulate her."

"If I were as wealthy as her ladyship, I might try," Juliet said wistfully. Although her eccentricity would probably take a different path, one strewn with books of all kinds.

As she rose to leave, Mrs. Burrell held up a hand. "A moment, if you please." She nodded to her maid. "Give us ten minutes."

Juliet resumed her seat as the maid left. "I want your honest opinion on Bianca," her mother said without any preamble. "How is she, do you think?"

"Living on her nerves," Juliet replied, glad of the opportunity to discuss her concerns. It was worth making a hurried toilet before dinner to do this. She valued her mother's opinion. "She's brittle, frenzied at times. The center of attention, as always, but not with any conviction."

Her mother jerked a nod. "Go on."

"I've seen nothing to suggest that Whiston has treated her badly in the last few days, but this stupid race took all his attention. I don't think she tried to talk him out of it."

Mrs. Burrell picked up a hare's foot from her dressing table and studied her appearance in the mirror. "Even though it could have killed him."

She shuddered. "Even then. There's no talking him out of his mad schemes. I think Bianca has learned that."

Her mother touched the hare's foot to her cheek, then put it down. "She should never have married him. I was wrong not to prevent it. I thought she could reform him, or she could at least live a good life apart from him, but he needs her."

At Juliet's quizzical raised brow, she continued, "He needs a constant, admiring audience, an acolyte. That's how he regards her. The girl he was previously betrothed to, she would have served him, though I don't doubt he would have run through her fortune in no time. Bianca does her best to follow his dictates, which I think is bad for her. I don't like to see her under his thumb. That's not how I brought you all up." She sighed and dropped her hands into her silk-clad lap. "We must wait. I thought she'd have produced a child by now. When she does, she will be in a better position to choose how she lives. But I see nothing, and she says there are no signs."

"That is a shame. Whiston expects her to produce an heir and cut out the claims of his cousin. He dislikes him intensely."

"In that, at least, we share the same opinion. A creeping, insinuating man. I catch him around the house sometimes. He comes in unannounced and prowls." She turned her head and met Juliet's eyes. "Be careful of him. I don't trust him."

"I don't like him either," she said. "I'll be careful, I promise."

"Now to happier things," her mother said, picking up a letter from her cluttered dressing-table. "I received a letter from your sister this afternoon, very closely written. She may persuade Knowsley to bring her to London quite soon, now that the birth is not far off and her bout of illness appears to have passed." She sighed. "Morning sickness generally only lasts for the first three months, but hers lasted far too long. We must pray she is past that stage now. She does not wish me to go to her, but once you are married I will write again. Though, indeed, she may well be here by then."

"She must not risk her health." Viola was in the last stages of pregnancy. It had always been a possibility that her loving husband would not let her take the journey to London, superior birthing attendants notwithstanding, and Juliet could understand his concerns.

"She includes a note for you." Mrs. Burrell passed her daughter a sealed note. Her mother had always respected her daughters' privacy.

As she passed her sister's chamber on the way to her own room, Juliet saw a maid entering with a brown bottle in her hand and stopped the woman. "Is my sister well?"

"Perfectly, ma'am," the maid answered. "She has one of her headaches, that is all."

And she was using laudanum for them. That would explain the brittleness, the sense of blurriness Juliet could not quite define. And laudanum was dangerous and highly addictive if taken on a regular basis. Everything fell into horrible, worrying place: the laudanum, the white lead in the thick cream Bianca had taken to using on her face, the lack of sleep, the frantic activity.

Now Juliet was seriously worried.

Chapter Sixteen

THE NEXT DAY, Tuesday, Val called at Whiston House to take Juliet driving. He had sent a note later in the day after the race, apologizing for not returning to ensure her safety, but he'd been assured by her footman that she'd come to no harm.

Juliet wondered what had been so important as to keep him away. Had he received news that he had obtained the post he wanted? Did he even need her anymore? Juliet knew him better than she had, enough to know he wouldn't abandon her, not now. But did he really want her, or would their marriage be one of duty, not the bliss she'd so briefly experienced?

She dressed in an ivory carriage-dress and pale blue spencer and waited for him in the hall nervously. He was on time at ten o'clock, early for a ride, but perhaps he wanted no witnesses to what he wanted to say to her. He was all smiles and handed her up with meticulous courtesy.

"I'm so sorry I couldn't see you yesterday. I had important business which took longer than I wanted."

"Oh? Did you get the post?"

"What?" He spared her a glance. "Oh, that," he said as if it was of no importance. "Not yet. No, I went to Doctor's Commons."

"What?" She clung to the passenger rail as he took a corner a trifle too sharply. That didn't make sense. Doctor's Commons was where people went to obtain a special license to marry. Or perhaps he had other business there. That wasn't all they did.

"After I saw the start of that mad race, I could not bear you staying in that house any longer. I don't like you there, and I'm sorry if you don't like it, but there it is."

He took another corner, and they were back in Grosvenor Square. He slowed the horses to a stately walk, then came to a halt, and turned to address her directly. "I sent word to your brother-in-law and your sister. You might have noticed that they left the house."

She shook her head. "I thought they were still abed." They often were.

"They're waiting for us."

"Where? How?"

"In the chapel. You need witnesses, and I assumed you'd like them to attend. Your mother said she would see to the details."

A conspiracy. But one so quickly and smoothly arranged she'd had no idea. She sat, hands folded in her lap, staring at him, trying to catch up.

He took one of her hands, folded it in his. "If you should mislike it, Juliet, then we will go ahead as planned. But I want you with me. After that farce of a race, I could not wait any longer. If you make me, I will wait. But you are the only person who can stop me doing this." He smiled, and like always, her resolve melted. "So, Juliet Burrell, will you marry me? Now, today?"

She tried to marshal her emotions. She had thought he would retreat into his rational, calm character, the one he maintained with everyone else. But she saw the warmth and desire in his eyes, the man he showed to nobody else.

For that reason, she gave him her answer. "Yes," she said.

HE DROVE THEM the short distance to the Grosvenor Chapel in

South Audley Street. She'd attended services there before.

Whiston was there to give her away. Today he was relatively sober, dressed with neatness and propriety, although his shirt points were high enough to reach his cheekbones and his neckcloth a masterpiece of precisely creased snowy perfection. His waistcoat was not as florid as he usually preferred, and his double-breasted coat sported a set of relatively modest buttons. He'd made an effort for her, and Juliet appreciated it.

But he was distant as she took his arm, no doubt still brooding over the events of the day before. He'd lost a lot of money in that race, and his pride was badly dented. But he was here, and so was Bianca.

She tried to remain cool, but here they were, and she was about to change her life.

Val wanted to protect her, she understood that, but his actions were somewhat—autocratic. Was he the kind of man who took the vow of obedience too literally? He might want an intelligent, poised woman to manage the social side of his position, but Juliet wanted more than that. She wanted a partnership.

Passion they had, but she'd seen from Bianca and Whiston that passion did not last forever. Love? She knew little about love.

Val had left her to go to the front of the chapel. It was a modern, classically decorated place, more intimate than the larger churches in London. When she entered the chapel with Whiston, all but the first few rows were unoccupied, and the galleries were completely empty. She took a couple of deep breaths, steadying herself.

Val looked around as they came in and a slow smile curled his lips. When Whiston gave her to him, putting her hand in his, she lifted her gaze to his, and found her strength there. In the calm and tranquility of the church, they pledged themselves to each other. For those precious minutes nobody else existed.

Twenty minutes later they emerged from the vestry, and the deed was done.

They went outside and into the carriage waiting there. Not the curricle, but a more formal vehicle. He handed her in himself.

As he settled himself in, she asked. "Why did you not wait until Friday?"

He grunted. "I could not bear the thought of you unprotected in that household for another day. I want to look after and care for you, and by accepting my suit, you gave me the right to do so. So when I discovered this could be done, I did it."

His impulsivity surprised her, but the speed and thoroughness of his actions did not.

"Personally," he continued as the carriage jolted into motion, "I think you are the most beautiful of the Burrell sisters. Or rather, you were."

"Burrell no more." She smiled.

"We will do well," he said, and it sounded as much of a promise as all the vows she'd just made.

She slipped her hand into his, and he clasped it warmly. "We have a wedding breakfast waiting for us. I wish it were not so."

"Why?"

"Oh, I'm sure you can guess, if you think hard enough." His voice warmed, and when heat rushed to her cheeks, he reached out with his free hand and touched her cheek. "Lovely," he murmured, and moved closer.

Unfortunately the carriage stopped, so she was balked of her kiss.

He exited first and helped her down by simply clasping her waist and swinging her down to the pavement. They were outside the office of a large legal concern in the Inns of Temple. The gracious houses here had an air of purpose. He led her inside where she found the papers of the marriage settlement waiting for her.

"We would have done this on Thursday," he said, "before our marriage, but I hurried them along."

Val signed all the legal documents arranging her portion and its disposal, her rights where Val's private property was concerned, all the ifs and buts that attended a marriage between those of his rank and hers. Her pin-money seemed much too large a sum, and her dowry was to be sensibly invested and put in her control, through three trustees, who, Val assured her, would sign anything she wanted them to.

Within twenty minutes they were done, and back in the carriage for the short journey to Langston House.

Again, Val alighted first, and helped her down.

He paused, gazing down at her until the door to Langston House opened and they turned and went inside. With the front door to the house closed he pulled her into his arms and, before she had time to take off her bonnet, he kissed her. Properly kissed her. No peck on the cheek, and in front of as many servants as stood there, he kissed her.

Heedless of anyone else, she flung her arm around his neck and held on. This was her wedding day. To hell with conventions.

Nobody said anything when he finally drew away. Still gazing at her, he pulled the bow of her bonnet free and helped her draw it off. He held it out for a servant and treated his beaver hat the same way. He never let his gaze stray from hers. Not until she looked down to undo the little buttons on her gloves. They went upstairs to the drawing room to the hushed silence of the servants below.

Had he done that for effect? Confused, as much by the kiss as by his reasons, she stood in the doorway with him and took the gentle applause of the guests waiting for them to arrive.

A PLEASANT MEAL that lingered into the afternoon gave Juliet the chance to take stock of what had happened. Wedding breakfasts could be elaborate affairs, but as her new mother-in-law explained to her, "We have a ball arranged for Friday."

The day she should have been married.

About twenty people sat down to the meal. Juliet marveled that Lady Langston—the dowager—could arrange it at such short notice. Her ladyship gave up the seat at the bottom of the table to her—the place where the lady of the house, the hostess, would sit. It was done so adroitly Juliet barely noticed until Val led her there.

"However," Val's mother said with a smile after she took her place halfway up the table, "I will not use 'dowager.' I'm far too frivolous for that!" and everyone laughed. Her ladyship was effortlessly elegant, and Juliet had to agree that she was far too lovely to be considered a dowager.

TWO HOURS LATER, the meal ended, and the guests dispersed, agreeing by mutual consent not to linger. Her mother embraced Juliet, tears in her eyes. "I won't wish you happy because I know you will be." Bianca merely hugged her tightly and told her she'd see her soon.

Val took her upstairs, and up again, to the bedroom level. "My mother has the suite on the floor below," he told her. "Can you cope with this smaller one?"

She looked around at the spacious sitting room. "I think I can manage," she said, smiling. This room was charming and understated. The furnishings were classical, with the occasional touch of gilding, but not as gaudy or as ultra-fashionable as the ones in the Whiston mansion. This house was smaller, too, but that was like comparing a sprawling medieval castle to an elegant modern country house.

Her heart beat faster. This was the middle of the afternoon. Surely, he wouldn't . . .

"Here." He took her to the left side of the suite and opened the door to a bedroom. They stood in the doorway.

"Oh!" The room was decorated in shades of green, mostly taken from nature. Chinese wallpaper was pasted on panels. Draperies of rich emerald hung over the bed and in front of the windows. A fire glowed in the grate. "I love it," she said.

"I'm afraid we'll have to share for now," he said, smiling, "but there is a dressing room each."

His mother, an arbiter of fashion, had no say in the decoration of these rooms. They reflected him, showing his quiet good taste and his deep appreciation of quality. "I . . ." she laughed, short and embarrassed. "This is new to me. I've never been in this situation before."

"I should hope not!"

"Oh, I did not mean in that way. I meant, well, my brother joined the army as soon as he could, and he is older than we are, and my Papa died some time ago. We've been a house of women. When we had a house," she reflected. "My brother bought the Edinburgh house back after my mother sold it to pay for our Season in London. So I suppose I do have a family home, but I've not had a place that truly belonged to me."

He took her shoulders and turned her to face him. "I am not your brother or your father. I am your husband, and I trust our relationship will be nothing like you have known before. It's new to me, too."

"Oh, but . . ."

"I have no mistresses, nor will I have any affairs in the future," he told her. "This I promise you. If you promise the same."

That came from the heart. Perhaps his mother's liaisons affected him more than he allowed people to see. She had no problem making this pledge. "Yes, I promise. That's what I want, too."

He pulled her close, bent his head and kissed her breathless. She responded with enthusiasm and happy anticipation of what was to come. Why would she want anyone else when she had him, when she had this? That promise had seemed important to him, and she was only too glad to make it.

He broke the kiss and stared at her as if reading her. Then he bent and swept her up. "Hands around my neck," he said, low and intimate. She thrilled to him, eagerly did as he told her and pressed close as he left the sitting room and took the few steps that led to his bed. He deposited her on the mattress, smoothing her gown down. After tossing his coat and waistcoat to the floor, Val turned her. "I had intended to take this slowly and carefully." His fingers shook as he unfastened the row of tiny buttons at the front of her spencer. "But to hell with that." He laughed. "I beg your pardon."

"Don't."

"Don't what?"

"Apologize for saying what comes to you naturally." Her gown came loose when he dealt with the fastenings in the same way. "I want you to be you. Say what you want to when you want to." She wanted to shatter the sheet of ice that shielded him from the rest of the world. She wanted it gone.

He paused, and she knew he was thinking. Could he let go completely? She'd caught a glimpse of it when they'd made love before, that fierce duel that had thrilled her to the marrow, even as she'd borne the pain of losing her virginity. The triumph of her achievement had kept her going.

She lifted up to allow him to slip her gown down her body. She needed to touch him, to see him. All of him. Frantically she pulled at his clothes, but he held her arms so she couldn't tug his shirt up. "No," he said. "Not this time. I want you naked, I want to see you, and I want us to slow down."

"Why?" Recalling last time, she didn't understand why she should wait. She wanted that feeling back as quickly as possible.

"It's better when you take your time."

Looking at his slow smile, she believed him.

"Now," he said, and how a man could look in control when his face was flushed with passion, and his shirt was hanging out of his breeches she'd never know, "My turn." His low voice melted her.

He slid off the bed.

He pulled out the long tails of his shirt, then walked to the dressing table, as if on his own. Glancing at her, he undid his cuffs, and dropped the studs in a little dish on the table. The room smelled of him, citrus, male, entirely foreign to her and thrilling. She watched, scarcely able to breathe as he unfastened his elaborately tied neckcloth, taking care to undo all the folds before he dragged it off, shook it to loosen the creases, and dropped it over the back of his chair. His shirt went next. He was now bare from the waist up. She drank in the powerful shoulders, the ridge of his spine, and the way his muscles flexed as he turned to face her.

He glanced at her, smiling, then set to unfastening the fall on his breeches. He peeled them and his stockings off in one movement.

Juliet gulped. Had *that* actually been inside her? All of it? It was red and rigid, and she wanted to touch it.

He put his hands on his hips. "Your turn."

When she reached for him, he took a step back and shook his head.

He didn't have to say anything. Closing her eyes, so she wouldn't have to see him, she reached behind and pulled her stay-laces undone. He already knew she could do that, so she couldn't turn her back on him and ask him to help. Embarrassment swept over her in a great wave.

"Think of the reward," he murmured, as she pulled the laces loose. "I will kiss every inch of your skin, touch and caress you, discover you, as I want you to do with me. We can't do that fully dressed, can we?"

Embarrassment left her as desire surged in. A rush of energy led her to pull off her shoulder straps and let her stays fall. As they fell, she reached under her shift and undid her garters. The first went quickly, but as she felt his burning gaze searing into her, she took her time with the other one, giving him tantalizing glimpses of what lay above. The silk stockings went. She pulled her only remaining garment—her shift—over her head, and let it drop to the floor, heedless of where it fell.

Then he was on her. But not with the thoughtless passion she wanted to release, the fast race to the peak and then the glorious release and the lassitude. No. He pressed her against him so their bodies met. Nothing was hidden.

His fierce gaze pinned her to the mattress as much as his body did. Reaching up, she wrapped her arms around his neck, but he slid down, leaving her embrace empty, and set about fulfilling his promise.

Had she thought Val had no passion, no emotion? It seemed a thousand years ago when she'd thought he was an entirely analytical, logical person who never lost himself in emotion.

He was certainly losing himself in something now. Grateful for the support of his shoulders, she gripped tight when he licked her breasts, sucked her nipples, turning every part of her hot and needy. She squirmed under him. "Val, please . . ."

"Breathless already?" He lifted his head, rested his chin lightly on her belly. "Let's see what happens next, shall we?"

By his grin, he knew already. He came back up the bed and kissed her, smoothed his hands over her body in long caresses that drove her wild. Restless and needy, she lifted her leg and hooked it around his. By the state of his body, he was as ready as she was. How was he holding out? How was it possible not to give way to this primitive urge, this terrible need?

He was breathless as he drew away and leaned over her, holding her gaze. His hair fell over his forehead, tousled by her fingers. His caresses became more intimate and focused, and she leaned back, opened her legs to accommodate his deft movements. "Should you like me to kiss you there?"

At the murmured words, a miracle happened and her need shot up to impossible levels. "Val, Val, please, don't stop . . . !"

His low chuckle was shaky. "Yes," he said. "Yes."

And with one swift, powerful movement, he made them one.

With a strangled cry she arched her back as thrills coursed

through her. Beyond words now, she held on and responded as he drove in and out, the action familiar, as if they'd done this more than just once.

"Do what you want. Bite, scratch, clutch. Show me, Juliet, let me hear you."

Heedless of anything else, her responses to him instinctive now, she felt her body following his lead, lifting and sending her higher and higher. If she'd been able to think, she'd have wondered at her ignorance of her own body and its actions. Hidden instincts, unknown until now, made her hold rigid, push back. She stroked him, gloried in that expanse of strong, powerful male, cupped his backside as, finally, she blossomed and gave him everything she had.

VAL LAY BACK, his arm curved around his wife, who lay tucked into him, sleeping, her breath warming his chest. Her response to his lovemaking shocked and delighted him. They had reached levels he'd never experienced before. And he'd hung onto his reserve, kept the part of him that enabled him to retain his sanity apart and watchful. It was a close-run thing, but this time he'd managed some self-control.

When he'd told her he'd arranged to bring the wedding forward, he'd sounded reasonable, but truly, his decision had been made in the throes of panic. He'd seen that shard of wood coming straight for her before he'd picked her up and presented his back to the flying weapon. Someone or something else must have deflected it or stopped it reaching them. If it had followed its clear trajectory, he wouldn't be here today.

She hadn't seen that. But the incident had pushed him into that decision. He wanted her as his wife. If he had to die, he wanted to do it after giving Juliet everything she wanted and more. So he'd hurried her into signing the settlements, which held considerable bequests buried in legal language.

He'd managed to rationalize his decision, but deep down he knew it was because he wanted to claim and protect her, to ensure she would never want again. And to end up here, of course. Since they'd first made love, he'd longed for her again.

He turned his head, studied the woman who would be the only one to occupy his bed from now on. So lovely. He knew she was beautiful, had braced himself for it, but he hadn't been prepared for the purity of her skin, the perfection of her figure. So smooth and silky, such wonderful curves for him to explore.

He let his hand glide over her forearm. Last year society had reacted to the astonishing beauties making their debut with jealousy, derision, admiration, and astonishment. As one of the first people to make their acquaintance, he'd had a chance to prepare himself for their public appearance, to keep them at a proper distance.

Urged on by his friends, he'd gone to the house he owned in Brook Street when they complained about the house being half empty. The previous occupants had stolen half the house's contents when they'd left. It was enough of an excuse to visit the family who had excited the interest of the few people who'd caught a glance of them in plain traveling dress as they'd arrived in a hired hack. The three of them and their mother, older but handsome in her own right, had set him back. Juliet had attracted him then. Shorter than her queenly sisters, her hair neither as fair as Bianca's nor as dark as Viola's, but with those diamond-brilliant blue eyes, she'd offered a softness he responded to.

From the first, Juliet had spoken as she felt, honesty in every word. That could be a problem in a diplomat, who used words as a weapon. Diplomats were the last line between two countries at war, and they were required to use tactics, strategy, knowledge, to prevent the loss of life in physical conflict. The wrong thing said at the wrong time could have tragic consequences.

When he'd chosen Maria, he'd used his head to analyze what she would bring to him in his chosen profession, her connections, her silent support. None of that with Juliet, and yet he'd married her. He still didn't understand why he'd felt such a deep urge to take of her and care for her, but he was coming to terms with it.

She stirred, and he murmured to her. No words, just a soothing sound. To his satisfaction, she moved into him and settled down again. Sounds came from the room outside and he recalled he'd asked for a cold supper to be laid out. She moaned and moved again. This time he failed to settle her. She blinked awake. "Oh."

"Yes, oh."

"I . . ." she smiled and settled in again. Another sound made her stiffen. "What's that?"

"The servants. They're laying out some food and wine for us. We might need them later." He caressed her. To his delight, she responded, moving closer and sliding her hand up his chest. His low growl of approval met with a "Shh! They'll hear us!"

When he laughed, she thumped his chest, until he grabbed her and pulled her close, so she couldn't do it again. Her breasts crushed against his chest; he felt the moment her nipples hardened. "What do you think they imagine we're doing in here?" His chest shook, and her hair fell over his face in a silky tumble of honeyed curls.

"Oh!" Leaning up, shamelessly using him to prop her elbows, she pushed back her hair and frowned at him. "I'm not used to it, I suppose."

"I didn't tell my valet not to come in tomorrow morning," he added, unable to resist the tease. "In fact, I'd rather he did come in. Hot water and fresh clothes will be very welcome."

"But he'll see—" Breaking off, she grimaced at him. "You're joking!"

"We can let the curtains of the canopy down when he comes in." He didn't mind teasing her, but he didn't want her upset. He glanced up at the dark blue velvet drapery suspended and tied back above the bed head. He'd had the old-fashioned four-poster moved out years ago. They could pull the drapes down at a pinch.

She sighed. "It's a matter of getting used to it. I suppose I could move to another room after . . ."

"No," he said firmly, drawing her closer. "I like you sleeping here. Unless you don't want to, of course. I'll tell Compson not to come in until I ring for him."

Grinning, she said, "If you can stand it, so can I."

"Talking about standing . . ."

She was still laughing when he kissed her.

Chapter Seventeen

FRIDAY ARRIVED, AND with it the ball to celebrate their wedding. The servants spent the day moving the furniture from the large drawing room and the music room next to it and decorating the house with huge swathes of flowers and silk drapery.

Val and Juliet kept to their suite, and food was served to them upstairs. His mother had foregone an elaborate dinner, presumably because she had enough to do without arranging that as well. What she'd done in so short a time was remarkable. And all in excellent taste, none of her experimental waywardness on display here.

With Juliet's hand resting decorously on Val's arm, they greeted the guests, accepting their felicitations. Nobody would know that two hours before they'd been stark naked, laughing and making love in the bed with the blue velvet canopy.

It was a rather distinguished guest list, considering the Foreign Secretary had chosen to attend. Combined with the wilder set led by the Duke of Whiston it promised to be an interesting evening. The wild set and the political set were not known for their closeness, although the gossip sheets sometimes tried to link them, and liaisons of all kinds were not unknown.

But not Lord Castlereagh. His wife stood by his side. Lady Castlereagh was the epitome of a political wife, constantly loyal to her husband and his allies, holding salons and dinners that were discussed for weeks after. She was also a Patroness of Almack's. Val had every expectation of Juliet reaching that level, given time or encouragement. But if she did not, they would cope. He would not push her to be something she wasn't, nor anything she did not wish to be.

As Juliet performed her curtsey and received the usual congratulations, her ladyship studied her closely. "I am pleased his lordship is married, at long last," she said. "I have been hinting this age that he should do so."

"I had only to meet the right woman," Val told her.

"I thought you had." Her gaze flicked to a corner of the room. Val followed her gaze and froze. Had his wife seen her yet? Lady Rotherham stood with her husband—and their daughter. Lady Maria wore a fixed smile and a white gown, which served to emphasize her purity. Was Lady Rotherham sending a message to them? Did she know her daughter had not spent a night alone with Val's secretary?

Society knew Maria and Juliet were friends, so not to invite them would have led to speculation, but nobody had expected them to come. Walter Norris should be here somewhere, but Val had not seen him yet. Her ladyship was still holding out against her daughter marrying a mere secretary, and as a result Val had to endure Norris moping about the office. He had no right to interfere, but he wished he could. Or that the young lovers would either agree to part or take matters into their own hands. He'd done his best to bring them together, although he had to admit he'd been somewhat distracted the past few days.

He caught a snippet of Lady Castlereagh's conversation as she spoke to Juliet. "I believe your husband had an interest in slavery at one time."

Quickly, he returned to full attention. "I beg your pardon, my lady, but no."

"Didn't you own a slaving ship once?"

Lord Castlereagh had stopped talking.

"Briefly," he admitted, "but when I owned it, it was a simple trader in inanimate cargo. However, I went aboard the ship once to talk to the captain about his next voyage, and I found the rings and chains below decks."

His wife's lovely eyes rounded, and she clapped her hand to her mouth. "The Dawn Trader?"

He nodded. "The trappings had been covered by the cargo, but that was not enough for me. I could not wait to get rid of it, and I lost it in a card game that same night. I would have cheated to lose that hand, but I didn't need to." He'd lost the game to Whiston, who had promptly sold the vessel.

"So you hate even a hint of slavery?" she asked him.

Lady Castlereagh tsked. "Do you not know your husband's family history at all?"

She turned to him, a question in her eyes. "I thought I did."

There was so much she, and everyone else in society, did not know about his family, but he would repeat what people did know. "My father was famous for his philanthropy and his support of the abolition movement. I was pleased to continue that part of his legacy. I always took care to keep my investments as clear of the despicable trade as I could."

She moved closer. "I've never had close contact with it, but I did read a lot. I've always agreed with the anti-slavers. I despise the practice. It is simply wrong to displace people from one country to another, and then treat them like property." She glanced at the Castlereaghs, as if afraid of saying something wrong.

"You know Russia still has slavery?" Lord Castlereagh asked.

He had his answer ready. "I do. But if I were sent there, that would be on behalf of the nation, not myself. While I can never condone the trade, I know how to conduct myself. Besides," he said with a smile, "far more battles are won with discussion than with argument."

"Indeed," said his lordship, who had heard that speech before. Her ladyship, who had not heard it, commended him on his professional attitude.

He was proud of Juliet and how she'd stated her opinion against slavery, and he did not care who heard her. Some members of the government thought they'd gone far enough with the Act of Parliament from nearly ten years ago. He did not. The vehemence of his own response upon seeing the hold of the ship had shocked him, but he had never made such direct contact with the slave trade before. Those rings and chains were witness to the horror that had taken place on that ship and would never be free of it. But he'd kept his personal revulsion to himself, because his career had always taken precedence.

"Perhaps we should leave the decisions to the people directly involved in the trade." The soft voice to his left told him Whiston's heir had arrived. He might have known Carrington, ever ambitious for preferment, would be lurking.

"In what way?" Castlereagh prompted.

Carrington cleared his throat. "Well, my lord, I know it is right and proper to ensure the welfare of the slaves, but they are considered essential to successful trade in some parts of the world. It may not be our place to advocate for all. Who are we to interfere with that system?"

"Good people who know what is right?" Juliet suggested.

Carrington shot her a supercilious glance, as if her opinions did not matter in the least. "We may not be so influential, if we take too liberal an attitude."

"So you would advocate for continuing the trade?" Lord Castlereagh asked.

Val waited for Carrington's answer with interest. Surely the man knew the Castlereaghs were in favor of abolition? Or did he not? If he had not done his research, he would not be a proper candidate for the FO. He seemed to be everywhere, poking his nose into everyone's business in his attempts for preferment. "While matters are still uncertain in Europe, I think so," Carrington smiled unctuously. "Not every country is fortunate enough to have the resources or the wealth of Great Britain."

Russia. Of course, Russia still had slaves.

Was Carrington angling for the Russia post? Pandering to Tsar Alexander might be a way of achieving it. "Does that indicate strength—or weakness, to abandon one's position in order to please a foreign potentate?" he wondered aloud.

Castlereagh nodded. "It is a difficult subject. I'm glad to hear your opinions, gentlemen."

At least he'd not lost his temper, though these days that rarely happened.

Juliet slipped her hand from his arm as the little group dispersed and they moved on. Carrington was smirking, no doubt assuming he had won the encounter. "I'll be back," she said with a soft smile. No doubt she needed the ladies' retiring room. He watched her go.

⇛⇜

JULIET HAD DECIDED to avoid the Rotherhams today, but when she saw Maria slip away, she could not resist. If Maria refused to speak to her, then there was less harm done if she did not do it in public.

A small antechamber was set aside for the ladies' use, and as she entered, Juliet saw Maria sitting at one of the mirrors, a maid in attendance pinning up a stray curl. She looked pale, and her white gown made her pallor worse. But she held her head high, and even managed a slight smile when she met Juliet's eyes in the mirror. She dismissed her maid with a few quiet words.

Juliet sat next to her, and knowing they did not have much time, didn't waste words. "So our ploy did not work immediately?"

"Not in the way we planned." Maria stared at her reflection, watching herself speak. "But there is another way."

"And that is?"

The cold expression on Maria's face chilled Juliet. "I have

received a flattering offer from the Marquess of Stonyhurst."

"But he's twice your age! Three times, even!" The Marquess was so much older than Maria. And he was not known for his kindness and generosity—more his spite. She vaguely remembered even Whiston saying as much, and his nephew, Mr. Fraser, had not spoken well of him at the Regent's dinner. Surely Maria couldn't be seriously considering an offer like that?

"Yes, that is true. And he is desperate for an heir. His son died a few years ago, and he lost his brother and two nephews at Waterloo." She turned to Juliet, smiling brightly. "Don't you see? My mother flatly refuses to allow Walter into the house, much less to let him pay his addresses to me. Not under any circumstances." She grimaced. "And my father agrees. There is no budging them. I cannot go on, Juliet." Tears filled her eyes.

Juliet groaned and reached out to put her hand over Maria's. "If you hold out, if you refuse to accept anyone else or admit that you had not spent the night with him alone, you can still win. Your mother still has your sister to place. Surely she would let you go."

Maria shook her head. "She wants us all married to peers of the realm. She's mad for a title. When you stole Langston, she was livid, determined to prove I would make a better match. And then—my courses came, and you know, I could not hide that from her. She was on the lookout."

Juliet listened in horror. In Maria's position she would have ensured everyone knew she'd spent the night with the man she professed to love, made it impossible for people to look away. Why had Maria not held out?

"You can refuse, you know. You are nearly of age. Only a year or so and you can marry anyone you choose."

"And lose everything else? How can you think of such a thing?"

Anyone would imagine nobody had done that before. "Walter Norris is a gifted and enthusiastic politician," she said. "He will care for you."

"I am not made for a politician's wife!"

"But you could be."

"Mama is delighted by the prospect of the Marquess." Maria closed her eyes, squeezed them tight before she opened them again. The glimmer of tears faded. "I have known the Marquess most of my life, although not well. We were able to have a frank conversation. He says he doesn't care where the heir comes from, and he will acknowledge any child of mine as his own."

"And Walter? Have you considered what will happen to him?" She could betray her love that way?

"He will accept the post of secretary to the Marquess. I will be a marchioness, which will make Mama happy, and I can still be with Walter. Better, because I will have a jointure and our son will become a marquess. Once I am a widow, I may marry whoever I please. It can't be long, can it? He must be seventy if he's a day."

So Maria had exchanged a love match for a clandestine affair, a true love for status and a title. And for this life of deception and lying, the true heir would be cheated out of his inheritance. Maria had just shown her the difference between diplomacy and deception. The lesson could not have been clearer.

Juliet got to her feet. She could hardly speak, such was the iniquity of the scheme. With a little resolve, Maria could have attained what she swore was her heart's desire. "I cannot wish you happy, Maria, because I do not think you will be. But you must do as you wish."

She left, bitterly disappointed with her friend.

So that was why Lady Rotherham had appeared here today, and most likely why she allowed her daughter to meet Juliet. Juliet no longer thought it an accident that she had found Maria alone. And it was confirmed for her when she returned to the drawing room in time to see Lady Rotherham watching for her entrance, a triumphant smile on her face.

She could not blame the lady for having ambitions for her daughters—Juliet knew what it was like to have an ambitious mother. But her mother presented possibilities. She did not force her children into doing what she wanted them to do rather than going where their hearts led them. In contrast, Lady Rotherham's blindness in fixing on a title and ignoring other possibilities showed a disregard for everyone but herself. And to ignore the happiness of her daughter and the man who loved her was heartless.

"Everything all right?"

She flashed a brilliant smile at Val. "Perfectly."

"Then let's go into supper."

Juliet looked up at him as they started to move. "Has Norris put in his notice?"

He stared at her, shock widening his gaze. "Yes, he has. How do you know?"

"Lady Maria Richards told me."

"Are they planning to run away again? Because if they are, I'm strongly inclined to let them."

She was tempted to agree with him. "There's more."

"I want to hear it. I lost an excellent political secretary today, one who could have gone much further."

"I'll tell you later."

They could say no more now—they had to get through the ritual of the ball first.

Juliet didn't think she'd have much inclination to discuss the tangled affairs of Maria Richards and Walter Norris, but she would have to tell him something sooner or later.

⇢⇒⇒≪≪≪

SHE SHOULD HAVE enjoyed the ball. It was for her, after all. But her natural reticence, which she'd fought against for so long, and her anxiety about her behavior and her conversation, put her on edge. Juliet determined not to let her husband down, to instead be the wife he deserved. So she smiled, nodded, and said "thank you" a great deal.

They'd been dancing and conversing for hours and she was exhausted, and she still had the night to get through. This morning, the thought of the ball had thrilled her. Now she only wanted to rest. Considering her resilience in most situations, perhaps the concentration on her and the insistence that she held the center of attention for all this time accounted for her weariness.

All the chatter began to merge into one voice, totally incomprehensible. She couldn't separate them, though she knew they were different people, but picking one thread out of the many was impossible.

Maria watched her. Juliet used the sight of her, fixed her attention on Maria alone, and found the strength to smile again.

Eventually, Val spoke to his mother, who promised to look after the guests.

Juliet turned to him. "Are we leaving?"

"Yes." A few people stood around, chatting, but they were definitely listening.

"We have a box at the theatre," he said.

She stared at him in surprise. "Do we?"

His laugh rocked the room. "My lovely wife is, as usual, scrupulously honest."

Then everyone laughed, and Juliet wanted the room to swallow her up. Of course he was giving a polite excuse, and again, she'd put her foot in it. But nobody seemed offended, so that was something at least.

Leaving the room, Juliet felt the waves closing behind them, the gossip swelling. They would not be missed now. "I'm sorry," she said.

"What for?"

Did he not remember? "The stupid remark I made when we were leaving."

He gave a short laugh. "That did nothing but good. I made the conventional remark, and you showed the company that we couldn't wait to be together."

"But that isn't true, is it? Is it?"

He caught her hand in his and held it fast. "Speak for yourself." His voice was lower and rougher.

That tone sent thrills through every part of her as her senses heightened. She'd thought the day had wrung her dry. She was wrong. They exchanged a look that said more than words ever could.

Then he took her into the carriage that waited outside for them.

"We really do have a box at the theatre?" she asked.

"No," he answered. "It's a surprise."

They set off.

"Tell me about Norris," he said.

So she did. It didn't take long. He grimaced. "I have lost an excellent secretary with a brilliant future because of a sordid scheme cooked up by the Rotherhams?"

"Basically, yes. And I have lost a friend."

He glanced out of the window as they rounded a corner. The pause was significant.

"Are you sure she was your friend?" he asked abruptly. "It seems to me she used you, first to get enough knowledge to attract me, and then to plead her case to myself and her mother. She seems to lean on other people."

"Not everyone can be strong and resolute," she said, trying to understand her erstwhile friend. "Maria is a sweet girl, with moderate understanding. She has some brilliant connections. She was kind to me when we first arrived in London. Her mother was a significant factor in our success."

"But she is being sold, or selling herself, as a brood mare to a man intent on spiting his heir. Who, I may tell you, does not give a button about the title. He'd make a better marquess than the current incumbent, but ironically, he does not want it. I doubt he'll object to this infamous marriage."

"All she had to do was hold the line," Juliet said. "She could have won through. Lady Rotherham has another daughter to settle and if Maria had only held fast, she could have prevailed."

"You are assuming she was prepared to give up her position in society and her comfortable life for the man she loves."

His dry remark made her stare. "She would not starve. You were giving him a seat in Parliament, were you not? And there were opportunities for him to earn more."

"Yes indeed, but Maria has been used to the finest of everything. This way she improves her social standing, and she has her man. Perhaps she is content."

They were coming perilously close to their first argument.

"Any children will not belong to Walter. How could he contemplate that?"

He clicked his tongue. "Currently he is mad for her. He'll take her under any circumstances. Let us see if that will last." He watched her, smiling. This close, their intimacy struck her hard. "Let's wish them to perdition for now. They will do what they want to, and we can do little to change it, even if we think it's folly."

She wondered if he thought it was folly to marry her. She had been under the impression their connection was to be temporary until that night when he'd taken her and the union had become permanent. Had he meant to? Would he come to regret the wildness that infected both of them every night?

They were reaching the outskirts of London. Juliet turned to Val, a question in her eyes.

He answered without her having to ask anything. "Very well. Here's the surprise. I'm taking you to our Thames villa. I share it with my mother and now you. It's a private home. Neither my mother nor I ever invite anyone there, apart from our closest friends." He smiled. "And you are definitely a close friend. Not many people even know about it."

So they were to have privacy. "I thought we would be staying in London because of Russia."

"Russia can wait. It's time we thought of ourselves. And

we're not going far. My mother knows where we are. If there's any news, she will send a rider to us."

He tightened his hold on her hand and pulled her closer, into his arms, and kissed her. They were in open country now, and effectively alone. She reached up, grasped his shoulder, and returned the kiss.

They spent the rest of the journey in delicious dalliance.

The carriage stopped, and after a pause, the door was swung open. They had arrived.

He got out first and helped her down. She paused, gazing up into his face. While not classically handsome, she preferred his lean features, the extravagantly winged brows, the dark gray eyes that gazed at her, if not with adoration, then certainly with warmth.

Then she turned her attention to the house. It was a modest-sized house, the exterior of London red brick, with white stone edging the doors and windows. The pleasant drive and gardens at the front were a welcome contrast to the lavish London houses in Mayfair. Lights glowed from inside, but the outside lanterns were not yet lit.

"It's lovely," she said. This was the house of her dreams. Unpretentious, elegant, and fitted perfectly with its setting.

"You are lovely," he murmured, his smile warming her inside and out. "Let's go and celebrate."

Chapter Eighteen

THEY HAD NEARLY a week. By the time they returned to London, Juliet was more accustomed to being addressed as "my lady" and to being treated as if sleeping with a man every night were normal. The change between that and the strict propriety society insisted on had taken some getting used to.

The villa had six bedrooms in all, including those belonging to Val and to his mother, and a collection of pretty rooms all devoted to quiet enjoyment. No state rooms, no grand reception rooms. If she could have lived in a house like this, Juliet would have been completely content. But she did not, and rather than the country gentleman she'd imagined for herself when she had first come to London, who might have a house like this, she had married an earl and become a countess expected to run houses four times this size.

But not this week.

On the way back to town, her hand tucked in his, she broached the subject. "I don't know how many houses you have, or what I'm supposed to do as Countess. I can keep accounts and inventories, sew, and cook. Mama saw to that."

"I'll arrange for you to meet the staff," he said. "Housekeepers, butlers, house stewards, land stewards." He did not seem the least perturbed by her confession. "You can go from there. Although if I am offered the Russia post, you might not see the country houses for some time. My mother will help if you wish her to. Otherwise, she declares that she will take herself off to one of her own establishments."

"Oh, I don't want to discommode her!"

He smiled and lifted her hand to his lips. "You won't. She rarely stays in the same place for long. She's a restless soul and has the fortune to suit her whims. I've been expecting her to tell me she is setting out for the Continent now the war is over. I suspect she will before too long. But she bids me tell you to make use of her while she's there. She is as eager to shuffle off that particular burden as you are to take it up."

"She is very . . ." Juliet hunted for the right word and failed to find it, ". . . unusual."

He let out a sharp laugh. "She is indeed. Wealthy, indulged, by her parents and by me, but she has kept her head through it all."

"Through it all?" Juliet repeated, puzzled.

He paused, released her hand, and gazed out of the window. "We've arrived," he said shortly.

What was he going to say? Juliet suspected, as she had before, some secret, something Val wasn't telling her, but she couldn't ask him now. They were indeed nearly back at the London house. Unfortunately, no sooner were they indoors, than Val had to go out again. The Foreign Office had requested his presence. Was this the news he was waiting for?

He was back in an hour. By then her mother-in-law was sitting with Juliet in a small parlor overlooking the garden at the back of the house. They had the windows open to better appreciate the mild weather and they were enjoying tea and gossip. By mutual agreement they did not discuss anything of note, only the on-dits since they'd left town and the latest fashions.

Lady Langston, after reminding Juliet that she would use the title of Dowager when she was dead, produced a stack of fashion magazines and pointed out a few garments she thought might become Juliet admirably. "My dear, you have the face and figure to carry off the most daring styles," she said. "A gown à la Russe, for instance, would look charmingly on you. The military style is becoming démodé, thanks to the end of the war. Fashion is definitely taking a different turn. Lady Langston cannot be out of the current mode, don't you agree?"

Since she would be in the public eye, especially if the Russian post came up, Juliet had to agree, but she was doubtful about some of the clothes. They were gently arguing over a white Meiningen gown when the door opened to admit Val.

He paused on the threshold. "What a charming sight! Even if my mother is trying to bankrupt me by urging a new wardrobe on you, my dear."

He had called her many things in the privacy of the villa, but this was the first time he'd called her anything fond in front of anyone else. The word, mild though it was, warmed her heart.

"Come in Val, let me pour you some tea!" his mother said briskly.

Juliet lifted the pot. "I'll do it."

He grimaced as he came in. "More tea. I've been drinking it all morning."

"Any news about Russia?" his mother asked while Juliet poured.

"Nothing yet, but the world continues to argue, dispute, and make unfortunate alliances. I have plenty to do. They asked me to come in to deal with another matter."

"Do you think our marriage spoiled your prospects?" When she handed him his tea, he didn't show any sign of disturbance. She was learning the small signs. He was not a demonstrative man, and that, at first, had fooled her into believing him cold. But underneath was something else altogether.

"No," he said softly. "You are lovely, intelligent, and I have all the contacts we need." A grin flashed across his face. "We are a team, Juliet."

"You are," his mother said, blatantly watching the exchange.

Not as intrusive as Viola's mother-in-law, who because of a disability couldn't move quickly, so she was present when Knowsley proposed.

Val sat and stretched his legs out. Typical male, to take up all the space he could. She'd learned that he was the same in bed. She had to fight for her space, especially when he slept, always on his back with his limbs stretched out.

To calm herself down when she recalled the glorious sight of her husband naked, she put her tea where she could reach it and picked up the gossip sheet by her side instead. "We've been gossiping and reading the papers. Bianca is featuring rather a lot in these. Not as much as Whiston, though. They say he has a mistress."

"He might." Val considered. "He's certainly a gambler. One can't go to the clubs without running into him making bets on flies and the like."

"Flies?"

"If there are more than one, they bet on which one will reach a spot first. It's ridiculous, especially the stakes. But don't worry, Whiston doesn't bet too much on that kind of thing. I don't think he enjoys gambling, to be honest. He fritters his money away in other ways."

"I've done my share of frittering," his mother commented. "You should try it. It's very enjoyable."

He met his mother's direct gaze and laughed. "So you have. I prefer other pastimes. Mama, you never spend more than you need to. But I've done the rounds of the clubs and coffee-houses. Whiston is dangerously close to the edge of disaster."

That didn't sound good. "Is Bianca in trouble?"

"We'll see," he said gravely. "I wouldn't worry too much, though. He'll always have what is entailed to him, and he is a duke; his estate is considerable. He can mortgage some of it, it's true, but I have no details about that. She'll never find herself on the streets."

"We'll look after her, won't we?" she asked.

Her mother-in-law leaned forward and patted her hand. "Of course we will, my dear."

JULIET VISITED WHISTON House the next day. She was on her own, because her mother-in-law was visiting a "friend," and Val had decided to collect gossip from the club. She called the carriage and traveled in style. She still felt like an impostor, riding in an elegant carriage with an earl's crest on the doors, dressed in the height of fashion. She was no longer the same woman who'd dressed in ten minutes in the dark and hurried out of lodgings in Dublin that were little better than a brothel. Or rather, their landlord wanted them to become so. With the sisters as the main attraction.

They were all different people now, surely.

That feeling melted away when she stood in the grand hall at the Whiston mansion, handing her hat and gloves to the footmen she knew well. They had joined the Burrell family in Edinburgh, and while they hadn't experienced the worst of the Burrell's adventures, they knew most of them. The sight of them brought her right down to earth.

Her mother called out. "Juliet! Up here!"

She sounded happy. Juliet dared to hope.

Bianca had guests. Three ladies had called, all of whom were delighted to see Juliet. More than delighted, Juliet thought as she sat in one of the chairs, which, she only noticed now, weren't in the best condition. Fine chairs, to be sure, but the fabric was rubbed a little, and the edges showed a few thin spots that would fray before too long. She would never have noticed that before her honeymoon. She'd grown used to wealth and luxury so quickly.

"You've landed on your feet," Lady Westbrook commented. She was the aunt of Viola's husband, a forthright gossip, and a lady who seemed to be everywhere, know everything. And a woman who spoke her mind. "I have to congratulate you."

Knowing her, she meant it. So Juliet thanked her, while wondering how she'd managed to obtain the reputation for being plain speaking instead of being insufferably rude.

"If I didn't know how devoted you are to one another, I'd suspect you made him a target." Before Juliet could protest, she added, "But I've seen you together. How could I doubt it?"

Her sharp look told Juliet that she had doubted it, and still did. Juliet was not so far gone as to respond in kind, although she was tempted. Lady Westbrook was a powerful figure in society.

"We are back in London now and attending to our duties. I have so much to learn, and I look to those older and wiser than I am to treat me kindly." Although she meant it, she hated the necessity, but if this helped her help her husband, then so be it. But she wouldn't lie. She wouldn't betray him. And she was determined that she wouldn't, absolutely wouldn't, say something she should not.

"Quite remarkable," said Lady Westbrook, getting into her stride. "Three sisters arriving from nowhere, becoming the toast of society, and each claiming one of the best prizes on the market!"

Now she was definitely provoking Juliet, but she refused to rise to the bait. "We were not exactly from nowhere," she murmured.

"Ah yes." Lady Westbrook plucked a tiny fan from her reticule and spread it, wafting it idly before her face. The breeze wasn't even enough to stir the lace on her tucker. "Cork, was it?"

"Dublin and Edinburgh. I loved Edinburgh. So many interesting people there! I daresay it is as fashionable as London, although the gossip isn't so amusing."

"Hmm. I've never been to either place. A bit out of the way, wouldn't you say?"

"Not if you live there."

Her ladyship closed her fan with a snap. Juliet had to admire her skill in cracking a fan so small, but she did not say that aloud. Her ladyship was glaring at her.

Somehow she'd done it again. Her resolve of only a moment before had come to nothing. "They are respectable cities, my lady, as respectable as any city can be." She felt her throat tightening, her hands clenching. Deliberately she took a deep breath and forced her hands to unclench.

Another fan snap came from her mother, who had echoed Lady Westbrook's action. "We lived in both cities long enough to appreciate them," she said coolly. "We still have a house in Edinburgh. However, we were more than glad to quit it for London. The wind whistles up the Royal Mile in winter so you'd believe you were in the polar regions, not a civilized place at all."

Someone managed a titter. "It is not a place I care to visit," Lady Loughborough said. "I prefer somewhere closer. Cheltenham, for instance, or Bath."

"Or even Brighton," someone else remarked.

The conversation flowed again, centering on various spa towns and their many advantages. As if Edinburgh and Dublin had not been mentioned.

Only when all the guests had gone did her mother enlighten Juliet. "Lady Westbrook has a sister," she said, leaning forward in a confidential manner, although, with the drawing room to themselves, she had no reason at all to do so. "It's very mysterious, but apparently she ran off with someone after her first Season. They got to Gretna Green, and the man, whose name I cannot discover for certain, abandoned her. She was forced to go to Edinburgh where a cousin of hers lived." She grinned. "Nobody knows for sure what happened, how she got there, or the identity of the man who vanished like smoke on a winter's day. But now Lady Westbrook intensely dislikes any mention of the place or of the people there."

Juliet groaned and clutched her forehead. "Not again!"

Her sister laughed. "Who cares?" she said. "It's not our concern. If she can't take comments about her past life, she should not delve into those of other people." Bianca went back to the sideboard and collected the sherry decanter.

"You don't want to make an enemy of Lady Westbrook," Mrs. Burrell said, accepting a glass of sherry from her daughter, "She can make an excellent ally. Do try to think before you speak, Juliet."

Juliet sipped her sherry. "I knew nothing about it," she said. She did think, always, but she'd had no idea of the connection.

"Evidently," her mother said.

Juliet stewed. On the one hand, she'd upset a powerful member of society. On the other, Lady Westbrook had no right to condemn a place Juliet was fond of. She tried so hard to get it right, and only succeeded in getting everything wrong.

VAL WAS SURPRISED to see Whiston in the Foreign Office, but there he was in all his sartorial splendor, standing in the doorway of Val's modest office. "Oh!" was his eloquent first response.

Whiston strolled in, plucking his snuffbox out of his pocket. Enameled with plaques of Venus and framed with diamonds today. "Very handsome," Val remarked.

"Charming, isn't it?" After helping himself to a pinch, and offering it to Val, who shook his head, Whiston snapped the box shut and examined it. He traced his finger over one of the figures on the plaques. "Smooth as glass," he said.

Val didn't bother to remind him that enameling was a form of glass. He pulled a sheet of paper over his work. "Is there anything I can do for you?"

"Not particularly. I dropped in to see my cousin. Family business." He stifled a yawn. "As boring as family business always is. But I can't find him, so I thought I'd give you the time of day before I went home. This is a dreary place, isn't it?"

"It's not something I generally notice." Val gazed at the dark, paneled walls and polished floor, the corners of the room dusty from perfunctory cleaning, and the faded, framed prints on the walls. He blinked in an effort to ease his tired eyes.

"Do you stay here all day like a clerk?" Whiston said, strolling around the room. "What's this?" He paused before a print, bent to read the title. "Walpole?"

"Our first Prime Minister," Val explained.

He was so close to finishing his report and then he could go home. He'd come in this afternoon to finish it, but apparently the task would take a little longer than he'd planned.

"Ah. And you come in early, like a good servant of the people, and stay until dinner time?"

"Hardly," Val said dryly. "I come when I have work to do and leave when it's done."

"You will be working all the time if you get the ambassadorial post," Whiston said. He perched on the side of Val's desk.

"I see it as serving my country." God, he sounded pompous! But he didn't know how else to put it. It was the truth. "I find the work fascinating and the rewards satisfying."

"And the work gives you international prestige," Whiston continued smoothly. "I'm sure you enjoy that. Russia is a civilized court. You'll like it."

Val wished Whiston didn't have quite such a loud voice. One never knew who was listening and the FO hated anyone to jump the gun. Just to be sure, he said, "It's by no means certain I'll secure the post. Many people are looking at it, not least your heir."

"Oh pooh!" Whiston waved away the suggestion. "You needn't worry about him. He can't leave the country until my darling wife gets with child and provides me with an heir apparent. No sign of that yet, though I daresay it'll happen before too much longer." His smile broadened, but it didn't reach his eyes. "How are you finding married life?"

Wonderful. "Perfectly satisfactory." Would the man never go? He could hardly reveal the work he was doing, adding to the record of spies in Paris. Britain had spies working all over Europe now, securely in place. Whiston's loose tongue would make mincemeat of the whole thing if he caught a glimpse of it, and it was so close to being done. Then he could pass the whole thing to Castlereagh and be done with it.

Whiston stifled another yawn. "I daresay after a year you'll be looking for entertainment outside the marriage bed. Most of us do, you know."

Had Whiston set up a mistress? He could barely afford his own household, much less add to it. But he could probably find a woman in society who would not cost him a bean. He did have a great deal of countenance and address.

He didn't ask, but Whiston told him anyway. "Lady Owen. Do you know her? Charming woman and most biddable." His smile suggested lascivious afternoons.

Would Val have to tell his wife? Only if it was true, he concluded swiftly. He wouldn't put it past Whiston to tease and lie in order to create trouble. If Whiston chose to dally with a woman in society, Bianca would inevitably discover it, sooner rather than later. There would be no lack of people eager to tell her, and they would do it in a friendly, sympathetic way. In the long tradition of people who did not want to be the bearer of bad news, he decided to wait and look for more reliable sources.

"I've met the lady." Lady Owen was pretty and with a compliant husband. She did not excite Val's interest in this or in any other matter. He moved the plain leather folder on his desk a fraction. Just straightening it and adding a gentle hint that he'd like to get on with his work.

Predictably, Whiston ignored the hint, but his gaze lingered on the folder. "My lovely Bianca is proving interesting, if not entirely satisfactory." He shoved his hands in his coat pockets and took a turn about the room, pausing to gaze out of the narrow window onto the quadrangle below. "I try not to resent her, but sometimes, especially when I have to deal with the duns, it is difficult. When I see her, though, all that melts away." He turned around. "I was intended to marry Lady Margaret Flushing, you know, but her parents wanted to wait until her come-out this Season."

Yes, he knew. The Earl of Knowsley had put paid to that, and a good thing too. "No doubt she has the fortune hunters thronging around her."

"Yes, her parents wanted to avoid that. Our mothers had a longstanding agreement. Which, in the end, came to nothing. I have naturally paid my respects, but nothing else. I can only wish her the best of good fortune."

"Indeed." He'd heard rumors about Lady Margaret, that her parents were looking around for another match for their daughter. Someone reliable, perhaps older, and with a fortune of his own. He knew, because he'd received tentative advances himself. He had not been tempted, even before matters between him and Juliet grew serious.

Perhaps he wouldn't tell Whiston.

Val leaned back in his chair, ignoring the creak of protest from the wood, and folded his arms. What did the man want? "I've never been interested in innocent girls fresh from the schoolroom."

Whiston began to answer, then narrowed his eyes. "Are you bamming me?"

"Not at all."

Whiston shrugged. "Have to go. See you in the club later?"

Without waiting for an answer, the Duke left the room, leaving the door open.

As if they were characters in a play, less than five minutes later Arthur Carrington walked in. At least he stopped to knock. Val wasn't sure why he'd bothered to get up and close it. "Have you seen my cousin?"

"Yes, a few minutes ago."

"Did he tell you what he wanted?"

"No." Perhaps his terse answers would encourage Carrington to leave. Val had had his fill of that family for one day. And he wanted to finish his list and deliver it before he left. Castlereagh already had most of it; this was the last part. However, at this rate he might as well start a salon for Carringtons instead.

"Ah. I wanted to speak to him about a family matter." He closed the door and walked forward. Val couldn't remember inviting him to do that. He suppressed his long-suffering sigh. "You are married to the Duchess's sister, are you not? It was her unfortunately brash remarks today to Lady Westbrook when she was the Duchess's guest that have now created trouble between the pair."

Bad news traveled faster than good. "Indeed? I don't consider my wife at all brash." He let the words sound mild, but he met Carrington's gaze and kept it, daring him to say more. "And surely calling her or her remarks unfortunate is a particular slur on me."

Carrington took a sharp breath. "I didn't mean it in that way. but you have to admit, your wife does occasionally say the wrong thing."

"Why would I admit that when it isn't true?"

Carrington's thin lips curved in a parody of a smile. "Since the Burrells first arrived in London, they've showed themselves to be not of the ton. I heard that the mother was from a distinctly bourgeois background, and that is why the Viscount disowned his son."

"In case you were wondering," Val said icily, "we are not French. Attitudes and assumptions like those destroyed the monarchy in France, together with a rigid system entirely dependent on birth. That was why idiots ran the country at the end of the 'eighties."

Carrington only shrugged. "It is a matter of opinion. But your wife does say the wrong thing rather too often."

"Repeating an incorrect assumption does not make it true. Wrong is a judgment, not an absolute." No apology then for his comment about Juliet. Carrington probably had a file with all her faux pas in it, so that he could brandish it at appropriate moments. And perhaps use it against them. Carrington was hard-working, he'd say that for him. But try as he might, he couldn't think of any other good quality in the man. "Wrong to one may be right to someone else."

"Spoken like a diplomat," Carrington said with a smile.

When he left, Val was tempted to open all the windows. Not that Carrington had a problem with body odor. He just looked as if he should.

Chapter Nineteen

HIS MOTHER'S ACCOUNT of Juliet's faux pas, which she'd heard from Lady Westbrook came as a decided anticlimax to Val. Not something he was used to with Juliet, he had to admit. "It serves Lady Westbrook right," his mother said tersely. "I know her ways. She was prying and poking, looking for something to gossip about. As if there were not enough already!" She smiled. "But without knowing it, Juliet turned the tables on her."

His mother put her hand over Juliet's. They were dining en famille tonight, so the leaves were out of the dining table, and they sat where they wanted to. And they could say whatever they wanted to. "That is what we will say, my dear. You knew nothing about her past." She paused, tilted her head on one side and studied her daughter-in-law. "Or did you?"

"No, nothing!" Juliet protested. "I was ready to sink when I heard the truth. I knew something was wrong, but I didn't know what, so I blundered about, trying to make everything right, and made it worse. I do that far too often. I've seen people cringe and wince when I say things."

"You speak the truth, that's all," her ladyship commented. "Some people don't like the truth."

Val wanted to get up and go to her. He hated her looking so distressed. "I don't care," he said, surprising himself that he wasn't more concerned about her perceived lack of diplomatic tact.

"We can turn it into a blessing," his mother said. She waved toward the buttered carrots, and Val obligingly helped her to some. Juliet had gone silent. "When—if—Juliet makes an untoward remark, we will simply applaud her and call her an original."

"Oh, please, no," Juliet said. "I don't want attention drawn to my fault."

Val saw where his mother was headed. "It's not a fault. You don't try to force your opinions on to people, you merely have them and choose to state them."

She gave him a tentative smile. "Yes. I'll smile and laugh it off." That was the best solution so far. But she knew if she went somewhere else—like Russia—she'd only make the same mistake again. She'd done it over and over.

She spoke to Val about it when they were in bed, after an evening at the theater and attending one ball afterwards.

"Please don't concern yourself," he murmured. "I rather like it. I think it could become a fashion. We shall make it so."

He made it sound like a casual oddity, rather than a genuine concern that was troubling her now. "People have never commented so on it before."

"You weren't the wife of a diplomat before. Nor a countess." He sighed. "You're a member of society now, not on the outside trying to push in." He kissed the tip of her nose. "Whether you like it or not, it comes with the husband you chose."

She laughed—yes, that was one way of putting it. "But shouldn't I learn to be more circumspect now that I am, as you say, the wife of a diplomat?"

"Good Lord, no!" He went up on one elbow to gaze down at her face. I'll introduce you to a few more diplomatic wives as they return home from assignments. They are not all perfections of probity and parrots for the British government. And without a little dissension and plain speaking we would not have the inoculation for smallpox, did you know that?"

She shook her head. He caught an errant strand of hair that had stuck to the pillow and wound it around a finger. "I wanted to do that for so long," he mused, before capturing her attention once more. "It was Lady Mary Wortley Montagu, the wife of the Turkish Ambassador who saw families using the technique of introducing cowpox to their children. That conveyed immunity to smallpox as well. Using her position in society, she insisted on use of the technique."

Her mouth formed an O. "She did?"

He nodded. "She stormed into society when they returned from Turkey, demanding that people listen. If she had behaved diplomatically and politely, that would never have been achieved. She reached the parts of society the doctors could not." He kissed her forehead. "So don't stop telling the truth and relating what you see."

His lips touched her cheekbone, her chin.

"Meantime, I think we can make better use of our time here than talking about spiteful gossips, hmm?"

As he was kissing her, before she lost herself in him, the thought crossed her mind—was that what he did—this turning of fault to fashion? Had he developed his own public face because of a private problem?

⇶⬿

JULIET WAS GOING down to breakfast the next morning when the doorbell jangled as if someone had grabbed the cord and hung on to it. Or perhaps they were swinging from it, because it did not end until a footman hurried to the door and opened it, but only slightly, so the caller couldn't see Juliet on the stairs. "Is she in?" a voice she knew well asked.

Juliet nodded and ran down the stairs to meet her sister.

Bianca was dressed as if she'd thrown on the first thing she could find, which was most unlike her. Worse was the slapped-on face paint. Although she had been painting heavily these days, she always took care with it. But not today. She flung herself into Juliet's arms and sobbed on to her shoulder. "Oh, Juliet! What will I do?"

Since she had no idea what had happened, Juliet couldn't answer. "Come into the breakfast parlor."

She led Bianca to the pretty room that overlooked the garden. As they entered, her husband looked up, startled, and waved at the footmen loading the sideboard with dishes. They left, but no doubt all the servants had noted Bianca's arrival and would spread the news around Mayfair before the clock had struck another hour. Well, that couldn't be helped.

Juliet had coped with Bianca's fusses before, ever since childhood when damage to a favorite doll would send her into absolute despair. No doubt she'd argued with her husband again. A tinge of uncertainty touched her, even though she tried to tamp it down.

When Bianca finally lifted her head, Juliet gasped.

Her mother-in-law got up from the table hurriedly and reached for a clean napkin.

Val exclaimed, "Good God!" and got up too, coming around the table to touch Bianca's chin. "What happened?"

No amount of face paint could hide the puffiness under Bianca's eyes, or the redness that rimmed them. Her complexion was blotched, red patches marring her customarily smooth, unblemished skin, and her pupils were like pinpricks. Anyone seeing her in this state could see what she'd been doing, what she'd been taking. Tears streamed down Bianca's face. Shocked, Juliet took the proffered napkin and dabbed gently at the tears, wiping away some of the face paint.

"He-he said it was all my f-fault!"

"Said what was all your fault?" Juliet prompted gently. She caught Bianca's hand and kept hold of it. Her sister was trembling.

"That we're in debt, that I . . . tricked him into marriage! He was furious. He said that it was my fault that we were so deeply in debt, my fault that we don't have an heir to confound Carrington." She sobbed into the napkin. "And I answered back. I shouldn't have done so, especially when he was in such a temper. But I'd just . . . I had a—headache, and I wasn't feeling myself. I should have waited until he'd calmed down. Then he wouldn't have been so c-cruel."

Val's mother left the room. Bianca didn't seem to notice but carried on. "I went on and on he said, and he . . ." She burst into another fit of weeping, but when she tried to knuckle her eyes like a child, Juliet pushed a fresh napkin into it, and dabbed gently at her sister's wet cheeks with another.

"L-last night, at the Owen ball, he went to L-Lady Owen, danced and flirted with her. And she's his m-mistress. Everyone knows, he says, but I didn't know. Not until then. So I threw that at him as well, and he said—he said I should learn to know my place." She touched the corner of her eye where it was raw and red from crying and winced. "He said she told him she was pregnant! He said I was a complete failure as a wife! No money, no b-baby. I wanted a baby so much!"

Val strode away and went to the window. He was controlling his own temper. Juliet saw him, silhouetted against the bright day outside, roll his shoulders, and clench his fists, once, twice, before deliberately relaxing them, stretching the fingers right out. There was the big difference between Val and the Duke of Whiston. While Val might have a temper, he controlled it.

"He said all that?"

Bianca, sodden with tears, head drooping, hair already tumbling down from its loose arrangement to tangle around her face and get caught on her wet cheeks, raised a hand and then dropped it heavily back into her lap. "When we were first married, he used to go away when he got angry, but now he just stays and shouts and shouts. And it's the truth—all of it. It's my fault it's all come undone."

Val turned slowly, stood before the window on the other side of the table, blocking the light. "How often does he—behave this way toward you?"

Bianca swallowed and glanced at Juliet before looking down again. "There is no pattern. Sometimes he won't do it for a while, weeks, and sometimes it's more like twice or three times in a week. He always begs my pardon later, goes down on his knees to me. He assures me he loves me, that it is all his damnable temper and he doesn't mean it. He might buy me a trinket, something we can't afford. And I always forgive him."

Val listened in horror to the narrative. He forced himself to listen passively. Then reason returned to him and he saw his way forward. Nobody should have to suffer such torture, but it was all too common in this world. He'd seen it, heard it, far too much. Closer to home, too. If he had not experienced this himself, he would have found Bianca's level of distress more difficult to understand. But he had, and he knew exactly what was going on.

Bianca swiped at her eyes. "But not this time."

Apprehension gripped Juliet. "What do you mean?"

"I ran," Bianca said in a small voice. "And I won't go back. When he told me about her baby, it was all I could think of doing. I didn't even get a carriage to bring me here. People must have seen, but perhaps they didn't recognize me."

Juliet's sigh sounded loud in the silence. They would, once the reports of the scene in this house became known. The whole of London would know. Not that it mattered now.

"He is so cruel when he is in a temper," Bianca said.

"Many people are," Val said, but he kept his tone soft, not revealing what the account was doing to him.

Juliet exchanged a glance with Val. He was angry, she could see it in the deepening gray of his eyes, and the twin creases between his brows. She shook her head in sorrow and returned her attention to her sister. "This isn't you, Bianca. These things he says—it's not what you are. Oh, my dear!"

"It's what I am now." Dry-eyed now, Bianca pleated the

napkin between her fingers. "As he says, he made me a duchess. I have to live up to my exalted status. So I smile, and I behave as if nothing is wrong."

"Does Mama know?"

Bianca shook her head. "Not all of it. Oh, she knows we shout, but not the rest of it. I'm worried she might try to tackle him herself." The corner of her mouth moved in the pretense of a half-smile. "He would probably throw her out of the house."

"Where is she?"

"Didn't she tell you? She's spending a few days with her friend Mrs. Robinson."

Juliet turned to Val. "She's an old friend of our mother's. Mrs. Robinson is married to a vicar, and lives quietly just outside London. She did tell me, but I forgot."

Had her mother been feeling the strain, too? Juliet would wager her best diamond necklace she was planning to do something about this situation. Perhaps she had gone to her old friend to ask for advice. How did someone who suspected such behavior effectively confront the husband of the woman he was legally entitled to insult and harangue? She had to have a plan ready.

"Could you have gone with her?"

"She asked me, but we had the Owen ball, and George was eager to go. I was, too, since Lady Owen is so amusing." Her voice shook on the last word. "He made his preference clear to all. That's when I knew for certain . . ."

"Then he's an idiot," Val said. "And worse."

"What will you do now?" Juliet said. "Of course, you can stay here if you wish, but, Bianca, he can compel you to return. We can't do anything to stop him taking you back. You could obtain a separation."

"No!" Bianca said in horror. "That can't happen! That kind of scandal would finish us all."

She had not thought of that when she ran off with Whiston in the first place, but then, the youngest of the Burrell sisters had always had an air of innocence about her. No more. She'd probably believed his promises of marriage, and to do her justice, Whiston could lie very well when he wanted something.

But they had no right to keep her, and if Whiston came here, they would have to let her go. He had not struck her or put her life in danger. If he had, they would have something to threaten him with.

However, if Whiston couldn't find her . . . and if they told a few lies of their own, something she would not hesitate to do if needful . . .

"The villa," Val said suddenly.

Juliet's head went up and she met his eyes, relief flooding her. Of course. "Yes." She turned back to her sister. "Bianca, do you want to get away for a while, somewhere he won't find you?"

Bianca nodded miserably.

"We have a place, not far from town. Val and his mother keep it for their own use." She bit her lip, remembering the happy time they'd spent there recently. "They don't take visitors there. It's entirely private."

Bianca nodded. "If he doesn't know where to find me, he can't bring me back, can he? I need somewhere to recover from this, from all this." She waved a hand, indicating the mess of her lovely face. "I can't thank you enough. I don't deserve such kindness. This is all my fault."

Juliet squeezed her hand. "No, it isn't! None of this is your fault." That admission of her sister's, so untypical, raised Juliet's ire. Her fault? Not in a million years.

She caught Val's gaze, but she couldn't read the message.

Her mother-in-law came back into the room with a basin covered by a towel. Heedless of the porcelain and mahogany, she swept the remains of their breakfast aside, and dumped the basin on the table. "Move aside, if you please," she said. Taking a washcloth and cake of soap, she gently began to clean Bianca's face. Bianca submitted to her ministrations, like a child patiently waiting for her mother to make her decent, but all the time longing to run outside and play.

Their mother had never allowed them to forget they were children, and she never let them see the strains she and their father were under. They protected their children, and the four were better for it. Apparently Lady Langston was cut from the same cloth.

"It's Lady Owen, isn't it?" she said as she worked. Bianca nodded.

"There," she said, leaning back. "You look respectable enough now." She turned her head and addressed her son. "I'm taking her to the villa. You will not tell anyone where we have gone."

"We came to the same conclusion, Mama," he said dryly. "The villa is the best place. I'm glad you've decided to go with her."

"What else could I do?" She returned her attention to Bianca. "My dear, you will have the time you need to rest, recover and decide what you want to do next. That is your decision, but you're not up to making it yet. We will support you." Those last words were so vehement, they startled Juliet.

"You've come across this before?"

"Yes." Juliet's mother-in-law lifted her sleeve. She always wore long sleeves, but then, many older women did, especially in this inclement weather. Juliet's breath caught.

Several scars marked her ladyship's wrists, one particularly harsher and whiter than the others. The dead skin stood out like a brand. "That was my response," she said tersely. "I swore then I would not stand by and see anyone do the same thing, try to damage herself because of the actions of another."

Juliet's thoughts whirled. The serene Lady Langston had tried to—harm herself?

"But that happened long ago," the older lady said, pushing down her sleeve as if the marks meant nothing. "What is far more important is now. Whatever the Duchess decides is up to her. We are fortunate to be able to offer a place of sanctuary for a week or two, but we cannot let her remain hidden there. He will discover the place."

"I have small mansions, houses by the sea," Val said grimly. "She may stay in any one of them she chooses."

"She could stay with Viola and Knowsley," Juliet said, referring to their other sister.

Bianca nodded. "I could. But it feels too much like running away."

Juliet held her hands out, palms up. "If it saves your sanity, then it will be worth it."

The color had returned to Bianca's cheeks and her eyes sparkled. Anger? Was she angry? That was more like the Bianca she knew. "It depends on your definition of sanity. Mine is to stand up unafraid, ready to face anyone in the world." Her head drooped again. "But I'm not ready. I don't know if I ever will be."

"You need rest," Lady Langston said. "You'll feel better when your body and mind heal. We will not tell Whiston where to find you. And when you are ready, we'll discuss what needs to happen next."

Bianca stared at her hands, now resting quietly in her lap.

A knock sounded on the door, but nobody came in. Only a voice through the woodwork. "The carriage is outside, my lady."

Lady Langston got to her feet and held out her hand to Bianca. "Come, child. We must make haste. We'll provide you with what you need."

If they didn't go now, Whiston could be on them. It would not be hard to guess where Bianca had gone. While Juliet didn't want to hurry her sister, at the same time a sense of urgency tightened her stomach. The last thing she wanted was for Bianca to return to her husband, to not have this precious time to think and reflect. He'd worn her down almost to nothing. She was in no state to fight back.

In the meantime she'd write to Viola. Her husband Knowsley had been Whiston's oldest friend, although he was a friend no longer. He would be able to protect Bianca, should she choose not to return. Or he could mediate, since he knew Whiston so well.

Bianca rose in the innately graceful way of hers and took Lady Langston's hand. She went out of the room with her, and Juliet followed.

A few minutes later, Juliet went back slowly into the breakfast room. "Thank you," she said simply. "The villa is exactly what she needs. Although . . ." she held out her hand in a gesture of helplessness, not knowing how to say what she felt.

He took her hand and raised it to his lips. "I know," he said softly. "And I know you'd rather go with her, but you know you cannot."

"Russia."

He shook his head. "No, not Russia. Someone has to stay to talk to him when he comes here. Family is far more important than Russia."

Did he mean that? It didn't sound like a platitude. "But this is my family."

"Which makes it mine. This comes closer than you know."

She waited, gazing at him. "Tell me, but only if you want to."

He inclined his head. "I want to." His eyes widened slightly, as if he'd surprised himself. "Yes, I do," he added, confirming what he'd said. "Let's go and sit down somewhere. Do you need any more to eat?"

Mutely, she shook her head.

He took her out of the room and into the small parlor on the ground floor. He waited until she'd chosen the sofa facing the window, and then joined her. She had a feeling she knew what he was about to tell her, but she prayed she was wrong.

Her prayers were not answered. "Your sister looks like my mother did after my father had finished with her," he said in a matter-of-fact tone. "More than once."

He and his mother knew because they'd encountered the situation before. They had suffered as Bianca suffered. "I'm so sorry."

"So am I." He stretched his arm over the back of the sofa, his fingers not quite touching her shoulder. "I was a child. I could do nothing. He told me I was a failure as a son."

"He put her down like that as well?"

He nodded. "I heard him often. He shouted, accused her of things she had never done, of behaving in ways she would never do. She bore it all for me, answered him so that his attention more often turned to her, not to me." He swallowed. "After I was born, my mother couldn't have any more children, and he blamed her. He treated her as if she meant nothing to him."

Sitting utterly, heartrendingly still, he closed his eyes. "It happens in many families. I recognized it in your sister immediately." He opened his eyes, and the bleak expression nearly finished Juliet. Until now she'd held back her tears, knowing they would mean nothing, but now one trickled down the side of her face.

He brushed it away with a soft touch, his expression back to his usual calm but she knew now, knew what was happening to him deep inside. "It is constant and relentless putting down, giving the feeling that the other person is never right, never does what is expected. Over time, it can turn a lion into a mouse, a lovely woman into a dowd. For my mother, she was never wearing the right clothes, never talking to the right people, always undermining him by speaking out—more and more, always dragging her lower. When he sent me to school, I was afraid he might grow even worse without my being around to deflect some of his tirades. So I contrived to be expelled. He wasn't happy." His mouth twisted. "For once I received the treatment he usually meted out to my mother, but then he turned back to her. It was as if she was the scapegoat."

He paused, as if searching for words. "That was worse, you see. I had to pretend I didn't know, or it was worse for her."

Juliet couldn't imagine much worse. And then she frowned as she recalled something else. "But your father was a philanthropist. He worked for the poor and the sick, was part of the abolition movement. He tried to persuade Parliament to pass laws. I've heard about him everywhere, especially since my name was first connected with you."

He paused, looked away and stared down at his hands, now clenched together tightly until the knuckles turned white. "Yes, he was. He enjoyed the adulation and praise, I think." He glanced back at her face. She didn't hide her reaction to his words. How could people have had no idea of this? How did a man hide behavior like that?

As if he knew what she was thinking, he said, "He never struck her. Ever. If he had, we could have perhaps done something about it. The law is against a man who beats his wife. His mouth twisted. "He had mistresses from time to time, but he was very discreet. He never brought that part of himself into our sphere, but he used their existence against my mother as a weapon. I think he only took the women to make them pregnant, to remind my mother she was barren."

"He got his pleasure from torturing your mother without laying a finger on her."

"I believe he did. And watching me react. Of course he knew that I knew what he was doing. His treatment of me consisted mostly of advice, dispensed regularly and often. The advice instructed me how to do things properly, and it undermined my confidence at every turn. But he was trying to mold me in his way, not break me down in the same way he did her."

He gazed at her, as if searching for something, waiting for her to understand.

The realization hit her like a lightning bolt. "Is that why you indulge her now? Why you don't stop your mother when she takes another lover, or behaves less than perfectly?"

"She deserves all the happiness she can find these days," he said. "Every bit of it. Everything, even her choice of furniture, builds her confidence back, turns her into the woman she should be, not the woman my father tried to make her."

Yes, she did. Juliet could barely imagine such cruelty. "Why did he do it?" She couldn't understand why a man reputed to be a great force for good in public life could behave like that in private.

He shook his head. "I started to understand it as I grew up, not that I ever condoned what he did. It was power. That, I think, was his motivation—the power, the control. Both the philanthropy and the treatment he meted out to my mother. That was where he found his pleasure." He turned to her, took her hand. "You must never fear that. *Ever.*"

The emphasis shocked her from such a cool and disciplined person. But now she understood it—both the intensity and the discipline. What he'd just told her explained a great deal about him, more than she could absorb all at once. But she admired him more than ever, for his compassion and understanding.

"I know," she said. "I know."

And she did. She could not think of anyone better to look after her sister at this time, when she needed someone to understand. She was glad her mother-in-law had gone with Bianca. And having experienced the peace and tranquility of the villa for herself, she knew it would go a long way towards healing.

Chapter Twenty

YESTERDAY HAD BEEN a difficult time for all of them. Having received the news that the Duchess and his mother had arrived at the villa and were being taken good care of, Val felt he could settle to some much-needed work. He had put it to the back of his mind while the family crisis burst into his life, but he needed to settle a few urgent points.

Last night he'd devoted himself to Juliet, and after a brief appearance at the opera, to which neither of them could settle, they had gone home. "At least people have seen us," he remarked as he led her to his room. They spent every night there, and it was becoming a matter of habit, as well as desire, something Val welcomed. Even on nights such as this, where all they did was sleep, entwined together in perfect harmony.

Small reminders, like her robe folded over a chair, and her slippers by the bed made him smile as his valet helped him prepare for the day. And as he gazed at his reflection in the mirror, he seemed to have a clearer vision, a calmer outlook. Perhaps, as Juliet had said, he'd needed to tell someone his secret, the one that had nibbled at his heart every day, taking part of his humanity with it. Now he'd told her, maybe he could find some peace. He had never believed in the power of confession, but he was rethinking it now.

Juliet had gone on a round of visits, trying to run her life as normal. She would be back for dinner.

Entering his study, he found his secretary there. Although Walter Norris had given in his notice, Val had kept him until it ran out, in the hope that he could persuade the young man not to abandon a promising political career and instead stay with him. Norris was shuffling through some papers but looked around and straightened up when Val entered.

"Looking for something?" Val enquired coolly.

"Yes, sir. A file has gone missing from the Foreign Office." He handed Val a note, scrawled in some haste, judging by the blots and splatters on the paper. It was cryptic, but he understood. "The One File is missing," it read. "Priority above everything else."

His heart sank. The list of French spies. There was only one copy of the file, because of the sensitive contents. Once Val had handed the final part to Castlereagh, it was circulated to a select list of recipients. Fewer than ten. It had been given to the recipients one by one, signed for and then signed again when it was handed back. "Who was the last signee?" he asked.

"You," was the terse answer.

So the onus was on him. He'd handed it to the next recipient, who'd signed for it without unsealing it. The person he'd handed it to was the Foreign Secretary himself, finishing the circle. Castlereagh was not likely to have purloined it.

This could be the end of Val's diplomatic career, but more importantly it could be the literal end of the people on the list, if it got into the wrong hands. "I have to go in," he said.

An hour later, he was back, and aware the hot water he was in had gone up to boiling. The list Castlereagh had received was not the list he'd sent out. It contained invented names, and it was not in a hand anyone recognized. Someone had intercepted the list and substituted a false one. That meant the list of agents in France was in the hands of . . . someone.

And because Val had been the last to receive the list, he was the person everyone was blaming. Something had happened. The man before him swore he'd read the correct list and was able to quote a few names. He'd given it to a courier, already sealed. The courier had delivered it to Norris, who'd given it to Val.

Who had unsealed it and read it. He'd opened the folder by himself and had no witnesses to it. He should have opened it with someone else present.

Too late now.

Was it Norris? What he knew of the character of the man mitigated against it, but Norris was not wealthy, and he might have wanted money in a hurry, perhaps to persuade reluctant parents that he was worthy of their daughter. Little though he liked it, Val had to stay wary of everyone in this situation, even Norris.

Norris was still in his study when Val returned, still shuffling papers, probably waiting on his return. He looked up eagerly. "Did you find it?"

"No. Somebody purloined it and substituted it to gain time. Who do you think it could be?" Waving Norris to a seat, he took his own behind the desk. Petitions, newspaper clippings, and handwritten notes he'd already replied to littered the surface. Nothing of note.

Norris swallowed. "I took the sealed file from the courier."

"Who was that?"

Norris frowned, pursing his lips in thought. "Mr. Carrington."

God damn, that man got everywhere. While he'd love to implicate the man, that was only personal prejudice. He had no proof, no suspicion even, that Carrington was involved in something like this.

A thought occurred to him. "Is Carrington short of money?" Whiston certainly was, but what about his cousin? The list would certainly sell. Hell, it could be put up for a secret auction. He could name a dozen people who would pay good money for it.

"Not short, no," Norris said. "He's careful with what he has, so he's not in debt or seriously incommoded."

"But the title he is heir to is a compromised one." In other words, the current Duke of Whiston and his father had run their wealth into the ground.

And what about Whiston? Would he be involved in such a thing? Although he and his cousin were constantly at odds, might they work together on this? His opinion of the man, never great, had suffered even more recently, but he had never considered him a traitor.

He touched his lips with the tip of his finger and pressed, his habit when in thought.

"Carrington is eager to pursue his diplomatic career," Norris said. "Would he risk it all for an opportunity like that?"

"Would he have known the contents of the folder?"

Norris shrugged. "He might. But the secret nature of it would tell anyone it could be valuable. I guessed what was in it."

Val winced and closed his eyes. "For the love of God, don't tell anyone else that." At least not until Val had explored all possibilities.

"Of course not."

Norris was leaving soon, heading north with the love of his life and her husband, which would make him a convenient scapegoat if there was another party out there looking for one.

ALL THROUGH DINNER and the token appearance in their box at the Theater Royal, Juliet was aware that Val was preoccupied about something—something new, not the trouble with her sister. She thought the tendons in his neck might snap under the strain. She also knew he'd refuse to tell her anywhere in public. So she waited, responded blandly to his equally bland questions, and forced herself not to ask what was wrong. She did her best to behave as if everything were normal. They went home early and were in bed before midnight.

They were coming to be in the habit of discussing matters

close to their hearts when they retired to bed, but usually it was after they'd made love, not before. Tonight was different.

"What is it?" she asked, leaning up on one elbow. She felt more vulnerable lying down, and if this concerned her sister, she wanted to be prepared. "I know something is wrong."

Juliet listened open-mouthed to Val's account of the events that had unfolded today.

"So do you think," Val concluded, "that Carrington or even Norris would actually take them?"

She'd had time to think during his brief outlining of the situation. "I think it's unlikely," she said. "Carrington is constantly lecturing his cousin on the right way of behaving, of avoiding scandal and being a true duke in word and deed."

She turned her head, saw him watching her intently. She took his hand, slid her fingers between his and held on. "He enjoyed dropping in at breakfast time, scolding us for staying up half the night while he was hard at work."

"He might look for a sum of money to support the title he values so much."

She nibbled on her lower lip. "I never thought of that. But Norris? No. He's taken a foolish decision, in my opinion, as bad as the one Maria took, but that does not make him a fool in other areas. You've trusted him. Before this fiasco you were willing to make him a Member of Parliament."

"Yes. You're right. I trust him with the most confidential matters. He knew about the list, and the names on it . . ." He closed his eyes. "I should not have told you even that much."

"Told me what?" she said softly. "I heard nothing. My mind must have drifted for a moment."

He pressed her hand warmly. "You are the perfect wife."

"I wouldn't say that. Thank you anyway. I do try to be. Is there anything I can do to help?"

He shook his head. "Not a thing. Just keep your ears open, though I doubt anyone will be discussing it openly. If it is even known the list has gone astray, people will come sniffing around.

In the wrong hands, it's valuable. And deadly," he added.

Deadly? To the people on the list or the people who knew about it? She prayed Val was not at risk. "You know I say foolish things sometimes. And you trust me with this?"

"Of course," he said without hesitation. "You know it's important, so you will not divulge what I've told you. I know that."

His assurance made her sure, too. She ventured a tentative smile. His was firmer, warming her heart. "Should I do anything?"

"No. You've already done a great deal by listening to me."

"It doesn't seem like enough. I feel useless. You've helped my family so much. I want to help you."

"I'll always need you." He leaned over, his heat and desire surrounding her like a protective shield, one they shared and both contributed to. "You should know that by now."

Willingly she lost herself in him, knowing he needed this as much as she did. The physical side of their marriage never failed to astonish her. Their kiss, starting in friendly warmth, continued seamlessly into passion, his clever tongue telling her without words how much he wanted her. That was before he rolled her onto her back and lifted her night rail, making her sit while he disposed of it. He caressed, stroked, teased until she cried out and called his name into the still night.

His growl, low in his throat, involuntarily told her, urged her to open for him, which she eagerly did. He touched her, ensuring she was ready, as he always did. His tenderness touched her, persuaded her that more than physical need controlled him, as it did her.

Rising over her, he took her with a mastery she reveled in. It was not always this way; sometimes she took control. At first shyly, not knowing if he liked it, if he wanted her to kiss him there, and there, but he'd soon persuaded her he enjoyed her attentions as much as she enjoyed his.

The merging of their bodies always came as a revelation to her, how close they had become. Tonight he needed her, he wanted mastery. Reassurance and love suffused her as he swiftly brought her to a peak of desire, holding her firmly as she fell apart under him.

Then it was his turn, as he arched up, throwing his head back as his body took over and flooded them both with passion.

He fell to one side, dragging her with him.

"I love you," she whispered against his chest.

But he was already asleep.

⟫⟫⟫✹⟪⟪⟪

"I'LL GO AND see my mother today," she told him at breakfast. She lifted the tea pot and when he nodded poured tea into the delicate cups and handed one to him.

"Is she back?"

"She sent a letter saying she would be in town today. I will have to see her about Bianca."

"I'll come with you."

"No." She put down her newspaper and gave him all her attention. "I can explain better alone. I won't tell her where Bianca is in case anyone is listening, but I'll offer to take her there."

"Of course. And I will handle Whiston."

"He called yesterday while we were at the theater."

"I know. I saw his card. If he tries his cruel tactics on you, leave at once." A tremor, so fine she could hardly feel it, rippled over him. Anger.

She hastened to reassure him. "I will be fine. Don't forget, we lived with them before you married me. He did not try to school us, only Bianca."

"I wonder why? My father wanted to control everyone around him, not just my mother."

She gave herself a moment to think. "Because he doesn't love me. I believe Whiston loves Bianca, adores her, and hates himself for doing so. Maybe he took a mistress to try to persuade himself he didn't need her. He doesn't behave like your father. There's nothing controlled about what he does. His rages are sudden, and soon over. I suspect he isn't entirely aware of what he's doing to her. It's all instinct. He has not learned to control himself. Why would he? He's a duke."

"Love doesn't display itself like that."

She wondered if his father's twisted relationship with his mother might have had a touch of love about it. Perhaps it began that way, but it was an unnatural, cruel kind of love and became something quite different. And from what he'd told her, his father manipulated and used the people he claimed to love, strove to control everyone around him. Of Val, of his mother, and everyone he came into contact with. Control and power, the power to dictate behavior, of the way people spent their lives.

"Whiston didn't care what I did or where I went." She picked up her rapidly cooling tea and took a sip. "He might suspect that I know where Bianca is, but he won't try to compel me to tell him."

"You seem so sure."

"In any case, he'll probably be out. He leaves after breakfast for his clubs and coffee-houses."

He met her gaze, and reached for her hand, clasping it in his. "I cannot be happy with you going there. Can you not ask your mother to come here? Send a carriage for her?"

"I could," she said slowly. "Or Mama might call of her own volition." But she wanted to go to Whiston House for another reason. She would not tell him, in case it came to nothing.

Last night he had discounted Whiston's involvement in the theft of the folder, but having slept on the problem, Juliet wasn't so sure. She knew how desperate Whiston was to make money. Few people knew how dangerously close he was to bankruptcy. Of course, being a peer and a member of the House of Lords protected him from being arrested for debt, but that was all.

And he'd had all those French documents—she'd seen him

stuffing his desk with them. The one she'd read was a deed, but there had been several others. Whiston claimed not to speak the language well, but if he knew what the lists were, he wouldn't have to speak it. He'd been in a great hurry to put that pile away, out of Juliet's gaze.

Would Whiston go so far as to conspire with his cousin and sell a valuable list?

No, she was almost sure he would not. He hated his heir with a venom that took Juliet by surprise sometimes.

However, though he might not scheme and plot to acquire such a list, he might take advantage of the theft if he found a way to do so. Not that he would wish harm on anyone else, but he did not think of the consequences of his misdeeds. Look at that disastrous race, for instance. He had not considered the dangers of doing such a thing, to himself or to other people. He would not think about the people on that list and the danger they could be in, only the money it would make.

"Take two footmen with you," he said. When she opened her mouth to protest, he said, "I insist."

She'd pushed him to his limits, and he was moving into protective mode. "I'll take care. And I won't discuss the papers with anyone."

He smiled. "I know you won't," he said.

Chapter Twenty-One

SINCE JULIET SENT a note to Whiston House after breakfast, her mother was expecting her when she arrived. She had taken one of the small parlors and ordered tea. There she was, arms folded, waiting. It was just as she'd always done when one of her children had transgressed—take a private room, speak to them alone.

"You should have written to me earlier," she said.

Juliet shook her head. "It's done. There was nothing we could do except help her. You didn't see her, Mama."

"I've seen her distressed before. You think I didn't know?"

"You'd not seen her like this."

Her mother winced. "I should have done something before now. Perhaps if I'd spoken to him or taken her away. Not to Viola, she's about to deliver her first baby, I can't put that on her, but Knowsley would have helped."

"So would Langston," Juliet reminded her, stung that she thought of Viola's husband before her own.

Her mother looked at her, met her gaze and nodded. "And he has helped. More than he needed to."

"I can take you to her." Juliet would not speak the location out loud. Anyone might be listening at the door in this poorly regulated household.

Since living in Langston's house, she had begun to understand how badly run this house was. The Burrells had never lived in a large household with a multitude of servants before, only stayed in them occasionally, when fortune smiled on them. They'd never known the complexities of the task, and so, when they'd come to Whiston House, they'd accepted what went on there as normal. It was far from that. Juliet was learning quickly, helped by her mother-in-law and her extremely competent housekeeper. She did not doubt the servants here sold what they could to the gossip-sheets, both to cover their arrears in wages and because they could. The atmosphere below stairs must be lethal.

Her mother shook her head. "Don't tell me. But I will go to her. Give me half an hour." At the door she turned and smiled, even though her eyes revealed the strain she was under. "Thank you for coming to tell me."

Then she was gone, leaving Juliet with her thoughts, half a pot of tea and a plate of stale scones.

But not for long.

Whiston burst into the room with the power of an arrow hitting its target. Behind him stood one of the footmen Val had set to watch over her. He was ready to lay hands on the Duke, should it be necessary. Juliet did not think it would be. Whiston had never offered physical violence.

Whiston looked ill, the dark circles beneath his eyes emphasizing the pallor of his complexion. He placed both hands on the table, palms down, leaning forward. "Where is she? Is she all right?"

"She's safe," Juliet said steadily. He looked like a madman. For the first time, a tinge of fear touched her. She'd never seen him like this before.

He closed his eyes. A single tear trickled from under the lid of his left eye. "I am sorry. I would do anything to take it back." He straightened up.

He swiped the tear away and opened his eyes again. "I called yesterday but you were not at home. All I want to say is that I will try to do better." He swallowed. "There are other matters we need to settle. I need to talk with my wife, you must see that."

"Eventually," she admitted. If they were to live apart, then they would have to make arrangements. If Bianca wanted to sue for a legal separation, a deeply impactful step, she would have to talk to lawyers. And so would he.

The agitation in his features told Juliet that Whiston was far from satisfied with her answer. "Is she close? Are you keeping her at your house? I need to see her!"

"She is not at our London house, no. And you will not see her until we are sure you will not hurt her again."

He could take them to court, accuse them of abducting her. But that would take time, and they could keep moving her, if need be.

He sighed, rubbed the bridge of his nose. "I see. But you would say that anyway, would you not? Though servants gossip. I daresay the whole of London would know if she were there."

"The whole of London will know everything, if you continue like this," she said acidly. Although her footman, a man she could trust, stood in the doorway, there was no telling who was standing in the hall, or beyond the servants' door.

He nodded. "Come into my study."

She wasn't about to make matters easy for him.

"One angry word and I will leave."

One glance at the footman, at his expressionless face and broad shoulders assured the Duke Juliet meant what she said. And his presence could save her from future histrionics.

Whiston led the way across the wide hall to a door on the other side which she knew to be his study. He opened the door and let her go in first.

The Duke's desk was as messy as always, but something was missing. It took Juliet a moment to recall what it was. The tantalus that always held three bottles, two of brandy, one of sherry, was missing. It had rarely been full, only in the mornings after the butler had refilled them.

He followed her gaze. "Yes. That's what I want to talk to you about." He opened a drawer, and scooped up a number of small, empty brown bottles. "And these."

Lord. The sickly sweet smell of laudanum wafted over her. She swallowed down her recoil. She'd never liked the stuff.

"Mine and hers," he said flatly. "Not that Bianca ever took it in great quantities. The habit is too easy to slip into. You may tell her, if you please, that I've had the house searched and these are going on to the rubbish heap. I am also restricting my drinking habits. I have overindulged recently, and I will do so no more."

Was he blaming alcohol for his transgressions? It could be part of the reason. Some people changed character completely when they'd had too much to drink. His tempers, his tirades, did they all happen when he was drunk? Juliet's mouth firmed. She could not say for sure.

If she'd not been bound up in her own problems perhaps she could have noticed more . . .

That was of no purpose now. The fact that Whiston had declared his intent spoke to his resolve as much as the spirits disappearing from the study did.

"I am truly sorry. I know I've said it before and not bound myself to my promises. This time I will. I do not expect Bianca to rush back to me." He bit his lip. "I don't want her to, not yet. I do not deserve that. I've allowed my habits to get the better of me, and from now on they will change."

Abstinence after a long period of indulgence would account for his terrible appearance. While she was beginning to believe him, Juliet didn't trust his resolve. It would be too easy for him to lapse, especially if Bianca returned to him too soon. "I will inform her of what you've told me, but don't expect an immediate reply."

He nodded, his mouth turning down at the corners in disappointment. "I only ask you to tell her that this time I am doing something about it, as she asked me to."

Neither of them had discussed the socially notable problem of Bianca's obvious absence, and Juliet understood his reluctance to do so. The word must be about that Bianca had left the marital home, though nobody would know precisely why.

The door opened and her mother, dressed in a bottle-green pelisse and smart hat, entered.

"You told her?" Mrs. Burrell asked the Duke.

"Yes," he said. He nodded toward the space where the tantalus had stood. "And I mean it. Bianca is more important to me than any stimulant. I will prove it."

"You'll have to," she said.

Apparently her mother had wasted no time with Whiston upon returning. Juliet longed to have been a fly on the wall when they had that conversation. Having undergone a few trials by Burrell before, she could imagine how it had gone. Even more so, because their transgressions had never been so significant.

"I will do everything in my power to win her back."

His eyes were bright with unshed tears. "It took this for me to realize how much I want her, how much I love her." He forced the sentence out, but he'd said it.

"You had no intention of marrying her," Juliet reminded him. "You meant to take her and abandon her."

"That was what I said," he admitted. "But I would have regretted my decision to the end of my days."

Words were cheap. Juliet would not believe him fully until she'd seen actual proof of his change of heart, and that could take months.

"What about your mistress, the one you flaunted in front of my sister?"

Whiston met her gaze directly. "She is gone."

"I thought she was pregnant."

He nodded as he sat down heavily at his desk. "Her husband has agreed to acknowledge the child. As he has for others she has borne other men."

A few papers slid, threatening to turn into an avalanche. Juliet slapped her hand on top of the precarious pile, before standing to take a stack of the papers and put them somewhere else. She dumped them on the floor, for want of a better place. "And tidy these," she said. "You need a secretary."

"I do," he said with a grimace.

A quick glance at the pile was all she could snatch, but it didn't appear to hold a list of names in French.

Juliet smoothed her skirts and turned to take a seat but paused, momentarily transfixed. There was something, there, sticking out of another untidy pile. French, she was sure of it. Her heart beating hard, she pulled it out. The document was filled with names. English names, followed by French names and French addresses.

This had to be what Val was looking for.

Juliet scanned the names, together with the addresses. They were in a hand she didn't recognize. A list of names and addresses, on foolscap instead of the creamy, smaller sheets that Whiston used.

"What's this?" she said.

He made to take the paper, but she pulled it out of his reach. He lifted an aristocratic brow, and dipped in the pile, finding another sheet similar to the one she held. He scanned the names. "I don't recognize it. Where on earth did this come from?"

He sounded completely bewildered. Instead of answering, Juliet said, "Who can come into this room?"

He waved the sheet of paper helplessly. "The servants clean it, of course. Most visitors go upstairs to the main rooms, though. I know I keep forgetting to lock the door, but very few linger on this floor. Why?"

Juliet thought over her answer carefully before responding. The last thing she wanted now was to blurt out the wrong answer, to give more out than she should. Even her mother didn't know about this. "Because I've been looking for this list. I thought it was lost."

There. She had not precisely lied, but she had implied the list was personal. Val would be proud of her. She was proud of herself. "May I take it, please?"

He made no move to hand her the sheet. His frown deepened as he examined the page in his own hand. "Why would you want a list of English people in France?" He turned back to the document he held. "Wait. I know that name." He looked up, blue eyes wide. "I know who he is and what he does. He's an old friend. We were at the same school for a time, before my father died." His tone changed, from abject misery to suspicion, his voice firmer, surer. "The other boys jeered at him because his father was poor and low-born."

So he had befriended the boy.

"I know what he was doing, and why his name is on the list." His gaze met hers directly. "Do you?"

She nodded. What would be the point of denying it? The boy had become a spy for the Crown.

Firm-jawed, he held out his hand. "Give the other to me. I presume your husband is involved?"

She nodded again. "He wants to take them back where they belong."

"Even if being in possession of them would implicate him?"

Good God, a sober Whiston was quick. Yes, if he knew what the list was, he must know whoever held it could be accused of treason.

He watched Juliet closely in silence for a moment then nodded decisively. "Then I will take them and dispose of them."

At that moment any doubts Juliet had about Whiston's loyalty to his country vanished. He would not willingly send men to their deaths just to make money. Women too. She was sure she'd caught sight of a few female names, although she wisely decided not to look at it again. She didn't want to know who they were.

"What are they?" her mother demanded.

"Government papers," Whiston said without taking his attention from Juliet. "I have no idea how they got here, but they will not stay here for long."

No, whatever else he was, Whiston was no traitor.

Whiston tunneled through the untidy stacks of papers on his

desk. Juliet helped him, tossing aside bills from tailors, accounts of rents from land-stewards, letters and other paraphernalia. More paper tumbled to the floor. They took no notice. Together they collected six sheets of paper. Juliet held two, Whiston had the rest.

They stood like duelists, facing each other. "Give me the rest," he said.

"What will you do with them?"

Mrs. Burrell moved to stand by her daughter's side.

With a jerk of his thumb, Whiston indicated the low fire burning in the grate. "Burn them."

"How will that help?"

He spoke slowly and carefully, as if addressing a child. "If you or your husband are found in possession of this list, you will be implicated. You don't want that, do you?"

"Did you take them?" her mother demanded.

The answer came immediately. "No. Even at my worst I would not stoop to such a despicable way of paying a few debts." Was she foolish to believe him? "Destroyed, these papers are a threat to no-one."

Presumably the Foreign Office had a way of contacting these people even if this list was gone. Perhaps, despite what Val had told her, there was another list, locked up tightly. Juliet found it hard to believe it had passed through so many offices with not one person taking a few notes. Officials tended to write everything down.

But destroyed, there was no proof this list had even existed. That made her hold her hand out. "I'll take them to him," she said, keeping her voice as calm as she could.

Whiston looked at her, studied her, and nodded. "Perhaps you're right." He still withheld the papers. She stood stock still, afraid that any movement could urge him into action. He was nearer the fire than she was. He could toss them in there and then they'd be lost.

After what seemed like an age, but was probably a matter of

moments, he walked around the desk. They were both standing before the fire. A spark spat out, making them both look around, breaking the spell.

"Careful!" Mrs. Burrell cried out.

Whiston turned to the fire. Before anyone could do anything, he tossed the sheets of paper on the fire. "Fate," he said, watching the paper flare up.

With a cry of alarm—"No!"—she rushed to the fire and grabbed the papers, pulling them toward her.

Her mother grabbed her elbow, pulling her back. "Leave them!"

As she stepped back, another spark spat, catching her gown, sending the stink of burning fabric into the air. In a panic, she batted at the small flame, but only succeeded in increasing it.

Whiston hurried to help her, pushing her away from the fire, but it had taken hold, flaring up her skirt. Her mother spun her around, away from the fire, as Whiston dragged his coat off, using it to smother the flame.

That, too, caught. Her mother dragged Juliet clear, but her skirt was on fire, heat scorching her legs and face. The papers scattered on the floor joined the fire, linking the different parts, sending up a greater flame that separated Juliet and her mother from the Duke, who spun around as his coat caught fire in earnest. He dropped it, but that only gave the beast more fuel. Paper after paper glowed and burst into flame.

Her mother pushed Juliet to the floor and came down heavily on top of her, in an attempt to smother the flame.

"Get out!" they heard, but Juliet, shocked into near insensibility, couldn't move.

"Go!" Whiston cried, and took a step back, away from them. Then he screamed, high-pitched, agonized. He was fully ablaze.

Behind her, her mother flung open the door, shouting for help.

How could this be the end of her? Dimly she heard cries of alarm, as servants burst into the room, adding more confusion and feeding the greedy fire with fresh air. The drapery around the window behind the desk had caught now, tongues of orange and red leaping up the soft green fabric, reaching out for more fodder, of which there was no lack.

Whiston was surrounded by flames. His hair was alight, his cries of terror and pain echoing around the room.

How could this happen so fast? Tears ran down Juliet's face, blurring her vision as someone beat at her legs, tearing the soft fabric of her gown, pulling it free.

The whole room was aflame now. They were going to die. Her last thought was of Val.

Chapter Twenty-Two

VAL WAS NOT happy. "I had no idea Bagot was back." He had taken himself to Watier's, and the witty, fashionable Adolphus Fraser who knew all the gossip worth knowing, chose to join him. He had a sense for gossip that rivaled a hound's sense of smell and was the cousin of the Mr. Fraser Val had met at the Regent's dinner.

"Sir Charles Bagot? I didn't know he was in the country," Mr. Fraser said.

"Newly arrived from the United States of America," Val said shortly. "He's been recalled. Castlereagh mentioned it casually."

"How casually?"

"So casually I knew he meant me to know." Val consumed the last of his wine in one gulp. "Bagot is competent, I have to admit."

"And he does pompous very well." Fraser smirked and sipped his wine. "Castlereagh has no tact." He poured them both another glass. "It's certain he meant you to know. I daresay his casual is akin to everyone else's maiden speech in Parliament."

"How would you know?" Val commented. "You haven't set foot in the place for years."

Fraser stifled a mock yawn. "My uncle gave me one of his Parliamentary seats, but the work isn't to my taste. So tedious. They say in twenty words what I can say in two. If I choose." He turned his glass, studying the ruby liquid. "Times are getting interesting again. Last year, with Princess Charlotte's wedding and the sensational arrival of the Burrells, we could hardly go a day without some scandal or other. This Season has been dull in comparison, but maybe it is finally revealing itself."

"I doubt it." Val did not sip his wine. He took a decent swallow, then put his glass down. He could sit here and drink and grouse and feel sorry for himself, or he could carry on. Bagot's return might not have anything to do with the plum position the Foreign Office was currently holding. "He's married to Wellington's niece. Perhaps Wellington called him home."

Lord Worsley grinned. "Perhaps they didn't like his never-ending sentences in America."

Val smiled in response. He was beginning to feel better. When he'd first heard the news, he was sure his expectations of obtaining the post to Russia were completely dashed, but now he was not so certain. He had not yet seen Bagot, so perhaps the man had another purpose.

A commotion by the door made him look around.

A bedraggled man stood there, in his silver and slate-blue livery. What was left of it, at any rate. He saw Val and made for him, shaking off the waiter who put his hand on his sleeve. His normally stoic expression had completely vanished, replaced by terror and distress. What looked like tears stained his grubby face.

"Foster? What is it?"

Foster swallowed. Val handed him the half glass of wine, which the footman gulped down. With little respect for manners, he wiped his mouth with the back of his hand. "It's Whiston House, my lord. It's on fire!"

The quiet murmur of gentlemen enjoying a quiet hour before dinner erupted in gasps, shouts of "Dear God!"

Chairs scraped back, men stood and went to the window, as if to see the fire from here. Smoke billowed from every chimney, every kitchen this side of the Thames. but at least there were no flames licking up to the sky from the direction of Grosvenor

Square.

"My wife?"

No, not that. Not her. Juliet could not have been there, he'd know it surely, feel the absence in his heart.

"Nobody knows what happened. There were too many people. They all came out of the houses, and started handing buckets of water about. I came for you. McCarrick is holding a cab outside for you."

Val was already halfway to the door. Foster hurried along by his side. People made way for them.

What had happened? They were running down the stairs now. The whole club was in uproar. "It could spread," someone in the hall said. "My sister lives close by. I must go!"

Val didn't waste words. He rushed past Foster and was out of that door and into the cab faster than anyone else could steal it. Even though McCarrick was holding it for him, he didn't trust the men from the club not to snatch the fare. He pounded the roof. Grosvenor Square!"

He felt the carriage shift as Foster quickly climbed up behind, and at the last moment McCarrick leaped in with him. "Sorry, my lord," he said, his Irish accent coming to the fore. Unusual for him, but the whole damned situation was unusual. Val swallowed his panic. The carriage set off at a spanking pace. He'd get extra for that.

On fire? How in hell did that happen? True, fires went off all the time, but surely they had blankets, sand, water, to put conflagrations out. Where was the fire company? "What do you know?" he demanded of McCarrick.

He listened to McCarrick's terse account. With every word his tension rose with his anger. He should never have let her go. The fire had started in Whiston's study. Had he done it deliberately? He recalled the mess there. All that paper was always a fire hazard. Oh God, Juliet!

The tang of smoke hit his throat before they turned into the square. Flames were licking out of a downstairs window. A single fire engine stood outside, the water pump emitting too little to make a difference to the conflagration.

A small crowd of people gathered around, servants and gentlemen jostling each other. Val elbowed his way through the crowd, ignoring the shouts and complaints sent up in his wake. Heat grazed his face as he went closer, forcing his way through to where servants gathered by the fire engine. They must have dragged it there themselves, since he could see no horse. How long had that taken? Why did they bother paying fire insurance if the bastards only sent one engine and that at their own pace?

"My lord!" A manservant hastened forward.

He didn't bother with the niceties. "Where is she?"

"They've taken your wife to your home, my lord."

Half a mile away. Panic seized him and without waiting to hear if Juliet was alive, or—God forbid!—dead, he set off at a run. When he heard feet pounding behind him, he stopped long enough to order Foster and McCarrick to stay and bring what news they could as soon as they knew anything.

Val belonged with his wife.

JULIET OPENED HER eyes when Val burst into her bedroom. They'd brought her home and laid her on her bed. Her mother had helped her undress, not allowing anyone else, not even her new maid, Bedford, to perform the task.

When Val came in, she thought it was the doctor, but she was soon disabused of that. He didn't seem aware of anyone else but came straight to her and took her hand. Warmth spread from him to her, and she began to come alive.

"What happened?" he said. "Grosvenor Square is in total chaos."

"Is the fire still burning?"

He nodded. "The fire company has arrived. I've left a man

there and he will inform us of events. It's too early to tell if the fire can be contained."

"How will we tell Bianca?"

"Tell her about the fire?"

He didn't know. There was no way of telling him gently, but she wanted to tell him alone. She glanced up and caught Bedford's gaze. The maid quietly left.

"Whiston is dead. We saw it, my mother and I." A tear escaped. She'd thought she'd finished crying, but apparently one remained.

Gently, he brushed it away with his knuckle. "You don't need to tell me everything now." But shock widened his eyes. He hadn't realized.

"I have to." Nobody better to share the burden with. The sight seared her eyes, so much she feared it would be there forever. "You know his study was full of papers he never sorted out. He told Mama and me that he wanted to turn his life around. For Bianca. He said he loved her dearly, promised to give up drinking, said he'd already given up his mistress." That might console Bianca when she heard the dreadful news. "He said he was appalled at himself when she left, that he was desperate to make things right." She lifted her free hand, waved it vaguely. Took a breath to hold the pain inside until she'd finished her narrative. "He seemed sincere. He dislodged some papers." She bit her lip. "I think he had the list you told me about. I found one of the papers. It was a list of English names and French address-es." She kept his gaze and saw when he flinched.

"It could be anything."

"I memorized a few of the names and addresses. Only three, but I thought if they matched . . ."

"Tell me."

When she did, his lips firmed and he drew a deep breath. "Yes. That's the list. How many sheets of paper?"

"We found six. I didn't tell Whiston what they were, but he guessed. He knew one of the names, went to school with the man, so he knew what he'd been doing. He said we should burn them. I said no, and in the confusion he tried to burn the papers in his hand. That's when it happened. The fire spat and there was no guard. One set my skirt on fire, and he and my mother tried to put it out. Then he caught. I must have dropped the papers I was holding." She pressed her hand to her eyes, unable to remember.

He moved her hand away. "It doesn't matter. None of it matters except that you're alive. Are you hurt?"

She swallowed. "A little. My mother has sent for a doctor."

She let him draw back the sheets and pull her night-rail up. He stared. "It looks worse than it is," she said.

The fire had scorched her legs, the right being the worst. It hurt badly, but burns always did, she told herself. If not for her mother she could have died with Whiston, so she counted herself lucky. "It could have been much worse, but my mother got me out of the room before the fire really took hold." She carried on as he examined her injuries. "Whiston was on the other side of the room, and he didn't come out." Another tear emerged. She brushed it away before he could see it, unwilling to give him more distress.

He murmured soothing words, but she brushed them aside. She had to finish her story.

"Foster picked me up and put me in the carriage with my mother. Then he and McCarrick went to find you."

Juliet was recovering from her shock quickly. After an up-bringing like hers, she'd had to learn that skill early. She had anchors in her mind that she could refer back to, memories. One of them, although she had not realized it until now, was the first sight she'd had of Val on their wedding day. She let her mind linger on it, kept it there while she went on. "I saw him in the middle of the flames, screaming."

"Oh, my love!" He took her into his arms, carefully as if she was made of porcelain, and she went. She rested against him. Had he realized what he'd said? Did he mean it? They had never actually said that before.

He was shaking. "You could have died."

That was true, but she hadn't. She curved her hand over the back of his head, tunneling her fingers into his smooth, thick hair. She reveled in her ability to do so. "Whiston did. What do we do?"

Gently he drew back enough so he could look into her eyes. "We wait for the doctor."

She needed him. This man, this earl, this honorable gentleman was her world now.

"I'll stay," he promised.

Although he hadn't asked for it, she gave him her opinion. "I don't think Whiston knew the papers were there. And as soon as he recognized them, and understood what they were, he wanted to destroy them. He knew putting them into the wrong hands would sign the death-warrants of the people on the list if they went into enemy hands. I told him no, I would give them to you."

"That would have been better, but they're gone now. Don't think about it."

"We have to!" She wouldn't let him act on his own. This was both of them together. "The Foreign Office will want answers, and we have to have them ready."

He studied her for a few seconds in silence, then gave an infinitesimal nod. "What have I married?" he asked, his mouth quirking in a smile. "What a woman!"

They kissed then, as tender a kiss as any she had ever known.

"So what now?" he said.

She had been lying there thinking about their next move, how she would proceed. "The list has gone. Is there a copy?"

"Not to my knowledge."

"The people must be warned. Who knows who saw it between its disappearance and now? It didn't occur to me at the time, but anyone could have taken a copy of that list before it reappeared on Whiston's desk."

"Yes, that aspect worries me. If I knew all the people on the list I could send messengers. But I don't know them all."

Doing that would disrupt Val's work, perhaps end his career, but she knew he would do what he thought was right. "Will you warn them if your superiors tell you not to?"

He said, "I won't condone silence."

No, he wouldn't.

"Do you think Whiston stole the list?"

"On balance, no. He came in not long ago, to see his cousin, but he was hardly ever in the Foreign Office."

He paused and so did she. She looked at him, seeing reflected what she had just realized. "But we know someone who was."

Chapter Twenty-Three

A DAY'S REST worked wonders for Juliet. Her spirits had revived, and she took her mother's attitude of "it'll all work out in the end" to be true. After the doctor had seen her, he dressed her wounds and ordered her to rest. They were, apparently, superficial, although she could expect a scar or two. They hadn't felt superficial to her.

Nevertheless she'd sent Val to the Foreign Office with some trepidation. And not a little effort, since he wanted to stay with her. But he fretted her, insisted on her eating, on staying in bed, on taking the greatest care. While she appreciated his concern, it was beginning to irritate her almost beyond bearing.

Her mother had gone to the villa, bearing the news, and later that day she sent a footman back to town, saying she would remain there for a day or two. The news had not felled Bianca, but there was no doubt she needed more time to recover from the news of her husband's death. Better to do that in private than in the full gaze of society's avid eyes.

After Val had gone, Juliet called her maid and dressed. Light clothing, which she allowed Bedford to choose, since she wanted to see what she would select. A muslin gown in muted shades of gray, an appropriate choice for a woman in mourning for her sister's husband.

She hovered as Juliet made her way to the dressing table, but did not offer support, waiting for Juliet to ask for it. She dressed Juliet's hair in a simple, pulled-back style and brought her tea over to the side table when the maid delivered it.

Juliet liked her new maid. Quiet, efficient, and stylish. As long as she was discreet, Juliet would definitely keep her past her month's trial. She was older than Banks, more experienced, and came with the best references possible. Juliet found her presence calming, which was just what she needed at this time.

Going into her boudoir, she settled down at the small writing table, a French piece of satinwood and gilt, set before the window. She needed to get her thoughts in order. With Whiston's death and Val's problems at the Foreign Office, together with her new status, she needed to set the way she would appear in public. Not to mention where. She had the butler bring up the letters of condolence that had arrived this morning, answering most with a brief note of thanks. A few invitations had arrived, too. Balls would not serve. Neither would the theater, but they would have to appear somewhere. Small dinners, perhaps. She set the invitations for the smaller events aside. They had arrived before the fire, of course, but they might prove useful.

Then she ordered black-edged visiting cards for herself, Val, her sister, and her mother. Bianca must be out of her mind with distress and worry. The smaller details would escape her notice, but somebody had to manage them.

The doctor called again and changed her dressings. Dr. Schovell had the darkest skin she'd ever seen, and the sharpest mind of any doctor she'd ever met. She did not like to ask how he'd begun his career, but he told her anyway, as he was working. "I began as a pageboy for a duchess, and when I grew too old, instead of throwing me out of doors she apprenticed me to a barber surgeon. I have progressed since then, and now I lecture at the College of Surgeons."

He beamed. She beamed back. She had found another gem. He was very gentle with her, binding her legs after bathing them and smearing some kind of soothing ointment on them.

"I'll come again tomorrow morning."

When she expressed surprise, he said, "We have discovered that keeping the wound clean is of the utmost importance. In times of war, medical advances are often faster than in peacetime. While I would not advocate it as a teaching method, there is no doubt that when needs must, discoveries are made. And one of them is the correct treatment of burns. Yours, my lady, will heal well now the blisters have burst. The granulation is excellent."

When she cocked a brow, he explained, "They're scabbing over well."

Ah, yes, she knew about that. Having a sister who'd needed toes amputated after she'd ignored the original, superficial injury, she understood what he meant only too well. Dr. Schovell promised to return every day until she recovered.

After he'd gone, she sent a note to Cerisot, her dressmaker. She'd have to have blacks made up. She'd have to send some gowns to the dyer's too. Sighing, she thought of all the lovely gowns she'd ordered recently. Whiston would not have objected to her wearing them, but the sticklers in society would. The rituals of mourning had never concerned her a great deal. They had never helped her handle her grief.

She couldn't believe Whiston was dead. Seeing him flare up like that, so fast, had shocked her to the core. When she closed her eyes she could still see the image. It was burned into her irises. She didn't tell Val she still saw it, had no intention of doing so. Why make two people unhappy? Her mother had to have seen it too and would have understood, but she'd gone where she was most needed. Juliet had a husband to take care of her; Bianca didn't, not anymore.

The screams. Would she ever stop hearing them?

Hastily she turned her mind to practical matters. They would need straw to lay down outside the house and an armature to put over the front door. No, the funeral furnisher would do all those things. Val's mother would know one. Juliet had had no need of one in London before. When her father died, their grandfather had seen to it that he received an adequate funeral. Adequate being the right word. They'd had the barest necessities. But at least her father had been taken to the chapel in the family castle, although his wife and children had not been invited to accompany him. The old man had his son taken there and interred.

This wasn't getting anything done.

The bell downstairs jangled and a few moments later a maid came up. "Please, your ladyship, there's a man to see you. He says he's the magistrate."

"Me?" Her first thought was to wonder what she'd done wrong, as the instincts of years of living on her wits caught up with her.

But no, she was a countess. She should behave like one. "I'll see him," she said, glad of her subdued clothing. It would give the proper tone. "Show him into the drawing room. I'll be down in a moment."

The drawing room would remind him who he was calling on. She would use every weapon in her arsenal to ensure she kept the upper hand. After checking her appearance in the mirror above the fireplace, she counted to fifty, and went downstairs, using the banisters as support, because her legs were stiff and aching, despite the doctor's careful attention. Her heart was beating wildly, her hands were shaking, but she clenched them into a fist, once, twice, until they steadied. What could it be now?

Pleased to see a footman in full livery outside the drawing room, she walked straight through, not giving him a signal, knowing he would open the door at exactly the right time. He flung open both doors and bowed as she went into the elegantly appointed, spacious drawing room.

A man stood there, dressed neatly, but with signs of wear on his black coat. The shiny spots at the ends of the sleeves, the collar, limp from pressing showed a garment at least a year past its intended use.

A portly man in late middle age, he bowed low. "I am the magistrate at Bow Street, my lady. John Birtle, at your service."

When she said nothing, he cleared his throat and carried on. "I understand you are the sister of the Duchess of Whiston?"

"I am."

"Would you know the whereabouts of Her Grace, my lady?"

"She accompanied my mother-in-law on a visit out of town. My mother has gone to bring her back. She will be with us by the end of the day."

He sighed. "I see. So she did not witness her husband's demise?"

"She did not."

"But you did."

She wouldn't let him see her distress. *Countess, countess*, she repeated in her mind. "I did, unfortunately. It was an accident. He was sorting out his paperwork, so there were a lot of papers piled around the room. When he went to burn one, the rest caught fire. My mother and I were at the other side of the room, nearest the door. We escaped. He did not."

"A sad business," he said. "I thought I'd seen it all, but not this. I have to inform you, your ladyship, that since this was a matter of sudden death, there will be an inquest."

She let out a breath. She hadn't thought of that.

"The inquest will determine if the Duke's demise was a result of an accident, or . . ." he faltered when he caught her gaze, "otherwise. If it is determined an accident, as I have every expectation it will, the matter will be at an end."

"I see." He didn't have to tell her what would happen if the coroner had a rush of blood to the head and declared it murder. Not that he would. Would he?

"I also came in person to tell you that you might be called to give evidence."

Oh no, not a public appearance. That would only increase their notoriety, add to the annals of the Burrell sisters. "If necessary, I will do my duty." Could she sound any more haughty?

The door opened behind her. Her husband strode in. His

mouth was a firm line, his demeanor at his most distanced. Funny how she could tell that so easily these days. He stood by her side and waited. The magistrate bowed and introduced himself, but his voice shook as he did so. "You have a good reason for disturbing my wife," Val remarked mildly.

"I came to forewarn her that she will be asked to give evidence at the inquest, my lord." He raised his chin. "It will take place this Thursday at the Crown and Anchor. At noon, my lord."

"You intend to compel her attendance?"

"No, my lord, not I. I am not involved until or unless the inquest brings in a verdict of unlawful killing."

She put her hand on Val's sleeve. "I want to do it," she said. "I want this matter cleared up."

"It will be a circus." He glanced at her, then turned his attention back to the magistrate.

"I'm used to circuses," she pointed out.

She could have sworn his mouth quirked, but she couldn't be sure. "I am aware of that."

"If the inquest determines foul play, her ladyship's presence could be required at the subsequent trial," Mr. Birtle continued. "I thought to inform you personally, my lord."

Val remained silent. He knew the power of silence, something Juliet was learning fast, but this time she spoke. "We appreciate the information. You may tell the coroner I have every intention of appearing at the inquest, if my evidence would help to bring this sorry matter to a speedy conclusion."

She was proud of herself. She'd thought about every bit of that sentence before she'd used it. Although she couldn't do it all the time, that was certainly a way out of her problem.

Val remained silent as a flustered Mr. Birtle bowed low and excused himself. He waited until the front door had closed before he spoke. "Are you sure you want to do this?"

She nodded. "I don't want Bianca bothered with this. She wasn't there, so unless they want to delve further, we can keep her clear of all this."

"That's very commendable of you." He leaned against the console table by the window, arms folded. She remained where she was, afraid to go to him, afraid of being rebuffed, even now. Had the scandals surrounding her family finally become too many to overlook? He seemed so distant. Her feeling of being an impostor returned.

Love had made her weak.

"The mob will be out in force. Are you capable of facing a London mob?"

She recalled a time when a cobbler had put their shoes on display and charged a penny a look. The mob had certainly been out that day. Juliet's anger had seen her through that encounter. The display had upset Viola deeply, and Juliet was beside herself with cold fury. Could she repeat it this time on Bianca's behalf? She'd have to, that was all.

"Yes, I am. I can."

"Even if I decide not to support you?"

She firmed her chin. "Yes. I know what I saw. It was nothing but a tragic accident."

"I see." He moved then, straightened up and strolled to where she stood. Then he put his arms around her and gently drew her close. "You're a brave woman, Juliet. Perhaps too brave. I worry about you sometimes." He laughed, but not without a tremor. "I understand your concern. I'll go with you."

She lifted her chin and gazed into his eyes. "Are you sure?"

"Of course." Effortlessly, he swung her into his arms. "Now you must go and rest."

He carried her all the way to her room and laid her carefully on the bed. "We'll dine privately at home. We've had enough excitement for one day."

JULIET REFUSED TO stay in bed the next day. Her wounds were

healing well. Dr. Schovell was very pleased with her. "I think your maid can change your dressings from now on," he said. "You may be able to leave them off in a week, but I'd like to see them before you take that step." She was sorry to see him go, but he was a busy man, with his practice and his lectureship. She couldn't expect such attention forever.

She dressed carefully, in a dark blue gown with the minimum of trimmings, because Bianca was coming back today. She had considered proper mourning, but she did not know her sister's wishes on the matter. Did she want everybody around her to wear unrelieved black night and day?

The carriage arrived while Juliet was consulting with the housekeeper about guest rooms and future meals. She stood, dismissing the woman, and went down to greet Bianca herself.

Bianca wore black. Her veiled hat, black gloves and gown were obviously not made to fit her, but they would serve. Not that either sister cared, but the public would, and those vicious critics who had set themselves against the Burrells. She walked up the stairs slowly, followed by their mother. The first thing Juliet did was to embrace her. "Oh, Bianca, I'm so sorry."

"Yes," came the muffled answer. "So am I." She stepped back a little and threw back her veil.

Juliet gasped. This was more the Bianca she knew. Bianca's eyes sparkled and her full mouth, set in a straight line, was firm. The sister she'd thought she would lose was back, even though she would bear the mental scars of his treatment for a long time to come.

"Yes," Bianca said. "Just so. I had time to think, and a marvelous woman to talk to. Your mother-in-law is a remarkable person."

"She is. So what did you decide?" Juliet led the way to the grouping of chairs away from the window, so they would not be overlooked. Although everything outside seemed normal, she'd wager Bianca's arrival had not gone unnoticed. They paused while a maid brought tea and refreshments, but Juliet dismissed her as soon as she'd laid down the tray.

"I had determined to return to the house and tell George that he would not speak to me cruelly again. I had a whole speech ready." She paused and lifted her teacup. So poised, anyone would think she was making a normal social visit. All except for the blacks. "I know there was a decent man under the drink and the worry and all the rest." She took a long sip of tea. "I determined that I would help him, but if he belittled me again, I would leave. I could do it, too. I have an income from my marriage settlement, so I have something to live on."

Marriage settlements could be discussed for weeks, months before the marriage and many considered them as binding as the wedding itself, but Bianca and Whiston had eloped. Still, Juliet was glad to hear there had been one. Bianca had some rights.

"You could come to us with nothing," Juliet said. "You know that."

"I told her that," their mother put in. She too, was dressed in unrelieved black. "And I have the Edinburgh house again."

Bianca put her empty cup carefully back in its saucer. "Thank you both. I do appreciate your offers. but I'm the Duchess of Whiston, and I will do my husband the honor of remembering that."

Even if he had not given her any, Juliet thought wryly, but didn't say it aloud. She admired Bianca's nerve and her determination, but she wondered how set her sister was, and how much she'd keep to her resolve once she'd seen the house and taken the enormity of the occasion fully in.

"The inquest is tomorrow," she said bluntly. There was no good way of breaking the news.

"Good," Bianca said. "I'll be there. Like this." She twitched at the heavy veil now thrown back. "I won't give the mob a chance to call me craven, or not fit to fill my position. All the things they will say anyway."

Bianca was no longer the despairing, weak wife of a man who spent more time drunk than he had sober. Her resolve had returned, and with it, the resourceful, courageous woman Juliet knew her sister to be. In short, a true duchess. Still, she didn't want her sister there tomorrow. "You weren't there. You don't have to go."

Bianca was quick with her response. "But you were, and you do have to attend."

Miserably Juliet nodded. "Val will be with me."

Bianca reached for the teapot, but their mother was already lifting it. "As will I be," she said.

"You should be with Bianca."

"We'll all go." Bianca sighed. "Let's put that behind us."

After her second cup of tea, Bianca put her cup down again. She'd eaten nothing, even though the maids had brought a cold collation. "I'm going to the house," she said. "Now."

Juliet's breath caught in her throat. "You don't need to do that."

"Do you know the state of the place?"

"Not in any detail," Juliet admitted.

Bianca nodded. "I need to know. I have to go there."

Juliet closed her eyes. How could she bear it? "Can't you wait a day? We've prepared rooms for you, won't you go upstairs and rest?"

"No," her sister said. "After, I would appreciate that, but I want to see it. I want to show myself and talk to the servants."

Since Juliet refused to be left behind, her sister and mother had to wait until she had changed into a black carriage gown and Bedford found a black bonnet and gloves. All plain, none of them especially distinctive. And perfectly black. "Did you send these to the dyer's?" She met her maid's gaze.

"No, my lady. Yesterday I went shopping for you. These are clothes from Cerisot, made for a funeral but never collected. I altered them for you last night. More clothes will be arriving for your inspection, my lady, mourning and half-mourning. And a supply of black bands."

Bedford's efficiency impressed Juliet. While she'd been making lists, Bedford had taken the practical route.

Outside her room, her mother-in-law waited. Juliet greeted her with a kiss on the cheek. "Thank you for doing whatever you did to help Bianca. My sister has returned."

"It was nothing," Lady Langston said. "I merely related my experiences and pointed out that I was still here, and I would help her whenever she needed me. Of course, we never planned for this." She lifted her hand in a sweeping gesture. "I left you alone with your mother and sister, but I wanted to know how you are. You should rest, but I presume you won't."

"I'm much better," Juliet said, touched by her mother-in-law's concern. "Truly. Doctor Schovell does not think it necessary for him to change my dressings himself every day. I am walking without pain . . . well, not much pain. The burns really were superficial. I can thank my mother for that. She threw me down and extinguished the fire on my skirts. It was Whiston who saved me, though. When I would have helped him, he pushed me away and told us to get out of the room."

Lady Langston smiled. "You have such a strong spirit. I believe you will make an excellent countess. A credit to the family."

"Thank you. I can't tell you how much I appreciate that." Juliet was truly flattered by her mother-in-law's words. "I've ordered guest rooms prepared, but I haven't had time to inspect them. Perhaps you could do that for me while I'm absent."

"Absent?" she said sharply.

Juliet grimaced. "Bianca wants to go to the house, see what state it is in. I can't let her do that alone."

"She shouldn't do it at all, but I know her a little better now. I can understand why she would do that. Your sister faces all her problems head on, does she not?"

Chapter Twenty-Four

JULIET WASN'T SURE her husband would approve of them going to the house, but he'd have to cope with that himself. She went downstairs and into the waiting carriage, thanking Foster who was on duty in the hall when he handed her a cane. Juliet had walked the distance before, although today that wouldn't have been suitable. And she doubted she could have managed it anyway.

They arrived in Grosvenor Square within fifteen minutes. At least the house was still standing. One side, the left side that had contained the small parlor and Whiston's study, was boarded up. Black scorch marks licked up from the ground floor, stains of the catastrophe. The door was closed. The black drapery woven into the railings outside and the doorknob spoke of the tragedy within. A footman stood outside. He straightened up before the ladies alighted. Juliet went with her sister to question him. "Is the house safe?" were Bianca's first words.

"Yes, Your Grace. The fire did not damage the structure of the house, but the rooms on that side are destroyed, and the advice we received from the firemen was that nobody should use the rooms on that side of the house until it has been cleaned and the beams examined."

The walls in the hall were blackened with smoke. The portraits that usually adorned the staircase had been removed, and only a bare minimum of furniture remained. The doors to the left side of the house were all firmly closed.

"Thank you." Juliet pressed his shoulder in a silent gesture of comfort before they climbed the wide steps to the front door.

Disdaining the bell pull, Bianca plied the knocker. "This is the first time I've used this," she mused. "I never had to wait for the door to be opened to me." She paused and Juliet knew she was thinking about the adventures that brought them to this point. Because she was thinking it, too.

A butler they did not recognize opened the door. His expression of stiff disapproval could be masking anything, or it could be just stiff disapproval. "Your Grace, Lady Langston, Mrs. Burrell." He stepped aside to let them in.

"What is it, Jodrell?" a familiar voice said. It was shortly followed by the last person any of them wanted to see.

"Where's Connors?" Bianca demanded.

"I dismissed him," Carrington said. He was wearing clothes Juliet thought she recognized, but she wasn't sure where. They were excellent quality, but obviously not made for him. The shoulders were too wide, the buttons around his stomach pulled at their buttonholes.

"Re-engage him," Bianca said, pulling off her gloves. She dropped them into the waiting hands of a footman.

Carrington lifted his chin and glared at her. "You are no longer the mistress here."

If Juliet hated him before, it was nothing to the way she thought about him now.

Bianca showed no emotion. Juliet was proud of her. "I am, until the will is through probate. And there is another factor."

Carrington tilted his head, regarding her as if she were an oddity. "Do tell."

Instead of answering, Bianca led the way into the breakfast room on the other side of the hall. Juliet and her mother followed, and Bianca made sure the door was closed before she spoke. "You had not considered the fact that I might be bearing the next Duke of Whiston?"

His eyelids flickered. He was nervous; he hadn't thought of that possibility. To do him justice, neither had Juliet. But Bianca was right. When a man died there was always a delay before the heir presumptive was allowed to take control of the title and inheritance. The possibility that the widow was pregnant was one of the reasons, and it provided for a decent period of mourning before the machine of the dukedom started up again.

"If that is so, I must be involved."

Bianca was quelling. "Not so. That depends on the dispositions set out in the will."

Of course Whiston would have made a will, but its contents remained to be seen. At least Bianca would have something, because she'd signed that marriage contract.

This time Carrington swallowed, his prominent Adam's apple bobbing up and down as if suspended in water. "We shall see. I believe you must tell me as soon as you know for certain."

"I would be bound to do that." She dismissed the comment with an aristocratic wave of her hand. "In the meantime, I will go upstairs and change."

"Ah."

That one syllable stopped her in her tracks. "Ah?" she repeated.

"My wife is upstairs."

"In my suite?" Bianca assumed the air of a queen.

"We thought we would . . ." he faltered as he met her gaze, then firmed his chin. "You have no use for such lavish luxury now."

"You think so? Were any of my belongings damaged in the fire? Is your wife assessing the damage?"

"Um, no." He was deflating quickly. He'd no doubt expected to find a subdued, grief-stricken widow who would turn to him for help. That was not going to happen.

"Where is your mother?" Mrs. Burrell asked. Of course, she would be bound to be here. The elder Mrs. Carrington had been one of Whiston's most voluble critics. She wouldn't miss the chance to gloat.

"She is taking stock of the damage and making an inventory."

"The inventory is already extant. I made it myself." Bianca walked to the door. "I take it you have not dismissed my maid?" She opened the door. "Please send my maid up to *my* suite."

Juliet and her mother exchanged glances. They would not have missed the potential scene for anything. Ten minutes ago they'd have said Bianca wanted support, but her anger carried her through magnificently.

Juliet stopped before she left the room. "My wounds are healing well," she said to a slack-jawed Carrington, "thank you for asking."

Her mother had already left. Juliet hurried after her.

Upstairs, Bianca was facing the younger Mrs. Carrington on the upper landing. This time she did not seek privacy. "Good day, ma'am. Thank you for your concern for my husband and myself. I will change now. Could you ensure my mother and sister have some refreshments served to them?" Thus the woman was relegated to the role of servant. Clearly, Bianca did not care how many bridges she burned. The Carringtons would never forgive her for this.

"I was not aware you were invited here," Mrs. Carrington said. Unfortunately for her, Bianca towered over her, and of course her beauty outshone the fussily gowned Eliza who, in other company, would present quite well.

"It is my house. I don't need to be invited here." She gave Eliza a sweet smile. "We have to wait until probate, of course, before we may use our new honorifics. I believe I will not take the title of dowager, when the time comes."

"Shameless!"

"Merely a woman who wishes to reach the sanctuary of her own bedroom," Bianca said. "You would have me weep and wail all over town? Would that not create more scandal?"

Eliza folded her arms. "I would think you are beyond worrying about scandal. Surely you have created enough for it not to bother you."

Bianca withdrew. "What you think does not concern me. You are welcome to stay here, of course, while we bury my husband . . ." For the first time she showed emotion. She closed her eyes and bit her bottom lip. "After that, we will see," she added, none too steadily. Then she pushed past Eliza and went into her suite. After a glance at Juliet, Mrs. Burrell followed her.

Juliet would not interfere. If her sister wanted her, she'd be here. So she went to discover how badly the house was damaged. After she'd taken stock, she went to the drawing room, where tea and bread and butter awaited her. The stink of burning paper and wood haunted the whole house, even in the drawing room. She hoped Bianca didn't mean to stay here. Carrington, his wife, and his mother entered the room a moment later. Each gave her a glare as they sat, and the elder Mrs. Carrington poured the tea. The cup rattled in the saucer as she brought it over, but even she would not break visitor etiquette.

"I do not believe your sister is expecting," Carrington said.

Juliet blinked at his abruptness. Did he want her to confess? Did he really think she would? "I do not know if she is or not. Neither, perhaps, does she. However, it is appropriate to wait, don't you think?"

His mother heaved a sigh. "Of course you are right, but surely that does not give her leave to occupy this house."

"That, surely, is her concern." Juliet would be surprised if her sister would choose to stay in this wreck of a building, but if she did, then she had the right. For now, at any rate.

The younger Mrs. Carrington took her turn. "We will also be staying here. Our old London lodgings are hardly sufficient for Arthur's new position, either as the heir presumptive or the holder of the title. If the Duchess is enceinte, then he will be required as a guardian to the child. And a trustee."

Juliet had the answer to that. "I fear not. The law says anyone who stands to directly gain from the death of the minor cannot act as a trustee. And surely the child's natural parent would be a better guardian."

She probably shouldn't have said that. Her rash words might only make matters worse for Bianca in this interim period. If Carrington believed he would gain in the minority of any child, he might accede to any demands Bianca might make. As it was, living here with him would make matters infinitely worse.

Ah well, it was said now. She went in for the kill. "Can it be you didn't know that?" Why not poke him a little? She had personal reasons for disliking him, as well as for supporting her sister.

Carrington looked chagrined, a deep crease forming between his bushy brows. "I was not aware of the particulars. I will have to look into it."

"A good idea. I'm sure Bianca will appreciate your support and help in the difficult time ahead." She was sure of nothing of the sort and wondered if Bianca would find an excuse to rid herself of them. However strong she seemed at the moment, her sister was vulnerable, already distressed from Whiston's treatment and attacks on her. Now she had to cope with his death.

The bell rang, and in a moment, Val came in, unannounced. "Ah, here you are," he said, going straight to Juliet. "I brought the larger carriage so we can all travel home together."

If Bianca came back with them, Carrington might make an effort to take over the house once more. As it stood, he was welcome to it in Juliet's mind. Perhaps living here with the place in this state would teach him a lesson.

Her mother soon followed Val. As he greeted the Carringtons with cool bows, forcing Carrington to stand and bow in return, Mrs. Burrell said, "Bianca is sleeping. She's had a trying time."

"Then I'll send the carriage back for you."

She gave him a weak smile. "Thank you, but there's no need. My daughter and I are both staying. Bianca is anxious to see the restoration of the damaged rooms done properly. I think the work will do her good. Keep her occupied."

"I see. Then I'll send the carriage tomorrow, for the inquest. You know she doesn't have to attend?"

Mrs. Burrell nodded. "She wants to." She sent the older Mrs. Carrington a hard stare.

"Inquest?" Mrs. Carrington said. "Do they suspect foul play?" She sounded eager.

"No." Val could rival Juliet's mother for cold stares any day of the week. "Inquests are held on the occasion of sudden, unexpected death."

The lady gave an exaggerated shudder. "Such a terrible way to go!"

"But he died a hero," Juliet felt compelled to say. "He ordered us to leave, not to try to—help him."

"And you did," Carrington's thin top lip curled in a sneer. "That could be seen as having contributed to his death."

Val responded to Juliet's wide-eyed shock with a short, humorless laugh. "Not a chance," he said. "If you try to accuse her of it, I will not let that go." He looked slowly at the three Carringtons, giving them each a straight-on stare. "You understand, I take it."

"I doubt you'll have the influence," Carrington said. "Although you may try."

A declaration of intent. A duel between the men, not a straightforward challenge with swords in hand, but the most unpleasant of challenges. If Carrington was not the duke, then he was one step closer to becoming one, that much closer to power. Only a frail baby could stand between him and the title he coveted so much. What an inheritance.

Juliet's mother intervened. "I am about to inspect the kitchens on behalf of my daughter. While she will remain in her room, I would appreciate a good dinner. My appetite is already keen. I presume you are staying for the meal?"

"We are staying here to support Her Grace and to ensure she is well," Carrington said smoothly. He had recovered his veneer.

It was a wonder Eliza didn't slip on the slime he left in his wake, since she tended to walk behind him instead of by his side.

"I will do that," Mrs. Burrell said, at her most haughty. "But if you insist on staying, you may not find your rooms comfortable. I will assign the best available to you. I will use the Duke's room, of course, since I will need to be close to my daughter."

The guest rooms, one of which Juliet had occupied until recently, were spacious and well-appointed, but since they were above the seat of the fire, presumably they would be a bit smoky. And probably rickety. Was that side of the house even safe to use? Not that Juliet cared. If the floor gave way under them overnight, all the better.

Juliet's mother had boxed them in beautifully. Good for her.

Chapter Twenty-Five

"THE LADY ASKED me to hand this to you personally, my lord."

Val took the card and glanced at it. "Thank you, Fotherington. No reply."

Juliet knew from his toneless voice the card meant something, but she said nothing until Fotherington had gone from the study. Their house, a smaller version of the Whiston mansion on Grosvenor Square was also different in subtler ways. It felt like a home, for one thing. Going indoors felt like a deep exhalation of relief.

"Who was the card from?"

"Lady Rotherham. She has invited us for dinner tonight."

"What? We have a number of other upcoming invitations, but they were given before the accident. I didn't expect anything new."

"She wrote a note on the back of the card. Want to hear it?"

"Of course."

He glanced down at the card. "'Terribly sad news. Only ten at dinner tonight. Close family. Condolences.' She wants the gossip."

A predatory woman. They would all be hunting them down now.

"So let's give it to her. And let her spread it."

He stared at her, open-mouthed. "You're serious?"

She nodded. "We are going to dinner with a close family friend who wishes to console us in our grief. If more than ten people are there, if she's trying to turn this into a circus, I can faint very convincingly, and you can take me home." She thought. "Besides, this might be a rapprochement on her part, and if we refuse, she might not take it particularly well."

He waited for what seemed like an age before he replied. The corner of his mouth turned up in a half smile. "I think that's appropriate. We dress in black, naturally."

"Of course."

So the night before the inquest on her sister's husband, Lord and Lady Langston went out to dinner. However, their unrelieved black clothing did not promise a convivial evening.

"I don't think Whiston would approve of all this black," she commented. Whiston rarely wore black.

"It's the dukedom, not the person that we're mourning." He leaned back, resting his hands on his lap, apparently at his ease. Nobody except Juliet would notice the slight deepening of the tiny lines at the corners of his eyes, or the tension tightening his upper lip. "We mourn the man in private."

Even the clop of the horses seemed melancholy.

"I think my sister still mourns him, despite what he did to her."

"It was a turbulent relationship. Whiston always seemed restless to me, always reaching for the next thrill, the next excitement. He found something in your sister that might have calmed him in time. If she had left him, that might have been enough."

"He had the decanters moved out of his study. He wanted to reform, he said, for her. So you could be right. Now we'll never know." She looked away, tears pricking her eyes. She hated this. He'd treated her sister badly, but Whiston was still dead before his time. Whatever he'd planned would never come to fruition. And those screams would stay with her forever.

"What do we say tonight?" he said.

"I was going to ask you."

"You know your sister best."

She grimaced. "But you know society best. Do we mention her potential pregnancy?"

He shook his head. "Unnecessary. Society will have noticed Carrington moving into the Whiston house. He seems determined to assume the title as soon as possible. Society will not approve of such unseemly haste."

"So we try to support him, but fail," she said. "Something like, "I am sure he is only trying to help," if the opportunity to use it arises."

The remaining daylight outside was testament to the progression of the year, and it enabled her to see his quick grin clearly. She loved that grin, such a fugitive expression that some people would miss it. "You will make the best diplomat's wife."

"I've always had to watch what I say. Sometimes I fail." She swallowed and paused. "I always do better when I plan what I'm going to say."

He didn't speak. Instead, he put his hand over hers, and pressed it warmly. "Never do that with me." He glanced out of the window. "Ah, here we are. Right on the stroke of half-past seven." As if bidden, a church clock struck the half-hour.

She let the reverberation fade before she allowed the footman to help her down the steps and on to the pavement.

"Here we are indeed," she murmured, as the door above opened, revealing the Rotherhams' butler.

In the drawing room they found her ladyship waiting for them, with her husband, two of her daughters and their husbands, Lady Maria and her brother Lord Greenfield, the heir to the Rotherham title. He was not yet married. Coming between the four oldest daughters and Maria, he had already begun a political career. He had natural gravity which he had developed into pomposity. Maria's betrothed was not present. Perhaps she'd seen sense and changed her mind. They were all dressed in subdued colors, and all wore black armbands. Bows and curtseys exchanged, they stood and spoke in quiet voices.

"I feel we should come to an understanding, to respect the late Duke," Lord Rotherham murmured to Val. "It would be what he wanted. Our son prevailed upon my wife to make the approach. We are of course deeply sorry that this tragedy occurred."

"It is a shock to us all," her ladyship added. "I had occasion to drive past the house today. It is in a sorry state."

Their son joined them. "It may need demolishing and rebuilding."

"Oh, I heard the damage was superficial," Mrs. Cholmondely, the oldest Rotherham daughter said. Although without a title, her husband was almost guaranteed to inherit an earldom in the fullness of time. Lady Rotherham's first triumph. Her husband, a jovial man, was doing his best to appear somber, but only managed boredom.

Juliet left Val to cope with the tedious discussion on the subject of the house and moved to talk to Maria. Maria gave her a tentative smile, so Juliet smiled back. "How have you been?"

"Perfectly well, thank you." Maria's red-rimmed eyes belied her statement.

Juliet lowered her voice. "If you wish to see me, send me a note."

"Oh, I wouldn't dream of bothering you at this sad time." Maria spread her fan. Was that a message? Juliet had the strong feeling Maria was being manipulated. Or was she? "I am perfectly happy, I assure you. I never expected everything to work out so well."

So well? Maria refused to meet her eyes, but Juliet persisted, trying to draw her out with conversation. "Thank you for your concern, Maria. It was a shock to us all."

"Are you recovered? I heard you'd been injured."

"I am well, thank you."

Had Maria been prevented from sending an enquiry to the

house, or did she forget until now? Juliet was seeing all kinds of things she'd never suspected before in her shy, sweet friend. The slyness, the tendency to adapt and comply with whoever was with her at the time—signs of these failings had passed Juliet by in her desire to find a friend outside her family.

Was she so easy to fool?

Dinner was announced, so they sorted themselves into rank and went in. Lady Rotherham insisted on formality even in small gatherings.

"Your sister was not living with her husband when the house caught fire?" Lord Greenfield asked.

"She was visiting a friend in the country, in the company of my mother-in-law. A few days only."

"I see. I heard differently."

She might have known someone would gossip.

"A madwoman rushed out of Whiston House, and raced through the streets," his lordship said. "Many people saw her. She had the appearance of your sister."

Inspiration struck. She was going to say her sister had heard some distressing news and had run for help. But her new idea was better. "That was not the Duchess. I'm afraid it was her maid. Bianca had given her leave to use her discarded clothes, as is usual with maids, but she transgressed—Bianca found her gossiping, and she dismissed her on the spot." The story would hold, she was sure of it.

"All maids gossip."

"They don't all sell the stories to the gossip rags."

A small silence fell. Lady Rotherham glanced at her son, then at Juliet. "Well indeed, that explains that story. All manner of gossip was spreading, but I told my son it was all a hum, and you have just proved that to be the case."

So Banks' timely dismissal would be useful after all.

They got into the carriage at the end of the evening with a deep sense of relief. "That was awful," she said, automatically moving into his arms.

He leaned his head back against the squabs and let out a long groan. "Yes it was. They only wanted information, all that they could get. We gave them what they deserved to know, which is little more than what they read in the newspapers. And you put paid to that extremely well."

⇶⇷

THEY LEFT THE Rotherhams to circulate their version of the story. They would not be disappointed. Having them to dinner was a coup for her ladyship, and she would pay them back by spreading the gossip far and wide.

When she slipped into their room that night he flipped the covers back and she climbed in, going straight into his arms again, where she found the most solace, the bliss she'd never imagined would be hers.

Turning to her, he took her mouth in a long, luscious kiss, which she returned eagerly. His taste, the feel of his body next to hers, then over hers, it was all so familiar and yet so very exciting. He kissed down her throat, seeking out the hollow at the base that was so sensitive. When he discovered her body, she did too, learning things about herself she'd never dreamed about. She welcomed him, touching him in places he enjoyed, like the space between his shoulder blades, which was sensitive to the point of tickling. Sometimes she'd kiss it, and make him squirm, and then they'd laugh together.

Was this the real Valerian, the man in the bedroom, or was it the cool, reserved man everyone saw outside it?

No. This was the man. His enjoyment of her, his ready laughter, the way he could caress, knowing just when to deepen his touches, when to climb over her, settle between her open legs and—oh yes, that was it!

She let out a long, heartfelt groan. She let her head go back on the pillow as he came back to her, joining their mouths in a kiss.

He kissed so well!

Bracketing her face with his hands, he kissed her and kissed her as he moved rhythmically inside her, unerringly reaching the place that touched her inner core, that would eventually drive her up and over. Juliet responded the best she could, wrapping her ankles around his calves, pushing back against him, reveling in the long, hard body bringing her up to fulfillment.

She caught her breath on a scream, gasped for breath as the tides rose, taking her with them. Opening her mind to the experience they were sharing.

Only this mattered. The thought came on her release, when she cried out, and called his name as she pulsed around him. He murmured hers, before he drove deep and came.

As he slid to one side of her and drew her close, she let out her troubles in his arms and sank into a blissful slumber, the best sleep she'd had for days.

VAL LEFT HIS wife still sleeping the next day. He dressed in his dressing room, usually meant for storing his clothes, but now it held a small dressing table and mirror, as well as a washbowl for washing and shaving. That created a few problems for his valet, but they would have to learn to cope, because it would be happening again. Besides, he was no fop. All he required were creaseless, neat clothes that would take him through the day. Compson was superb at producing those and dressing him quicker than he could manage himself. He also delivered an excellent close shave, something that took Val much longer to achieve.

Downstairs he found his mother taking a long, leisurely breakfast. She had gathered all the morning papers, and by the look of them had already read most. He helped himself to a plateful of eggs, bacon, chops, and some potato concoction that looked tasty, and took a seat close to her. The table in here was a round one, so when they had informal dinners, they tended to use this room. No worries about precedence.

"Anything?" he asked her as he scooped his first forkful into his mouth.

"Gossip," she said, waving an elegant hand. "Mostly about the fire. A great deal of speculation filling space and meaning nothing. Some malicious, but we could expect that. Juliet's story about her sister's maid has taken. Good idea, that. Unfortunately, they're also reporting the place where the inquest will take place."

He sighed. "A shame, but inevitable. It will be a circus. Astley's without the horses."

"The horses will be outside," she said absently, leafing through another paper. "I shall go."

"Mama!"

"If the Duchess and Juliet are attending, then I will go, too. Might as well make it a good circus."

He subsided, knowing if he protested, she'd only insist. He knew that look, when his mother could not be persuaded otherwise. His right to order her to stay away did not enter the equation for either of them. Long ago, he'd promised her she would never be under a man's jurisdiction again, unless she chose to be so.

Wisely, he kept his peace. "I've given orders not to disturb Juliet until absolutely necessary. She needs her rest."

His mother twinkled at him. "Kept her busy, did you?"

Val closed his eyes and pinched the bridge of his nose. "I won't dignify that with a reply."

She chuckled. "I love to see you so disconcerted. What, did you think I assumed that you and your lovely wife retired to separate rooms for the night? The maids are abuzz with the information that you regularly share the same bed. And what will you do there? Sleep?"

Val kept his eyes closed. "Are you sure you don't wish to retire to the dower house and become a respectable member of the local community?"

She snorted. "You couldn't pay me to live in that hovel. And the biddies in the country are no better than the highest in the land. That is, they're equally malicious. The center of their group is when they meet to change the flowers in church every Friday. That's why Lent and Advent are relatively peaceful times—no flowers."

Val listened, fascinated, at least to the last part of what she said about Advent. Opening his eyes, he met her guileless gray ones. "You could be a grandmother this time next year." Meet fire with fire.

"So I could." Serenely, she reached for the coffee pot. "I've already faced that possibility and dealt with it. I will take younger lovers. That will balance everything out."

She was, indeed, incorrigible, but he loved her all the same.

He accepted the coffee she handed him. "Do you think the Duchess will cope with the events of the day?"

"No doubt," she replied without pause. "She's a strong woman. Before we received the terrible news, she'd decided to come back to London and face her husband. She would have told him that the minute he tried to belittle her again, she would leave and not come back."

"With your help." Bianca's determination had all of Val's admiration.

She gazed at him over the rim of her cup, the steam from the coffee making her eyes appear unsteady. "She made the decision on her own. I advised she remove to the house in Brighton for the rest of the Season, but she rejected my offer. If he had harangued her again, I have places she could have gone. Heavens, I could have bought one for her. Not that I'd tell her so."

"Juliet says she still loved him."

"Undoubtedly. You can love what is bad for you."

Given that opening, he dared to ask the question he'd been

dying to ask for years, but, respecting his mother's privacy, had not. "Did you love my father?"

"To the day of his death." She put her cup down in the saucer. "And yet I knew he could destroy me in one of his rages. He loved me too."

Val grunted. He couldn't say anything until he'd swallowed the food in his mouth, but he wanted to rave at her. By the time he'd taken a mouthful of coffee and cleared his mouth, his temper had subsided. This was an old story. Neither of them could do anything about it. "Were you willing to walk away?"

"He would not let me. I learned other ways of defending myself." She caught his gaze, kept it. "Just because people do the same things, it doesn't mean they do them for the same reasons. Whiston adored Bianca, but he was spoiled, wanted his own way in all things. Your father did it for power. He knew what he was doing, learned the best way to control everyone around him, and reveled in it. At home he was cold, analytical. He wanted dominance, he wanted never to be challenged, he wanted to be master of everyone and everything. I asked him once why he did not strike people, because, you know he never did." Val nodded. "He said that was crude, unworthy of him. His way was subtler and longer lasting."

"Why was he like that?"

"I neither know nor care, but it was something to do with his upbringing, I think. His own parents were draconian. Perhaps he decided at a certain point that nobody would control him anymore. Which was strange, because I felt exactly the same. That resolve kept me going in the worst of times. And you, dear boy, and you."

Her words touched her son. She'd never explained her side of the story until now.

Such a tragedy, one only too common, and it drove women to employ subterfuge and guile, where they should have recourse in the law. "Thank you, Mama.

He got to his feet. "I thought I'd look in on the clubs, get a sense of people's mood."

"You're not going into the FO?"

"No."

Truthfully, he did not want to face two problems in one day. He would devote the proper time to it tomorrow. With Bagot returning from America, his expectations for the ambassadorial post had taken a step back. If he had to fight for it, then he would, but not today.

Chapter Twenty-Six

LATER THAT DAY, as Juliet and Val arrived at the Crown and Anchor, the howling mob was present in force. The crowd surged forward as they left their carriage, and two sturdy footmen not in livery stepped forward immediately to prevent anyone getting too close. A chill crept up her spine, sending fingers of dread through her. The mob was a dangerous creature, and while these people were here to drink in a scandalous situation, at any moment they could decide to take matters into their own hands and become one, which was why the mob was a singular object. "They" became "it."

That was why the time the three sisters had visited the cobbler's was so frightening. Before they'd arrived, the spectators had already become the mob, threatening to overwhelm them. They'd reached for the Burrells, pulled at them, grabbed their clothing.

Inside the inn, matters weren't much better today. It was crammed, the heat suffocating, even though the windows were open. At the front the coroner sat in state on a temporary platform, a scarred inn table provided for his document. Another chair was set out, presumably for any witness. The jury, a group of men, sat at the front. On the other side were the witnesses.

At least the coffin wasn't set on a trestle, the previous custom at inquests. As far as Juliet knew, the coffin was at the morgue, awaiting interment to the family vault in the country. She assumed he would be buried with his ancestors.

Bianca already sat at the front, heavily veiled, and like Juliet, was dressed in black. It would be a difficult task to get to the empty chairs set next to them. The inn was relatively spacious, and most of the furniture was removed for the event, but the beer kegs were still set against the wall, and people were still buying the various beverages the inn had to offer.

However, forging a path proved easier than she'd imagined. Several burly men ruthlessly shoved back the crowd. They were already present and had places in the crowd that must have been worked out in advance, because suddenly there was a clear, if narrow, path to the front. Bianca did not turn to watch, but Juliet felt her acknowledgment. The crowd was hardly silent, either. She did her best to block out the raucous cries.

Grim-faced, Val helped her sit, and the proceedings began.

The coroner, a weaselly little man who sat bolt upright in his uncomfortable wooden chair as if it were red hot, gave her a terse nod.

Several people stood and gave evidence. A servant in the house related his account, the butler had his say, and then came Bianca's turn. She stood, and answered the question, "Could you tell us where you were on the day of your husband's death, Your Grace?"

The honorific sounded like a parody. Bianca answered steadily. "I was spending a few days with the Dowager Countess of Langston in the country."

"Why were you not with your husband?" The coroner made it sound like a crime.

"Because I was tired. I needed to rest."

"Was there any particular reason you were tired?"

Bianca's breath stirred the heavy black veiling draping her hat. She had not folded it back to answer, and so far the coroner had not asked. But now, she pulled it away from her face in a dramatic gesture that made the crowd gasp.

Her beauty shone in this place. Despite her red-rimmed eyes and the light covering of face paint, she glowed. She waited until the sound subsided. "No." She stared at the coroner, daring him to ask more. Juliet held her breath.

"So you were not there on the day of your husband's death."

"I was not."

Carefully, she lowered the veil over her face again.

With visible regret, the man dismissed her and turned to his clerk, who called out, "The Right Honorable, the Countess of Langston, please take the stand!"

Juliet emulated her younger sister and stood at the place she had recently vacated.

"Where were you on the day of the Duke of Whiston's death?"

Juliet bristled. He knew. Everybody knew. "I was with him in his study."

"What were you doing there?"

Had he the right to ask that? "I visited him to discuss my sister."

"What about your sister?"

Damn, she should have rephrased that. "If he had heard when she was returning to town."

"She did not tell you?"

"Was she supposed to tell me before she told her husband?" There, that shut him up.

But not for long. "Are you accustomed to privately visiting men you are not married to?" The slow drawl and the sideways wink at the audience demonstrated his implication.

She showed him the Countess, staring down her nose at him. "My mother was also present."

He deflated a little, his shoulders drooping. Did he think he'd uncovered a scandal? There was one, but not the one he was pursuing. He evidently thought Juliet was having an affair with the Duke. Dirty little man. "A mere social visit, then?"

"Indeed."

"And could you describe in detail what happened?"

She could. That did not mean she would. "He was going through his accounts, so there was a great deal of paper around. He was disposing of the irrelevant ones by burning them. The fire spat a spark that set my skirt alight, and he came to help me."

"How did His Grace suffer such terrible injuries while you were not harmed at all?"

"I was harmed. My legs were burned." She waited for the gasp, which duly came. "His Grace ordered my mother and me to leave. They were his last words. He gave his own life for ours."

He would die a hero, if she could help him to. God knew he was far from that, but being the widow of a heroic man would work much better in Bianca's favor. She had a husband to mourn, and there was no reason she had to do it in disgrace.

The coroner nodded sagely. Perhaps he was sensing the mood of the crowd, which had changed since she'd come in. "So noted," he said. "So you are saying the event was a tragic accident?"

"I am, sir." Maybe the "sir" would sweeten him.

"And your mother will corroborate your statement?"

"She must do that for herself."

Finally, he let her go and called up her mother.

Mrs. Burrell repeated the events in her own words, but essentially she told the same story. The only thing they left out was Whiston's treatment of Bianca. And why should anyone know that? It was hardly likely to happen again, so best to let things lie. He was wrong, but he was dead. And any shade cast on his corpse would only make Bianca's lot worse.

The jury took less than ten minutes to come to their verdict: "Accident."

There was a rush for the door, then the remainder of the crowd quietened down. Juliet felt washed out. Bianca had been admirable. She could only see a shadow of her face now, under the thick black veiling.

The coroner came over to give his condolences. Probably

eager to avoid any lingering resentment. Juliet felt some, for his weak attempt to place her with Whiston while Bianca was away, so she chose to greet him coolly.

BIANCA AND HER mother came back with them. Bianca didn't say a great deal on the way back, just leaned against the squabs, veil thrown back and eyes closed.

Outside the house stood a traveling carriage, a little the worse for wear, but they recognized the crest on the doors. In days gone by Juliet would have flung herself out of their carriage and rushed up the stairs, but the Countess of Langston did not do that, especially when the house was being watched. Juliet and Bianca exchanged a glance, and their mother made a wordless sound of pleasure.

Mrs. Burrell entered the house first. A few people on the street stopped to stare, but not as many as earlier. Interest was already moving along. Word spread fast. Of course there'd be gossip and speculation, but it would fade, especially if a juicy scandal appeared in the next day or two.

They went straight upstairs to the main drawing room.

"Viola!" Mrs. Burrell cried.

Viola sat on one of the sofas. She needed the space, since she was big with child. Very big. She had her feet up on a footstool, and a table by her side held tea and cakes. Her husband stood just behind her, hovering as if afraid she would drop the baby at any moment.

Mrs. Burrell pressed Viola back in her seat when she would have risen and kissed her cheek warmly. "How are you, my love? Why are you here?"

"You thought you could keep me away?" she demanded.

"Viola will give birth in town," Knowsley said in more measured tones. They had a London house close to Whiston House in

Grosvenor Square.

Juliet went over to give her sister a hug.

Viola was the dark version of Bianca, tall and elegant with the dazzling blue eyes all the Burrells shared. Her dark hair contrasted with Bianca's fair locks. Juliet was the lesser sister, not as tall, not as strikingly lovely, but she had never felt the loss.

"Oh!" Juliet drew back, startled as something prodded her middle.

"Did the baby kick?" Viola asked with a laugh. "I'm so used to it, I almost don't notice these days. I'll be glad when it's over."

"You traveled in this state?" her mother said, appalled. "You should have stayed put. You're much closer than I thought to birthing the child."

"How could I do that when we heard the news?" Viola held out a hand to Bianca, who went to their sister and pressed her hand warmly. "I'm perfectly healthy now. At first, I admit, I suffered, but once the baby settled I was fine. Gerald fusses too much." She gave him a fond smile, which he returned, their exchange as easy as breathing.

For the first time that day a tear trickled down Bianca's cheek. Juliet felt helpless, sensing Bianca's loneliness as well as her sorrow. She could do nothing except be present for her sister. It did not seem fair that she and Viola were so happy in their marriages.

Her sister appeared uncomfortable, shifting her position, not at all the graceful Viola Burrell of a year ago. Although the day was not warm, she was lightly dressed and carried a fan, which she plied regularly. Women did come to London to give birth, since all the best midwives were here, and most refused to travel to their potential clients. Bianca supposed they preferred to keep to where they could attend the most childbirths. And also, it had to be said, closer to the research establishments and large hospitals. Not that a lady of Viola's quality would ever dream of attending one of those.

"Will you stay here?" Juliet asked, without consulting her

husband first.

"I've ordered our house opened," Gerald said, his deep voice reverberating around the room. "But we would appreciate a room here for a night or two, while the servants get everything ready."

"With the greatest pleasure," Val said. "We're honored to have you. I would prefer that Mrs. Burrell and Bianca stayed here too, but they are insisting on remaining at Whiston House."

"We have to stay in possession of it," Bianca said, "or he will overrun us."

Nobody needed to ask who "he" was. Val's expression froze, a sure sign he was not happy.

"And if he does that," Mrs. Burrell added, "he will try to claim Bianca's other rights, and whatever her husband bequeathed to her in his will."

Bianca grimaced. "Which won't be much. He may have left me everything he could, but the debts must be paid. After that there isn't a lot left. Tomorrow, I'll collect the jewelry he gave me and bring it here, if I may. That is about all of value I can expect. Though I have my portion, so I won't starve."

Gerald sighed and shoved his hands in his pockets. "He had such promise. When his father died, George said he would build the dukedom to what it once had been. He did start to do it, but he met too many temptations along the way. He was an immensely charming man, and that, I think, was his downfall. I'm so sorry all this happened."

As were they all, but Gerald had once been George's close companion. After his parents died, Whiston was brought up by Gerald's parents. They went to school together, sowed their wild oats together. Unfortunately, Whiston never stopped sowing them, while Gerald grew out of that reckless phase.

"I loved him," Gerald said, "but that does not mean I was immune to his faults. And he had many. He hated not getting his own way in all things. Because of his position, his good looks, and his charm, he usually did. When he did not, he could be cruel.

But I know his parents' deaths made him feel helpless, tossed about by fate. He swore he would never let that happen again."

"He was an eternal child," Bianca said. "He darted from one project to the next, from one thrill to the next. I fear I was one of them." Her jaw trembled, but she kept her head up, and her eyes free of tears.

"Everyone wanted you," Gerald pointed out. He strode around the large room, like a wild beast in a cage, stopping to face Bianca. "Because that was so, he wanted you too."

She nodded. "I know it now. I won't be fooled that way again. I thought him sincerely in love with me, as I was with him. Because I was, you know."

Juliet grasped her sister's hand. "We know, my love. We're here now, for you."

Of course the papers made hay with the inquest, but try as they might, they could not dig up any more scandal than was already there. Many resorted to talking about the race through London, describing it in detail, and pointing out Whiston could well have been killed. They praised his control of his horses and carriage but failed to mention that everyone who'd heard about the caper had kept out of the way. "We may skate through this pretty well," Val said, folding the paper and setting it down.

"Are you going into the FO today?" Juliet asked.

Val turned his whole attention to her, trying to discern her mood. Last night he'd thought her calmer, more accepting. Beneath her serene surface was a woman seething with passion, something he appreciated every time he took her in his arms. But that passion also led to high emotions.

"I want us to get as far back to normal as possible," she explained. She returned his regard, letting him see her. "And there is an important decision being made that you should not let pass."

She was right. Without him, people would spread rumors and they would gain hold. Wild stories circulated around the Foreign Office. He'd never forget the one about Napoleon being hidden somewhere in Whitehall before his transportation to St. Helena. Some people remained convinced the man they took to that remote island was not Bonaparte at all, but an impostor, an impersonator.

He should be there to scotch whatever stories they had concocted about him, but he had not thought of it seriously until Juliet suggested it.

"We'll keep Juliet company. We won't be going anywhere," Viola said, glancing across the breakfast table at her husband, who nodded. "Gerald won't let me go very far."

"No," he agreed. "I won't. When you go upstairs for your rest this afternoon, I'll walk over to the house and see the progress. Apart from that, I won't be going anywhere, either."

So Val agreed to go. After a quick trip upstairs to change his coat to a black one and tie a black armband around his sleeve, he tapped his beaver hat on and left the house. He appreciated the half-hour walk. The day was dull, as usual these days, but at least it was not raining. He acknowledged a few people but did not stop for any of them.

As he approached Whitehall, his apprehension rose. Since his marriage, he'd felt confident about his position. Juliet had proved an asset, polite but not easily fooled. Her outspokenness did not deter the likes of the Duke of Wellington, who appreciated intelligence and plain-speaking. Yes, his choice was sound, despite the present situation. Her appearance at the inquest caused a flurry of attention, but she had acquitted herself well. And now Whiston's death had been declared an accident, they could arrange for his funeral and then get on with their lives.

Try as he might Val felt little pity for the Duke. He had brought his fate on himself. He appreciated Whiston's bravery at the end, and did not believe him to be a spy, but as for the rest— the man was a liability. He had nearly killed Juliet's spirit, and Val could not forgive him for that.

The FO appeared the same as always. The tall, stuccoed building with its ranks of windows stood in the midst of history. Across the road, the Admiralty held sway, with its parade ground in front. Further up, the Banqueting House, a constant reminder to republicans and monarchists alike of what can happen when the establishment is turned upside down, stood in serene glory.

Inside the Foreign Office, activity bustled. The porter at the desk nodded to Val, who nodded back. Few others had the time to acknowledge him. Val had always appreciated the relative anonymity that ruled here. As he crossed the marble hall to the corridor he required, a sense of serenity and order eased through him, the impression of timelessness in the midst of change, a balm to his soul.

He went into the maze that lay behind and around the marble hall. A tangle of corridors, some dating back to the great fire that had destroyed the Palace of Westminster, some new, or tacked onto the old ones. There was no sense or organization in them, but Val had walked through them so often that he didn't have to think about it. His office led off one of these nondescript, down-at-heel corridors.

His first surprise was discovering the door was unlocked. The second was the person sitting behind his desk. "Good morning," said Arthur Carrington.

Val tossed his hat on to the hatstand by the door. "Good morning. May I have the pleasure of knowing why you're here, in my office?"

"I needed to speak to you."

"And where you found the keys?" He thought he'd tracked down all the keys, but apparently not. Only he and his secretary were meant to have copies.

Carrington shrugged. "If a person knows where to look, it's easy to find a spare."

Interesting—not in a good way, either—but the admission added to Val's suspicions. Carrington could creep, sneak and inveigle his way into most places. Who better to steal a set of papers, copy them and insert them where they would be of most use? To him, not to the country.

"What did you want to say?"

"That a man should be careful." He got to his feet. For a change, he was wearing a decent suit of clothes, but they hadn't been made for him. Someone taller and broader in the shoulder had worn them first. Whiston, Val concluded heavily. Carrington had raided the wardrobe of a dead man, literally stepped into his shoes. Despicable worm.

Carrington prowled toward him. Val held his ground. "You and I know I will soon inherit the title of the Duke of Whiston."

"Do we?"

He smiled. "Oh yes. We will give the ladies a chance to mourn the worthless being who came before me, but then I will take control of the dukedom and the entail."

Should Val mention Whiston had mortgaged and borrowed on the worth of the things he couldn't sell? No, let this weasel find out for himself.

He had reason to know that the Duchess was not pregnant. His mother had confided the truth to him, with the Duchess's permission, that her courses had come while they were staying at the villa. In time, this grasper would indeed be the Duke.

"I'm sure you'll do as you will, of course. I don't see what business it is of mine, except that my wife is the Duchess's sister."

"So you don't take sides?"

"Do I need to?" he shot back.

Carrington shrugged. The bottle-green coat did not move with his shoulders. "If you do, you won't win."

"Win what?"

Carrington strolled back to the desk. "That is the question, of course." He touched a paper on the desk. Val was not alarmed. He never kept anything important in plain sight. Though this man's ability to find keys was somewhat alarming. "I have some unfortunate, and delicate information. I have already told Lord

Castlereagh."

Val remained silent.

Carrington glanced at him. He was smiling, but not with amusement. "I know about the papers that went missing." Of course he did. "I've been helping to search for them." He glanced down at the documents on Val's desk again. "I found one in a most unfortunate place. In the late Duke of Whiston's study."

"Indeed?" Val tried to sound mildly surprised. "How on earth did it get there? If you're right about it, of course. Not many people had access to those documents."

"No." He drew the word out. "But he did spend some time here. I myself saw him in this office."

So he had. He'd arrived immediately after Whiston had left. "He was my brother-in-law."

"And it was the time when you had possession of those documents, was it not?"

Val disliked the way the conversation was going. He needed to talk to Castlereagh before this poison reached his ears. "Around that time, yes. Other people had access to this office, too."

"Including your secretary, and one or two others. Do you really think they had any reason to steal the papers?"

"Did Whiston?"

"They would have fetched a pretty penny to the right people."

Val gritted his teeth, forcing himself not to call the blackguard out, or merely punch him where he stood. But although that would bring comfort to his soul, it would not help his reputation, or Whiston's. "Do you really think Whiston would have done that?"

"Why not?"

Anyone who thought like that would assume anyone was capable of such an act, that there was no one who was not able to be tempted into transgression. That, more than anything else the man had said, convinced Val that Carrington had stolen the papers. But he had no proof, none at all. It infuriated him this man would inherit a title that was still one of the most prestigious in the land.

Carrington shrugged, but Val's sense of unease followed him to the door. As he reached it, he turned. "Oh, by the way," he said, as if he had just thought of something. "Bagot has been offered the post of Ambassador to Russia. I heard his mission to the colonies—the United States, I mean—was not entirely successful, but the Russian post will suit him excellently. Friends and relatives in high places, eh? What chance do the rest of us have?"

He stood with his back against the door and lowered his voice. "I heard you were in contention for the post, my lord. However, your unfortunate choice of spouse and events following on your marriage did not sit well with Castlereagh."

Val took the seat behind his desk and folded his arms. "Is that so?"

"Indeed. I was with Castlereagh when he said it. He said he held you in high esteem, but he could not consider you for this post or any other, as long as your association with that scandalous family continues. Perhaps it was because I had just informed him of my suspicions about the Duke of Whiston."

With a smirk, he turned and left the room.

Val had had enough. He knew where his true loyalties lay.

He picked up his pen and wrote a series of short notes in the cipher he knew by heart. The basic code would do. "You have been found out. Leave immediately. Tell others."

Then he made a list of all the people on that list that he could remember. Nobody had given him leave to do this, but it was the right thing to do.

When he'd done, he called for his secretary and gave him the list and the notes. "See these are sent off at once," he said. "Do not tell anyone who is not authorized to know."

Those notes would be on their way by the end of the day, passed down the chain he himself had created to pass urgent messages quickly. The recipients might not get the notes themselves, but they would get the messages.

After taking three deep breaths, Val pulled a fresh sheet of paper towards him. He picked up his pen and wrote without hesitation.

Dear Lord Castlereagh,

I was delighted to hear about the new appointment of the Envoy to Russia. I am sure your choice will be a great success.

I have informed the people on the list of the lapse we discovered. I did so with their wellbeing foremost in my thoughts.

Considering certain remarks about my wife and my private life, I must conclude that you no longer have the confidence in me that you used to. Understand, sir, that whoever the person is, I will not accept any aspersions cast on my wife or her family. The rumors that my brother-in-law was involved in the theft of certain items from this place are lies. Since we evidently disagree on this topic, I have no choice but to tender my resignation, effective immediately.

While he did not entirely believe what Carrington had told him, the words gave him the impetus he needed. And they were typical of what Castlereagh *would* say. Sending his warnings would certainly be grounds for dismissal in any case, so he would walk before he was pushed.

He would not wait on any other developments. Castlereagh had made his choice of envoy, and Val did not want to drift around the offices waiting for an appointment that might never come.

He signed his name and title with a flourish, something he rarely did here, usually making do with his initials. He sanded the letter, folded it and sealed it, using his personal seal that was engraved on the gold ring he habitually wore, not the seal of his position in the Foreign Office.

Still seething with fury, he left his office, locking it behind him, although that seemed a useless gesture now, and left.

He didn't look back.

Chapter Twenty-Seven

JULIET WAS STEALING a few quiet moments in the downstairs parlor when she heard the front door slam. That was a rare occurrence, so she put her book aside and went to the door. She paused before opening it—it could be trouble of some kind—and listened. She had to step back quickly when her husband barreled through. He caught the door before it hit her, and came in, closing it behind him.

"What's wrong?" She read his mood instantly. He was worried, no, angry.

He took her by the shoulders, then slid them down to her waist. "Less now I've seen you. I met Carrington in my office. He got there before I did, because he used a key he shouldn't have." He tipped back his head and exhaled. "No, he's not worth the trouble. I'm just angry he will have the dukedom to shield him. Privilege!" He almost spat the word.

She framed his face with her hands, making him look at her. "You're right. It doesn't matter. The papers are gone now, so nobody can sell them or pass them on."

His mouth flattened. "They might have been copied."

Juliet caught her breath. "Yes."

He drew her closer. "I sent messages to all the people I could remember on the list. All my people in Paris and the few I remembered from outside. Without instructions to do so. It was

288

not mine to do, they were not in my control, but I did it anyway. It's something I would be dismissed for."

"I'm proud of you," she murmured, and kissed him softly on the lips. He'd put lives before duty.

"When Castlereagh finds out, he'll be anything but proud," he said wryly. "I don't regret it. They will be warned. What happens next is up to them. Most, I imagine, will come home or leave their current situation."

"But they will be alive."

"Yes. Many in the Foreign Office consider them expendable. They lie for their country, cheat and steal for it, so they are not honorable, by the standards of the people we know. But they went, and they faced danger, which is more than many of the gasconaders in the office would have done. They deserve something for that."

"Gasconader?" She frowned.

"Sorry, military term. Blusterer, boaster."

"Ah yes. Parliamentary generals." They laughed softly. They hadn't laughed like that for days, but the bitter tone in his voice remained.

"I've resigned," he said. "If I had not, they might have asked me to leave. Politely, of course, considering my position and rank."

"No!" Releasing him, she stepped back. "I know what that position means to you."

He stayed where he was but put his hand on the back of a chair. "It did. It filled the void after my father died and I discovered what my mother had suffered. I went to work at the Foreign Office because I wanted to help, wanted to do good for people."

"I know," she said softly.

"I can let go now," he continued. "I don't need it anymore."

"What are you saying?"

"I'm saying I have you. Some said you were not the right choice for me. I know people have been talking about you, about all of you—the scandalous Burrells. They've talked about you since you arrived."

She was used to that. Because they had no wealth, few connections, society had proved a hard hill to conquer. She shrugged, but it always stung, and he could see it.

"No, they're wrong. And if they can't accept it, then they're of no importance to me."

Had she cost him the position he valued so dearly? She feared he was putting a brave face on it. And she felt so badly for him. "You could go back."

"I don't want to, not on those terms. I won't betray people who depend on me, and I won't listen to lies about my wife."

"They're not lies." She'd faced her truth years ago. "They're right."

"Not about everything. Whiston's death was not your sister's fault, neither was it yours."

"How can you be so sure?"

He stroked her, as if calming an agitated cat. "Because I am. Because I love you. Juliet, you are more important to me than anything else."

She listened in awed silence, hardly believing him until his lips covered hers and he followed his words with action. By the time he'd removed her tucker and exposed her breasts to his hungry hands she was convinced. That, and the murmurs of love he uttered between soft kisses to her neck, lips and breasts convinced her beyond doubt. "I love you," came as balm to her hurt soul. Years of insults, slights, and disparagement melted away under his adoration.

Juliet responded, adoring him in her turn, stroking and touching, gasping when he hit a particularly sensitive spot.

When he lifted her and took her to the sofa, neither registered the potential dangers of being discovered by others, so lost in one another as they were. He came down over her, pushing up her skirts, caressing her legs and finding more sensitive spots on the way. She'd thought they'd explored each other's bodies thoroughly. She discovered she was wrong.

Her sighs and gasps melted with his, and when he pushed into her she lifted her knees automatically, welcoming his hard length, enclosing it within her, claiming it for her own. And with it, the man himself and everything she was. She let go of her doubts, her reservations and finally put herself into his keeping.

"Everything I have is yours," he murmured. "Everything I have belongs to you."

"And I you." She pushed her hand into his thick hair, letting the silk run between her fingers as he bent his head and gave her everything he had. "I love you so much, Valerian."

Then words left them as they entered the world they shared, the one they thought they knew. Juliet found more there, as if a barrier had given way and they had now become truly one. She arched her back, pushing up, trying to take as much of him as she could, to absorb him, make him irrevocably a part of her.

He caught his breath on a cry, so it came out as a choke, deep in his throat, and she felt him pulse deep inside her, as she reached her own peak and came with him.

He slumped over her, boneless, as he gasped for breath. In an instant he lifted up on his elbows and claimed a deep kiss.

"You are wonderful," he said when he lifted his head. He kissed the tip of her nose. "Never let anyone tell you anything different."

"Oh Val!" Her fears disappeared under his warm, loving gaze. As long as he continued to look at her like that she could bear anything, do anything.

Someone came to the door, rattled the handle. Val glanced down at her, grinned and sat up, taking a few hasty steps to the door. A voice murmured outside, she couldn't catch the words, and the person, whoever it was, went away.

Val secured them from further intrusions by the simple expedient of dragging a chair over and pushing it hard against the door. He turned to her, smiling broadly. "There."

"Do you think they heard us?" She searched wildly for her partlet. The white silk seemed to be nowhere in sight. How could she get upstairs in this state?

"Probably," he answered. "It didn't seem important at the time." He came back to her and caught her hands. "Shall we retire upstairs, my love? We have nowhere to go, nothing to do until dinner, so we could put that time to good effect."

She saw what she was searching for in a heap by the table. He followed her gaze and grabbed it, waving it at her. "I prefer you like this."

With a growl she snatched the offending object from him and stepped up to the mirror by the window. Fortunately the room overlooked the garden at the back of the house, not the front. Even better, there was nobody outside. Her hair was half up, half down, and her gown had been pushed down. She wore only light leather stays today, and he'd made short work of them, loosening them enough to give him access to her breasts.

With shaking hands, she folded the silk and wrapped it around her neck, drawing her bodice back into place and using what pins were left to hold it, at least for now. "What were we thinking?"

"Just what we should," he answered. Having tucked his shirt back into his breeches, he seemed almost normal again, except for his ruffled hair and his waistcoat, which hung loosely from his shoulders. He fastened it, and found his neckcloth, wrapping it loosely around his neck.

She envied him. With a few swift moves he'd restored himself to respectability. She would have to take much longer to do the same.

Gently he moved her hair aside and kissed her neck. "We only need to be decent. We're not going far."

"I—I'm not used to this." She'd thought that she was beyond embarrassment, but she'd never been in quite this situation before.

"Good. You might want to get used to it, though, because I see it in our future."

The mirror told her she was blushing.

THEY WOKE TO a discreet tap on the outer door to the small sitting room, then an even quieter tap on the bedroom door. Val was about to say "Come in!" when Juliet clapped her hand over his mouth. He grinned under her hand, and she released him. They were naked, the bed covers tossed and creased, and the room bore all the evidence of a meal taken hastily and a bottle of wine drunk at leisure. She had told him to instruct his valet to leave them strictly alone when they'd retired upstairs, and although he laughed, he acceded to her wishes.

Val found a robe and went outside to consult with Compson. He returned a few minutes later and laughed. Juliet had straightened the covers and found her own robe. She sat in front of the mirror, brush in hand, wondering where to start.

"You're laughing a lot."

"I have good reason to." He came over and dropped a missive on the dressing table. "Castlereagh wants to see me in an hour. Should I go?"

She answered immediately. "Oh yes, I think so. You can tell him to his face what you said in your letter. And use choicer language if you want to."

He eased his hip onto the table, and his robe came loose. She tried not to look at what reached her eye level. They had no time for that now. "I've ordered you a bath, and breakfast will be served in the sitting room when we're ready for it. Now, I think we have ten minutes . . ."

Fifteen minutes later, a more relaxed Juliet left her husband to dress and went into the sitting room where she found her breakfast, a choice selection of the repast usually served downstairs. She tried to behave like a countess to her maid, who condescended to serve her personally. Juliet discovered exactly how hungry she was.

As she dressed, she planned her day.

Her first call was to her sister at the Whiston residence. The hall still smelled of charred wood and paper. That stink would linger for a long time. A new door had been put on the openings to the part of the house worst damaged by the fire. At least Bianca didn't have to look at those. Upstairs, Bianca and their mother waited for her in the drawing room with the inevitable tea.

After kissing her sister and mother, she sat and prepared to listen. Bianca, still dressed in unrelieved black, looked even more beautiful than usual, if somewhat pale, which was to be expected. "So how are you managing?" she asked.

"Well enough," Bianca said, with a glance at the door.

"I brought Foster with me," Juliet said. "He's outside. He has instructions to look after me. I trust him."

Bianca visibly relaxed, slumping a little. "I'll be glad when this part is over. The lawyer is coming today, to tell us where we stand. After that, I'm free."

"She's coming with me," their mother said. "We'll go to Knowsley's first, to help during Viola's confinement. Then we're moving to their country residence as soon as they can, and after that, perhaps Edinburgh."

Bianca closed her eyes. "I want to rest and think. That's all I want to do."

She looked exhausted, fragile, defeated. Juliet hated that one of the people she loved most was in this slough of despondency. "It won't be long until you can."

"I've ordered repairs done to the damaged rooms. I want his office completely cleared and redone."

A good plan. That way, she wouldn't have the constant re-minder. As Juliet had arrived, she'd seen people drifting around the square, their gazes intent on the house. They wanted to see the scene of the tragedy, bathe in its notoriety. Juliet had wanted to yell at them all, tell them to go. Instead, she'd lifted her chin and walked up to the front door, seemingly oblivious to the people hovering, the ones who muttered, and the occasional shout.

She was, after all, still a Burrell.

They were interrupted by a maid bringing a card. Apparently the lawyer had arrived. Bianca asked for fresh tea and for the man to be shown up. "I might as well get this over with," she said resignedly.

Mr. Bright came up, a small man carrying a large leather folder. He had a pair of gold spectacles pinching the top of his nose and wore severe black and white. With a black armband, she noticed, as Bianca asked him to sit.

He refused a cup of tea. "Your Grace, I'm not sure I can divulge to you anything but the personal property your husband left to you."

"That will do," Bianca said, apparently composed, but she folded her hands tightly in her lap. "Please let me know what I can expect."

He sighed, and drew a parchment document out of his file, weighed down by a heavy seal. "Your husband rewrote his will in the week before his death. When you were away from home, Your Grace."

Bianca nodded but said nothing. The news came as a shock to Juliet, and, she presumed, to her sister, since she had said nothing.

"I informed him of his situation, but he was insistent. He has left everything not specifically in the entail to you."

"What?" she said. She looked dazed, and swayed where she sat before she regained her rigid posture.

"There are a number of manors, two larger houses, and some land. He did not leave this property to any child you might bear, but to you personally. The partnership I have the honor to belong to are appointed trustees."

"But—the debts?" Bianca said, her voice barely a breath.

"Ah, yes, that is the rub," Mr. Bright said regretfully. He readjusted his spectacles. "Unfortunately, His Grace and his father before him borrowed on the property. All of it. What was not sold was mortgaged. I'm afraid when the creditors are taken care of, and the bank is paid, there will be very little left."

"And the estate?"

"Yes, the entail. I should inform the heir to the dukedom—that is, if you are not . . ."

Bianca sighed. "I am not." That was the first time Juliet had heard the news first-hand. "But," her sister went on, "I wish to take the time assigned to me to put my affairs in order. I will accompany His Grace's body to its final resting place in the family vault, then I will return to London for a while before I do anything else, and I do not want any unseemly displays from the heir presumptive before that is done."

The Whiston main estate was not far from London, perhaps a day's journey at this time of year. So by the end of next week, Carrington could be told he was the new Duke of Whiston. That didn't leave much time.

"I understand, Your Grace. I was told Mr. Carrington was not at home. Would it be convenient for me to call back tomorrow?"

"Indeed it would. I'll let him know."

Mr. Bright expressed his condolences once more and left.

Bianca passed her hand over her eyes. "I just want to get this over with. I'm barely holding together."

"Oh, my dear!" their mother said, moving to take Bianca in her arms, but the Duchess held up her hand to stop her.

"Please, Mama. It won't be long now. If I can bury poor George, then I may leave in peace. I just want to be alone to mourn and to think. I didn't imagine for a minute there'd be much left, and when Carrington hears what George did in his will, he'll be furious, even though most of it will have to be sold. I don't want to be here when the storm breaks."

"What can I do?" Juliet asked.

"Nothing, but thank you," Bianca said.

"We moved most of her personal property to Viola's house," her mother told her. "Some jewelry, a few bonds, not much at all really. She is supposed to receive a generous allowance, but I doubt that will be forthcoming."

"I'm not banking on it," Bianca added. "But there'll be

enough to live quietly for a while."

"You're always welcome with us." Juliet knew her husband would agree with her. She tried not to recall her own happiness. It didn't seem fair.

"Thank you, but I want to support myself," Bianca said. "To prove to myself that I can. I have the title. I can use that." She stopped abruptly and bit her lip before continuing. "We've known worse, haven't we?"

"Come to Edinburgh with me," her mother suggested. "Come home."

The house in Edinburgh was the nearest place to a home that they had ever known as a family. "Yes," Bianca said with a little sigh.

Juliet had to speak. She didn't want her mother and sister to discover her own bad news from someone else. "The position Val wanted has gone to somebody else. And I think I helped to lose it for him." She lowered her head. "I read the Foreign Secretary a lecture on slavery, and while he is against the trade, I do not think he appreciated my speech. Slavery is still practiced in Russia."

"And what about the papers and George's acquiring of them?" her sister asked. "I cannot think where he got them from."

"Neither did he," Juliet said, "which is why I think somebody else took them there."

Bianca clapped her hand over her mouth.

Their mother said the two words. "Arthur Carrington?"

Juliet nodded. "But there is no proof because the papers were destroyed in the fire. All we can say for sure is Carrington touched them. But so did others."

The women sighed, almost in unison. "Is there nothing we can do?"

"I don't know," Juliet confessed. "Val has gone to the Foreign Office to see the Earl of Castlereagh. He resigned yesterday."

Chapter Twenty-Eight

VAL STRODE INTO the Foreign Office, prepared to do battle. Apparently the news of his resignation had not traveled, because the guard on the door merely touched his hat as he walked in. For all its confusion and grubbiness, he'd miss this place.

Castlereagh's office was considerably easier to find and better appointed than the one Val used, but he did not want all the pomp and circumstance that would go with such a post. Parliamentary politics were not of interest to him, and the Foreign Secretary bestrode both parliamentary and foreign affairs. He supposed Castlereagh deserved an interview.

The outer office was full of clerks standing at their desks, scratching pens over paper and parchment. A large table to one side held supplies of ink and inkwells, unsharpened pens and knives, just in case the clerks did not have their own. The place had the bitter smell of ink, magnified because there was so much of it.

The scratching stopped as the men watched Val walk through and then into the smaller room to the Earl's secretaries. One stood, and went to the inner door, tapping respectfully before going in. He was back in less than a minute. "My lord, his lordship would be delighted to see you.

"Good. I'm delighted to see him." He doubted Castlereagh

would be quite so delighted when he'd had his say.

Castlereagh stood when Val went in, and he briefly wondered about precedence. That part of his title never bothered him much. His mother usually put him right. Although Castlereagh was a viscount, he was the heir to a marquessate, and so technically held the rank of earl. But he was not a peer of the realm. Dammit, nothing of that idiocy belonged in this place, only outside it.

"Glad you could come. Brandy? Tea?"

Val declined refreshment and they both sat. The large desk contained stacks of files, all neatly arranged, and the inevitable red dispatch box that members of the government used to carry official papers. This one had been well-used, judging by the dents and grazes it bore.

He leaned back, crossing one leg over the other, waiting for the hammer to fall.

"This," Castlereagh said, waving a paper at him, "is what you sent me yesterday. Did you mean it?"

"Every word."

"Who told you these things?"

"What things?" He had no intention of giving anything away.

"That your wife is unsuitable for an ambassador, that your brother-in-law stole the file that went missing. Those things."

Val had no objection to telling him. "Carrington. Soon to be the Duke of Whiston, when probate is through."

Castlereagh grimaced, his gray eyes cold. "I knew it. I've sent for him, but I wanted a word with you first."

Val didn't especially want to spend any time in the same room as Carrington, but he would wait, for Castlereagh's sake. "Speak, then."

"I freely offer my apology that this was ever suggested to you. None of it came from this office and never would. And you may inform your wife of that. However, I think the true apology should come from the source."

For an instant, Val had a glimpse of the anger and turmoil

behind the cool exterior. Castlereagh was a man of passion and ability combined, one with deep melancholy moods, but here, in the FO, he tended to keep his passions to himself. His eyes now showed the man within until the shutters came down again. Val recognized it because he did that himself.

"Carrington."

"The same." Castlereagh leaned back, leather creaking from his chair, and steepled his fingers. "There is more I wish to say to you, but—"

A tap on the door announced the entrance of the secretary, followed by the man himself. "Mr. Carrington is here to see you."

"Please show him in."

Neither man stood to welcome Carrington, although he stood in the doorway, apparently waiting for them to do something. When he became the Duke, he would be insufferable. Val would do his best to avoid the blackguard.

"Carrington. Do sit down."

Carrington took another chair and kept his distance from Val. The feeling was mutual.

"You wished to see me? I am, as you may imagine, somewhat preoccupied these days."

"Indeed you are," Castlereagh said. "My condolences for your sad loss."

"Thank you."

Castlereagh tapped the letter on his desk. "Langston here has tendered his resignation."

Was that pleasure Val saw in Carrington's eyes? Did the man want to step into his shoes? Of course he did. He always had.

"I am not minded to accept it," Castlereagh went on. "The reasons given are not valid."

"Which are?" Carrington asked.

Val didn't mind telling him. "Reports about my wife and the speculations about the file that went missing." Which must be an open secret by now, making Val even more glad he'd contacted the people named.

"The one that appeared in Whiston's study?"

"That one," Castlereagh said. "Its disappearance has caused us a great deal of trouble." He glanced at Val, his eyes hard and steely. "Langston here contacted all the people on the list."

"I did."

"Commendable initiative," Castlereagh said.

So he approved. Whether he did or not, Val would have done it anyway. Too many people despised and denigrated the people doing a necessary job. Too many people would have left them in place to be captured or worse.

Carrington shot him a sly look. Val pretended not to notice. "That puts the French organization in chaos," Carrington said.

"We will deal with that. As soon as the folder went missing, they were in danger." He glanced at Val. "I continued the good work Langston had begun. I had a copy of the complete list, locked in my safe. I used that to contact all the people there, to tell them they were no longer safe, and they should return home, or find a place of safety."

Val wanted to cheer.

Castlereagh continued. "In the interval between them disappearing and then being found, any number of copies could have been made. And sold." He let the last two words drop into the sudden silence.

Val knew better than to break it. Let Carrington believe they had caught him.

Castlereagh cleared his throat. "Naturally, the list is now worthless." Smoothly he went on, as if Carrington's goggle-eyed, slack-jawed response had gone unnoticed. "I called you in, Carrington, because it is highly likely you will inherit the title of Duke of Whiston. I would not like you to believe that you would not have it for long."

"Eh?"

Now the viscount gave a smooth smile. "I'm sure you're aware that the papers were discovered in Whiston's study. And anyone in possession of them illegally is technically guilty of treason. You recall what the punishment for treason is?"

Carrington swallowed. Had he not considered that eventuality? If Whiston had lived, if he'd been caught in possession of the papers and found guilty of treason, the results would have been inevitable.

"As well as the death penalty, the offender's property is forfeit. And that includes any titles he might hold." Carrington allowed another silence to fall. "However, we at the Foreign Office do not believe Whiston was aware he was in possession of the papers. We believe somebody else put them there, either to implicate him in the crime, or to conceal them until they were ready to pass them on. It could be anyone, of course, even a servant."

He leaned forward, resting his elbows on the desk. "The title is safe, and so are the people named in the papers. We will consider the matter closed. Unless, of course, I have reason to reopen the case."

Carrington sucked in a breath, loud in the silence. "Thank you, my lord."

"Not at all. I am sure you will find future events far too challenging for you to spare us any time. You will be busy, either helping the widow to raise the new duke, or becoming the duke yourself. Life is about to change for you, Arthur Carrington."

Thus, he dismissed the man who most likely stole the papers. With a threat, to keep him in line.

Carrington had no choice. He got to his feet and bowed. "I must thank you for your generosity," he said hollowly, and left.

They waited a moment, and then Castlereagh raised a brow. "I take it you would not refuse that brandy now?"

"I would welcome it."

They sipped and appreciated the fine French brandy.

"One thing about the war ending, we can obtain the best vintages once more," the viscount said contemplatively.

The vintage was indeed a good one, but at the moment, Val would have taken a shot of the roughest spirit. That interview, delicately done, demonstrated Castlereagh knew who had stolen the folder.

"I think he planned to implicate Whiston," Val said. "The Duke was always on the brink of bankruptcy. Carrington must have feared for his inheritance, and then, after Whiston married, feared he would not inherit at all. He could find himself with a nursery full of infants between him and the dukedom."

"He could indeed. Although I would say that given the choice, I would not wish to inherit an impoverished title. Did you know nearly all his property is mortgaged, even the entail?"

Val nodded. "We fear his widow will be left with nothing, but that is in confidence, you understand. She will not lack." He met Castlereagh's gaze. The man nodded.

"A sad end. When one title holder chooses to deplete the property, it can often be recovered, but when the next holder does the same, it will take many years to bring it back in order. The new Duke will find his task a hard one. Even worse when government influence is denied him."

So that was Carrington's punishment. He could be convicted of nothing, as matters stood, and their actions had rendered the papers, and any copies of them, worthless. And the new Duke of Whiston would never be trusted again.

Good.

"My lord, there is another matter I wish to discuss with you," Castlereagh said, "but I would prefer your wife to be present."

Val frowned. "I beg your pardon?"

"Is it possible to request her presence?"

"I suppose so."

What on earth would involve Juliet?

Juliet had only just arrived home. She had not even removed her pelisse and bonnet before she received a summons, in the form of a polite request, in her husband's distinctive scrawl. She knew him well enough now to read between the lines. He needed her. So she climbed into the carriage and ordered the driver to take her to Whitehall.

The stately buildings lining the wide thoroughfare always awed her. Nearly all of them were offices of government.

An official greeted her effusively as she tried to look like a countess, something she was getting more used to. She followed him down narrow corridors to her husband's office. He was waiting for her, too, and dismissed the official with a smile and a nod.

"Come," he said. "Castlereagh refused to tell me what he wanted until you arrived."

He hurried her along yet another corridor. "And it concerns me? Is this about Whiston?"

They passed several people, but her husband did not acknowledge any of them. "I don't think so. That seems settled. He came to the same conclusions we did. And Carrington is no longer welcome in government."

They turned into a wider, better-appointed corridor. Juliet doubted she could ever find her way out of this place on her own. "Government? Even if—when—he inherits?"

"Yes. The general view is that he will have too much to do to bother with government concerns. I assume he'll take his place in the House of Lords eventually, but as long as this administration remains in power, he will not be a part of it. He will be denied government influence, which means bonds, investments, preferences."

"And rumors and gossip?"

"Precisely."

Goodness. How much could change in the course of a conversation.

"He did not accept my resignation," Val said as they reached a pair of white-painted double doors. "If I insist, he'll have to. Perhaps he wants to appeal to your better nature."

"I don't have one."

They entered the office laughing. Not for long, though, as a neatly dressed gentleman took them inside the inner sanctum. The room was well-appointed, with a massive mahogany desk dominating the spacious room. The large windows overlooked the Admiralty with its parade ground. On her first visit to London, she'd visited it to watch the guards parade and practice their drills. That seemed so long ago now.

"Ah, Lady Langston." Lord Castlereagh got to his feet, all smiles. "Welcome. I'm very grateful you agreed to come at such short notice." Instead of bowing, he came around the desk and shook her hand. "Would you like tea?"

"No, thank you. I've just come from Whiston House, and we drank tea all afternoon. I'm awash." He shared her smile. He had a charming smile, which he should deploy more often.

"Very well. Please take a seat."

She took the leather office chair her husband held for her. He sat in its twin, close to her.

"Lord and Lady Langston," Castlereagh said. "You may have heard that Lord Bagot has been offered the post of envoy to Russia. The Tsar asked for him specifically, and I brought him home from the United States earlier than I'd planned."

"The Tsar asked for him?"

Castlereagh shrugged. "He expressed a preference. The Tsar is a brilliant man, but he can be difficult. Apparently he met his lordship in Vienna, and formed a liking for him. Bagot is experienced and capable. I believe he will work well in Russia." He leaned back, keeping his attention on them. "Which leaves a vacancy in the United States."

Juliet gasped. "My brother is there with the army."

"I am aware of that. It was one of the factors in my decision. We are about to sign an important treaty with the Americans and begin a new era with them. The wars are over. However, the French are still a threat, so we need someone capable and sympathetic. Your brother, my lady, is about to be promoted to

General."

"Oh my goodness!"

"He earned it."

This was all going so fast. But if they were to go to America, she could see Frank again, and Cecilia, his lovely wife. How did Val feel about this? She spared a glance at him. He sat, seemingly expressionless, but she saw the gleam in his eyes. He wanted this.

Could she leave her sister in her grief? In the care of her mother and sister, yes she could. She was sure of that. Her head spun, and she had to fight to clear it, and concentrate on the important things. "When would you want us to leave?"

"As soon as possible," Castlereagh said. "But that, of course, is up to you, especially in these sad circumstances."

It took but a small nod for Val to say, "Yes, my lord. We accept the offer."

Epilogue

Late August 1817

"I F YOU NEED anything don't hesitate to write," Mrs. Burrell said as the carriage drew up at the Pool of London. The forest of masts was still there, seemingly exactly as they were when the Burrells had first come here in search of materials they could make over for their London Season. They didn't need that now.

Although still in mourning, Bianca had come to see them off. So had Viola, but only when she'd promised her husband she would tell him the minute she felt tired, or ill, or anything at all. Juliet gripped her hand. "I'm so glad we got to see your baby. I would have felt cheated had I not seen him for myself before we left."

Viola had been delivered of a healthy baby boy a mere three weeks earlier. Although her pregnancy had been difficult at times, the birth had not. "Easy," the midwife had called it.

Once Juliet and Val left, Viola and Gerald would return to the country, where no doubt Gerald would spoil Viola and their son until they begged for mercy.

Juliet had bidden farewell to her colorful, endlessly kind mother-in-law at the house. She would miss her, but Lady Langston had found a new love to occupy her time and affections.

No doubt his charms would fade in a month or two, but for now she was happy, and that was all that mattered.

Val swung Juliet down from the carriage, holding her until she found her feet on the slimy cobbles. "Here we go on our new adventure," he murmured to her. "We're traveling on the best ship I could buy."

"You bought a ship?"

"Her," he corrected. "Yes, why not? The United States is a large place, so we shall most likely need it to travel up and down the coast. Not too far down, though. And it may find some trade to offset its cost. The Canadian fur trade is flourishing."

"Oh, yes." She had not for a minute considered he meant the slave trade. He had continued to oppose any trace of it, and she knew he'd assured himself that this new ship had no connections with it.

They walked slowly toward the fine sea-going yacht, where the captain, dressed smartly, awaited to welcome them personally. It might be two months or more before they saw land again. But she would not be afraid, not if she had Val by her side.

As she always would.

Author's Note

I did take a liberty with this storyline. Lord Bagot didn't actually return to Britain until later in the year, but he did take up the position of Envoy to Russia and made a great success of it. But I had to fit my hero in somewhere and having her brother over there was too good to miss!

The rest of the story is as factual as I could make it. Castlereagh was a bad-tempered, highly strung man who did a great deal for his country, and eventually committed suicide after his mental state deteriorated.

The three sisters are loosely based on the Gunning sisters, who took London by storm in the mid-eighteenth century. There were three of them, but since the third, Anne, married a country gentleman to suit herself, she is rarely remembered next to her sisters. One of them died young, but my sisters aren't about to do that!

And since I've been asked more than once—a "raree show" was a raucous, rowdy show, sometimes by street performers. You'll find lots of references to it in contemporary literature. Journalists often compared debates in Parliament to a raree show, and since the MPs sometimes came to physical blows, you can understand why!

The mob was still an influence in London. The worst mob violence was in 1780, the Gordon riots, which went way beyond the original reason for it. Buildings were destroyed, breweries broken into to fuel the mob's fury. Although the Riot Act was read, threatening to set the army on the mob, and often suiting action to words, nothing really helped until the creation of a regular police force in the 1830s.

About the Author

I write stories, and I always have. And I love a happy ending, especially a well-deserved one.

I'm an award-winning, best-selling author of historical romance. I fell in love with the eighteenth century when I was nine years old, and it's my dream job to write about the people who lived and loved back then.

I used to work in marketing, and I have more letters after my name than in it, but I don't use them much anymore.

I live in the UK with my family, including my muse, Frankie the Nonsense, a ragdoll with no decorum. I love traveling, and I get over to the States at least once a year.

My website is at lynneconnolly.com. SItwitters @lynneconnolly and my Facebook page is here: facebook.com/ lynneconnollyuk. My blog is at lynneconnolly.blogspot.com.

I also have a newsletter. If you'd like to join it, email me on lynneconnollyuk@yahoo.co.uk or fill in the form on my website.